# THE SONG IS YOU

• • • • • • • • • • • • • • • • • • • •

*Studies in Theatre History and Culture*

Heather S. Nathans, series editor

# THE SONG IS YOU

*Musical Theatre and the Politics of*

*Bursting into Song and Dance*

· · · · · · · · · · · · · · · · · · · · · ·

BRADLEY ROGERS

University of Iowa Press, Iowa City

University of Iowa Press, Iowa City 52242
Copyright © 2020 by the University of Iowa Press
www.uipress.uiowa.edu
Printed in the United States of America

Design by Ashley Muehlbauer

Printed on acid-free paper

*Library of Congress Cataloging-in-Publication Data*
Names: Rogers, James Bradley, 1982– author.
Title: The Song Is You: Musical Theatre and the Politics of
Bursting Into Song and Dance / James Bradley Rogers.
Description: University of Iowa Press:
University of Iowa Press, 2020. |
Series: Studies in Theatre History and Culture |
Includes bibliographical references and index. |
Identifiers: LCCN 2020006578 (print) |
LCCN 2020006579 (ebook) | ISBN
9781609387327 (paperback) | ISBN 9781609387334 (ebook)
Subjects: LCSH: Musicals—New York
(State)—New York—History and
criticism. | Sex role in music. | Music and race.
Classification: LCC ML1711.8.N3 R64 2020 (print) | LCC
ML1711.8.N3 (ebook) | DDC 782.1/409747—dc23
LC record available at https://lccn.loc.gov/2020006578
LC ebook record available at https://lccn.loc.gov/2020006579

The text of a musical show is woman.

—NED WAYBURN

What all the rest of us knew was that the essential purpose of a musical comedy book was to be interrupted. Its very quality lay in its interruptibility. . . . It was an endless series of open doors, an airy and unimportant artifice, an invitation to *freedom*.

—WALTER KERR

I'm perhaps the only member of the cheering congregation who worried a bit because it failed to "live up to the sum of its component parts"—whatever that may really mean!

—ROBERT GARLAND, on *On the Town*

And do not despise public taste in that haughty, youthful way of yours, because that's silly. . . . Therefore do not grumble at public taste, but rather follow it. I do not mean pander to it. It must be left to your own good judgment to distinguish between its healthy appetite and its sick fancies.

—"A DRAMATIST," *Playwriting: A Handbook for Would-Be Dramatic Authors*

Just think of a grown up man saying, "I should worry," when anybody would know that "Ish Ka Bibble" is the proper form. It should be the height of everyone's ambition to make the language they use sound like a musical comedy.

—MARIE ERHARDT, 1914 student essay on slang, quoted by David Gold

Mildred Natwick in *70, Girls, 70*. Photograph by Martha Swope, ©Billy Rose Theatre Division, New York Public Library for the Performing Arts.

# CONTENTS

# ACKNOWLEDGMENTS

The 1968 musical *Maggie Flynn* features "The Thank You Song," in which Maggie leads the orphans in expressing their gratitude for everything ranging from their nose—for "sniffin' out a dumplin'"—to even their kidneys. Anyone familiar with my extreme sentimentality might be expecting a similarly exhaustive set of acknowledgments—all the more so in a book that emphasizes the profound ecstasy of applause. Only the contractually delineated word limit of this manuscript—to which I am perilously close—is reining in my natural impulse to expound even more effusively upon the many debts I owe.

First, of course, my family—virtually all of whom have been conscripted into sharing my love of musical theatre at one point or another. My mother drove me to school every day as I played *Destry Rides Again* and *I Can Get It For You Wholesale*. When I was four, I presented her with a "book" I wrote; now I can finally give her a real one. Delo took me to see my first show at the Flat Rock Playhouse, and Suzanne and Kevin welcomed me to Tampa so that I could write these final pages. My aunt Jeannie agreed to buy me my first CD (Smithsonian's Cole Porter compilation) and my first libretto (*Gypsy*), and my aunt Jan was willing to take me to see *The Fantasticks* for my high school graduation gift. My sister once got roped into playing Name That Tune while I played Broadway melodies on the piano, and even my father did not escape: I once guilted him into letting me play *Coco* as he drove me to Roanoke for the GRE.

I wouldn't trade Timmy Yuen—who understands better than anyone the value of bad theatre—for all the *grisbi* in the world. *Hic, haec, hoc,* sir. And who but Sam Nystrom would text me with his discovery that Allyn Ann McLerie was sometimes billed as Allyn McLerie? Sin twisters, always. Matthew Sugarbaker deserves my deepest appreciation for having sat through everything from *Einstein on the Beach* to *Classic Uggams*. As I thank my seat partners, I must also express my gratitude to Sarah Frith Kenny and R. Brent Vann, who in my senior year actually agreed to let me write and put on my high school's first musical—a production that set me down this path.

Intellectually, this book owes its greatest debt to Suzanne Cusick, whose brilliance, generosity, and sense of humor remain the gold standard to which I aspire. The confidence that Linda Williams had in my project, and the joyful conversations we shared as I was making my first discoveries, inspired and sustained me to the end. Rita Felski, Jonathan Flatley, Shannon Jackson, Victoria Kahn, Michelle Kisliuk, Fred Maus, Shannon Steen, Renate Voris, and Jennifer Wicke all changed the way that I think. And I capped my graduate study with a seminar taught by Richard Taruskin, whose intellectual and rhetorical gifts provoked me to think anew about argument.

Judith Butler, Alexander Doty, and Victoria Kahn read fragments of this project in its most embryonic state; and John Clum, Tom Ferraro, Mary Francis, Louise Meintjes, David Savran, Millie Taylor, and Jacqueline Waeber read later versions of the manuscript. I am grateful to them for the generosity with which they shared their time and their considerable insight.

At the Jackman Humanities Institute in Toronto, I was surrounded by wonderful, sharp colleagues and friends: Robert Gibbs (who joined in a lusty chorus of "God Bless the Human Elbow"), Tania Ahmad, Nicole Blackwood, Stefan Dolgert, Charlie Keil, Andrea Most, Atsuko Sakaki, David Francis Taylor, and Kim Yates. An offhand comment from Alan Bewell helped me to reconceive the project. I still miss Monica Toffoli and Cheryl Pasternak, who brought me so much support, warmth, and laughter.

Jody McAuliffe, Neal Bell, and Frank Lentricchia were incredible champions of mine as I moved to Duke University. Torry Bend and Jeff Storer nurtured my passion for musical theatre, and my colleagues Sarah Beckwith, Sara Berghausen, Cyndi Bunn, Claire Conceison, Chris Chia, Thomas DeFrantz, Ellen Hemphill, Margo Lakin, Esther Kim Lee, Michèle Longino, Jules Odendahl-James, Miriam Sauls, Dierdre Shipman, Helen Solterer, Coco Wilder, and Darren Gobert have helped to make Duke an intellectually enriching home. To Priscilla Wald I owe an incredible debt; she always went well beyond the call of duty in caring for this institutional orphan.

This project owes much to the help of librarians: Pam Howie, Mark Horowitz, Walter Zvonchenko, Arianne Hartsell-Gundy, Cheryl Thomas, and Linda Purnell, Amy Ravenal-Baker, and Cheryl Wilkins of the wonderful interlibrary loan department at Duke University. I am also grateful for the fellowships that I received—from the Mellon Foundation, the ACLS, the John W. Kluge Center at the Library of Congress, and the Harry F. Ransom Center—that made this research possible in an age of austerity. Portions of earlier versions of chapters 1 and 3 appeared as "Redressing the Black Crook" in *Modern Drama* 55, no. 4, 476–96; and "The Interpellations of Interpolation" in *Camera Obscura* 23, no. 1, 89–111, respectively. I appreciate the permission of the presses to reprint excerpts of them here.

Other sources of support along the way: Dennis Best, Rod Bladel, Ken Bloom, Aaron Boros, Matt Buckley, Leslie Butler, Tim Carter, Irene Chien, Andrew Clark, Marianne Constable, Josh Daughtry, Marcy Edenfield, George and Agnes Eichler, Abigail Fox, Joe Gram, Analia Howard and the crew at Claymakers, Judy Ison, Alicia Jiménez, Kim H. Kowalke, Bennie Leonard, Josh McAlpine, Michael Malone, Taliyah Roach, Patrick Roberts, Allison Hayden Russo, Michael Schulson, Jasmine Swope, Susanna Moross Tarjan, and Ami Wong; and the staffs at the Bateau Ivre in Berkeley, Parker & Otis in Durham, and Konditori and Bien Cuit in New York, where I wrote much of what you will read in these pages.

I am lucky to count Anita Gillette, Karen Morrow, Nancy Dussault, Rita Gardner, Sondra Lee, Faith Prince, and Vicki Clark as friends. Through these incredible women, I learned so much about the joys of musical theatre. Bambi Linn is a hero of mine, and getting to know her and her wonderful family—Joe, Elisa, Jennifer, and Sophia—has been such a blessing. Just when I thought that this book might never see the light of day, a card arrived from Bambi: "Try harder!"

To my inner sanctum—Benjamin, Gaal, Allen, Stephen, Tyler, Colin, Sarah, Shana, Maxine, and especially MCR—you have given me a life beyond this book, which is the greatest gift of all.

Heather Nathans worked miracles in getting this book between two covers and has single-handedly renewed my faith in the profession. Thank you, thank you, thank you. I also owe deep gratitude to Daniel Ciba, Karen Copp, Ann Przyzycki DeVita, Susan Hill Newton, James McCoy, Jacob Roosa, Meredith Stabel, and the University of Iowa Press for having made this process end on such an unexpectedly painless note.

This book—and so much else—would not exist without John Mason Kirby, who has given me a home in New York. Much of this book was written at his kitchen table, fueled not only by the everything bagels that awaited me every morning but also by his profound insights about theatre, words, and life. His energy suffuses every page of this book.

Whenever my grandmother and I spoke on the phone, she always wanted to know about the book—and she was always finding "treasures" at yard sales and the like that she thought might be helpful. As I was finishing the manuscript, she was diagnosed with brain cancer. Grandma said to me—as only she could—"You've got to hurry up and finish this book so I can read it before I lose my marbles!" Sadly, she did not live to see the book in published form, but her devotion to it is here. After she passed away, I was cleaning her house at the same time that I was finishing the introduction. In her living room, I discovered a set of cassettes of Broadway songs that she purchased for me at a thrift store—and there in the liner notes was just the quote I was searching for, a quote that now appears in the introduction. How I wish the grandfolks at home could only see. . . .

# THE SONG IS YOU

Sally Ann Howes, Edward Mulhare, and Reginald Denny in "The Rain in Spain." Photograph by Friedman-Abeles, ©Billy Rose Theatre Division, New York Public Library for the Performing Arts.

# INTRODUCTION

## Bursting into Song and Dance

When *My Fair Lady* opened in 1956, critics gushed over the perfect unity of its form. Robert Coleman, a columnist for the *New York Daily Mirror*, wrote that the "Lerner-Loewe songs are not only delightful, but advance the action as well. They are ever so much more than interpolations, or interruptions. They are a most important and integrated element in about as perfect an entertainment as the most fastidious playgoer could demand."[1] *New York Post* critic Richard Watts, Jr., echoed Coleman in lauding "the enormous value of being a perfectly integrated score,"[2] and John Chapman elaborated even further in his review for the *New York Daily News*: "Not since 'Guys and Dolls' have all the elements of a big musical production—the stars and the chorus, the sets and the costumes, the dances and the plot, the melodies and the lyrics—been blended so artfully and so enjoyably."[3]

The claims of these critics exemplify a significantly larger theme in musical theatre historiography: the venerable hermeneutic canard of "integration," which generally involves a series of related claims that are often invoked to validate or legitimize musical theatre, claims that the musical numbers "advance the story," that the musical moments do not "interrupt" the narrative, that the various elements of the genre—dance, music, spectacle, design, and so forth—have become increasingly unified in the service of the dramatic action.[4] However, "integrated" is perhaps the last word that would come to mind if one were asked to describe an episodic form that *alternates* between scenes of dramatic dialogue and scenes that feature singing and dancing. Given that this interruptive rhythm is unmistakably the palpitating, irregular heartbeat of the genre, any claim of integration—a claim that invokes unity and continuity, denying any fragmentation—necessarily misses what is most distinct about the form.

Indeed, when the critics of *My Fair Lady* claim that the show was integrated, they deny this interruptive quality, suggesting instead a subtle seamlessness of the narrative surface. With this in mind, we might look more closely at a number that even Alan Jay Lerner, the show's librettist and lyricist, referred to as an "impromptu outburst" in the show: "The Rain in Spain."[5] It was apparently an "impromptu outburst" not only for the characters but for the creators as well: calling it an "unexpected visitation from the muses," Lerner described the song as "happen[ing] so spontaneously and easily that we were suspicious of it."[6] Might a subterranean suspicion extend to the song itself and similarly haunt all "outbursts" of musical theatre? "The Rain in Spain," which critic Wolcott Gibbs described as "just about the most brilliantly successful scene that I recall seeing in a musical comedy"—makes explicit the functional logic of every outburst of musical theatre, of every moment when the characters burst (out) into song and dance, despite what the discourse of integration would suggest.[7] Exploring this functional logic of "bursting out" entails exploring the kinds of performances that these moments engender.

My Fair Lady posits, both spatially and temporally, a world in which performances occur one after another, in seemingly endless chains. The show begins outside the Royal Opera House in London's Covent Garden, where the audience is leaving the auditorium only to find street entertainers picking up the "business of show" right where the opera left off. The endless domain of theatrical space is mirrored in the circularity of theatrical time: the opening scene of My Fair Lady is indicated as taking place "after theatre," such that the spectator's "beginning" of theatre is already "after theatre." In this way, the spectator is conscripted into a world in which it is always the time of theatrical performance. And there in Covent Garden, where Henry Higgins and Eliza first cross paths, the crowd watches as Higgins guesses, based on speech patterns, the neighborhoods in which various people in the crowd reside. And it is there that Higgins himself—cold, distant, unfeeling Higgins—is mistaken for a performer. As the stage directions indicate, "[p]opular interest in the note-taker's *performance* increases," after which Colonel Pickering inquires, "May I ask, sir, do you do this sort of thing for a living on the music halls?"[8] "I have thought of that," Higgins replies. "Perhaps I will someday."

But of course the plot will focus less on Higgins's ability to perform than on Eliza's. Referring to her as a "squashed cabbage leaf," a "disgrace to the noble architecture of these columns," and an "incarnate insult to the

English language," Higgins makes the startling claim that he could pass Eliza off as the "Queen of Sheba"—indeed, that Eliza could successfully imitate exotic foreign royalty.[9] Enticed by Higgins's suggestion that with his tutelage in elocution she could secure more respectable employment, Eliza returns to Higgins's home the next day to engage him as her teacher. Pickering, meanwhile, is intrigued by Higgins's boast and volunteers to pay for all the related lessons and costs. And so begins Eliza's laborious training, involving endless recitations of vowels, incanting "H"-heavy words before a flickering flame, mimicking the cadence of a xylophone, and reading a poem with marbles in her mouth.

Then, after a seemingly unrelenting stretch of exercises, Eliza emerges victoriously with her pronunciation of "The rain in Spain stays mainly in the plain."[10] This evolves into an ecstatic tango, whereupon "Pickering jumps to his feet and the three sing out joyously." During an instrumental interlude, the stage directions indicate,

> Higgins takes a handkerchief from his pocket and waves it in front of Pickering who charges it like the finest bull in Spain. Higgins turns and grabs Eliza and they do a few awkward tango steps while Pickering jumps around like a flamenco dancer shouting "Viva Higgins, Viva!" Higgins swings Eliza onto the sofa and joins Pickering in a bit of heel-clicking. . . . They throw themselves into a wild jig and then all collapse back upon the sofa engulfed in laughter.[11]

A tango? The culmination of Eliza's attempts to imitate Higgins, a British man, is a tango? The play is structured to give the sense of interminable ennui at her inability to mimic Higgins, and yet, at the very moment when she finally mirrors his precise elocution, the moment when she successfully imitates him, what do the three do? Yet *another* imitation! This time, Eliza, Higgins, and Pickering jubilantly indulge their kitschiest fantasies of Spain, home of the infamously soaked plain. Distilled in this number is what I argue to be the logic central to all musicals: the transitive force of musical imitation, with one imitation prompting yet another, bodies imitating other bodies, all unleashed in the moment of bursting into song. These performances—these bodies imitating other bodies—are precisely the performances unleashed every time the musical bursts (out) into song and dance. Eliza's triumph is marked not by her assumption of a stable new identity as a proper British woman, but instead by the beginning of yet another imitation. Impersonation begets impersonation in a chain whose unfolding constitutes the most primal pleasure of musical theatre.

This transitive chain, which began with Eliza imitating Higgins, now moves into a startling elaboration, with Higgins midwifing an elaborate psychic imitation in which Pickering becomes Eliza. Pickering's indulgence in cross-ethnic impersonation—charging like a bull and shouting "Viva Higgins, Viva" during the tango—provides a visual and corporeal model for the cross-gender impersonation that follows. As soon as "The Rain in Spain" concludes, Higgins announces that he is ready for yet another imitation: "the time has come to try her out."[12] He immediately begins planning for Eliza's appearance at the ball, asking Pickering, "Where does one buy a lady's gown?" Colonel Pickering—visiting from India—volunteers, "Whiteley's, of course." Higgins, despite having directed the question at Pickering, is nonetheless puzzled by Pickering's ready answer to his question. When asked how he could know the answer, Pickering defensively dismisses it as "common knowledge." Empowered by Pickering's explanation, Higgins "stud[ies] Pickering carefully" as he begins to muse about the sartorial direction in which he will steer Eliza: "We mustn't get her anything too flowery. I despise those gowns with a sort of weed here and a weed there. Something simple, modest and elegant is what's called for. Perhaps with a sash."[13] The stage directions indicate that Higgins "places the imaginary sash on Pickering's hip and steps back to eye it," his satisfaction indicated by his appraisal: "Yes. Just right." Then Higgins leaves, prompting the most incredible action yet: "Pickering looks down at his hip to reassure himself the sash is not there and follows after him." Why would Pickering be so seduced by Higgins's gesture as to believe that he is wearing the dress that they envisioned as clothing Eliza?

As Higgins projects Eliza onto Pickering, approvingly placing a sash on his feminized body with a certainty that confuses even Pickering himself, the show that famously voices the query "why can't a woman be more like a man" seems just as concerned with turning a man into a woman. The ease with which Pickering is convinced that he is Eliza is not accidental— for the text has prepared us for this elision. In the scene preceding "The Rain in Spain," Higgins and Pickering eat dessert while Eliza practices.

Amidst Eliza's Cockney failures, Pickering tastes one of the desserts and exclaims, "First rate! The strawberry tarts are delicious. And did you try the pline cake?"[14] The Colonel's "pline," his unconscious slip into Eliza's mode of speech, which prompts Higgins to "loo[k] at him in horror," makes Pickering's eventual assumption of her body all the more satisfying.

*My Fair Lady*'s obsession with bodies mimicking—and in a sense becoming—other bodies is not accidental. Indeed, the series of performances unleashed in "The Rain in Spain" merely renders explicit the complex psychic operations unleashed every time a musical bursts into song. Revising the widely held belief that musicals burst into song when words will no longer suffice to carry the emotion, I argue instead that musicals burst into song—and dance—when one *body* will no longer suffice to carry the emotion. To satisfy our desire to exceed the expressive limits of a discrete body, we must create complex psychic relationships across different bodies. Just as "The Rain in Spain" prompts everyone involved to "become" bodies different from their own, the same is structurally demanded of spectators every time the musical indulges its genre-defining impulse to burst into song.

Further, these moments of bursting into song are fundamentally eruptions of the nineteenth-century entertainments that compose the musical form: melodrama, minstrelsy, and burlesque. In *My Fair Lady*, for example, what is "The Rain in Spain" but an instance of Spanish minstrelsy, followed by psychic drag in which Colonel Pickering is fitted with the outfit that Eliza will wear as she promenades—a bodily display not unrelated to burlesque—down the staircase at the Embassy Ball? Given, then, that the narrative surface of musical theatre is punctured at regular intervals—punctured precisely by explosions of the erotic energies borne of burlesque and minstrelsy—the radical relationships made possible by these moments of bursting into song are indebted to the bodily relationships of those older forms. Wherever and whenever contemporary productions take place—whether on Broadway, in a high school auditorium, or in a church basement—the musical reintroduces us to the bodily structures and psychic pleasures of the nineteenth-century entertainments that constitute the form. In incorporating these older forms—and the bodily practices that constitute them—the genre thus invites complex identifications with bodies that it positions as spectacular: black bodies, Latinx bodies, women's bodies, and a broader range of bodies positioned as sensuous repositories of spectacular excess.

These nineteenth-century cultural genres are profoundly mutable and can take on a wide range of forms. Minstrelsy, for instance, encompasses not only blackface but indeed any form of racial or ethnic drag that finds spectacular or erotic pleasure in imitating certain bodies. The tango of "The Rain in Spain"—an eruption of pseudo-Spanishness in a play set squarely in London—participates in a longer lineage of similar eruptions of Latin-ness in musical theatre (that themselves fit into an even broader lineage of the more general "exotic" number, a trope that includes not only "Latin" numbers, but also, for example, so-called "Oriental" numbers, among others). Almost all of the great musical theatre composers at one point or another wrote Latin numbers of this style, including: Victor Herbert, whose "Cuban Song" was featured in the 1897 musical *The Idol's Eye*; Sigmund Romberg, whose "In Brazil" was featured in his 1922 musical *Springtime of Youth*; George Gershwin, who wrote "Argentina" for *George White's Scandals of 1922*; Richard Rodgers, whose 1926 musical *Peggy-Ann* included a song titled "Havana"; Irving Berlin, who wrote "Latins Know How" for his 1940 musical *Louisiana Purchase*; and Vernon Duke, who wrote "Who Started the Rhumba?" for *Banjo Eyes*. Cole Porter indulged Latin rhythms often, whether "Begin the Beguine" in the 1935 *Jubilee*, "Visit Panama" in 1940's *Panama Hattie*, or "Sing to Me Guitar" in *Mexican Hayride*. Much was made of Richard Rodgers's musical *Too Many Girls*, which was a huge break for Desi Arnaz and featured "All Dressed Up in Spic and Spanish" and "She Could Shake the Maracas." The tango was introduced to American audiences precisely through the dancing of Vernon Castle in the 1913 musical *The Sunshine Girl*, and Carmen Miranda would popularize Latin numbers through her iconic "South American Way" performance in the 1939 production *Streets of Paris*. Such numbers continued through the 1950s and beyond, in musicals like *Wish You Were Here* ("Don José of Far Rockaway"), *Bells Are Ringing* ("Mu-Cha-Cha"), *Wonderful Town* ("Conga"), *The Pajama Game* ("Hernando's Hideaway"), *Damn Yankees* ("Whatever Lola Wants"), *Once Upon a Mattress* ("Spanish Panic"), and *She Loves Me* ("Ilona," a beguine).[15]

As Brian Herrera has shown, numbers like these, with their "congas, ruffled shirts, and arbitrary *olés*," are often ones in which "Latin-ness floats freely as a vague abstraction and operates primarily as a dramatic device or staging strategy."[16] My work, which focuses on the broader conventional category of "exotic" numbers, similarly understands such numbers to operate from a place of aggressive incoherence, an incoherence that makes possible the identity play at the heart of these numbers.[17] As such, I aim to understand what this "dramatic device or staging strategy" accomplishes in the context of these shows, something that I pursue from a structural point of view. In other words, what prompts the recurrence of such a number, in which representations of Latin-ness are pointedly removed from any context and repurposed as camp signifiers of erotic energy? "The Rain in Spain," with its invocations of flamenco, tango, and a charging bull, functions in precisely this way—and its effect in *My Fair Lady* points toward how this kind of number invites audiences to participate in a complex form of identificatory play.

Walter Kerr wrote that "there is no controlling the joy in the theatre" when the three performers begin "The Rain in Spain"; he described the number as "the kill," the moment when the show, and the performers, completely captured the audience.[18] Moss Hart's wife, Kitty Carlisle Hart, called *My Fair Lady* her "favorite musical, the best ever written," noting, "I've seen it a hundred times, and every time they start 'The Rain in Spain,' no matter who is playing in it, the audience is lifted two feet off their seats. They levitate, and they stay up there for the rest of the performance."[19] This levitation is *our* hearts taking flight and *our* wings spreading, just as those of Eliza do. When her "heart takes flight," Eliza reveals the central principle that governs musical theatre: that the chains of impersonation fuel the chains of desire that set the musical in motion. The desire at the center of musical theatre is precisely the creation of complex relationships across bodies, through impersonation and projection—as modeled in the cross-gender, cross-racial, and cross-ethnic performances that relentlessly populate the genre.

The result of the transitive power of imitation for the spectator is the very same as it is for Eliza and for Pickering: nothing short of the dissolution of identity. As Higgins remarks to Pickering, "What could possibly matter more than to take a human being and change her into a different human being by creating a new speech for her?"[20] Just as Eliza's imitations bring her a "new speech" that "change[s] her into a different human being"—prompting the same for Pickering—the impersonations of musical theatre make the very same transformation possible for its spectators, performers, and artists.

It is precisely through this complex play with identifications that the musical models how calcified structures of identity can be dissolved. Its interruptive form, with its oscillations between book and number, explicitly challenges the idea of a singular subjectivity as it requires spectators to switch between different modes of engagement. However, the form is more complex still: because these eruptions are eruptions of minstrelsy and burlesque, they are at the same time eruptions of cross-racial, cross-ethnic, and cross-gender impersonation that demand spectators to participate in these particular kinds of identity play. As the musical deploys these various forms of imitation in rapid succession, it asks audiences to undertake an increasingly vertiginous set of identifications and misidentifications that reach across different gendered, raced, and sexualized bodies. Crucially, I argue, these operations occur in transitive chains. In other words, imitation begets imitation, both vertically—from creators to performers to spectators—and horizontally, in the sense that the forms of imitation depicted rarely occur in isolation. In *My Fair Lady*, these transitive chains occur both in the movement from cross-racial ("Viva, Higgins, Viva!") to cross-gender impersonation (the be-sashèd Pickering as Eliza), as well as in the movement from creators to performers to spectators. Indeed, the Spanish tango that provokes Colonel Pickering's transformation into Eliza prompted a similar operation during the scene's very first embodiment: Nancy Livingston, who was married to lyricist Alan Jay Lerner at the time, recalled years later that Lerner and composer Frederick Loewe ecstatically acted out the scene when they first composed it, with Lerner undertaking his own cross-gender performance as he played Eliza.[21]

If the moment of creation found Lerner undertaking a cross-gender performance, the original Broadway production would extend the same opportunity to director Moss Hart. During the rehearsal period, the inexperience of Julie Andrews, the actress playing Eliza, became a point of major contention, with star Rex Harrison threatening to leave the production "if that girl is here on Monday giving the same goddam performance."[22] Hart agreed that Andrews "didn't have a clue about playing Eliza," and he dismissed the entire company and spent a weekend trying to transform

Andrews into Eliza. In this story, Andrews—the tentative naïf unprepared for the rigorous demands of Broadway—essentially becomes Eliza, while Hart, not unlike Higgins, "bullied, cajoled, pleaded, scolded, [and] encouraged" the actress for two days. Having earlier voiced a desire to "*paste* the part" on the jejune performer, Hart would end up modeling Eliza for Andrews, essentially asking her to imitate him imitating Eliza. As Andrews recalled years later, "I remember when he snatched Eliza's purse from my hand and he hit out at an imaginary Higgins, to show me how he wanted it done. . . . And then, I have a picture of him holding Eliza's teacup, very prim and proper with that ring finger extended. At times he actually became Eliza Doolittle and I just kind of stood back and watched."[23]

This same transgressive energy that moves from the creators' own bodies to those of the actors, and on to the characters, will reach the spectators as well. Writing that "The Rain in Spain" was the pivotal moment of the show, Walter Kerr implicitly suggested the kind of transitive chains that clearly inform the genre: when Eliza successfully imitates Higgins, Kerr writes, "Suddenly her delight becomes yours," and when the Spanish-inspired tango begins, "the audience erupted right along with the characters." That is the power of musical theatre: as the characters erupt in song and dance, we erupt as well. These transitive links spread across the footlights, enlisting the audience in keeping alive the chains of impersonation, the chains of affect across bodies—thereby inviting the spectator to new modes of subjectivity. Indeed, the work of the musical is to seduce its spectators into a dizzying set of identifications and misidentifications, so dizzying as to unsettle any sense of stable subjectivity. These ricocheting networks of imitation work to reorganize desire and ultimately identity. In this way, as the form is brought to bear on *our* own bodies, the song is you.

This radical play with identifications, then, is predicated on the genre's deployment of bodies. In particular, it is predicated on the deployment of bodies that the genre marks as spectacular, as ones that step out of the narrative and invite a different kind of engagement. These spectacular bodies—the broad range of bodies that the genre posits as spectacular vehicles of sensuous excess—derive their spectacular nature from the cultural logic of the nineteenth-century forms, burlesque and minstrelsy, out of which the genre emerges. Thus, an irony lies at the heart of the genre's radical potential: the genre's progressive potential to dissolve the very category of identity itself is made possible by the imitations and transformations borne by these older, seemingly regressive forms.

The spectacular bodies that stop the show—the bodies of performers, and the imagined bodies deemed worthy of spectacle—produce the ruptures in the narrative, and in channeling desire, they also produce ruptures in the spectator's sense of subjectivity. Because this division between narrative and spectacle circumscribes how certain bodies are apprehended and suggests that certain bodies are precluded from certain kinds of agency, it fuels anxieties of exploitation. As the musical endlessly grapples with its own economy of appropriation, it must always contend with the inescapable link between its most progressive political possibility—the shattering of stable identity—and its most regressive political possibility: that this shattering is made possible by the very bodies whose labor is appropriated by the genre. Given this dynamic of power, the genre is understandably preoccupied, indeed obsessed, with the *labor* of the bodies that permit these identifications. Because the genre's sites of rupture always activate both the progressive and exploitative possibilities, the musical inescapably pairs its ecstatic joy with a deep ambivalence about the potential exploitation involved in achieving this effect. For example, as we will see later, because it channels queer desire through the female performer, the genre is obsessed with the *labor* of women's bodies that makes this identification possible. The specter of exploitation is always in play at the moment of bursting into song, since the musical can never fully dissociate these two qualities of cross-body identification—the progressive and the exploitative.

Just as Eliza is the vehicle for Pickering's transformation, the plot reveals a tremendous anxiety over her labor. While the first act, which concludes as Eliza successfully "impersonates" a Hungarian princess, is about imitation, the second act concerns credit and acknowledgment for the work of this impersonation. To be sure, the second act opens with a meditation on this very issue, with Pickering incanting, "Tonight, old man, you did it! You did it! You did it! You said that you would do it, And indeed you did."[24] Higgins interrupts Pickering's celebration, urging him to "give credit where it's due. A lot of the glory goes to you," thereby suggesting bizarrely that Pickering "did it." But what, exactly, might Pickering have done? The stage directions indicate that Higgins's comment causes Eliza to "flinc[h] violently," her severe physical reaction perhaps prompted by the ongoing inability to draw meaningful boundaries between her performance and that of Pickering. Pickering's having paid for the experience, and the ease with which he becomes her, may explain Eliza's strong desire to delineate the nature of her own work and identity, a desire that extends to the materials that enabled her own transformation. For example, when she storms out of Higgins's apartment, she queries him as to whether her clothes belong to her or to Colonel Pickering, whose subsidizing of the experience has occurred in both the fiscal and psychic realms. Might the clothes be his because he purchased them, or because he was implicitly fitted with them? Significantly, it is her claim in this regard that she might be charged with "stealing" that "deeply wound[s]" Higgins and prompts the outflow of feeling that will contribute to resolving the play.[25]

As Eliza works to discern the credit and the material possessions that are rightly hers, she also works to clarify the nature of her labor by distancing herself from any semblance of prostitution, which the text repeatedly introduces and tries to suppress. The sexual overtones of the play's premise are introduced from the very beginning, when Higgins picks "her up off the kerbstone," and recur in Eliza's own worries that he will drug her, and in Pickering's concern that "no advantage" be taken of Eliza. The arrival of her father—whom she has already disavowed by telling Higgins that she has no parents—feels much more akin to the arrival of her pimp. After Eliza has taken up residence with Pickering and Higgins, Alfred Doolittle suggests an "arrangement" with the two men whereby he would "let her go" for five pounds. When Pickering vouches that Higgins's intentions are honorable, Doolittle replies, "Of course they are . . . if I thought they wasn't, I'd ask fifty." Noting that his own labor—the "sweat of his brow"—has cultivated Eliza to the point where she's "of interest to you two gentlemen," Doolittle asks for his own reward. (It is worth noting in this context that the resolution of the play will find Higgins inexplicably securing an income and "respectability" for Alfred Doolittle as a professional speaker, removing the first stated need for Eliza to work: "A man was made to help support his children—but / With a little bit of luck / . . . . They'll go out and start supporting you!") The nature of the transaction is clear to Higgins as well: later in the play, when Eliza leaves, Mrs. Pearce reminds Higgins that he has no basis for reporting her to the police, to which Higgins replies, "The girl belongs to me! I paid five pounds for her!"[26] Eliza's own anxiety about her labor and identity, and the show's broader thematic preoccupation with these issues, point to the genre's anxiety about the transformations that are so central to its affect and effect.

Every "outburst" of musical theatre invites the kind of psychic maneuvers that are made explicit in "The Rain in Spain." Indeed, every moment of bursting into song works to reconfigure the relationships between the bodies, onstage and offstage, of musical theatre. With this in mind, we can see how the claims of integration made on behalf of *My Fair Lady*, by misrepresenting how musical numbers function, work to deny the complex identificatory work made possible by the eruptions of gendered, raced, and sexualized bodies. The narrative continuity imagined by integration would suggest that these unruly spectacular bodies, now safely integrated into the narrative, no longer invite the same kind of identifications that they did when positioned outside it. Those who suggested that musicals had attained integration were ultimately suggesting a kind of authorial—and spectatorial—control or power, but the form is of course always eruptive, the bodies are always beyond control, and those powerful identifications are always in play. Indeed, integration is thus an attempt to obscure the fact that the musical's most profound effects emerge precisely from the disjunctions of its form.

The disjunctive nature of musical theatre has been widely noted.[27] While some of playwright and theorist Bertolt Brecht's writings offer an antecedent, more specific writings about the disjunctive form of musical theatre have emerged in recent years, beginning with D. A. Miller's brilliant *Place for Us*.[28] There, Miller characterizes integration as the "'dramatic model' of a show whose musical numbers . . . now had to be strictly rationalized by the dramatic situation," likening it to a "protective coloration."[29] Noting the genre's "frankly interruptive mode-shifting," he writes that the young gay fan of the genre would find "not the integration of drama and music found on the thematic surface, but a so much deeper formal discontinuity between the two."[30] This emphasis on formal discontinuity would be picked up in Scott McMillin's 2006 *The Musical as Drama*, where he writes that when a musical is working well, I feel the crackle of difference, not the smoothness of unity, even when the numbers dovetail with the book. It takes things different from one another to be thought of as integrated in the first place, and I find that the musical depends more on the differences that make the close fit interesting than on the suppression of difference in a seamless whole. *Difference* can be felt between the book and the numbers, between the songs and dances, between dance and spoken dialogue—and these are the elements that integration is supposed to have unified.[31]

Within a broader argument that "[t]he musical's complexity comes in part from the tension between two orders of time, one for the book and one for the numbers," McMillin fixates on "repetition" as a critical concept, writing that "usually the book sets forth the turn of plot and the number elaborates it, in the spirit of repetition and the pleasure of difference."[32] Millie Taylor has argued that while a text may be "integrated" in the sense that "all the elements support an understanding of a narrative," there is not necessarily any *one* narrative that the piece supports.[33] Thus, for her, musical theatre, with its "narrative construction that is comprised of disruptions, discontinuities and gaps," offers the pleasure of interpretive freedom made possible by the various disjunctive elements of the genre that "have the potential to challenge the experience of narrative certainty."

For D. A. Miller, the contradictions between book and number ultimately render the form a repository of queer desire, which in his account involves a fantasmatic mother-child relationship between the diva and the gay fan. While not focused on issues of sexuality, McMillin similarly sees a relationship between spectatorial identity and the formal structure of the genre. For him, the pleasure in musical theatre comes when "characters break out in song and dance, adding musical selves to their book selves."[34] He finds in the musical form a Kierkegaardian pleasure in repetition and doubling whereby the genre, through its constitutive repetition, is capable of recognizing that "I am what I am and then some."[35] Like Miller and McMillin, Stacy Wolf also argues that the disjunctive form is somehow connected to identity. For her, the "fragmented form of the musical invites extravagant identifications, aggressive reappropriations, and elaborate forays into fantasy," complexities that she deftly exploits to provide a series of readings that illuminate the rich possibilities afforded by the genre from a feminist, lesbian spectatorial position.[36]

David Savran points the way to a broader critique of integration as well, but while Miller and Wolf focus squarely on the genre's relationship to gender, Savran's emphasis is on race. His enlightening materialist analysis of *South Pacific* explores the interplay of the piece's sociological and racial politics in relation to integration. As he writes, "*South Pacific* is in fact a perfect illustration of the sleight of hand responsible for producing the illusion of the so-called integrated musical. For none of their other works is as much the jerry-built collage that *South Pacific* is."[37] In Savran's sharp reading, the "liberal, anti-anti-miscegenation politics of *South Pacific* are thus played out not only on the level of content but also in the very form of the musical, which promiscuously mixes high drama with low and uses several quite distinct musical styles."[38] Savran concludes that "a so-called integrated musical like *South Pacific*—which could more accurately be described as a segregated musical—carefully displaces anxieties about the expropriation of African American, artisanal forms onto the happy natives of Bali Ha'i, who are all too willing to commercialize their charms."[39] I too am concerned with issues of race and class, but I am not as engaged as Savran is with the sociological dimensions of high culture and low culture, nor with ascribing ownership to certain cultural elements that are used in the genre. My work focuses instead on the bodies that enact the eruptive moment, and my concern with materiality emerges in considerations of the labor of the bodies that structure the genre. Indeed, while my work builds on the insight of all these scholars—especially Miller—this study is distinguished by its broader historical focus on, and its structural analysis of, the *laboring spectacular bodies* that populate the form and generate its pleasures.

Like Savran, I also take the claims of integration seriously—but not because I believe that they are "correct"; I do so because I understand them as defensive reactions to the musical's most radical powers.[40] Thus, in this study, every invocation of "integration" becomes an aperture through which the genre's disruptive, disintegrative energies are inadvertently revealed. By attending closely to these moments, this book articulates the disintegrated unconscious—a logic of identification and labor—that suffuses the musical form and triggers the anxieties that prompt critics to declare that the genre is integrated.

*The Song Is You* consists of a single argumentative arc structured in three parts. The case studies and arguments of chapters 1 through 4 form the infrastructure for the synoptic account of the genre that I articulate in chapter 5, while chapters 6, 7, and the conclusion explore (mostly recent) responses to the ethical issues that I explore in chapter 5. Chapters 1 through 4 use historically informed case studies of musicals like *Show Boat* and *Oklahoma!* to show how the discourse of integration is fundamentally concerned with anxieties related to the laboring bodies who perform and experience musical theatre. Beginning with an examination of *The Black Crook*, long cited as the first musical, I argue that the foundational gesture of the genre is the eruption of the burlesque bodies of women into narrative—and that claims of "integration" in shows like *Oklahoma!* respond to fundamental anxieties provoked by the eruptions of these women's bodies. Chapters 1 through 3 show how the discourse of integration works: to insist that the radical energies of women's bodies can be contained; to distance the performers, and by extension the genre, of musical theatre from the socially marginalized form of burlesque and the related threat of sexualized labor; and to disavow the ways in which the form facilitates identifications between (male) spectators and the women performers who are situated outside the narrative. By exploring *Show Boat* and the theories of director Rouben Mamoulian, chapter 4 shows how these same issues explored in the first three chapters regarding women—ones of identification, control, and labor—emerge in the context of (spectacular) black bodies.

The fifth chapter subsumes the concerns of the first four, arguing that a radical aesthetic of disintegration—a disintegrated logic of identification, control, and labor—underpins musical theatre and also generates the anxieties that provoke integration. Chapter 5 argues that this aesthetic of disintegration makes possible the complex identificatory play that works to dismantle the idea of subjectivity. However, because this identificatory play is accomplished through spectacular bodies, the most radical possibilities of the genre are thus predicated on the regressive entertainment forms that mark certain bodies as spectacular. As the genre's liberating transformations of identity are always haunted by the exploitations that make them possible, the musical develops an anxiety about the laboring bodies that make possible these profound psychic transformations. An ethical dilemma thus lurks in the heart of the genre.

The final two chapters and the conclusion explore responses to this dilemma. Chapter 6 focuses on David Henry Hwang's revision of Rodgers and Hammerstein's *Flower Drum Song* to see whether an artist can solve this dilemma through a sensitivity to representation; that is, whether the existing formal structure of musical theatre can accommodate an "authentic" content. Chapter 7 moves from content to form, asking how the through-sung form of musical theatre revises the "across bodies" aesthetic of musical theatre and might thereby offer a different approach to resolving the dilemma. I conclude by exploring three musicals—*Passing Strange*, *Jelly's Last Jam*, and *Soft Power*—that aim not to supply a "better" content, nor to abandon the form, but that instead aim to work through it, revealing a way forward for musicals to address this dilemma while affirming the political pleasures of the genre.

Before elaborating some of this study's broader findings, I should first articulate a few caveats and clarifications. First, my claims about the disjunctive or spectacular nature of the genre in no way contest the obvious truth that the artisans of the musical—distinguished creators like Otto Harbach, Oscar Hammerstein, and Stephen Sondheim—have made extraordinary leaps in dramatic characterization and in the use of songs to continue the thematic concerns of the drama. These writers articulated their genuine dramaturgical ambitions, often explicitly discussing their work in the terms of narrative integration. Indeed, Geoffrey Block has provided an excellent assemblage of comments and writings by various composers, lyricists, and book writers that demonstrate their collective interest in achieving "integration."[41] By suggesting a complex logic that undergirds integration, I do not mean to question the honesty and earnestness with which such claims were put forth. Even when authors realized that the term could be deployed for the purposes of elevating or marketing musical theatre, "integration" was not a disingenuous hoax perpetrated upon a naïve public. What I do mean to suggest is that the broader underlying goal to "tame" these musical outbursts, to gain control over the musical numbers, is a response to the powers inherent in the aesthetic of "bursting into song and dance." My goal is to articulate these powers.

Second, when I insist upon the genre's oscillations between narrative and spectacle, I do not mean to suggest that moments of song and dance have no storytelling capacities whatsoever, for they certainly do. However, I do mean to suggest that these elements, when present in song and dance, are relegated to a position significantly subordinate to the more powerful engagement that the spectacular bodies of those numbers make with audiences. My premise is that the rhetoric of integration is a systematic denial of this other spectacular mode in favor of a totalizing view of narrative—a hierarchy that runs so obviously counter to the musical's manifest priorities and pleasures.

Third, as a further clarification, the rhetoric of "bursting" is not meant to deny the manifold styles of musical theatre, which have different approaches to the introduction of song. Some numbers announce themselves with a *fortissimo* cymbal and a *tutti* chorus, while others tiptoe in with a melodic verse that elevates speech ever subtly into song. However, my thesis is centrally concerned not with any particular *quality* of interruption, but instead with the very *fact* of interruption—with the inevitable deferral of one mode of presentation while another mode engages spectators differently. Thus, while not every number bounds on the stage with a shocking jolt, it is not accidental that the expression "bursting into song and dance" is a conventional term in popular discourse for describing this fundamental trait of musical theatre, regardless of the styles of the eruptions in any one show. Indeed, the popular imagination has articulated—correctly, I believe—precisely how the genre is working, an articulation that informs this study.

Fourth, the concept of integration in musical theatre emerges in the early part of the twentieth century, in concert with such broader dramatic developments as the well-made play, with its emphasis on the "solid structure of dramaturgic technic,"[42] and in parallel with the emergence of the unitary subject of modernism. In discussing an early work like *The Black Crook*, a work that predates discussions of "integration," I do not mean to deny that spectatorial traditions were different in the nineteenth century. I do, however, mean to point out the raw elements of the form that were ready-made templates for later developments in musical theatre. On a related note, while this book is deeply invested in the historical archive, I do not necessarily move in a chronological fashion, either across the book or within individual chapters. At times, I bring different pieces together in the same paragraph in order to illuminate recurring themes, structures, and forms. By foregoing a certain kind of conventional temporality, I hope to have instead identified a set of structural concerns that recur across periods, styles, and genres.

Last, I access answers to these formal questions both through examining archival materials—newspaper reviews, contemporaneous magazine articles, writings by artists and critics, as well as manuscripts and drafts—and through close readings of musicals. These close readings of musical theatre texts help us to understand what the form permits, encourages, demands—thereby tracing the possibilities of the form itself. It might initially seem paradoxical that a book emphasizing the limits and failures of narrative should be invested in interrogating plots. However, musicals are always in a sense telling stories about musicals, and attending closely to these stories can reveal how the form works at a more fundamental level.

As for the study's broad findings, I make six related claims. First, I argue that the politics of musical theatre are linked to its aesthetic of failure: the musical links narrative failure, bodily failure, and the failure of subjectivity. The moment of bursting into song and dance occurs not when words alone are insufficient to convey a certain emotion—as an oft-repeated description of the genre would have it—but instead when a torrent of desire builds within us to exceed the limits of our discrete bodies. Thus, the genre links narrative failure—the insufficiency of a single mode of presentation (e.g., dialogue) to convey the drama—and bodily failure—the insufficiency of a single body to experience it. Through this bodily failure, we are delivered to a different kind of subjectivity. In this way, the eruptive form of musical theatre—its constant oscillation between narrative and spectacle—works to create a similar sense of rupture in the subjectivities of its spectators, creators, and performers.

Second, in this moment of bodily failure, we are invited to try on other bodies. The musical theatre form is an apparatus that facilitates psychic relationships across different kinds of bodies. These psychic relationships are modeled by the cross-gender, cross-ethnic, and cross-racial performances that the genre relentlessly indulges. This "trying on of other bodies," which forms the infrastructure of the genre, is indebted to the nineteenth-century cultural traditions of burlesque and minstrelsy, which mark certain bodies as repositories of erotic energy, and thus as spectacular points of sensuous identification.

However, minstrelsy becomes more complex as it, and similar forms, are enfolded within the form of musical theatre. Historically, minstrelsy invited its performers (and, by extension, its spectators) to apply the make-up and thereby try on *one* other body, and to feel power in the taking-off of the makeup (and the other identity)—thereby emphasizing that one is ultimately *not* that other identity. The musical, by contrast, asks us to try on a dizzying *series* of bodies in such rapid and incoherent fashion as to undermine the idea of identity. This is crucial, as the musical, with its endless predilection for bursting into song and dance, is constantly asking spectators to associate not just with one other body but with *many* other bodies. This complexity is modeled by the genre's own investment in transitive chains of imitations—as seen in what I will call its exotic/erotic performances, its almost inevitable linking of cross-gender and cross-racial performance. In both these moments of "cross-" performances—which are themselves *failed* performances of gender, ethnicity, and race—and in the psychic operations that they engender, one impersonation prompts yet another, ricocheting desire from body to body to body. As the number of impersonations grows, the musical promotes ever-changing cross-identifications, thereby endlessly reconfiguring reified social categories like gender and race—ultimately dissolving the very concept of stable identity itself. This is the work that the musical undertakes every time it bursts into song and dance. By facilitating this powerful work of dissolution for the duration of the aesthetic experience, the musical can help the spectator to rehearse a utopian vision of new subjectivities, pleasures, and relationships—a vision that the spectator of musical theatre might work to realize outside the theatre as well.

Third, the power of the musical is derived from this aesthetic of dis-integration—from its ability to destabilize identity through the manifold identifications solicited by the formal structure of failure. Integration, however, denies narrative failure, suggesting instead that the (otherwise disruptive) spectacle has been subsumed into a totalizing, uninterrupted narrative order. By denying the narrative failure, integration also denies the identifications made possible by the musical form, suggesting instead not only a sophisticated model of authorial and spectatorial control but also a stable subject.

Fourth, the narrative view implied by "integration" profoundly misrepresents the role of narrative and subjectivity in musical theatre. The musical is designed not so that narrative may triumph—as the discourse of integration would suggest—but so that it can fail. Indeed, the genre's deep investment in adaptation—with the pleasure of seeing how well-known narratives will be broken up by the form—testifies to the ways in which musical theatre posits narratives precisely to see how they fail. Further, just as the musical posits a narrative so that it may pleasurably fail, it also posits a subject position precisely so that this subject can pleasurably fail. The musical, in other words, finds pleasure in the immolation of the unmarked subject that it puts forward. This narrative subject—the subject defined in opposition to the spectacular—is immolated precisely through the work of the spectacular performers. Integration, however, denies the work of these bodies and shores up this subject, suggesting that this subject position has been unaffected by the work of the spectacular bodies onstage.

Fifth, because spectacular bodies effect this immolation of subjectivity, they undertake subversive work every time they burst into song and dance. Whether spectators find such work transcendent or they find it unsettling, there can be no doubt that these bodies accomplish the genre's most profound effects. Because the genre's radical possibilities are thus predicated on the marking of certain bodies as spectacular—a marking that ultimately permits a different kind of relationship with these bodies—the genre is haunted by its own potentially exploitative consumption of certain laboring bodies. Thus, the genre's progressive politics—its modeling of the destabilizing of identity—is made possible by its foundations in these ostensibly regressive forms, burlesque and minstrelsy among them, that mark and deploy certain bodies as spectacular. As a result, the genre is obsessed with the labor of these spectacular bodies, an obsession that materializes in its plots.

Sixth, if the musical's form exploits certain bodies, the very same form opens up the possibility to critique this exploitation. Indeed, the genre's aesthetic of failure makes possible a reflexive critique of the musical's own failures. I conclude by looking at three musicals—authored by African American and Asian American artists—that force a reexamination of the genre's conventions, pleasures, and effects.

While the argument will unfold over seven chapters and countless examples, its insights are all present in the moment when Eliza bursts into "The Rain in Spain." When lyricist Alan Jay Lerner's wife Nancy Livingston heard her husband and composer Frederick Loewe jubilantly perform the material moments after they wrote it, she recalled telling them, "You have created one problem." The problem? "This number will stop the show."[43] And of course she was right—the number, according to stage manager Jerry Adler, was "a showstopper."[44] Indeed, all of these great joys and attendant anxieties of musical theatre emerge precisely from the moment of stopping the show, from the "impromptu outburst" that characterizes not only "The Rain in Spain" but every eruption of song and dance in musical theatre. The form of musical theatre thus models not only an aesthetic form but also a form of subjectivity, and the goal of this book is to understand both by thinking through the actual *work* of musical theatre.

The "Postcard Girls" of the dream ballet in the 1979 Broadway revival of *Okla-homa!* Photograph by Martha Swope, ©Billy Rose Theatre Division, New York Public Library for the Performing Arts.

# 1

# THE DANCING
# TABLEAU OF
# *OKLAHOMA!*

Foreswearing its earlier addictions to vaudeville and burlesque, the musical finally matured when *Oklahoma!* "integrated" its various art forms—so the histories tell us. The critics who attended the opening night performance in 1943 certainly thought so: Lewis Nichols, writing in the *New York Times,* asserted that "Mr. Rodgers's scores never lack grace, but seldom have they been so well integrated as this for 'Oklahoma!,'"[1] while Howard Barnes similarly observed that "[s]ongs, dances, and a story have been triumphantly blended at the St. James."[2] This attitude was taken up in academic treatments of musical theatre as well. In his magisterial *American Musical Theatre: A Chronicle,* Gerald Bordman discusses the "excellent totality of *Oklahoma!,*" writing that "much ballyhoo ensued over how well the songs and plot were integrated. They were."[3] In *The Broadway Musical,* Joseph Swain muses that *Oklahoma!* "survives . . . because of its own integrity,"[4] while John Bush Jones, in *Our Musicals, Ourselves,* describes *Oklahoma!* as a "totally integrated musical."[5] And for Stanley Green, "what was unique about *Oklahoma!* was the synthesis of its component parts into a complete theatrical entity of great beauty and imagination."[6]

In praising the show, critics paid particular attention to Agnes de Mille's choreography, especially the famous dream ballet that closed the first act. Burns Mantle went so far as to write that *Oklahoma!* "is a combination of Lynn Riggs' 'Green Grow the Lilacs' and Agnes de Mille's 'Rodeo' ballet, if you can picture the combination. And a mighty sweet joining of the arts of drama and the dance."[7] Calling the dream ballet "spine-tingling, out of this world," Burton Rascoe noted that de Mille's choreography, "carried out to perfection by her ballet, is actually the biggest hit of the show."[8]

I want to probe what is meant by the claims that *Oklahoma!* is integrated, which—as these reviews would suggest—involves accounting for the role of dance in the piece. In this context, we might look more closely at Peter Riddle's laudatory claim that in *Oklahoma!*, "Rodgers and Hammerstein chose deliberately to eschew most of the conventions that had developed ever since *The Black Crook*."[9] Riddle's invocation of *The Black Crook*—an 1866 production often cited as the first musical—takes us to the nexus of a wide range of issues concerning musical theatre, dance, and women's bodies. However, the relationship of *The Black Crook* and *Oklahoma!* is far more complex than mere eschewal or rejection. On the contrary, *Oklahoma!* achieves its potency—its alleged "integration"—precisely by engaging with the infrastructure first laid out in *The Black Crook*. The historical circumstances surrounding *The Black Crook* involve the profound erotic energy of female dancers transcending the narrative—a scene that *Oklahoma!* will revisit. However, *Oklahoma!* revisits this scene precisely in order to insist that this energy can be contained—an insistence that is both asserted thematically in the plot of *Oklahoma!* as well as promulgated through the discourse of integration. However, the plot—much as it may work to disavow the radical power of women's bodies—cannot override the work of the form, just as integration cannot either.

It might be surprising to incorporate *Oklahoma!* into a genealogy that dates to *The Black Crook*, if for no other reason than the almost farcical circumstances of its birth. On May 21, 1866, a kitchen fire broke out in the restaurant of Manhattan's Academy of Music, quickly spreading to the auditorium and finally the stage. According to the *New York Times*, the theatre's windows "vomited great tongues of living fire" as the conflagration engulfed the distinguished venue.[10] One of the first grand theatrical buildings erected in New York City, the Academy was now in ashes—a fact which was of no minor significance to Henry C. Jarrett and Harry Palmer, two American producers who had already signed an agreement to present a ballet production at the Academy. At the time of the blaze, the two men had just returned from Europe, where they had travelled to the great opera houses, recruiting some of the continent's finest dancers, including Rita Sangalli and Maria Bonfanti, for their production.[11] Now in desperate need of a theatre to house the contracted dancers, Jarrett and Palmer ingeniously approached William Wheatley, a producer who was leasing Niblo's Garden, one of the largest, most luxurious, and well-ventilated stages in nineteenth-century New York. Seeking to install their production at Niblo's, Jarrett and Palmer proposed that Wheatley join the two men in producing a spectacular drama that would include the dance troupe as well as the fancy scenery and costumes that they had commissioned in Europe. Wheatley agreed to the proposal and suggested that *The Black Crook*, a manuscript submitted to him by Charles Barras, might be suitable for their joint endeavour.[12] Niblo's box office manager Joseph Whitton later wrote that as he read the play, he saw "what Wheatley had already seen, that here was the very piece to fit the Ballet—a clothes-line, as it were, on which to hang the pretty dresses, besides affording abundant opportunities for scenic display."[13] While Whitton and others have noted that the play was not particularly original or inventive, Wheatley was somehow able to persuade the duo to pay the playwright $2,000 for the use of his text.

Barras's play was classic melodrama, with a plot centering on Rodolphe, a young artist whose beloved, Amina, is betrothed to Count Wolfenstein, the "all-powerful lord of this wide domain."[14] After challenging Wolfenstein, Rodolphe is abducted by the Count's underlings and held prisoner; meanwhile, the sorcerer Hertzog, otherwise known as the Black Crook, conjures up the dark spirit of Zamiel with the hopes of restoring the potency of his spells. Zamiel offers the Black Crook a renewable lease on life: for every year he is to live and be powerful, he must offer up one soul to Zamiel. Once the Black Crook agrees to the pact, Zamiel advises him to begin his soul-hunting by preying upon the desperate Rodolphe. At the vault in which Rodolphe is imprisoned, the Black Crook lures Rodolphe to pursue riches which would enable him to snatch Amina from the clutches of Wolfenstein. The Black Crook misleads Rodolphe by suggesting that these riches can be plundered from a cave long guarded by superstition—but which can be safely breached with a talismanic ring that he gives Rodolphe. Knowing that in fact fairies will kill anyone approaching the cave, the Black Crook is thus leading Rodolphe to his demise. As Rodolphe nears the grotto, the fairies notice the ring of the Black Crook, but Stalacta, the Fairy Queen, intervenes because Rodolphe is none other than the young man who saved her earlier that day in the forest from a serpent. She requites his act by replacing the false talismanic ring with a genuine one. After further brushes with Wolfenstein and his grunts, Rodolphe survives, and watches with Amina as Zamiel kills the Black Crook.

However boilerplate a melodrama it might have been, Barras's libretto nonetheless provided a coherent structure into which Wheatley shoehorned Jarrett and Palmer's distinguished company of European ballerinas and all of the scenic wonder they had secured while abroad. As George Odell writes in his encyclopedic *Annals of the New York Stage*, Wheatley "incorporated [Jarrett and Palmer's] effects and their really gorgeous ballet in an absurd melodrama by Charles M. Barras, a melodrama more ridiculous than any burlesque melodrama could possibly be. But it served as a connecting link for the progression of dances, scenes and episodes that made *The Black Crook* the unique thing it was."[15]

The story of the creation of *The Black Crook* seems almost apocryphal, yet thus was born one of the most renowned productions of the nineteenth century. Opening on September 12, 1866, the piece went on to run for over a year, with revivals throughout the decades that followed. Nearly a century later, its significance was validated by the emerging field of theatre historiography, whose practitioners almost invariably cited *The Black Crook* as the genesis of American musical theatre. Writing in 1950, Cecil Smith begins the first major history of the genre, *Musical Comedy in America*, by writing that "[f]or all important purposes, the history of musical comedy in America starts with *The Black Crook*, as everyone has always said it did," adding that he sees the story of musical theatre stretching from "*The Black Crook* at one end to *South Pacific* and other contemporary musical comedies at the other."[16] However, less than twenty pages later, Smith tempers this claim, writing that "to call *The Black Crook* the first example of the theatrical genus we now call musical comedy is not only incorrect; it fails to suggest any useful assessment of the place of Jarrett and Palmer's extravaganza in the history of the popular musical theatre."[17] The piece, Smith wrote, "contained almost none of the vernacular attributes of book, lyrics, music, and dancing" that distinguish the genre. Smith's contradiction—that "the history of musical comedy . . . starts with *The Black Crook*" and that it is incorrect "to call *The Black Crook* the first example of . . . musical comedy"—is telling.

In writing the first history of the genre, Smith is attempting to encapsulate the genre within a coherent narrative. Just as the ballet dancers fractured Barras's melodramatic narrative, the dancers seem to occupy a similarly uneasy place in Smith's narrative. Indeed, his ambivalence about *The Black Crook*—his equivocal veneration and denigration of the show—can be traced to the legs of the female dancers, as they resist the narrative totality that he seeks to impose. Smith himself seems to admit that the legs of the dancers are the problematic element, as he follows his comment that *The Black Crook* "contained almost none of the vernacular attributes of book, lyrics, music, and dancing which distinguish musical comedy" with a concession: "True, it thrust two hundred legs upon the gaze of the beholder," he admits. Though Smith goes on to claim both that legs are not essential to musical theatre and that *The Black Crook* did nothing special leg-wise, the very fact of his concession alerts us to the fact that the legs *are* centrally important to musical theatre.

This fact also bubbles to the surface in theatre historian Julian Mates's legendary complaints about *The Black Crook*. If Smith is ambivalent about the place of the 1866 show in theatre history, Mates is unequivocal: "nothing about *The Black Crook* justifies its position as the precursor of our modern lyric stage," he argues, suggesting that *The Black Crook* is a relatively unremarkable show that should be situated in a longer lineage of musical theatre.[18] Mates argues that "*The Black Crook* added no new elements and no new ways of integrating spectacle, music, and drama," before noting a page later that "if *The Black Crook*'s integration of dance and drama has any claim to originality, it lies not so much with the ballet as with the cry, 'Bring on the girls!'" Dismissing *The Black Crook* as a "girlie show," Mates writes that "no proof exists that the road which leads to burlesque carries either scholar or tired business man to musical comedy."[19] However, this scholar wishes to differ. Indeed, I will argue that the road which leads to burlesque carries all number of travellers precisely to musical comedy. Mates's comments about "integration" point to the historiographic trouble: the legs of *The Black Crook*—its bodily pleasures—resist any high-minded and cerebral narrative of formal integration. By properly considering the bodily pleasures of *The Black Crook*, we might better appreciate how it can be understood, as Christopher Morley wrote in 1929, as "the grandparent of modern musical comedy"[20]—and how it sets the stage for the alleged integration of *Oklahoma!*

To understand the role of *The Black Crook* in this historical narrative, we must return to the most prevalent theatrical form of the nineteenth century: melodrama. I see the musical as inheriting its fragmented structure from the narrative-spectacle dichotomy of melodrama, whereby embodied tableaux would interrupt dramatic scenes. These tableaux were brought to life by the dancers of *The Black Crook*, women whose sexualized bodies transported them beyond the realm of narrative. As they moved beyond narrative concerns, these women transcended the passive roles to which they were relegated and instead assumed a tremendous power in the act of performance—thereby generating the constitutive formal structure of *bursting* into song and dance. In contrast to the critics who dismiss *The Black Crook* as nothing more than a glorified burlesque show—and therefore irrelevant to the history of musical theatre—I see the elements of *The Black Crook* inflected by burlesque as directly responsible for its place in the development of musical theatre. Furthermore, any claim that *Oklahoma!* is integrated must be understood within this historiographic context.

Musical theatre inherited its interruptive structure—its alternation between narrative and spectacular modes—from melodrama, which featured a similar structure in which narrative scenes were punctuated by embodied interruptions in the form of tableaux. These interruptions were part of a broader aesthetic tradition in the nineteenth century that foregrounded interruptive rhythms. Indeed, as early as the late eighteenth century, sentimental novels had popularized a formal structure that interrupted seemingly simple narratives with episodes known as tableaux, essentially ekphrastic passages in which an object or event was held up for extended description and contemplation. The juxtaposition of these two modes, narrative and tableau, brought into sharp relief the different functions of each. As David Denby argues, "sentimentalism has its roots in narrative, and in a type of narrative which is at heart very simple. But . . . sentimental narratives are constantly punctuated by *tableaux* of various kinds, which appear to function precisely in a spatial rather than a temporal dimension, and to imply a mode of perception radically opposed to that of narrative."[21] Noting how literary tableaux are often considered to have evolved from the practice of plate illustrations that accompanied many short narratives, Anne Patricia Williams writes that the tableau works "to deny the power of language to capture subjective feeling."[22]

The tableau—this emotive, visually descriptive fragment standing in opposition to coherent narrative—was taken up as a theatrical device in melodrama, which was even more adept at foregrounding the inadequacy of language, since it deployed the non-linguistic modes of music and bodily gesture. Melodramatic scenes were often interrupted by tableaux, painterly moments in which the characters briefly adopted and held a pose that captured the relational dynamics in play and gave what Peter Brooks described as a "visual summary of the emotional situation."[23] *The Black Crook*, of course, participates in this conventional use of the tableau, as for instance in its deployment of the well-established tableau of astonishment. After Wolfenstein confronts Rodolphe at a ball, for example, Rodolphe kisses his ring, instantly summoning Stalacta and the fairies. Following "*Exciting action*," the script continues: "Wolfenstein, *guards, and gentlemen shrink back appalled.* Hertzog *stands, the embodiment of baffled rage.* Von Puffengruntz *on terrace, faints and falls into the arms of* Barbara, *who fans him. Tableau and quick curtain.*"[24] Here, as is customary in melodrama, the bodies of the tableau distill the relationships between characters and condense the moment's emotional vectors into a composed stage picture. Insofar as tableaux like this one marshal the visual and musical resources of the stage and the immediacy and temporality of the theatrical situation, the tableaux of melodrama were able to affirm and indeed magnify the sense of interruption that was so prevalent in late-eighteenth-century culture, thereby laying the foundation for musical theatre.

While it might at first seem an antiquated relic, the tableau thus remains a central part of contemporary theatrical life in musical theatre, indeed in every moment when the dramatic narrative stops and spectacular bodies burst out in song and dance. Every time the form bursts, we feel how the tableau felt, as we experience bodies fragmenting narrative. In other words, the disintegrated structure of the musical, with its split between dramatic scenes and song and dance, emerges directly from melodrama's long-standing investment in the visual deployment of bodies in tableaux to interrupt narrative.

However, *The Black Crook* transforms the spectacular tableau of melodrama by drawing on, and extending, the pleasures of the related posing traditions of the *tableau vivant* and the *pose plastique*. While the melodramatic tableau focused on moving bodies brought still, the tableau vivant and pose plastique—which informed how *The Black Crook* would have been understood—offered the related visual pleasure of seeing still pictures and statuary, respectively, brought to life by alternately mobile and immobile bodies.[25] Further, these posing entertainments shared with melodrama a deep investment in the visual display of mythic and ideal subjects. In *The Black Crook*, the European pedigree of the dancers, the classical gestures evoked by the solidly Romantic style of ballet, along with the well-circulated image of ballet as ethereal and otherworldly, all contributed to understanding the dancers' movements as classical statuary in motion—taking to its logical conclusion the impulse behind the tableau, the tableau vivant, and the pose plastique. In other words, the women of the ballet were statues brought to life. To understand how motion could be the logical conclusion of the various seemingly static tableau phenomena, we might reconsider the relationship between stasis and movement in these posing traditions.

In referring to the tableau, critics frequently foreground its stillness; however, in contrast to this emphasis on the tableau's static qualities, Philippe Hamon usefully defines the literary tableau as a "'lively and animated' description of actions, passions, physical or moral events."[26] Though seemingly contradictory, these two qualities—static, yet also lively and animated—are, in fact, easily reconciled: as tableau interrupts narrative, it is precisely *narrative* that becomes static; meanwhile, the tableau activates a dynamic affective force. As Denby notes, "its function is to freeze narrative, to suspend temporal progression so that the set of forces which the narrative has brought together in a particular moment may be allowed to discharge their full affective power."[27] Resisting the inertia of narrative, which serves to defer affective release, tableaux allow the reader to amplify, savor, and metabolize the emotional forces conjured by the text.

Just as the literary tableau in this way oscillates between stasis and action, the melodramatic tableau similarly participates in a much more complicated relationship between stillness and animation. While the seemingly still image of the tableau sublimates potential energies and suggests incipient action, other related tableau entertainments—foremost among them the tableau vivant and pose plastique—attempt to realize, however briefly, this incipient action, indulging the related pleasures of paintings and statues brought to life.

This elaboration of the tableau structure was part of a broader aesthetic interest in animating what had previously been static. This dialectic between stasis and motion that I am attributing to the pose plastique and the tableau vivant was also present in the period's deep investment in enlivening or animating classical statuary.[28] The intellectual father of the tableau vivant, Goethe, describes much the same dynamic when he says of the Laocoön: "To seize well the attention of the Laocoön, let us place ourselves before the groupe [sic] with our eyes shut, and at the necessary distance; let us open and shut them alternately and we shall see all the marble in motion."[29] William Hazlitt echoes these sentiments when he observes that, in certain of the Elgin Marbles, "the whole is melted into one impression like wax; there is all the flexibility, the malleableness of flesh . . . and the statue bends and plays . . . as if, instead of being a block of marble, it was provided with an internal machinery of nerves and muscles."[30] No wonder, then, that Goethe himself was fascinated by the similar aesthetic offered by the posing traditions. The late eighteenth and nineteenth century craze for posing began when Goethe popularized the "attitudes" of Emma Lyon Hamilton, in which she would adopt a series of classical poses in a private salon.[31] While the Pygmalionesque fantasy of vivified statues is a venerable one, it took on an especial intensity as the basis of a number of very popular entertainments in nineteenth-century America.[32] The associations that attached themselves to these American entertainments would govern how *The Black Crook* was received, in a context that was simultaneously artistic and erotic.

By 1831, Mrs. Ada Barrymore appeared in New York, advertising a series of "tableaux vivans" [sic] likely adapted from the work of Andrew Ducrow, the celebrated British equestrian artist who had presented his "personifications" and "living statues" within dramatic presentations.[33] During the 1830s and 1840s, tableaux vivants and poses plastiques became quite the craze, occasionally presented in broader dramatic structures like pantomimes but usually presented as entertainments unto themselves. These early incarnations of tableaux vivants and poses plastiques generally focused on moral and didactic edification, advertising themselves as being inspired by the "classical" and "ancient" work of the "celebrated masters."[34]

In adopting these poses, women became the virtually immobile objects of the gaze of men. While men were invited to gaze upon women's bodies, women were denied the power of looking. As Mary Chapman notes in her study of tableau vivant manuals, women's eyes "are perpetually 'modestly cast down' and 'face[s] . . . bent downward as if blushing.'"[35] Indeed, the Victorian affinity for tableaux vivants celebrated how women's movements could be halted when they embodied statues. In this way, the passivity associated with the retiring heroines of melodrama found its ultimate expression in the poses of tableaux vivants, entertainments in which women's bodies were mobilized in order to be immobilized. By embodying the mythic and ideal figures of statuary while silent and still, women accessed the otherworldly realm so central to melodramatic experience. While part of the pleasure of these posing traditions focused on activating the statues, another pleasure was to be found in silencing and paralyzing the female performer, diminishing her power and reducing her to the model submissive Victorian woman. As Chapman has observed, many tableaux vivants performed "the virtues of the cult of true womanhood: piety, purity, submissiveness, and domesticity."[36] Chapman reveals that even the most adventurous and powerful female figures in myths were depicted in tableaux only in their most passive moments, often repenting for their unfeminine transgressions just as they were dying. This approach to depicting women foregrounds how the posing traditions sought to bring myths to life, such that the powerful performer could be tamed into a silent, passive woman.

By 1847, some presenters began to capitalize on the possibility of these entertainments to reveal feminine form, and thus began the long-standing tension, nearly inherent in the genre, between mythic ideality and erotic materiality, between poetry and pornography. The sexualized dimensions of the posing traditions would have given spectators a context for understanding the tableaux of *The Black Crook*, which, to be sure, was notorious for its extensive display of women's bodies. Reporting on the production, the *New York Times* wrote that "such dancing has never been seen here; such unembarrassed disporting of human organism has never been indulged in before."[37] Elsewhere characterized as consisting of "lithesome limbs and lovely lasses," the "unembarrassed disporting" in the show prompted the *Clipper* to salute "the symmetrical legs and alabaster bosoms so lavishly presented to our view through the liberality of *The Black Crook*."[38] Much was made of the near nudity of the dancers, as for example in a *New York Times* comment about the "witching *Pas de Demons*, in which the Demonese, who wear no clothes to speak of, so gracefully and prettily disported as to draw forth thunders of applause."[39] A more precise account of the bodily display of *The Black Crook* comes from Reverend Charles Smith, a preacher who, after visiting the show himself, all too predictably warned others not to subject themselves to its immorality. Smith preached that "the first thing that strikes the eye is the immodest dress of the girls; the short skirt and undergarments of thin gauze-like material . . . ; the flesh colored tights, imitating nature so well that the illusion is complete; with the exceedingly short drawers, almost tight fitting . . . arms and neck apparently bare, and bodice so cut and fitted as to show off every inch and outline of the body above the waist."[40] For Smith, the indecorous nature of these costumes was only amplified when in motion: he complained of "ladies dancing so as to make their undergarments spring up, exposing the figure beneath from the waist to the toe, except for such covering as we have described . . . ." The coupling of men and women added insult to injury; "when a danseuse is assisted by a danseur," he noted, "the attitudes assumed by both in conjunction suggest to the imagination scenes which one may read of in descriptions of ancient heathen orgies."[41] Equally incensed was a writer for the *New York Herald*, who complained of the "indecent and demoralizing exposition" of *The Black Crook*, opining that "we can imagine that there might have been in Sodom and Gomorrah such another place and scene, such another theatre and spectacle on the Broadway of those doomed cities just before fire and brimstone rained down upon them and buried them in the ruins."[42]

However, these views, though very widely held, were not universal. The *New York Daily Tribune* dismissed such screeds with its sentiment that "[a] ballet is a ballet. So long as it is not indecent, there is nothing more to be said about it . . . . Youths who can be injured by looking at a lot of dancing girls must be made of very worthless materials."[43] This kind of ambivalence received its clearest articulation in Olive Logan's 1869 account of *The Black Crook*, in which she testifies that the show's scandalous display of the feminine corps was tempered by the art involved:

> When the *Black Crook* first presented its nude woman to the gaze of a crowded auditory, she was met with a gasp of astonishment at the effrontery which dared so much. Men actually grew pale at the boldness of the thing; a death-like silence fell over the house, broken only by the clapping of a band of *claqueurs* around the outer aisles; but it passed; and, in view of the fact that these women were French ballet-dancers after all, they were tolerated . . . . Those women were ballet-dancers from France and Italy, and they represented in their nudity imps and demons. In silence they whirled about the stage; in silence trooped off. Some faint odor of ideality and poetry rested over them.[44]

Logan's sense that the dancers balanced their "effrontery" and "boldness" with "ideality and poetry" revisits the complex interplay of sexuality and art that pervades the piece. This complex balance and interplay was captured by the phrase "model artist," which was a generic term for the posing entertainments that distilled these tensions—and the genre's relationship to burlesque—even more precisely than did the related terms tableau vivant and pose plastique. In its earliest appearances, the term "model artist" emphasized the artistic qualities of the performers; yet, as the century progressed, it often came to connote a number of down-market, salacious variations on this erstwhile upstanding genre. The *New York Clipper* explicitly referred to the dancers of *The Black Crook* as "model artists," asserting that the "imported model artists" did give "variety" to the proceedings, but also "pander[ed] to a taste already sufficiently depraved without this incentive to greater lewdness. It will not be surprising if a revival of nude model artist exhibitions throughout the city should follow this exposition of undressed dancing girls at Niblo's. The one would draw as well as the other."[45] Charles Smith, the moralizing preacher who warned of the immorality of *The Black Crook*, condescendingly characterized the dancers as such: "Model artists they are, poor things," he wrote.[46] And Mark Twain, writing about his trip to see *The Black Crook*, explicitly associated the show's dancing bodies with the posing entertainments by humorously comparing the dancers of *The Black Crook* to model artists: "When I was here in '53, a model artist show had an ephemeral existence in Chatham street, and then everybody growled about it, and the police broke it up . . . people wouldn't go to see it. But now they call that sort of thing a 'Grand Spectacular Drama,' and everybody goes."[47] He writes that "those girls dance in ballet, dressed with a meagreness that would make a parasol blush. And they prance around and expose themselves in a way that is scandalous to me."[48] Comments like these make clear that the musical numbers of *The Black Crook* were indeed seen as part of the tradition of eroticized and vivified tableaux vivants, which we can now see as part of the broader tradition of burlesque. It was the display of women's bodies in motion—often dismissed as the burlesque element—that permitted the women's bodies to attain the "escape," the "beyond," that was the signal effect of the tableau. It is precisely through the burlesque element, through the deployment of erotically charged bodies, that *The Black Crook* transcends its narrative and makes its most potent aesthetic gesture: a bursting into song and dance that mirrored the scene of its emergence, when the ballet fractured the narrative of Barras's melodrama.

However, by incorporating this burlesque tradition within the melodramatic structure of musical theatre, *The Black Crook* transformed this tradition and realized a very different potential. If the women of tableaux vivants subordinated themselves in submissive stillness in order to access the ethereal realm of the ideal, the musical reversed this tendency and afforded women profound agency. Unlike all of the retreating, wilting, dying heroines of melodrama and the passive spectacles of the tableaux vivants, the dancers of the musical were active, vibrant, and erotically potent. Their bodies, sexualized on display, were endowed in the moment of performance with a profoundly empowering license.

Such an attitude of empowerment extended beyond the stage as well. Indeed, it is worth noting that the principal dancers of *The Black Crook* were in fact exercising profound agency in their lives. To have elected to come to America in the first place was an act of deep courage and adventurousness. As Barbara Barker noted, "the ballerinas left secure employment in state-supported theatres with their knowledgeable, partisan audiences and the fixed order of established traditions. . . . They had no guarantees except handwritten contracts for six months' employment, which might or might not be good."[49] And while these particular contracts *did* prove valid, the dancers of *The Black Crook* found opportunities to advocate for dancers and their rights. In several instances, Giuseppina Morlacchi defended younger dancers from capricious managers, as in one case when a manager demanded that a young dancer pay for a broken prop, despite the fact that it had in actuality been broken by a worker at the theatre. As Barker reports, Morlacchi "insisted that the girl's money be refunded. When the manager refused, she broke her engagement and left the theatre, taking the girl with her."[50] Maria Bonfanti also made valiant efforts on this front, participating in the Sorosis Club, a proto-feminist organization that hoped to attain better rights for women workers, including women in the theatre. And of course, being a performer—and thus a female worker in the public sphere—was an act of resistance all its own in the nineteenth century. These women went even further, with Bonfanti opening a dance school and Morlacchi sometimes "teaching the local mill girls to dance."[51] All three of the principal dancers had gained national attention and commanded salaries that were substantial for their time. Both onstage and off, *The Black Crook* provided new opportunities for empowering women.

In a similar vein, it is not coincidental that the historiography of black musical theatre begins with the 1890 production *The Creole Show*, which James Weldon Johnson characterized as the first show to "glorify the coloured girl."[52] The show's veneration of black womanhood—and Johnson's citation of this veneration as the show's most distinctive contribution—reveals that in this period of segregated performance, black musical theatre developed similarly through a focus on the exposure of black women's bodies. And just as the dancing white women of *The Black Crook* offered a powerful alternative to the retiring heroines of melodrama, the dancing black women of *The Creole Show*, with their "robust, expressive working women's bodies offered contrast, foil, and supplement to the frail, sickly, and sexually constructed literary heroines" of that period, as Jayna Brown has written. For Brown, the sexualized black bodies of the chorus girls "reflected a wide trajectory of black, and black female, mobility," becoming "important figures of hopeful migratory movement, urban ebullience, and promise."[53]

While dance afforded the dancers of *The Black Crook* and *The Creole Show* a quite literal "escape" from the social strictures of their time, it is important to note that the narrative structure of the musical provides a structural possibility of "escape"—an opportunity for these women's bodies to transcend the confines of the narrative and assume power in the act of performance. This is precisely how musical theatre developed its odd oscillation between treating women as passive objects of the narrative and celebrating them as powerful performing subjects—this oscillation being a central source of the affective disintegration whose pleasures structure the genre. In this way, the genre's constitutive sense of disintegration can be traced to this transformation of women's bodies in tableau culture. Every disintegrating moment will, like this one, be borne of the transformations of *bodies*, made possible at this structural juncture between narrative and spectacle.

*The Black Crook* thus helps us to trace what I think to be the most direct ancestry of the musical: its emergence from melodrama through the bodies that enliven the tableau. The musical, in other words, is a melodrama in which erotically charged dancing bodies transport us beyond the realm of narrative. *The Black Crook* inaugurates the form of musical theatre, which as a genre works to modulate into corporeal terms the conventional melodramatic understanding that music is invoked when words will no longer suffice: it is precisely through the bodies of the performers that *The Black Crook* and its audiences access the realm of "beyond." In its reworking of melodramatic traditions, *The Black Crook* sets forth the historical and formal significance of dancing female bodies to the genre's constitutive disintegration.

Given that women's bodies produce this disintegration, these bodies unsurprisingly become the terrain upon which claims of integration are made in relation to *Oklahoma!* In other words, *Oklahoma!* does not merely reject *The Black Crook*—nor does it pursue some revolutionary, sui generis path that ignored everything that preceded it. Instead, the formal structure outlined by *The Black Crook*—in which interludes of dance released women from the passive roles to which they were often relegated—in fact provides the very infrastructure for Agnes de Mille's extraordinary work in the 1943 musical *Oklahoma!* In this way, the earlier work became a useful historiographic foil, a vehicle for articulating the power of *Oklahoma!* that simultaneously obscures the formal similarities between the two.

To be sure, de Mille's work in this show has long been considered a landmark in musical theatre choreography, with Richard Kislan writing that de Mille's work "functioned onstage in so substantial and valid a way as to secure for the choreographer the status of coequal to playwright, composer, and lyricist in the making of a musical show."[54] This achievement was generally understood as having "integrated" dance. As Ethan Mordden notes, "director Rouben Mamoulian and choreographer Agnes de Mille found a way to mesh their work, to hold all of *Oklahoma!*'s staging in balance the way its authors had matched the score to the book."[55] However, we might look closely at Mordden's next line: "True, one piece did stand out: the dream ballet, 'Laurey Makes Up Her Mind.'" It is precisely this dream ballet—this exception to his rule, this eruption of dance, this "standing out"—that links *Oklahoma!* to the musical in which dance first fractured the narrative: *The Black Crook.*

Just as the eruptive structure of *The Black Crook* gave control to women, the dream ballet—with its title, "Laurey Makes Up Her Mind"—explores a dynamic of empowerment. Indeed, Laurey is not merely "making up her mind" in the sense of deciding between Curly and Jud. She is "making up"—in the sense of creating or generating—her mind. Only in this dance, only through the dancing body, does Laurey conjure—or articulate, even to herself—her deepest thoughts and desires. As Roger

Copeland observed in *Dance Magazine*, "it was de Mille's dream ballet *Laurey Makes Up Her Mind* which first suggested that even a frivolous, simple-minded ingénue like *Oklahoma!*'s Laurey might possess a complex and turbulent inner life."[56] Indeed, *Oklahoma!* insists that the dancing body is the medium through which a (female) desire can transcend the otherwise controlling narrative.

However, the significance of de Mille's use of the dancing female body to articulate desire must be understood within the broader context of *Oklahoma!*, which is at every moment concerned with the sexualization and trafficking of women's bodies. As soon as Will Parker arrives back in town from Kansas City, he shows the rest of the townsmen what he bought for the father of his beloved Ado Annie: "The Little Wonder," a kaleidoscopic toy that, when turned, reveals a woman undressing. Drawing the men of the town around him, they share in the images of women disrobing. Will then sings about all the ways that they've gone "about as fur as they c'n go" in Kansas City, recalling seven-story skyscrapers, radiators, gas buggies, and telephones.[57] However, the modern achievement that receives his most extended description is the "bur-lee-que" he attended, where he watched a "fat and pink and pretty" woman "prov[e] that ev'rythin' she had was absolutely real."

Though Will may put a relatively benign spin on viewing the bodies of burlesque, the farmhand Jud lends a foreboding coefficient to every incident of gazing at women. In the first scene, Laurey confesses to Aunt Eller her fears about Jud, noting that he makes her "shivver ever' time he gits clost to me," later confessing alarm over the "pink covers off *Police Gazettes*" that adorn the walls of his smokehouse abode.[58] Jud also reveals that "The Little Wonder," which Will had understood as a mere novelty, in fact possesses a much more sinister dimension. As Jud describes it to the Peddler, "it's a thing you hold up to your eyes to see pitchers, only that ain't all they is to it . . . not quite. Y'see it's got a little jigger onto it, and you tetch it and out springs a sharp blade . . . . Y'say to a feller, 'Look through this.' Nen when he's lookin' you snap out the blade. It's jist above his chest and, bang!"[59] In *Oklahoma!*, women's bodies are seductive—but lethal. And significantly in this case, they are lethal insofar as they provide a visual distraction that, through a toy, enables one man to extend a blade and penetrate another.

No doubt sensitive to this broader anxiety about these bodies, Curly tries his best not to participate in the ongoing focus on women's bodies. In the smokehouse, when Jud offers him a postcard, Curly covers his eyes: "I'll go blind!"[60] Set amidst an atmosphere rampant with sexuality, Curly's moralizing scenes are well matched by Laurey's naivete. After Ado Annie confesses that she "like[s] it so much when a feller talks purty to me I git all shaky from horn to hoof," she follows by asking Laurey, "Don't you?" Laurey's obliviously sterile reply, "cain't think whut yer talkin' about," precedes her counsel that Ado Annie "jist cain't go around kissin' every man that asts," prompting Ado Annie to launch into her celebrated defense of why she "cain't say no."[61] Ado Annie's song is but one of the highlights in a play that is fundamentally about Laurey's journey from sterility to some kind of sexuality.

Meanwhile, Ado Annie is not the only character to bring sexuality to Laurey's experience of the world. When Ali Hakim comes to peddle goods to Aunt Eller and Laurey, he asks Laurey if she wants anything, prompting her to elaborate a litany of her desires. With the stage directions indicating that she "work[s] up to a kind of abstracted ecstasy," Laurey says she wants "things I cain't tell you about—not only things to look at and hold in yer hands. Things to happen to you. Things so nice, if they ever did happen to you, yer heart ud quit beatin."[62] In response, he offers up the Elixir of Egypt, smelling salts that purportedly help one to see things clearly and make a decision.

When Laurey inhales the Egyptian potion—thereby incorporating this exotic brew hawked by the Persian peddler into her own body—the concoction becomes a philter, unleashing her own subconscious desire, as explored and revealed in the dream ballet through her terpsichorean counterpart, the dancing Dream Laurey. Through the dream ballet, the most celebrated sequence of the show, Laurey tells her own story. As it turns out, her story, the story of her sexuality, surprises even her: she might desire Jud. This desire for Jud is a desire for someone dangerous, but that danger is mediated through the book's racialized depictions of Jud as a kind of animalistic threat. Not only does Curly first refer to Jud as "bullet-colored," but the stage directions for "Pore Jud" indicate that Jud repeats lines "reverently like a Negro at a revivalist meeting."[63] Referring to Jud staring at her "like sumpin back in the bresh som'eres," Laurey tells

Aunt Eller that she "hook[s her] door at night and fasten[s] her winders again' it. Agin' *it*." As Andrea Most observes, Jud "is dark and evil . . . . His sexuality, like that of the stereotypical male racial other, is threatening."[64] Laurey's desire for Jud thus stands in for a romance whose psychic power is surely mediated through social prohibitions.

Indeed, de Mille herself wrote that Laurey was drawn to Jud's "absorption in sex, a mysterious and forbidden kind of sex."[65] As Laurey recoils at the revelation of her desire, the *Police Gazette* girls—the women depicted on the magazine covers in Jud's smokehouse—enter, having come to life as dancing burlesque performers. Here, *Oklahoma!* makes explicit its relationship to *The Black Crook*. Revisiting the founding gesture of the genre, the static images come to life—and form what de Mille called a "whore parade."[66] To a can-can arrangement of "I Cain't Say No"—the very song that Ado Annie sang to the aloof Laurey—the burlesque dancers ruffle their skirts in Laurey's face, almost inviting her to participate. Writing that Laurey "somehow vaguely and secretly . . . identifies" with the "Postcard Girls" of the dream ballet, de Mille—and her choreography—suggest that Laurey desires to become one such dancing burlesque girl herself.[67] In writing her desire with her body, Laurey escapes from the confines of the narrative, which presents her as something of an icy cipher, and explores the realm of her desire, which is populated not only by her fascination with Jud's racialized body, but also by her own related desire to become a sexualized dancing girl who would attract him. De Mille's extraordinary work in *Oklahoma!* thus makes explicit what every dancing female body can do in musical theatre: protest the confines of narrative by articulating her desire in dance. Thus, "Laurey Makes Up Her Mind" is in a way the genre's most reflexive number, grappling as it does with what happens when women's bodies unleash the power of the musical form.

While virtually everything else in the show presents women as objects, the ballet emphasizes the possibility, however fleeting, for women to assert themselves as subjects. De Mille's uncannily instinctive understanding of the form's possibilities—and of Laurey's dilemma—comes from how those possibilities aligned with her own philosophies about the female dancer, who, de Mille felt, could use dance to resist the confines, sexual and otherwise, imposed on her. De Mille wrote that young girls want to become "[generically] DANCER in the permitted dress, exposed legs, free and floating arms, aerial skirt . . . because it produces effects of transformation as recompense for all they find insupportable in woman's traditional lot." Chief among these insupportable conditions was the place of women in a sexual economy traditionally governed by men's desires. De Mille understood dancing as a bodily pursuit that offered women "satisfaction and control" as well as "power and Dionysian release on their own terms" in a sexual culture that was otherwise "unsatisfactory, uncertain, and expensive to the individual."[68] She emphasizes the empowering dimensions of dance in her claim that "[a] dancer can do more than pray or hope; she takes matters into her own hands." The musical form thus offers a ready-made template for de Mille to explore her sense that women are drawn to dance because "it is escape, it is protest."[69] This is what happens in every moment when the characters burst into song and dance.

De Mille was hired to choreograph *Oklahoma!* after Rodgers and Hammerstein saw her ballet *Rodeo*, which Theatre Guild co-producer Lawrence Langner suggested would show her "ability to handle Western material."[70] However, I would argue that *Rodeo* was just as relevant because of its complex portrayal of female desire and loneliness. Significantly, the ballet presents the story of a Cowgirl whose gender presentation is unlike the more conventionally feminine girls in the town. The Cowgirl longs to attract the romantic attention of the Wrangler, and the piece concludes when she dresses in a more conventional feminine style and outdances the other girls. While *Rodeo* does give voice to an unconventional presentation of sexuality and of loneliness, it ultimately restrains this presentation and resolves on a note of conformity. *Oklahoma!* participates in a similar logic: while "Laurey Makes Up Her Mind" articulates a range of unspoken desires, as embodied most dramatically in Jud's dancing Postcard Girls, Laurey is ultimately unable to join their dance. Intimidated by her inadequacy among these experienced women, she recoils yet again. Her desires thus revealed, the rest of the play will focus on containing that desire, on suppressing the show's broader suggestion of female sexuality.

While the dream ballet brings down the first act curtain, the second act opens onto the joyous "The Farmer and the Cowmen," which, through discussions of women, pokes fun at the foibles of the two groups. All is fun and games until Carnes and Cord Elam make remarks about the "ole farm womern," inciting a riot. "You cain't talk that-a-way 'bout our womern folks!"

exclaims one, and a "free-for-all fight" ensues.[71] Aunt Eller—with the help of a pistol—resolves the situation by forcing everyone to resume singing. The song concludes with lyrics about how "when this territory is a state, / And jines the union jist like all the others, / The farmer and the cowman and the merchant / Must all behave theirsel's and act like brothers." The refrain reminds us that this tranquility is accomplished precisely through the exchange of women: "Cowboys, dance with the farmers' daughters! / Farmers, dance with the ranchers' gals!"[72]

Indeed, the union of the nation requires the same thing as the union of the plot: that women be married off. The aggressive sexuality of women must be contained domestically, and the plot of *Oklahoma!* is resolved in the quick succession of three related elements: Curly's not-guilty verdict, Ado Annie's entrance, and the pulling on of the fabled surrey. First, the verdict resolves the issues surrounding the death of Jud, whose definite extermination ensures that Laurey's errant desire for his sexual, racialized body is contained.[73] Second, the comic parallel of this desire, Ado Annie, enters with Will, "holding hands soulfully. Ado Annie's hair is mussed, and a contented look graces her face." Quizzed about their whereabouts, Ado Annie says that "Will and me had a misunderstandin'. But he explained it fine."[74] As they walk upstage, "tell-tale wisps of straw are seen clinging to her back," prompting laughter from the crowd. With Ado Annie's scandalous tendencies thus safely limited to her betrothed, the surrey is pulled on, and Curly and Laurey head off for their honeymoon. The entire second act has thus worked to contain and dismiss the specter of female sexuality—associated with Jud—that the dance unleashed. This thematic resolution creates the perception that an integration has taken place. And we can see how the emergence of this kind of "integration" makes perfect sense in 1943, when, as David Savran observes, "in reaction against the unprecedented economic mobility of women during the Depression and WWII," the integrated musical "endeavoured to reassure audiences that an independent-minded, unruly, or shrewish heroine would be tamed by the final curtain."[75]

While de Mille's dance explicitly articulates how the dancing female body unleashes a form of desire, the discourse of integration works to insist that the form can contain that desire, a goal shared by the plot itself. However, no matter how insistently they declare it, neither the narrative nor the discourse of integration can match the powers of the spectacular domain, thereby unsettling any sense of firm resolution. Is the explosive ballet, with its intense depictions of Laurey's sexual desire for Jud's racialized body, so easily dismissed? Having articulated such vivid fantasies, can Laurey's prim white femininity seem so certain and secure?

The ostensible integration of *Oklahoma!* involves an inexplicably demonstrative affirmation of narrative—which denies both the spectacle itself as well as the powers and desires articulated therein. The claims of integration suggest that the form has contained the women's bodies, a suggestion mirrored in the plot's containment of their desires. However, just as the spectacle inevitably overwhelms the narrative, so too does the form overwhelm any claims to integration. In this way, *Oklahoma!* accomplishes its pleasures precisely through the same mechanisms that were first enumerated in *The Black Crook*, a show whose legacy suffuses the entire genre—and whose history is intertwined with *Oklahoma!* in unexpected ways.

With long-running revivals produced in all the major cities of the country, *The Black Crook* ran almost continuously throughout the latter half of the nineteenth century but received its most prominent revival in 1929. Christopher Morley, who had been attempting to start a legitimate theatre in Hoboken, New Jersey, recalled that

> from the beginning we had had a hankering to revive *The Black Crook*. I'm afraid it was only a name to us; if we had really studied the matter we should have recoiled from the heavy cost of such a production. But ever since boyhood we had heard rumors of the famous old extravaganza, of the prodigious scandal it caused in its prime.[76]

Notably, Morley and his associate Cleon Throckmorton leased for their production the Lyric Theatre of Hoboken, which Morley writes had been featuring, among other entertainments, "lectures on physiology—For Men Only," thus situating *The Black Crook* yet again within the context of posing model artists.[77]

However earnest Morley's intentions might have been, though, the production was ultimately mocking in tone. Critic Edward B. Marks complained that Morley's production was "no extravagant spectacle starring world-famous ballet dancers, but instead a tongue-in-cheek satirical production which pointed up the plot—that outmoded atrocity—and omitted all that made the original production a success."[78] In his view, the production fully achieved its goal, which was to "mak[e] the modern audience feel far superior to those creatures of bygone days who thought this hysterically funny drama was good enough to run for 475 performances." While Marks may have been spot-on in noting that Morley's production was a tongue-in-cheek satire, he was a bit off the mark in claiming that it starred no world-famous ballet dancers: its choreographer, who also danced the part of Queen Stalacta, was none other than Agnes de Mille, making her choreographic debut.

Yet de Mille's association with *The Black Crook* would not end with Morley's production. In the winter of 1950, Jerome Chodorov, the writer who would later pen the book for *Wonderful Town*, purchased a copy of Cecil Smith's *Musical Comedy in America* and thought that the story behind the making of *The Black Crook* would be a fine basis for a musical comedy. De Mille was hired to choreograph the show, which was eventually titled *The Girl in Pink Tights*. While Sigmund Romberg wrote the score with Leo Robin, it was Chodorov and Joseph Fields who would have to assume responsibility for the book, which modulated the oft-told story of *The Black Crook* into a sublimely corny key.[79] Actor-cum-playwright Barras was transformed into Clyde Hallam, "a handsome young actor who has come home in uniform after many long and weary months in a Johnny Reb prison camp."[80] Once back, he presents the owner of Niblo's with *Dick the Renegade*, a Wild West melodrama he wrote while in confinement. Outside the theatre, Clyde meets Lisette Gervais, "a truly beautiful and fascinating girl," who is the prima ballerina of a French ballet troupe about to perform in a rival theatre. Clyde and Lisette get in a slight tiff—she even calls him an "animal-trainer"—yet they are clearly intrigued by each other. These flickers of attraction are fanned when the Academy of Music goes up in flames, with the brave Clyde rescuing Lisette from the conflagration. With the Academy in ruins, the producers agree to merge their shows, provoking Clyde's indignation. Furious with Clyde, Lisette refuses to relinquish her place at the centre of the spectacle and decides to entertain the advances of a theatrical financier named Van Beuren. After much anguish, a dejected Clyde finally goes to the premiere. During the curtain call, Lisette unexpectedly defers to Clyde and gives him center stage. In the immortal phrasing of the souvenir program, "Lisette and Clyde know that though they may hurl names at each other again and again, theirs is really a true love."

Writing in the *Daily Mirror*, critic Robert Coleman advised readers to "leave your super-critical faculties at home, come to the playhouse prepared to enjoy yourself, and you'll have a wonderful time."[81] Director Shepherd Traube told Gilbert Millstein that the show was "an affectionate look backward."[82] De Mille's dances, however, ranged from the "straight" to the "satirical," with reviewer Coleman noting "a charming, sentimental pas de deux" as well as a "hilarious" parody of a "corny bacchanale."[83] Indeed, while de Mille did provide some serious ballet, her choreography seemed to mock *The Black Crook*. According to George Jean Nathan, de Mille's parody "may be sufficiently described as the kind in which one of the more awkward girls periodically breaks down giggling and in which another girl dubbed 'a messenger from Heaven' floats back and forth on a tangled wire desperately kicking out her legs in all directions. Agnes de Mille is responsible for the jewel."[84] Dance critic Frances Herridge complained that "[t]he lengthy spoofing of old-time interpretative dance in 'Bacchanale'—usually so easy to laugh at—is too broadly slapstick to be funny."[85] *Herald-Tribune* dance critic Walter Terry, too, felt that de Mille's impulse was satirical, even though he enjoyed it. De Mille, he observed, had "done a great job of satirizing the kind of spectacle which astounded New York in the 1860s in such extravaganzas as the famed 'The Black Crook.'"[86] De Mille's choreography exaggerated the differences between the frivolity of yesteryear and the seriousness of contemporary ballet, but it was precisely *The Black Crook* that made possible her extraordinary work on *Oklahoma!*, and indeed that made modern dance—with its deep emphasis on the subconscious—so assimilable to the musical theatre form. It seems de Mille might have unconsciously absorbed the lessons of *The Black Crook* not only in her work on *Oklahoma!* but also in the show she choreographed in its wake: *One Touch of Venus*. Written by Kurt Weill and Ogden Nash, the show featured Mary Martin in the role of a statue of Venus who comes to life. Venus spends the show persuading a contemporary barber to marry her but realizes—through a dance—that she cannot stomach the banal suburban life in Ozone Heights that a marriage with him would entail. As before, the dancing body articulates its own desire as only it can. John Chapman wrote in his opening night review of the show that "Venus comes to life in the delightful show which opened last night at the Imperial Theatre—and so does the musical comedy stage."[87] And indeed, since *The Black Crook*, it was ever thus: when the statue comes to life, so does musical theatre.

Carol Channing as Dolly Gallagher Levi. Photograph by Friedman-Abeles,
©Billy Rose Theatre Division, New York Public Library for the Performing Arts.

# 2

# BRING ON THE GIRLS

*The Princess Theatre and the (Tired) Businesswoman*

As discussed in chapter 1, the foundational gesture of musical theatre is the eruption of burlesque, the moment when the sexualized bodies of women transcend the narrative. The radical desire unleashed in that moment of bursting into song and dance is precisely what the plot of *Oklahoma!*—and the discourse of integration—work desperately to contain. The primal scene of musical theatre, *The Black Crook*, fueled deep anxieties about sexualized women, as manifest, for example, in the rumors about its dancers. An 1866 article in the *New York Clipper*, the foremost theatrical newspaper of its day, claimed that some of the performers in *The Black Crook* "commence their other operations and sell themselves to the first bidder" as soon as the curtain goes down, noting that "yes, among the dancers and ballet girls exhibiting their shapes at the theatres on Broadway may be found quite a number of prostitutes."[1] This eagerness to link the dancers of *The Black Crook* not only with burlesque but with sexual labor is a manifestation of broader anxieties about the *labor* of the working women who performed musical theatre.

These anxieties also emerge in the genre's thematic obsessions with strippers and prostitutes, and its recurring trope of other women in the labor force being misperceived as "fallen" or as prostitutes. For example, the classic 1954 musical *The Pajama Game* opens with Mr. Hines "pranc[ing] on," and stating directly to the audience, "This is a very serious drama. It's kind of a problem play. It's about Capital and Labor. I wouldn't bother to make such a point of all this except later on, if you happen to see a lot of naked women being chased through the woods, I don't want you to get the wrong impression. This play is full of symbolism."[2] Indeed, the "naked women" turn out to be precisely the "Capital and Labor" on which the piece focuses. The curtain goes up to reveal the pajama factory, where "factory Girls are busy sewing, while others are sorting and inspecting pajamas."[3] The play focuses on a factory strike, the resolution to which comes when Sid Sorokin is able to examine the company finances, which have to that point been under the control of Gladys, who keeps the ledger "key around [her] neck."[4] After Sid gets Gladys drunk, she surrenders the key, ultimately announcing, "Oh, dear, a fallen woman—that's what I am—I lost my key."[5] When Gladys, the working woman, analogizes herself to a different kind of working woman—a prostitute—the strike is resolved, permitting the rest of the women to return to work as well. A labor strike is also central to the 1959 musical *Fiorello!*, which features a woman worker on a picket line being (mistakenly) arrested "not for picketing—for soliciting."[6] Perhaps the best encapsulation of this dynamic comes from producer Cy Feuer's account of the genesis of the 1953 musical *Can-Can*:

> [co-producer] Ernie [Martin] and I . . . read one story about hard-working laundresses [on the Right Bank of Paris], who, after a day of working in a literal sweatshop and leading a hard and horrible life, would go at night to a nightclub, the Moulin Rouge, to relax and to dance. Their costumes, or lack of them, were kind of shocking, even for Paris. They wore no panties and would roll their stockings up only to high on the thigh. "There's a musical in there somewhere," Ernie and I said to each other . . . and that was the beginning of *Can-Can*.[7]

Feuer correctly observes that the essence of musical theatre exists at the intersection of working women and their sexualized bodies.

No show distills this logic more efficiently than *Hello, Dolly!*—a musical squarely about work. The 1964 musical features a running gag in which the title character, Dolly Gallagher Levi, dispenses a seemingly endless series of calling cards announcing the motley array of services that she can provide. In addition to "marriages arranged," she is also available for

"Financial Consultation," "Instruction in the Guitar and Mandolin," "Short Distance Hauling," "National Monuments Restored," "Fresh Country Eggs," and "Poodles Clipped," among others. When asked what benefit she reaps from this industry, she replies: "a living." Indeed, Dolly announces in the very first scene that she is "tired of living from hand to mouth"—hence her desire to "marry Horace Vandergelder for his money."[8]

Dolly is not the only one attempting to marry into the Vandergelder family. She pursues this task in parallel with Ambrose Kemper, a "poor struggling artist" in love with Vandergelder's niece, Ermengarde. Hired by Ambrose to facilitate his engagement, Dolly announces that "the first thing to do is make you financially independent. I know! I'll find you a job."[9] Only in the topsy-turvy world of musical comedy could financial independence be assured through a career as a performer—but this is precisely what Dolly directs Ambrose to undertake, turning him into an entertainer who will perform at the Harmonia Gardens Restaurant.

In the published version of the play—indeed, in the play as it is customarily known and performed—Dolly instructs Ambrose to compete in a polka contest at the restaurant so that he can win a solid gold cup. At the opening night performance in 1964, however, there was no polka contest. Indeed, for all of the performances in 1964, for all of the entire year Carol Channing performed Dolly on Broadway, there was no polka contest. The polka contest was a substitution made in 1965 for what had been, for the previous year, a scene featuring—as announced in the program—"Tableaux Vivantes." In this original version of the show, we find Ambrose singing "Come and Be My Butterfly," a number that echoes the elaborate transformation scenes in shows like *The Black Crook*. Where the 1866 show featured a sumptuously produced "[s]ubterranean gallery of emerald and crystal stalactites" home to "fairies, sprites, water nymphs, amphibea, gnomes, etc., bearing treasure . . . ,"[10] Ambrose's song similarly tells of "a shady glade where the elves abide / Where the water sprites and the nymphs reside."[11] A picture frame drops in from above, framing the posed "Living Flowers," who are joined eventually by butterflies and moths. During a dance break, a "cocoon is wheeled on and opens with a familiar cry to reveal Ermengarde."[12]

Never quite satisfied with the scene, director Gower Champion finally replaced the tableaux vivants with a polka contest when Ginger Rogers assumed the role from Channing in 1965. As in the genre of musical theatre itself, the tableaux vivants gave way to dance. However, even as Ambrose undertakes a different form of performance, he still works at the Harmonia Gardens—despite his own objections toward performing there. He complains to Dolly about the lack of respectability of the venue, and its unsuitability for Ermengarde: "I'm sorry, Mrs. Levi, but no fiancee of mine is going to set foot in a . . . in a pleasure palace!" When Dolly defends the restaurant as a place that she enjoyed with her late husband, Ambrose notes that "working there" is an altogether different pursuit. Dolly persists, arguing that "it's the only way to show Horace Vandergelder we mean business!"[13] Given the structural alignment of Ambrose and Dolly—both wanting to marry into the Vandergelder family, both using the Harmonia Gardens as the venue to accomplish this goal—Dolly's insistence on defending the Harmonia Gardens becomes more complex. If Ambrose must work at the restaurant, what kind of work does Dolly perform there, and why is the venue—and this "business"—of suspect character?

This question was answered most efficiently when the original cast was ready to run through the title number for the first time. Not yet having composed music for Carol Channing's descent down the staircase, composer Jerry Herman asked rehearsal pianist Peter Howard to improvise entrance music. According to David Payne-Carter, "As Channing descended the stairway, Howard broke into burlesque music. . . . The idea was kept, orchestrated, and the music accompanied Channing down the stairs on opening night."[14] Payne-Carter suggests that this burlesque introduction added a "dimension of which Herman and [director Gower] Champion had never dreamed," but I would argue that Howard clearly intuited what was in fact the most logical introduction for Dolly—for the work she does is precisely the work of burlesque.

Nowhere does the genre salute its foundational gesture—the eruption of burlesque—more flamboyantly than at the Harmonia Gardens. Only in the context of burlesque can we make sense of the otherwise inexplicable and inexplicably long title number, with its endless struts around the *passerelle*. The inflection of the restaurant with burlesque overtones explains Ambrose's rejection of it as a "pleasure palace" and as a place unfit for his future wife. Further, other moments reinforce this association of the restaurant with burlesque: as the title number concludes, Vandergelder bumps into Dolly wearing her red sequined dress. Not initially recognizing her, he pardons himself with "Excuse me, girlie," while his date, Ernestina, asks to dance the "hootchy kootchy."[15] In an earlier draft of the show, the link between the restaurant and the sex industry is made explicit: as Horace arrives at the Harmonia Gardens, "one of two passing ladies of the evening winks at him, hums a few suggestive notes, twirls a pink parasol, and finally opens her coat to reveal a dazzling electric blue sequined gown. That is enough for Vandergelder, who assumes she is Ernestina, gives her his arm, and they start in."[16] Indeed, the Harmonia Gardens, in its function as a public space, is a place where, despite the ever-present male waiters, women *work*—as women do at Mrs. Molloy's Hat Shop, where Irene Molloy complains to her assistant Minnie Fay that "all millineresses are suspected of being wicked women. That's why I can't go to restaurants or balls or theatres . . . that's all the proof they'd need!" She explains that she is going to marry to escape the millinery trade, as she "can no longer stand being suspected of being a wicked woman with nothing to show for it."[17]

Irene's comment about not being able to visit "restaurants or balls or theatres" helps us to understand Mrs. Levi's dilemma as well: Dolly's triumphant return to the Harmonia Gardens is thus not merely her much-touted "rejoining the human race," but a return to the public sphere in which her presence carries a scandalous current, a current that will be neutralized by her marriage to Horace, just as Irene's will be neutralized by her relationship with Cornelius Hackl, Vandergelder's clerk.[18] *Hello, Dolly!* is above all a play about the working woman, the associations—both sexual and more generally scandalous—that attend the working woman in the public sphere, and the desire to neutralize the socially fraught qualities associated therewith.

The genre's thematic obsession with working women testifies to its own anxieties about its own working women, the actresses whose laboring bodies generate its most profound effects. And because the laboring bodies of its women performers draw their profound power precisely from their associations with the erotic and spectacular dimensions of burlesque, the bodily exhibitionism central to musical performance can never be divorced from the threat of sexualized labor. Similarly, because the narrative of musical theatre is fractured by these allegedly déclassé presentations of women's bodies, the eruptions of musical theatre are thus perceived as socially suspect. Unsurprisingly, then, the first attempt to "integrate" musical theatre would aim precisely to dissociate the genre from the socially marginalized field of burlesque. Indeed, the Princess Theatre Musicals sought to lift the entire genre into repute precisely by lifting its working women into repute as well. The "integration" of the Princess Theatre shows was thus not a profound transformation of musical theatre form, but instead an attempt to reconceive the presentation of bodies in musical theatre as artistic and highbrow, indeed as part of a broader project of moral and social uplift.

The term "Princess Theatre Musicals" refers to five musicals: *Nobody Home* (1915), *Very Good Eddie* (1915), *Oh, Boy!* (1917), *Oh, Lady! Lady!!* (1918), and *Oh, My Dear!* (1918). As the name suggests, these shows were all produced at the Princess Theatre, a small house built in 1913 on 39th Street between 6th Avenue and Broadway. Inspired by the Grand Guignol Theatre in Paris, the Princess was an intimate auditorium, with only 232 seats distributed among thirteen rows of orchestra seating and a small balcony.[19] The stage itself was about half the size of the auditorium, and as such precluded productions that required grand spectacle. A review of the theatre's inaugural production, for example, noted that "the limitations of the Princess stage" placed "the firing squad perilously close to the doomed men."[20]

The Princess Theatre Shows have long been considered an early landmark in integration, a primitive adumbration of the revolutions to come with *Show Boat* and *Oklahoma!* Even at the time of their production, they announced the ostensibly revolutionary structure of their shows. As phrased in the souvenir program for *Oh, Boy!*, "stage traditions received a memorable and impressive shock that eventful night in the latter part of April, 1915" with the production of *Nobody Home*, which "was the first glimpse New York audiences had of a new form of stage entertainment, which was destined to revolutionize modern musical comedy and lead to many imitations."[21] This treatment of the shows as revolutionary was picked up in many histories of musical theatre, with John Bush Jones, for example, echoing the common claim that the Princess Theatre Musicals were "a rudimentary form of what in later years has generally come to be called the 'integrated musical.'"[22]

One of the most fascinating aspects of the Princess Theatre Shows is how the various histories of musical theatre have misframed the shows as the "Bolton-Wodehouse-Kern" shows. While Guy Bolton was present for the entire series, Kern left after the fourth show, and P. G. Wodehouse was brought on for the last three only. The central figure in the Princess Theatre story is not the "men who invented musical comedy," as one book title phrases it, but a woman—Elisabeth Marbury, who reinvented the portrayal, management, and marketing of women in theatre. The radical work of the Princess Theatre productions is not to be found in a radically innovative integration of song and scene accomplished by its male creators; the actual revolution of the Princess Theatre musicals, on the contrary, was to distance musical comedy from burlesque precisely by distancing its *performers* from the specter of burlesque. The Princess Theatre Shows reinvented the genre precisely by reframing the laboring bodies of musical theatre. The savvy Marbury cultivated a new (paying) audience for musical theatre by reimagining the musical's relationship with women—women as characters and as consuming spectators, but above all as working women performers. As the employer of many women in her theatrical enterprise, Marbury passionately advocated for better conditions for women workers, and in the process, she aimed to fashion a respectable popular theatre fit for an upwardly mobile audience composed, in part, of women consumers.

All of Marbury's innovations were aimed at elevating musical comedy precisely by distancing it from its "common associations" with burlesque. Recalling that her pursuit of producing musicals was "met with considerable disapproval on the part of [her] friends," Marbury triumphantly notes that "musical comedy lost its commonplace atmosphere and through the joint efforts of my associates and myself it was raised from the ranks into the realm of a different and better form of entertainment."[23] With her remarkable business acumen, Marbury presciently recognized the market for, and undertook efforts with women to create, just such a form of musical theatre, a "better and different" musical theatre that is often recognized as the first "integrated" musical theatre.

Marbury was responding to anxieties about the dancing in musical theatre. Deeply concerned with the morality of social dancing, Marbury felt that musical comedy had led working people astray by misrepresenting questionable dancing as acceptable in society. More than a year before she produced her shows, she wrote that

> It is not difficult to find the explanation of some of the undesirable dancing. A working man and girl go to a musical comedy. From their stuffy seats high up under the roof they look down upon the dancers on the stage. These are—so the program tells them—doing modern ball-room dancing. The man on the stage flings his partner about with Apache wildness; she clutches him around the neck and is swung off her feet. They spin swiftly or undulate slowly across the stage, and the program calls it a "Tango." The man and girl go away and talk of those "ball-room dances." They try the steps; they are novel and often difficult; they have aroused their interest. The result is that we find scores of young people dancing under the name of "One Step" or "Tango" the eccentric dances thus exaggerated and elaborated to excite the jaded audiences of a roof-garden or a music-hall. There is no one to tell those young people that they are mistaken in their choice of the steps, that "society" does not do those dances.[24]

For Marbury, the vulgarity of musical comedy had deceived young people—particularly young working-class people—through its presentation of allegedly disreputable dancing. Notably, her invocation of "Apache wildness" refers to the Apache dancing fad of the time, a dance whose moves were inspired by the interactions of prostitutes and pimps. Thus, Marbury thought it necessary to provide a kind of artistic education to these young people, revealing to them the kind of movement appropriate to high society, thereby making it possible for them to change their station.

Marbury's concern regarding these ostensibly unrefined forms of dance was directly related to her ideas about uplift for the working class, particularly working women. She felt that "the lure of the rhythm, the sense of flinging aside the weariness of the working-day, is as strong in the heart of the girl behind the counter as in that of the girl in the private ball-room. The man who labors in the humbler callings is as interested in his girl friend and as anxious to dance with her as the young man in what we call 'society.'"[25] Marbury defended the working class from accusations of crudeness, arguing that she does not "believe that all those young persons, the fathers and mothers of to-morrow, who are working and striving to earn honest livings and to rise in the world, connect their moments of recreation with suggestive ideas and unworthy ideals."[26] Claiming that for workers, dancing "means something different from the dull daily round," she sought to "establish once and for all a standard of modern dancing which will demonstrate that these dances can be made graceful, artistic, charming, and, above all, *refined.*"[27] When shown how to dance with taste and modesty, these dancers, she wrote, would be like the "child of the tenement . . . delighted if put into a beautiful, clean, and airy play-room."[28]

Marbury undertook several enterprises to confront the popularity of questionable dancing, most notably her personal stewardship of the dancers Vernon and Irene Castle. Under Marbury's vision, the Castles became national figures in the promotion of ballroom dancing as a wholesome, socially sanctioned form of entertainment. Marbury traced her interest in managing the Castles to a speech at the French Academy in which the author Jean Richepin had decried the "vulgarization" of modern dances, arguing that popular social dances in their purest form actually had a noble lineage that could be traced to "the tombs of Thebes, from Orient to Occident, and down through ancient Rome."[29] Given this distinguished pedigree, Richepin argued that "centers should promptly be established in every capital of the world where the grace and beauty and classic rhythm to which the modern dance so naturally lends itself should be developed and emphasized."[30] Marbury took up Richepin's commission when she noticed an unoccupied building across from the Ritz Hotel. As she recalled, "the thought of making it into a smart dancing centre flashed upon my mind and simultaneously the personalities of Vernon and Irene Castle, whom I had already seen in Paris as an attraction in a restaurant."[31] She envisioned—and soon realized—the vacant building as the "Castle House," which would offer both instruction in dancing as well as afternoon tea socials featuring the Castles. Marbury's work with Castle House aimed above all to bring "refinement" to the modern dance. For example, she wrote that "the much-misunderstood tango becomes an evolution of the eighteenth-century Minuet" under the Castles' elegant modulations. With "no strenuous clasping of partners, no hideous gyrations of the limbs, no abnormal twistings, no vicious angles," the tango as taught at Castle House was "courtly and artistic."[32]

Ultimately, her desire to offer instruction in more sophisticated and socially acceptable forms of popular dance came from her conviction that "the attempt to start a moral campaign against all modern dancing is destructive . . . unless we offer something better in its place."[33] Marbury urged women's groups to take up the cause of dancing, counseling "the women of every city [to] open properly conducted dancing-halls for young people where they can dance to good music under refined supervision."[34] Writing that "the best course in the interest of morals is to encourage dancing as a healthful exercise and as a fitting recreation," Marbury opened just such a dancing-hall with Elsie de Wolfe, their friend Anne Morgan, and Mrs. W. K. Vanderbilt, although the lack of alcohol on the premises brought a swift conclusion to their enterprise.[35]

Though her dancing hall was in the end unsuccessful, Marbury would ultimately achieve its goals through her work in musical theatre, which she saw as one such "something better" to be offered in place of the vulgarity then commonly perceived in popular dancing. Though it has gone unremarked, *Nobody Home*, the very first Princess Theatre Show, which was "destined to revolutionize modern musical comedy," was clearly inspired by her obsessions with improving the reputation of musical comedy and of its dancers by distancing them from their traditional associations with burlesque.[36]

The plot of *Nobody Home* concerns Violet Brinton's engagement to dancing teacher Vernon Popple, an engagement that scandalizes her aunt and uncle, Mr. and Mrs. Amorini, since Vernon is a dancer. When he offers to give up dancing so as to meet their standards, they continue to interrogate him as to his "habits and—ahem—morals."[37] After questioning him about drinking, smoking, and gambling, Mrs. Amorini holds up a magazine featuring a photo of Tony Miller, the female star of the Winter Garden revue, and asks, "Do you know such women as *this*?" Violet slyly prompts Vernon to deny knowing Tony, since Mrs. Amorini would think that affiliating with a female dancer was a sign of compromised integrity. The first act climaxes when Freddy unknowingly repeats that Vernon and Tony have known each other for years, scandalizing Mrs. Amorini. Amidst a series of mistaken identities and comic exchanges, the plot concludes when Violet's uncle surprises everyone by blessing the marriage.

Notably, the entire plot is driven by Mrs. Amorini's disdain for performers. Upon her arrival at the hotel, she complains to her husband that "there are actresses in that room, and they are smoking. I'm not sure we did wisely in letting Violet come to New York."[38] When Mr. Amorini looks at a travel magazine that contains a picture of the Winter Garden chorus girls, Mrs. Amorini exclaims, "Disgraceful!" Later, when Vernon explains the situation to Tony Miller, he says that Violet's family is "very straight-laced"—which Tony immediately interprets as "prejudiced against actors." Vernon follows this by noting that "they're terribly down on all women who have publicly climbed the ladder of success." Tony concurs: "It is rather unladylike—with so many men at the bottom."[39]

However, we quickly learn that Mr. Amorini does not share his wife's suspicion of performers. While she unleashes her harangue about the dancers, her husband absent-mindedly mumbles agreement, comically revealing that he in fact holds the very opposite view. When she dismisses his travel guide, which contains an advertisement for a musical revue, as disgraceful, he agrees with her in comic fashion:

> But I agree with you. It's terrible. Look at this costume. And THIS. Oh, here's one that's worse than any. Let me see if that really IS the worst. (Scans the picture very closely.) I'm not quite sure. Oh, here's the very worst of all. Miss Tony Miller—Tony Miller, the Queen of the Revue. I really think we ought to go to the Winter Garden tonight, so that we can warn our friends in Grand Rapids against the performance.[40]

When Mr. Amorini—at his request—is introduced to Tony, Mr. Amorini recalls, "I remember you one year ago at the Winter Garden. Oh, what a beautiful costume. I shall never forget it."[41] In fact, he goes on to recall another scene involving "that little military costume and the chorus all military, one, two, three, four, salute march and the hero," going so far as to re-enact the scene, with him posing as the hero, opposite Tony as a nurse. Mr. Amorini, unlike his wife, expresses and even embodies his desire to become a performer, signals his newfound appreciation of performers, and blesses the marriage. The show is resolved with a general celebration of the chorus girls as respectable.

The narrative energy of *Nobody Home*—its interest in valuing dancers like Tony Miller—mirrored Marbury's own attempt to reimagine the societal image of dancing and to dignify dancers. Given that the chorus girl—and the genre—had long been shadowed by an association with burlesque, Marbury's elevation of the chorus girl—and of musical theatre—would come precisely by distancing them from this affiliation and demonstratively associating them with class, style, and individuality. Marbury described her revolutionary form of theatre as "that form of entertainment which has been so successfully imitated ever since, namely a comedy with music in which each extra girl became an individual, dressed according to her personality, and was not given a uniform costume."[42] The revolution implied in such a view becomes clearer when we consider the more commonly held view of the period—as expressed, for example, in a 1911 magazine article by Glenmore Davis: "The members of a chorus, as a general rule, are incapable of independent playing. They are parts of a whole and are theatrically useless when not surrounded by the other particles. Seldom—very seldom—do they learn to act or to demonstrate any other ability capable of lifting themselves out of the ensemble."[43] As Marbury lifted women out of the ensemble, she felt that she was instructing them how to accomplish a parallel elevation in society.

Just as Marbury sought to improve the dancing of the working girl, she also sought to improve the working conditions of the dancing girl. She even avoided the term "chorus girls," preferring instead to refer to them as "'small part' members of our cast."[44] Determined to "become their friend as well as their manager," Marbury insisted on fair salaries and humane working conditions. She felt that her efforts would elevate the "young, impressionable" performers, whom she referred to as "chameleons," claiming that "they are too often reflections of the atmosphere around them. Let this be one of refinement, and they will quickly respond to it."[45] Elsewhere, she referred to them as "mirrors of their associations," noting that they are "tender and plastic, and when they become hardened it is generally because contact of an undesirable nature has made them so."[46]

Rather than placing the blame on the character of these performers, Marbury felt the culprit to be the rude and boorish behavior of the men who generally oversaw theatrical productions on Broadway. As she wrote in a 1917 article for *Harper's Bazaar*, while "women of education and of breeding" are encouraged "to adopt the stage as a profession, . . . no influence to-day so discourages such candidates as this entirely unnecessary and demoralizing atmosphere which is creeping into our theatres through these men of smaller power into whose hands managers have confided their interests."[47] She criticized their disciplinary methods, noting that "discipline should not mean either blatant noise, vulgar personalities nor turbulent terror. . . . It should be weighted with moral authority, not arbitrary power; with dignity, not disturbance."[48] She once wrote that she hoped to "introduce that humane principle of Henry Ford and Thomas Mott Osborne," complaining to an interviewer that performers were being treated by theatre managers "in a manner that would not have been possible with . . . even Osborne and his convicts at Sing Sing."[49]

Marbury modeled instead an employment arrangement with a strong degree of pastoral stewardship; speaking of her relationship with "Miss Marbury's Girls," she explained that she wanted each of her "girls,"

> while confiding to me her standards, at the same time to feel my standards for her. I wanted her to realize that the moment she received salary from me she had become to me an entity, that her difficulties became mine to solve, that her discouragements became mine to combat, that her physical weakness became mine to consider. She was no longer to be one of an impersonal group, but an individual—"just a girl," if you will, but a girl who was to realize a responsibility due to herself, a girl who was not a stage accessory, but a human being throbbing to respond to her innate ideal and to her own vision.[50]

Marbury had a maternal defensiveness when it came to the women in her theatrical companies, arguing that "they are not of a coarse fiber, on the contrary, they are incipient artists, with all the sensitiveness which that implies."[51] She was quick to dismiss the kind of notoriety that had long attended chorus girls, as in the cases of Evelyn Nesbit and Nan Patterson, two of the "pretty maidens" in the musical *Florodora*, who had gained widespread notoriety through their connection to two murder cases.[52] Writing in 1920, Ned Wayburn summarized how the scandalous press coverage of the time led the public to believe that "the chorus girl was a high-tensioned vampire, with no other thought in her head but dissipation and no other aim in life but a round of pleasure."[53] Marbury, however, writing that "a great deal of misapprehension has been formulated regarding the immorality of the stage," rejected such claims by asserting that the behavior of those in the theatrical world was far superior to "the lack of ethics condoned by modern society."[54] She noted in particular that "the manners and deportment of the average show girl would often put to shame the conduct of the débutante." Marbury's advocacy for the women in her employ lifted her to ever loftier rhetorical heights: "They are 'just girls' if you will, but believe me that the majority of them are first and foremost human beings with arms outstretched to the sunlight and with souls looking heavenward for that something better which we all want to find."[55]

In Marbury's mind, that "something better" to which these women should aspire was high society, which was also the audience she sought to cultivate. The souvenir program of *Oh, Boy!* noted that "to look over an average audience at the Princess is like reading a page from the social register of New York," going on to boast that

> more than eighty-seven per cent of the patrons of this theatre attend in their own limousine cars. The traffic congestion of automobiles in front of the Princess . . . has been such that the police department was compelled to make Thirty-ninth street a "one-way street" in order to adequately handle the great number of private cars which line up for several blocks east of the theatre. Naturally, with such a clientele, it is obvious that the Princess is in reality "New York's smartest playhouse."[56]

The program also claimed that the "elites" sought to attend the Princess for two reasons: because of the nature of its smart and clean musical comedy, "which appeals to the refined and intelligent"; and because of the theatre itself, which is "the intimate, drawing-room type of theatre, with a limited seating capacity which gives one the atmosphere of an exclusive social function in a private mansion." In her quest to lift musical comedy from the proverbial gutter, Marbury herself would frequently invoke the "drawing room," writing, for instance, "I will guarantee that you can take my boys and girls off the stage and put them in any drawing room or ballroom in New York, just as they are dressed, and their costumes will be in perfect harmony with the occasion and surroundings."[57] Newspaper writers took note of the productions' elegance in similar terms, writing that "the dances and the songs charm by their freedom from even a suggestion of vulgarity. They could be used in the most collet monté drawing-room without shocking anyone."[58] If the Princess Theatre Shows were motivated by a desire to elevate the disreputable eruptions of burlesque, one can see a parallel aim in Marbury's comments that seek to elevate the social standing of the actresses. In other words, the "perfect harmony" of the actress in the social setting mirrors the ostensible harmony, or integration, of these shows—an operation that is precisely one of reconceiving how bodies were perceived within a broader context, be it one of society or of narrative.

Marbury's interest in developing a "respectable" form of musical comedy that would attract new audiences was an American attempt at an approach that several British impresarios and artists had undertaken in the second half of the nineteenth century and the beginning of the twentieth. Given Marbury's transatlantic work managing writers and artists, she was surely familiar with these enterprises—as would have been Jerome Kern, who had worked in London preceding his Broadway debut. Of particular note is the work of director George Edwardes, who, as the proprietor of the Gaiety Theatre, essentially pioneered a form of musical comedy that surely inspired many elements of Marbury's entertainments.[59] Edwardes's musical comedies sought a "respectable" audience by distancing his shows from the burlesque overtones of the Gaiety shows helmed by his predecessor, John Hollingsworth, whose shows emphasized the "full breasts and well rounded thighs" of the chorus.[60] By contrast, Edwardes—as Marbury would go on to do—"picked his chorus girls carefully so that each girl stood out as an individual type: all of them were statuesque creatures who knew exactly how to wear their clothes," which were elegant and fashionable.[61] Edwardes's reforms were inspired in part, as Noël Coward recalled, by the "healthy, clean-limbed but melodious high jinks of Gilbert and Sullivan," with whom Edwardes worked early in his career as an assistant stage manager for Richard D'Oyly Carte.[62]

Indeed, Edwardes's approach mirrored that of librettist and lyricist W. S. Gilbert, who was eager to distance his work in comic opera from his own earlier work in burlesque. Dismissing the sexuality of the burlesque, Gilbert boasted that his and Sullivan's more wholesome form of comic opera had far exceeded the popularity of burlesque "without the adventitious aid of sprawling females in indecent costumes."[63] These developments at the Savoy were themselves influenced by Thomas German Reed's "Royal Gallery of Illustration," which disavowed the connotations of theatricality, presenting instead the "pretence that the artists were essentially portraying *themselves*—respectably behaved and attired members of the bourgeoisie—in fictionalised comic situations."[64] While Marbury would bring a unique contribution in her work as an employer of women, there is no doubt that her interest in changing the depictions of women and cultivating female audiences was pioneered by German Reed, Gilbert, and Edwardes, and on the other side of the Atlantic by vaudeville impresario Tony Pastor, who sought to cultivate a family-friendly vaudeville suitable for women.

Though these artists certainly provided Marbury the inspiration and template for her theatrical enterprises, she had, since the beginning of her time in public life, been involved in developing venues for women in the public sphere. For example, in cooperation with her friend philanthropist Anne Morgan, whose father was financier J. P. Morgan, and Mrs. J. Borden Harriman, Marbury established the "first social club for our sex in the City," the Colony Club, which included a "restaurant, lounge, swimming pool and gymnasium."[65] And indeed, Marbury hoped that larger audiences of women would follow from her attempts to change how women were presented onstage. A press release announced that "for years theatrical managers have been providing light amusement for the tired business man. Miss Marbury has discovered and developed the style of production that appeals to the tired woman, and when you possess a play that women want to see, you needn't bother about the men; they'll have to come whether they want to or not."[66] As confirmation of Marbury's success, we might note a review that opined that *Nobody Home* "offers mild stimulation for the tired business man and harmless diversion for his intellectually languid sisters."[67] In a similar vein, one review of the Princess production of *Nobody Home* noted that "this musical comedy should offer a peculiar appeal to the tired business man. It will waft away his troubles without stimulating him. It's as soothing as reading Jane Austen, and when he reaches home, the good man will sleep well, for *Nobody Home* is the reverse of a tonic."[68] Of course, musicals have long been relegated to the position of entertainment for the tired businessman, owing this characterization not only to the simplicity of the plot and the general air of diversion but also to the notorious displays of women's bodies. In this critic's view, however, the fatigue of the proverbial tired businessman is assuaged not with the legendary legs of the chorus line but with something more akin to the pleasure of reading Jane Austen, pleasure generally associated with the novel's historically female audience. Here we begin to see a shift, however subtle, with the musical increasingly depicted as fit for women, and producer Marbury depicted as cultivating a respectable place for women in theatre—as spectators, artists, and professionals. In a newspaper feature about Marbury titled "Woman Making Theater Her Own Institution," author Archie Bell took note of May Dowling, Marbury's press agent, who, he wrote, "has done better work on the road than nine out of ten advance managers."[69] Deeply committed to creating opportunities for women in public life, Marbury took great pride in her chorus members, once boasting that "many girls made their début with me, and how often do I see a name heading a program only to recognize it as one of those whom I discovered, and to whom I gave a first chance."[70]

Chief among those whom Marbury gave a chance was her life partner, Elsie de Wolfe, who designed the sets for *Nobody Home*.[71] Marbury's and de Wolfe's relationship, which Kim Marra has called their "Boston marriage," was widely recognized in the public eye, with the press referring to them as "bachelor girls," "bosom friends," and "those fair inseparables."[72] As Marra notes, whatever the precise nature of their relationship, they were clearly "significant others," and Marbury was deeply invested in assuring de Wolfe professional success, well before Marbury enlisted her to design *Nobody Home*.

While Marbury first met de Wolfe during one of de Wolfe's performances as an actress, Marbury would soon steer her to a new career, much as she would do with other women throughout her life. De Wolfe recalled that she had always been "sensitive to her surroundings" and that her "senses [had] always been visual."[73] Noting that she was "thrilled" by "visiting old houses," de Wolfe wrote that during a time in London, she "realized that a house, inside and out, if it is to be authentic in its dispensations, must be in harmony with the life which goes on within it."[74] She read voraciously on matters of period architecture and "interior arrangements," and practiced her knowledge when theatrical producer Charles Frohman "sometimes gave [her] a hand in the stage sets."[75] While she was still an actress, de Wolfe began to counsel her friends on these matters, and eventually, during a conversation with de Wolfe and their close friend Sara Cooper Hewitt about the importance of beauty in one's surroundings, "Elisabeth, seconded by Sara, exclaimed, 'Elsie, that is just your *métier*! You have a natural gift for color and arrangement. Why not go ahead and be America's first woman decorator?'"[76] Deeply supportive of de Wolfe's professional ambitions, Marbury helped to secure for her the job of decorating the Colony Club that Marbury had helped to found, a commission that de Wolfe felt "started [her] on [her] way."[77]

While Marbury's investment in virtuous femininity was central to the effect of *Nobody Home*, it is worth noting that the visual element of the presentation—which de Wolfe orchestrated—was not insignificant.[78] As one reviewer wrote, "'Nobody Home' differed from the rest of its kind in that it was done in miniature."[79] The miniaturization of musical theatre would have been particularly striking since this deviated considerably from the convention of grand spectacle then dominant in musical theatre and the musical revue. In a particularly insightful article in *The Green Book Magazine*, author Channing Pollock writes that

> condensation has become the theatrical order of the age. In these days, when apparently nobody can build a playhouse too small for the audiences that come to it, New York finds itself with six theaters whose aggregate seating capacity is less than that of the Lyric. Until recently these stages have been devoted exclusively to an intimate type of drama. No one has thought of using them for musical comedy—certainly not for the currently popular "revues" which, with their elaborate "books," their "scores," and their dependence upon sirens and scenery, really require the spaciousness of the New Amsterdam, the Winter Garden, or the Hippodrome.[80]

The Princess Theatre's revolution must be understood in the context of its assault on the twin pillars of the spectacular: the denuded chorus girl and the grand scenic spectacle. A contemporaneous article in *Arts &* *Decoration* on Joseph Urban's stage settings celebrated how Urban's designs for the *Follies* made the impression that one was "on the threshold of a new age in the art of musical comedy."[81] The article, after describing Urban's work in florid detail, noted that "it is as impossible to imagine the Ziegfeld show without its Urban settings as without its girls." By contrast, the modest size of the Princess Theatre precluded any kind of visual excess, and in its spatial dimensions it promoted a sense of withheld modesty that mirrored the restrained attitude of the women. The Princess Theatre shows thus presented themselves as coherent alternatives to spectacular excess—mediated through its presentation of the white female body.

This "new form of stage entertainment" said to "revolutionize modern musical comedy"—a revolution pioneered by two queer women—was a revolution in the genre's relationship to women, both onstage and off, in characterization and in labor. Marbury simultaneously sought to refashion her chorus girls as fit to enter high society and to cultivate that high society as her audience. Meanwhile, she went to extraordinary lengths to reframe the relationship between the manager and the working woman. However, as would often be the case, the revolution—which was a revolution in how the musical engaged with the bodies of the women who performed it—would be mischaracterized as having been principally a revolution in abstract dramatic construction effected by men.[82] In 1918, the *Dramatic Mirror* interviewed Guy Bolton about "the seemingly successful attempt at world domination in the musical-comedy field by Messrs. Bolton, Wodehouse and Kern."[83] Bolton advances the conventional logic of dramatic integration when he argues that "we endeavor to make everything count. Every line, funny or serious, is supposed to help the plot continue to hold. This is, of course, true of all drama, but it seemed never to have been applied to musical comedy before." However, Bolton seems to assume that songs must be written before the show, writing that "if the songs are going to count at all in any plot, the plot has to be built more or less around, or, at least, with them." Thus, once Bolton receives the songs from the composer, he has to "reconstruct the entire plot, practically working backwards and forwards from the songs, as the case may be, to get the proper intervals of time between them." He sums up this complicated dramaturgy in his claim that "drama is much easier to write than a musical comedy. Poor old Ibsen didn't have to count his pages back to the last number or count the minutes since the girls were on last, when he was doing his bit."[84]

This disconnect between Bolton's grand artistic ambition and his actual work is also apparent in his brief discussion of the individual shows. Of *Nobody Home*, he says that despite their goal of overthrowing the conventional interpolated comedy, there "still had to be the same haphazard plot . . . ," and while there was a "definite thread of a story," "there were the same irrelevant scenes, too." Bolton seems to experience similar complications with the next Princess Theatre show: "In 'Very Good Eddie,'" he notes, ". . . it was easier to work out our theory of giving the public a real 'honest-to-goodness' plot with characters, but it was difficult to get altogether away from the irrelevant scenes." However, Bolton felt that his next show, *Oh, Boy!*, "had nothing irrelevant in it." Bolton invokes the central tenet of integration when he writes that "the plot was connected, and every song and lyric contributed to the acceleration of the action," mirroring our modern conception of integration by suggesting that the songs are essential to the dramatic logic of the play. However, in further elaborating this claim, he argues precisely the opposite: "We tested the play out one day to see whether it could stand the test of making sense, or at least coherent nonsense, as you will, without music. And it did."[85] Indeed, Wodehouse and Bolton would later write of *Oh, Lady! Lady!!* that "the integration of book and music was better than in *Oh, Boy!*," with "the story—for a musical play—exceptionally strong, so much so that [Wodehouse] was able later to use it for a full length novel, *The Small Bachelor*. . . ."[86]

Bolton is not being disingenuous. Rather, the profound dissonance between his claim about the songs furthering the action, and his claim that the action is totally comprehensible without them, reveals one point of confusion in the logic of integration. Bolton is trying to elevate the genre by denying what is undeniable: the rupture of the musical numbers. Implicitly confronted by this tension, he paradoxically concedes that "the plot in all these musical comedies seems tenuous, but that is not the fault of the plot. It is due to its musical accompaniments—their interruptions of the plot. However, if the plots of any of our musical comedies were taken and were played without the musical accompaniment they would still, I believe, have some reason for existence as comedy." In this way, he is really concerned with the quality of the comedic book, rather than with any relationship between the book and the musical numbers—hence his interest in "realism" and in plots that "deal with subjects and people near to the audience." Spoken as this was in the aftermath of World War I, it is unsurprising to see Bolton's idea of "realism" to mean home-grown characters as opposed to imitations of European royalty. As he phrased it, "Let us laugh with the U.S.A., instead of at Europe, Asia and Africa in our musical comedies."[87] He was interested in different kinds of laughs as well, making modest strides at writing more organic, character-driven comedy. These are incremental steps in dramatic construction—not the revolutions that Bolton purports.

However, Bolton and Wodehouse would return to the Princess Theatre Shows once more, in a memoir written forty years later—and offer an entirely different tone. Their book opens with an imaginary scene in a "smoke-filled room in a hotel" during the out-of-town tryout of a musical. Having discovered a lull in the show, the various creators and performers debate how to enliven it. The solution, they write, comes from

> a man in shirt sleeves, chewing an enormous (unlighted) cigar. He is fifty-five years old and for twenty-five of those years he has been an impresario of musical comedy. Lending to the discussion the authority of long experience and uttering the slogan which he probably learned at his mother's knee, he says: "Bring on the girls!"[88]

Wodehouse and Bolton remark, "And how wonderful those girls always were. . . . A hundred shows have been pushed by them over the thin line that divides the floperoo from the socko."[89] In mock gratitude for such work, Wodehouse and Bolton dedicate the title of their book—*Bring on the Girls!*—to them, thereby misremembering the entire enterprise of the Princess Theatre Shows. To the degree that the show was invested in "bringing on the girls," it was in a sense entirely contrary to what is evoked by this passage.

Marbury's shrewd efforts to reframe and reconfigure the labor of burlesque were a harbinger of the "revolutions" of integration that would recur again and again, which are always about the laboring bodies of the theatre.

However, despite the seemingly disingenuous nature of Bolton's comments about "the girls," he nevertheless reminds us that the undercurrent of burlesque is always present in musical theatre, always ready to bubble to the surface. It is there every time Dolly Levi struts down the stairs of the Harmonia Gardens. Indeed, it is there every time the genre "brings on the girls," every time a woman's body returns to the spotlight, where we beg her never to go away again. But what prompts this solicitousness on our part? The answer may be broached in an early draft of *Hello, Dolly!*—the same draft that explicitly articulated the threads of sexual labor that would be sublimated in the final script. This earlier version elaborately depicted the consequences of Dolly's return to the restaurant, culminating in farcical disorder when Cornelius and Barnaby try to evade Vandergelder's detection. When the young men express concern that Horace will catch them, Irene Molloy instructs them to put on her and Minnie's coats and veils so that they might depart unnoticed.[90] After the women dress the men, Minnie says, "Irene, doesn't Barnaby make a lovely girl? He just ought to stay that way." Even "Barnabetta," as he is now sometimes called, gets into the act, saying, "Well if I have to stay a woman, Cornelius, I think you'd better take me home. It's awful late for a young girl to be out. I wouldn't want people to talk. . . ."[91] In this moment, an identification with the female body—in the form of material and psychic drag—becomes a kind of corollary to the eruption of burlesque, an unexpected logic to which I will now turn.

Myron McCormick as Luther Billis as Lutheria Billis in *South Pacific*. ©John Swope Trust, Craig Krull Gallery.

# 3

# HIS INNERMOST BEING

*Brecht, Musicals, and the Politics of Identification*

In his memoir, *Musical Stages*, Richard Rodgers gave his own account of integration, writing "that's what made *Oklahoma!* work. All the components dovetailed. There was nothing extraneous or foreign, nothing that pushed itself into the spotlight yelling 'Look at me!'"[1] In Rodgers's telling, integration is threatened precisely by the potential for an element of the show to behave like a narcissistic performer, seeking to escape from the demands of the piece and selfishly occupy the spotlight. Rodgers's comment tellingly reveals that the anxieties that motivate the discourse of integration are precisely anxieties about *bodies* that escape and that seek recognition. In this chapter, I want to think about how this metaphor actually functions quite literally, and what is made possible when a performer—a female performer—steps into the spotlight and solicits attention, and why some may find this unsettling, prompting them to advance the idea of "integration."

The opening night reviews of *Oklahoma!* suggest that the show's ostensible cultivation of an ensemble cast instead of star performers was central to the broader claims made about the show. Indeed, while contemporaneous critics generally singled out stars when writing reviews of other shows, a surprising number of the reviews of *Oklahoma!* contain an implicit or explicit appreciation not of particular stars, but instead of the cast as an ensemble. As Howard Barnes wrote in his review, "there are no particularly well known performers in the piece, but that is all to the good in a show which has inherent theatrical excitement."[2] The excitement previously generated in stars, it was thought, could now be generated more organically in the "integrated" content of the show. Revisiting the New York production more than a year after it opened, Barnes wrote that "certainly [*Oklahoma!*] is not dependent on any particular set of principals, let alone a star. It is a show first and foremost—an exercise in performing only according to the standards of particular presentations."[3] When *Chicago Sunday Times* critic Robert Pollak reviewed the traveling production that visited Chicago in December of 1943, he wrote that

> "Oklahoma!" was born star-less on the last day of March, 1943, and it is star-less still. Many a fat and sassy musical has come to life only because Ethel Merman or Victor Moore was handy at the time. But the idea of "Oklahoma!" glittered like Orion long before this premiere . . . . They collected a cast of young and capable principals who were willing to work hard because they believed that "Oklahoma!" was going to be a wow and reveled in its sturdy, American quality.[4]

A 1945 review in the *Boston Globe* of a traveling production similarly remarked, "As for the cast—here is definite proof that 'Oklahoma' is a great show. There isn't a single star in the billing . . . yet they seem as talented and fresh as the original company which was here in 1943."[5] And in 1947, critic William Hawkins of the *New York World-Telegram* revisited the Broadway production, praising "the spirited exactness of the whole company as an ensemble . . . here the show remains the thing . . . ."[6]

It was the "sturdy" quality of "the show" that "remains the thing" with *Oklahoma!* In venerating the ensemble and dismissing stars and divas like Ethel Merman, these reviewers reveal that the metaphor Rodgers used to discuss integration—preventing anything from hogging the spotlight and yelling "Look at me!"—was true in a literal sense: the goal of "integration" was precisely to stifle a certain kind of bodily solicitation. In this chapter, I will extend Rodgers's claims and show how integration is motivated not only by the performers who ostensibly seek attention but also by the spectators who answer this solicitation. To understand how this works, I turn to a production that opened not long after *Oklahoma!* in 1943: *A Connecticut Yankee*.

While *Oklahoma!* marked Rodgers's first effort with Oscar Hammerstein after having worked with Lorenz Hart—a professional split thought to coincide with the split in musical theatre history between piecemeal and "integrated," between primitive musical comedy and "mature" musical theatre—Rodgers did in fact work with Hart once more, when the two wrote a few new songs for a 1943 revival of *A Connecticut Yankee*. This revival was to star Vivienne Segal, a famous performer for whom Hart had written a new song, "To Keep My Love Alive." While Rodgers was apparently willing to siphon Hart's emotional reserve for songwriting, Rodgers found Hart's emotional state to be disturbingly unstable. According to Samuel Marx's and *Carousel* actress Jan Clayton's account of the incident, Rodgers ultimately forbade house management from allowing Hart to enter the theatre on opening night. Rejected at the door, Hart went across the street to a bar and began to drink; after a while, he returned to the theatre and was able to slip in through an unattended door. When Segal began to sing "To Keep My Love Alive," "[Hart] began his familiar pacing, at first nervously and then frenetically and finally joining in with her singing, louder and louder."[7] Per instructions given earlier to house management by Rodgers, Hart was removed, and the audience grew silent. Within a couple of days, Hart admitted himself to a hospital, his death following shortly thereafter.

Hart's ability to sing along with the diva is precisely what is at stake in the spotlight—in the "Look at me!" moment—and indeed his singing along is precisely what the discourse of integration seeks to disavow. The older tradition of burlesque-inspired musical comedy embraced a bolder recognition of the diva outside the narrative order of the musical play. Segal was more than merely a part of a plot: she was also a performing body, a body able to escape her position as narrative object and instead present herself as a defiant musical subject, one with whom Hart could identify and sing along. This is precisely the power of the performing body that bursts into song and dance, a utopian mobility that challenges any pretense of musical integration. Identification with the diva, as in the case of Hart, emphasizes the potential of the spectacular musical register to promote a signifying order—and a signifying subject—different from the more conventional signifying order of narrative. If the beauty of the female diva occurs in her carnivalesque oscillation between narrative object and defiant spectacular musical subject, then the female performer embodies the genre's uneasy yet productive split between narrative and spectacle. The representational possibilities of theatre, and of the performing woman, are pushed to their respective limits simultaneously in the musical form. Integration, however, works to deny this dynamic.

Given the inevitable failure—the structural impossibility—of attempts to "integrate" music and spectacular female bodies into the narrative economy of the play, why invoke such an odd discourse? And why are artists, critics, and spectators invested in containing the performer—and consequently in containing the spectator who wishes to sing along? To understand this dynamic of regulation, I return to another set of terms frequently invoked to describe *Oklahoma!*—as suggested in Burton Rascoe's comment that the "joy of the production . . . is in its total effect."[8] Rascoe's mention of "total effect" echoes the Wagnerian concept of *Gesamtkunstwerk*, or "total art-work," a concept that has been explicitly invoked in relationship to *Oklahoma!* by numerous critics. As John Bush Jones writes, the "concept of the integrated musical is similar to Richard Wagner's ideal of the *Gesamtkunstwerk* . . . [in which] the individual elements of composition and production—music, lyrics, story, characters, ideas, and point of view—all harmoniz[e] to present [the musical play] to the audience."[9] By assimilating operatic terminology, those championing "integration" were able to endow the musical with the legitimacy associated with a high art. Further, Scott McMillin and Stacy Wolf, who have also written about the Wagnerian strain in the use of "integration," demonstrate the usefulness of Bertolt Brecht's critiques of Gesamtkunstwerk for thinking through the general politics of musical theatre. As Wolf writes, "gleefully divided and contradictory, musical theatre is, as Scott McMillin points out, indebted to Brecht's theories of 'alienation' and not to Wagner's 'total artwork,' despite mid-twentieth-century artists' citing Gesamtkunstwerk as their ideal."[10]

However, I want to return to the writings of Wagner and Brecht to reveal something quite different: unexpectedly shared anxieties surrounding music and female bodies, anxieties that catalyze the discourse of integration in musical theatre. Both Wagner's ideas of Gesamtkunstwerk—as well as Brecht's ostensible critiques of those ideas—help us to understand the relationship between integration, the spectacular performing bodies of women, and the potential for men to identify with them.

For composer Richard Wagner, the curious nature of musical moments in theatre, the fundamental oddness of singing in a drama, could be squelched by seamlessly integrating these moments into the piece as, he argues, composer Christoph Gluck did before him. In *Opera and Drama*, Wagner celebrates Gluck's "reproducing the feeling of the text as truly as possible through the medium of musical expression . . . ." Gluck's object, Wagner continues, "was to speak in music both correctly and intelligibly."[11] Gluck himself writes that he attempted to "divest [his music] entirely of all those abuses (introduced either by the uncomprehending vanity of the Singers or by the Composers' excessive wish to please) which have so long disfigured the Italian opera."[12] In a similar vein, Wagner writes that "if we consider honestly and unselfishly the essence of music, we must own that it is in large measure a means to an end, that end being in rational opera the *drama* . . . ."[13] In a view that strikingly resembles common critiques of frothy musicals of the 1920s and 1930s, Wagner felt that many opera composers arrived at projects with music written well in advance, music that paid scant heed to the dramatic particularities of any given piece. For Wagner, music should not flaunt itself; instead, it should serve the drama.

Crucially, it is through *gender* that Wagner elaborates his theory of opera composition. According to him, the opera composer is well situated to submit to the poet in order to render organically expressive music. Composers working in the older mode of composition, however, "could never succeed, on account of standing in a fundamentally wrong relation to that element of poetry which was alone capable of bearing fruit; having, in his unnatural and usurping situation, robbed it, in a certain sense, of its productive organs."[14] Poetry, for Wagner, contains a certain spiritual kernel of the entire drama; this kernel is capable of penetrating the composer to provide a proper operatic offspring. The parthenogenetic hysteria of traditional composers, though, does nothing but produce illbred children outside the logical economy of rational opera. It is hubristic, Wagner argues, for music to believe that it could retreat to its own devices and create a true drama; true operatic music cannot exist without having been inspired, or fertilized, by the poetic lyrics and text, which combine with the music to form a synergistic drama.[15] This synergistic drama engenders the Aristotelian totality that Wagner sought to reclaim in opera.

Wagner is emphatic about this point: "Music is the female—destined to bring forth—the poet being the real generator; and music had, therefore, reached the very summit of madness when it aspired, not only to bear—but also to produce."[16] For him, music alone could not tell stories, and its goal was to serve the text, to become a vessel for narrative. "Music," Wagner writes, "is a woman. The nature of woman is love; but this love is one of conceiving, and of unreserved devotion in conception. Woman only attains to full individuality at the moment of this devotion."[17] Music, then, in its absolute attention to the poetry, in its complete devotion to bringing the poetic narrative to life, comes into its own; similarly, a singer fulfills her role in the drama by championing the text and effacing her own presence. This attitude—that music and the (female) singer should become narrative vessels—is precisely the attitude of integration.

Given Wagner's embrace of the values that also undergird integration, we might look to German playwright Bertolt Brecht's critique of Wagner's Gesamtkunstwerk to better critique the values of integration. However, I want to argue that Brecht's critique ultimately *extends* part of Wagner's claims. Indeed, *both* Wagner and Brecht share a distrust of music that they both analogize through the body of the female performer. Through a close reading of Brecht's writings, I show how he actually *furthers* Wagner's claims about the female performer. Ultimately, it is by bringing Wagner and Brecht together that we can understand the relationship between integration, female performers, and male fans.

Brecht argued that Wagner's Gesamtkunstwerk was an undesirable and in fact unrealizable goal, thereby striking a sturdy blow at the ideology that champions integration. Whereas Gluck and Wagner view the traditional conception of opera—one that celebrates certain musical moments or performers, perhaps at the expense of the overall drama—as a great evil that must be overcome, Brecht views opera's lack of integration instead as its fundamental strength. For him, opera is senseless, and it is therefore at its best when it interrogates and deploys the "senselessness of the operatic form" as an aesthetic phenomenon.[18] The musicality of opera is what gives it this senselessness: "A dying man is real. If at the same time he sings we are translated to the sphere of the irrational."[19] For Brecht, the degree of unreality is directly proportionate to the amount of pleasure that opera affords; as one increases, so does the other. While he ultimately abandoned opera as a viable form of epic theatre, Brecht did sustain an interest in using songs in his theatrical projects.

Part of the reason that Brecht so championed music as a central element of his epic theatre was that he could deploy music as one way of underscoring "unreality." He could seize upon this unreality, alienate it—in other words, bring a particular kind of attention to it—and thereby metaphorize the entire theatrical project. By foregrounding the essentially theatrical elements of theatre, Brecht was able to catalyze a consciousness of the narrative modes through which the drama was being presented. This represents Brecht's great revolution in dramatic practice: the musical moments were recognized and valued precisely *because* they were profound ruptures in the narrative. Though Brecht did seek to deploy the oddness of music to a particular end, his understanding of music as narrative rupture represents a direct critique of Wagnerian integration and thus obliquely criticizes the understanding of music that enables critics to discuss musicals as integrated. However, despite Brecht's sophisticated understanding of, and investment in, music, he does not ultimately seem able to embrace the political possibilities of the fully "disintegrated" musical form. He and Wagner are far more alike than previously thought, and by tracing Brecht's own anxieties surrounding music and the female body, I will show what "integration" wishes to deny, what transpires when someone says "Look at me!" in the spotlight.

Though the centrality of music to Brecht's epic theatre has been widely appreciated, it appears upon closer analysis that Brecht in fact retained a great deal of suspicion toward music in and of itself. He was quite wary of the autonomous art music of his time, writing that

> Most "advanced" music nowadays is still written for the concert hall. A single glance at the audiences who attend concerts is enough to show how impossible it is to make any political or philosophical use of music that produces such effects. We see entire rows of human beings transported into a peculiar doped state, wholly passive, sunk without trace, seemingly in the grip of a severe poisoning attack.[20]

For Brecht, then, art music—music *qua* music—was basically a disguised form of Aristotelian theatre. Indeed, he went so far as to write that this "music is cast in the role of Fate."[21] The idea of fate, of course, was anathema to Brecht's theatre of social transformation; by labeling this music as fate, he was relegating music—because of its affective power—to complicity with the status quo. Brecht concludes this discussion by complaining that "such music . . . seduces the listener into an enervating, because unproductive, act of enjoyment. No number of refinements can convince me that its social function is any different from that of the Broadway burlesques."[22] What, then, is the social function of the burlesque?

Brecht suggests an answer to this question elsewhere when he elaborates his understanding of the connection between music and fate. With their desire for catharsis, Aristotelian plots, he suggests, are structurally founded on "lead[ing] the hero into situations where he reveals his innermost being." Brecht goes on to explain that

> All the incidents shown [in an Aristotelian drama] have the object of driving the hero into spiritual conflicts. It is a possibly blasphemous but quite useful comparison if one turns one's mind to the burlesque shows on Broadway, where the public, with yells of "Take it off!," forces the girls to expose their bodies more and more.[23]

The spectator of the Aristotelian drama, then, is very much like the spectator of the burlesque show. As such, Brecht's distrust of music as fate is mediated by the presence of the female burlesque performer. However, the question that emerges is why—in his indictment of the psychologizing dimensions of Aristotelian theatre—would the "innermost being" of the hero turn out to be like the "exposed" body of the burlesque performer?

The answer may be found when Brecht follows his analogy of classical drama and burlesque with some additional thoughts on the role of fate and identification in Aristotelian theatre: "Everyone (including every spectator) is then carried away," Brecht writes, "by the momentum of the events portrayed, so that in a performance of *Oedipus* one has for all practical purposes an auditorium full of little Oedipuses . . . ."[24] If Aristotelian theatre demands this sort of identification with the hero, then what must the burlesque theatre demand of its audience? Surely that it simultaneously desires the body it views and that it quite possibly *becomes* the body it views.

This is the great danger of burlesque in musical theatre: it inspires the male spectator to identify with the female body! The pleasures of burlesque seem to be not unlike the pleasure that Lorenz Hart got by singing along with Vivienne Segal; to be sure, such a psychic cross-dressing seems to provide one way of understanding what Brecht called the "enervating" pleasures of art music and burlesque and what Wagner called music's "robbing of the productive organs." Brecht's disdain for burlesque was motivated by the various identificatory pleasures, bodily and musical, that ran counter to the cognitive pleasures he sought to deploy in his epic theatre. Brecht, Wagner, and the integrationists meet on this ground: all find these kinds of pleasures imminent and alarming, hence the (unsuccessful) disavowals implicit in the discourse of integration.

These fears about identification—with both music and the female body—led Brecht to try to control the use of music in his epic theatre. By adding a dimension to the textual presentation, Brecht explains, music is able to be "gestic," to "conve[y] particular attitudes adopted by the speaker towards other men."[25] This juxtaposition and unexpected contrast is what Brecht means when he refers to his epic theatre's "radical separation of the elements."[26] This radical separation, of course, stands in direct contrast to Wagner, a fact that does not escape Brecht: "So long as the expression 'Gesamtkunstwerk' (or 'integrated work of art') means that the integration is a muddle . . . the various elements will all be equally degraded."[27]

However, despite Brecht's professed appreciation of this musical dimension, his writings nonetheless betray his fear that music has an unbelievable power to efface the meaning of the text. His distrust of music seems to transcend genre; writing about older (pre-Wagnerian) operatic music, he writes that part of the problem with conventional opera was that "rational elements" and "solid reality" are "washed out by the music."[28] Indeed, he seems to deny this music the possibility of communicability, for even when music mirrors the text, as in the old opera, it still—despite mirroring the text—obscures it. Brecht's epic opera, by contrast, would "communicate," he writes.[29] This "communication" seems to be predicated on muting the power of music.

Brecht seems to champion the disintegrating quality of music at the same time that he reins in its power; his radical separation seems to be less a strict separation than a subjugation of music to text, precisely in the style of Wagner. Despite arguing for the strict separation—and ostensible equality—of music and narrative, Brecht's own description, in fact, privileges the text, arguing that music must "take the text for granted," must work from this text to present another dimension. However this additional musical dimension might function, however this gestic quality might work, it works in relation to the language of the text. This hierarchy results from the fact that Brecht seems paradoxically to think that music actually *is* capable of expression without an underlying situatedness or textual basis; in "On the Use of Music in an Epic Theatre," he remarks that "serious music . . . still clings to lyricism, and cultivates expression for its own sake."[30] Brecht is ultimately wary that the emotive force of music can overwhelm a listener and limit the possibility of critical distance.

Brecht's theatre, then, does succeed in separating the elements, but it does so only insofar as the musical, the irrational, can ultimately be subjugated by the rationality of the textual—a logic not unlike the logic by which integration seeks to subordinate spectacle to narrative. Brecht's basic problem with Wagnerian opera is not so much that the arts are "fused," as he seems to claim, but rather that the musical inevitably overpowers the verbal. He is uncomfortable with the power of music to render everything else a slave to its siren-like allure, just as the enervating influence of the female body impaired the effectiveness of the drama and of the dramatic spectator. Nonetheless, because music carries so much affective and signifying weight, it can still be useful to Brecht's theatrical project. Thus, he seeks not only to separate the elements but also, at the same time, to instill a sense of deference within music. He faced a startling dilemma: the very musical elements that could activate the "dramatic" realm were precisely the ones that he felt had to be controlled.

Wagner and Brecht thus help to illuminate the theatrical and intellectual traditions out of which emerges the ideology of musical "integration." For Wagner, as for those who champion "integration," the bizarreness of the musical drama could be tamed by integrating this musical element into the larger drama. To use Wagner's terminology, such an integration would keep music in its proper place: as a woman devoted to bearing the fruit of the drama, as a woman who never attempts to produce such fruit by herself. Music, for Wagner, is a means to an end. Though Brecht insightfully calls attention to the impossibility of Wagner's ideas about the

Gesamtkunstwerk, Brecht's ideas—though they have long been framed as a robust critique of Wagner's (misogynist) reflections—often reinscribe the problem of dramatic music and musically dramatic women. For Brecht too, because of the ultimately programmatic demands of his epic theatre, music is a means to an end. His view of the affective power of music meant that the linguistic text had to come first, and that the music—and the female musical performer—had to work carefully to avoid usurping the role of the textual, such that "communication" could occur in the form of a message.

This profound connection between Brecht's attitudes about musicality and about female bodies certainly inflects our understanding of his dictum that the musical gest emphasizes "showing":[31] the demonstrative quality of music is not a strictly aural phenomenon; it is mediated by the spectacular presence of bodies, especially those of women. Whatever their limitations, though, Brecht's thoughts about music, theatre, and performance insist that an inherently disruptive spectacular musicality can never fully be exiled from musical theatre. No matter how much artists, critics, and spectators may claim that musicals are integrated, they cannot be.

Further, this disruptive musicality is embodied by the sexualized burlesque performer whose body solicits identification—and by the male spectator who identifies with (and, in a sense, becomes) this sexualized burlesque performer. In this way, the musical theatre form thus presents a socially sanctioned venue for a socially unsanctioned desire. Brecht's fear—that male spectators identify with the sexualized female body inspired by musical burlesque—is borne out by the uncanny repetition of a trope in which invocations of burlesque are followed by sexualized panics or moments of drag. Each instance of this trope in musical theatre brings to the surface this dynamic of gendered impersonation that exists at a psychic level as well.

The 1962 musical *A Funny Thing Happened on the Way to the Forum,* for example, announces its investment in burlesque—in the *labor* of burlesque—shortly after its curtain is raised, when we are told that the show takes place around three houses, including that of Lycus, "a buyer and seller of the flesh of beautiful women."[32] The play makes a joke of the commercial nature of the enterprise, as for example when reference is made to the women's "uh . . . business."[33] Later, when Pseudolus prepares the women for the arrival of Miles Gloriosus, he admonishes the courtesans to "remember who you are and what you stand for. Now, will you all please strike . . . vocational attitudes?"[34]

One of Lycus's women has attracted the eye of a young man, Hero, who agrees to free his slave, Pseudolus, if the slave can procure the girl for him. The plot focuses on the various complications Pseudolus encounters as he tries to acquire the girl for Hero. After Lycus offers him three other women—including Gymnasia, who, after doing a "bump," is herself described as "a giant stage on which a thousand dramas can be played"—Pseudolus learns that the girl his master desires is a virgin from Crete who has already been sold to the military hero Miles Gloriosus.[35] Pseudolus schemes to make her seem less desirable to Miles by suggesting that a great plague is ravaging Crete and will likely fell the girl at any moment. The culmination of his plan requires his fellow slave, Hysterium, to don a white virginal gown and pretend to be the plagued corpse of the young girl that Miles had purchased. In other words, a play that places women's bodies at its center—and that thematizes their sale—also makes a grand spectacle of a man becoming a woman.

This is not merely an isolated gag in the play; a whole array of forces seem eager to turn Hysterium into a woman. Long before Hysterium assumes his drag, the myopic Erronius bumps into Hysterium and excuses himself with "Pardon me, young woman," an appellation Erronius later repeats.[36] Domina, Hero's mother, also joins in on the act. She welcomes Miles Gloriosus's arrival by telling him that her father was a military captain. When she notes that she "entertained over two hundred officers" on the last anniversary of his death, Miles replies, "Two hundred? By yourself?" Domina dismisses his suggestion: "Of course not. Hysterium here was a big help," prompting Hysterium to "smil[e] proudly, then reac[t] painfully."[37] Similarly, Hysterium protests when Pseudolus, in a moment of subterfuge, refers to Hysterium as his eunuch. Pseudolus dismisses Hysterium's concern by saying, "You know it's not true, and I know it's not true, so what do we care what they think?"[38]

Pseudolus moves well beyond these allusions, ultimately transforming their energy into a form of material drag. When he needs a body to feign being the dead virgin, "a gleam comes into his eye" as he "starts running his hand over Hysterium's shoulder and chest."[39] Before long, Hysterium will emerge in a virginal gown and wig, protesting that the captain will never believe that he is a "beautiful dead girl," to which Pseudolus counters, "He will. You're delicious." When Pseudolus tries to assuage Hysterium's anxiety by assuring him that Miles won't try to kiss him, Hysterium objects: "How can he help it if I'm so delicious?"[40] Finally, when Pseudolus serenades Hysterium with "Lovely," the show's love song, the stage directions indicate that the impersonation is becoming real: "Hysterium is becoming convinced."[41] This impersonation now successful, the end of the play will find Hysterium himself giving voice to the desire that his cross-gender performance has unleashed: "Why do older men find me so attractive?"[42]

Thus, *Forum* makes explicit the logic that motivated Bertolt Brecht: the spectacular display of women's bodies—as embodied in the women of the house of Lycus, one of whom is analogized to a "stage" after performing a burlesque bump—prompts men to identify with, and in a way become, those bodies, unleashing a form of errant desire. In a play featuring characters with suggestive names, it seems fitting that "Lycus" suggests the confluence of desire (liking) and identification and impersonation (like).

Those who insist on "integration" are responding to the possibility articulated in *Forum* and in Brecht—the potential for the musical form, with its interruptive elements, to make possible these identifications and thereby unleash a form of desire. This specter of errant desire is unleashed every time the musical bursts into song, every time the narrative mode is interrupted for musical spectacle. Those who advance claims of integration are attempting to disavow not only the escape of the performer into the spotlight but also the escape of the spectator into new identities through bodily identification and performance.

Fears relating to musical narrative are actually fears about the kinds of desires that are structurally unleashed when the narrative fractures. For example, we might look to the circumstances of the show's origin: as *Forum* came nearer to being produced in 1962, Sondheim reports that he experienced "a rapidly burgeoning panic, which [he] attributed to hysteria from the excitement of finally launching [himself] as a composer."[43] Not trusting his own rationale that the panic was just a function of his impending debut, Sondheim asked James Goldman to read the show and listen to the score. Sondheim reported that "after reading it, he praised its brilliance; after hearing the score, he was equally enthusiastic. I started to glow in relief, when he added, 'The problem is that they don't go together.'"[44] Elaborating Goldman's claims, Sondheim voices two related complaints about the show: first, that *Forum* demands songs that are the antithesis of the Hammerstein style; and second, that the pace of the show is damaged by musical interruption. In his words, the first complaint is that one-dimensional characters, like those in *Forum*, "do not give rise to songs that move like Oscar's one-act plays, nor do they allow for the subtext and resonance that Arthur Laurents had taught me to appreciate."[45] As Sondheim put it, the musical numbers do not "have a sense of urging the show ahead." This is related to his second complaint, which he notes is "one of the problems with writing a score for a farce," namely "that it interrupts the action instead of carrying it on. It interrupts because it's not about character, those are not songs that develop people and story."[46] Thus, Sondheim complains about having to write for *Forum* precisely the kinds of numbers that he feels it demands. How, though, can a musical be thwarted by the kinds of songs that the form is said to require?

While this contradiction might be said to reside in complications specific to musical farce, I think it is symptomatic of a more general anti-musical attitude, held by Sondheim and many others, that many well-constructed plays function better without music: as he put it, "the tighter the plotting the better the farce, but the better the farce the more the songs interrupt the flow and pace."[47] The fear is that the songs interrupt the tight plotting characteristic of successful dramatic works. Tellingly, Sondheim suggested to Burt Shevelove that *Forum* might be more successful as a play—and he made a similar comment to Arthur Laurents about *Gypsy*.[48] I would argue that Sondheim's anti-musical sentiment is rooted in his own contradictory relationship to the musical form: he misapprehends the value and success of his own brilliant score precisely because it resists the narrative function he desires to give it, and it resists the broader narrative impulse he wishes to elevate.

The anxiety that prompted Sondheim's own "hysteria"—that the spectacular musical episodes interrupt the narrative, thereby interrupting the swift resolution toward which the plot is racing—is precisely related to the anxieties that we see unleashed in Hysterium's drag. To understand how this broader narrative concern is related to issues of gender and sexuality—and to reconsider Wagner's and Brecht's ideas in a different context—I turn to narratology, in particular to the work of Judith Roof, who has explored the "heteroideology" of narrative.[49] Roof writes that "our very understanding of narrative as a primary means to sense and satisfaction depends upon a metaphorically heterosexual dynamic within a reproductive aegis."[50] For her, narrative is structured precisely around the idea of an end, which "appears to give us a sense of mastery over what we can identify as a complete unit."[51] This heteroideology, born of the Oedipal resolution implicit in narrative, "replays the triumphant discovery of identity and moves toward an end that resounds with a sense of completion and fulfilled desire."[52]

However, narrative closure is predicated on the overcoming of obstacles, of course, and in Roof's view, "narrative's heteroideological closure" structurally demands the production of homosexuality. This homosexuality, she writes, represents "an omnipresent anxiety . . . about mastery, control, and production that surfaces at the last point where narrative feigns failure."[53] Thus, homosexuality—in the form of the threat of narrative sameness—is the obstacle introduced as the energy that must be overcome and contained in order to sustain the heteroideology of narrative. The feeling of narrative closure is generated through the containment of "perversions," which she defines as sources of narrative's "potential dissolution," which include the homo energy of sameness. In other words, these perversions of narrative must be contained.

Roof's narratology focuses on literary examples, but her broad principles, the frame of her argument, and the terms of her debate are productive ones through which to discuss musical theatre. Sondheim's own anxieties—that the swiftly resolving romantic narrative of Hero and Philia will be thwarted by the one-dimensionality and the lack of movement of the songs—are precisely the concerns about "sameness" that Roof argues are the threat of homosexuality to narrative closure. In a more general vein, though, I want to make three claims about musical theatre narratology in relation to Roof's argument—claims that will bring together the concerns about gender and the concerns about narrative.

First, Roof understands conventional narratives to introduce perversions precisely to be controlled in the moment of heterosexual closure. Musical theatre certainly has a structural investment in introducing "perversions" in the form of narrative failure—indeed, these are the musical numbers—but I would argue that these are not subsumed in musical theatre into a moment of closure. Instead, musical theatre *privileges* this energy and does not contain it. The powerful spectacular explosions of song and dance dominate the narrative that ostensibly envelop them. The narrative frame pales in comparison to the spectacular episodes: as extreme examples of this phenomenon, we might consider any of the countless examples where the narrative and spectacular components stand almost in contradiction, as if daring the spectator to believe the pallid narrative episode against the sensuous power of the spectacle. One might look, for instance, at *Gypsy*, a play whose climax occurs in "Rose's Turn," but which then has a brief scene appended thereto, as a mere coda. In the exhilarating burlesque finale "Rose's Turn," Rose sings, "I had a dream— / I dreamed it for you, June / It wasn't me for me, Herbie. . . ." before declaring, "Startin' now it's gonna be my turn!" Then, she incants, "For me—For me—For me—For me—FOR ME!" After this explosion, after the orchestra crescendos, after the singer has unleashed such vocal fury—there is quiet. Louise then enters, saying, "You'd really have been something, Mother [. . .] if you had had someone to push you like I had . . . ," prompting Rose to declare, "If I could've been, I would've been. And *that's* show business . . . I guess I did do it for me."[54] We are left with both "It wasn't for me" and "I guess I did do it for me." But who could believe the flaccid lines of dialogue when given the choice to pledge one's allegiance to the existential terror of "Rose's Turn"?[55]

If the musical can in this way eagerly dismiss the narrative, the archetypal boy-meets-girl narrative of musical theatre needs to be reconsidered. What does it mean that the musical is organized around a heterosexual narrative that it constantly interrupts, fragments, and upstages? By privileging its moments of musical spectacle, the musical endlessly queers the heterosexual narrative that serves as its frame. Indeed, the genre introduces heterosexual narratives precisely to deviate from them. *Gypsy* illustrates this point as well, as it posits an amorous relationship between Rose and Herbie—a relationship that it demonstratively marginalizes—as the show thematizes the incompatibility of marriage with burlesque. In other words, the show insists that marriage, the resolution of the heterosexual plot, is made impossible by the theatrical genres of spectacle. When Rose and

Herbie agree to get married, Louise urges them to "do it today!" Rose declares, "Not while we're in burlesque," to which Herbie replies, "The day we close." With her agreeing that "it's a deal," the two "shake hands and suddenly kiss."[56] But of course show business dominates, and when this inevitable truth is finally made explicit, Herbie walks out.

Thus, the frequent complaint that musicals feature only flimsy plots, "a narrative thread" introduced merely as a pretext for song and dance, might in some way speak to an essential element of the genre: the heterosexual narrative is there precisely to fail, precisely to reveal the superiority of the spectacular explosions that emerge from its failure. In light of the genre's deep interest in the failure of heteronarrative, the insistence on integration—an inexplicably forceful affirmation of the supremacy of narrative—feels almost desperate. This desperation results from the incompatibility of integration with the musical's relationship to spectacle, which in Roof's terms are "perversions." While narrative seems to structurally demand the introduction of perversions in order to *contain* them, I would argue that musicals *thrive* on perversions, and uses narrative (and integration) in order to make them possible.

At the same time that integration denies the genre's indulgence of these "perversions" of spectacle, that very same discourse might be said paradoxically to *encourage* these perversions, by providing yet more cover for the extraordinary transgressions that the musical form may cloak. In this way, we might understand the musical as a genre of the closet, a genre whose pleasures lurk at once in plain sight and completely underground, awkwardly obscured by the rhetorical fig leaf of "integration." Just as musicals need narrative in order to resist, we might imagine that, in a Foucauldian turn, the discourse of integration *produces* the disintegration it seeks to deny.

This same logic of identification, labor, and desire is apparent in *South Pacific*, which juxtaposes two commercial enterprises—that of Bloody Mary and Luther Billis, both of whom are in the business of manufacturing souvenirs. When Captain Brackett chastises Bloody Mary for employing the natives to produce grass skirts—"causing an economic revolution on this island"—Billis volunteers that the "demand for grass skirts can now be met by us Seabees!"[57] Captain Brackett dismisses Billis's suggestion but exiles Bloody Mary from Navy property. However, the skirts—themselves a token of burlesque—stand in metonymically for the real item being exchanged: women's bodies, especially those of "exotic" women. (The play even explicitly suggests that bodies are the real item of commerce through Bloody Mary's other great souvenir—"a real human head"—which Billis will also try to imitate.) Once the skirts are exiled, the focus is squarely on the exoticized women. On Bali Ha'i, we find Bloody Mary pairing her daughter with the handsome Lieutenant Cable, persuading him to marry her daughter by assuring him of her economic security: "Lootellan, I am rich. I save six hundred dolla' before war. Since war I make two thousand dolla' . . . war go on I make maybe more. Sell grass skirts, boar's teeth, real human heads. Give all de money to you an' Liat. You no have to work. I work for you . . . ."[58]

If Bloody Mary is thus conducting an economic transaction of a woman's body, her rival Luther Billis is offering a rival product that, like his imitation human head made of a shriveled orange coated with shoe polish, is but a facsimile of the real thing: himself as a woman. Billis is engaged in the related act of identifying with, and presenting as, a woman's body. He has already convinced Lt. Cable to come to Bali Ha'i by noting that the women "dance with just skirts on," whereupon Billis "starts [to] dance as he hums the melody seductively."[59] This impulse will be most fully indulged in the "Honey Bun" production number, which features "Lutheria" Billis dressed as a "South Sea siren in a straw-colored wig, long lashes fantastically painted on his eyelids, lips painted in bright carmine, two coconut shells on his chest to simulate 'femininity' and a battleship tattooed on his bare midriff."[60] The number concludes as Nellie—wearing an oversized sailor suit that echoes Bloody Mary's own outfit of an "old Marine's tunic" and a "G.I. identification chain from which hangs a silver Marine emblem"—urges everyone to "Put your money / On my Honey-Bun!"[61]

The presence of Billis in drag brings forth the desires from the soldiers who are watching his performance, as when he "feel[s] a hand thrust up his skirt." Billis's impulse to punch the soldier is foiled by his sense of a higher purpose: as the stage directions indicate, "he can't get out of line and spoil the number; 'On with the show!'" Indeed, Billis's theatrical obligation to stay in the line of girls "dressed in home-made costumes representing island natives" keeps him "grim and stoic—even when another boy lifts one of the coconuts in his 'brassiere' and steals a package of cigarettes therefrom." [62] This kind of sexualized contact seems to be the very fear that horrified Captain Brackett when Billis indicated that the Seabees could make their own grass skirts and supplant the business of the locals like Bloody Mary. It ultimately involves the men either becoming women or desiring the men who pose as women—a feat made explicit through the ready vehicle of a musical number: "On with the show!" But it is telling that Billis is impersonating not just any woman, but indeed a "South Sea siren"—in other words, an exoticized body marked doubly as spectacular. The ethnically exoticized nature of this erotic spectacle is not accidental and points toward the significance of race in the logic of integration.

Pearl Primus in the 1946 revival of *Show Boat*. Photograph by Vandamm Studio, ©Billy Rose Theatre Division, New York Public Library for the Performing Arts.

# 4

# THE RHYTHMIC
# INTEGRATION OF
# BLACKNESS

*Rouben Mamoulian and* Show Boat

The first three chapters explored how women's bodies fracture the narrative of musical theatre, making possible complex forms of identificatory play while also provoking anxieties about the kinds of sexualized labor associated with these bodies. As adumbrated by the example of *South Pacific*, this logic of identification, control, and labor is a raced logic. This chapter explores two sites of integration—the theories of director Rouben Mamoulian and the claims made about the 1927 musical *Show Boat*—to demonstrate how "integration" is concerned with the kinds of identifications that the form permits with black bodies. I begin by showing how Mamoulian, whose theory of rhythmic integration was based on Russian aesthetics, reframed this concept as distinctly American by invoking stereotypes about the rhythmic faculties of African American performers. Juxtaposing Mamoulian's ideas with the contemporaneous production of *Show Boat*, I argue that "integration," which was deeply invested in the pleasures and fears that circulated about black bodies, ultimately works to shore up the white subject of musical theatre.

In 1943, magazine writer George R. Brooks interviewed Rouben Mamoulian about his work as the director of *Oklahoma!* When Brooks queried
Mamoulian as to "the keynote of a successful musical . . . Mamoulian
gave the answer simply: 'Integration.'"[1] Mamoulian could give the answer
"simply," precisely because he had been rehearsing it for years. From the
time of his arrival in America in 1923, Mamoulian—the Armenian-born
director whose stage works included *Porgy and Bess*, *Oklahoma!*, and *Carousel*—seized every opportunity to advocate for his theory of integration.
Indeed, virtually every Mamoulian production proudly announced its
ostensible integration: in 1935, for example, discussing his production
of *Porgy and Bess,* he opined that "the highest fulfillment and glamour of
the living theatre lies in the fusion of drama, music and dancing. I have
tried, as much as I could, to achieve this exciting unification of theatrical
elements."[2]

Mamoulian emphasized the importance of rhythm to his theory. As he
explained in 1943, "'Oklahoma!' differs from other light musical works
chiefly in the stress that it puts upon rhythm . . . . Through the songs,
through the dance, even through the speech we capture the mood of rhythm
. . . ."[3] These kinds of claims were being trumpeted by newspapers as
early as 1924, when Mamoulian wrote that he sought "to produce operas
as music-dramas, to have music, singing, dramatic action and scenery
blended into a perfect rhythmical harmony."[4] As one writer put it in 1927,
"Mamoulian's theatrical theories are few. Chief among them is a persistent
and uncompromising belief that there should be rhythm to all plays."[5]
For Mamoulian, the rhythmic essence of his plays was nothing less than
the foundation:

> Strip "Oklahoma!" of its rhythmic essence and you probably would
> have only a sort of Western with songs and dances transferred to the
> stage. But the conjoined efforts of the authors, the dance and mu-
> sical directors, the cast and all, as welded together, yield something
> utterly new in its appeal to audiences mainly, I believe, because of
> the emphasis they put on the rhythmic element.[6]

Mamoulian claimed that his interest in a rhythmically integrated theatre
"draws on sources nearly as far back as my arrival in this country when I was
associated with the Eastman Theater in Rochester."[7] At George Eastman's

invitation, Mamoulian came to America in 1923 to teach opera and theatre at the Eastman School of Music, where he gave lectures on dramatic art and rehearsed operatic scenes as well as "other sorts of stage divertimenti," which "ranged through many styles and subjects, from serious musical moments, to comic ballet, to little stage anthologies of folk song suitably dramatized."[8] His aesthetic goals regarding integration became pedagogical ones, and he set out to institute a training program that mirrored the unity he sought in productions, arguing that the school "shall unify the elements of music, dance and dramatic action by training in pantomime and in silent action to music."[9] Of particular significance was Mamoulian's production of Maurice Maeterlinck's play *Sister Beatrice*, which local press accounts reported "will try to combine the spoken drama, the dance and music, and out of these elements achieve an organic and unified whole."[10]

Crucially, Mamoulian claimed that his unique form of rhythmic theatre was distinctly American in conception. As he wrote, "For many years now I've been passionately interested in working out a form of musical theatre that would be authentically American [. . .] there was a need and an opportunity to produce a form of musical presentation which could blossom on our own soil and by appealing to large masses of people, as something of their own."[11] Elsewhere, Mamoulian refers to his "rhythmic integrated" plays as "a form of production which is intrinsically American in a young, but indigenous American theatre."[12] Much was made of the fact that Mamoulian's "authentically" American theatrical works were the brainchild of an immigrant. "After the successful stage productions of 'Oklahoma,' and 'Carousel,'" noted one account, "it is an acknowledged fact that Rouben Mamoulian, born in Tiflis, educated in Paris and Tiflis, is today's greatest interpreter and exponent of Americana."[13] In one interview, Mamoulian defended the immigrant perspective, writing that "spiritual and emotional kinship" are more consequential for understanding a country than is actually being from that nation.[14] He regularly suggested that as a foreigner, he was especially sensitive to American values, traditions, and sensibilities—with one writer noting that Mamoulian "felt that Americans had lost sight of the real potentialities of Americana by being too close to the scene."[15] This was a common refrain, and became a regular part of the mythology that circulated around the director, who, it was said, "created a kind of musical comedy that is as American as 'Yankee Doodle Dandy.'"[16]

However, the most fascinating element of this "authentically American" art form—this art form that, as he put it, "draws on sources nearly as far back as my arrival in this country when I was associated with the Eastman Theater in Rochester"—is that it came straight from Moscow. In his earliest interviews, Mamoulian is quick to profess his theatrical bona fides, noting that he trained at the Moscow Art Theatre with legendary director Evgeny Vakhtangov. After Mamoulian established himself in Rochester, references to his Russian training dry up rather quickly. However, as I will show, Mamoulian's celebrated innovations in this "distinctly" American art form were in fact derived directly from his Russian training, bringing a complex and fascinating global dimension to this conventional form of mainstream American entertainment. Just as complex was Mamoulian's use of black bodies to transform this Russian aesthetic into an American one.

Evgeny Vakhtangov, Mamoulian's teacher, was a significant figure in the Moscow Art Theatre, generally recognized for having bridged Stanislavsky's interest in dramatic truth with the theatrical dimensions of Meyerhold's vision. Calling his approach "fantastic realism," Vakhtangov founded his sense of theatricality on principles of rhythm which were profoundly influential in Russian aesthetics of the time, coursing through different circles in various permutations. These philosophies of rhythm would have come to Vakhtangov principally by way of Sergei Volkonsky and Vsevolod Meyerhold. Volkonsky, a leader of the Russian Imperial Ballet, lectured on eurhythmics, a kinesthetic mode of teaching music, at the Moscow Art Theatre, and later taught speech and rhythmic exercises in Vakhtangov's own studio. Vakhtangov's correspondence reveals that he highly regarded—and recommended to others—articles that Volkonsky published between 1910 and 1914 on François Delsarte and Émile Jaques-Dalcroze, the founder of eurhythmics. Meyerhold, meanwhile, became fascinated by rhythm through George Fuchs, the great artist and critic who founded the Munich Artists Theatre. In his *Stage of the Future*, which "made the deepest impression" on Meyerhold, Fuchs claimed that the actor's "art has its origins in the dance" and that the most significant means of theatrical expression is, in the phrasing of Edward Braun, "the rhythmical movement of the human body in space."[17]

Thus, Vakhtangov was immersed in philosophies of theatrical rhythm that deeply informed his directorial practice. As Nick Worrall notes,

During rehearsal, Vakhtangov tried to teach his actors to live and breathe rhythmically on stage. He invited practical exercises involving the moving of furniture, laying the table, cleaning the room, etc., to music. It was necessary to learn not only to move in a certain rhythm, but to live in it. He taught that every individual, every nation, every phenomenon of nature, every event of human existence, possessed its own especial rhythm. To discover the rhythm of the play was the key to the success of the production.[18]

Describing Vakhtangov's production of *The Dybbuk*, Yosef Yzraely notes that Vakhtangov, in adapting the play, took a chant that was merely used as an incidental gesture and extended it throughout the entire scene, thereby "devising a rhythmic musical form."[19]

Having studied with Vakhtangov, Mamoulian's philosophy of rhythmic integration had a most distinguished lineage in aesthetics, coming to him through his teacher's interest in Fuchs, Meyerhold, and Volkonsky, among others. However, when asked about the origins of his obsession with rhythm, Mamoulian never cited this pedigree. Instead, he trotted out any of several anecdotes about his childhood. As one such reminiscence went,

> The seed of my work was planted within me by a physics teacher. . . . In explaining sympathetic vibrations, he told us that a regiment must break step while crossing a bridge, because the rhythmic force of "in step" marching might cause the bridge to collapse. This set me thinking. If the sheer force of rhythm can destroy a great structure of concrete and steel, there must be a power in rhythm that can be used constructively. From that time on, I determined to find out how to build rhythmically.[20]

Elsewhere, he wrote that "I have always been impressed, too, with the Latin quotation that water, dripping on a stone drop by drop, will eventually break the stone, not because the drop is stronger but because of the frequency and orderliness of the rhythm."[21] We are similarly told that Mamoulian's "belief in the mathematical *rightness* of a marching universe, of organized *tempi*, dates back to his childhood in Tiflis, where he was born. In a great thick-walled room of his grandfather's house, he used to lie awake at night, listening to a ponderous old clock and following, with his eye, the weave and pattern of the tapestries which soared above his bed."[22]

Mamoulian's stories of his precocious childhood work to disavow his training in Vakhtangov's studio, obscuring his artistic lineage in the interest of promoting himself as a directorial iconoclast. However, there is no denying that many of his directorial "innovations" with rhythm flagrantly echo those of Vakhtangov. The extent of this "influence" can be found in Mamoulian's most invoked example of his own philosophy—the "Noise Symphony" in *Porgy*, a show that Mamoulian said was "utterly stylized from beginning to end. Every grouping, every position, every action, every movement . . . was stylized."[23] When asked to give concrete examples of how his theories of rhythm manifested themselves in practice, Mamoulian invoked the "Noise Symphony" almost without fail; only two or three other examples make even occasional appearances. This uniformly praised number, which Mamoulian sometimes called his "Occupational Humoresque," was a precisely choreographed number that brought Catfish Row to life through a musical mosaic of such mundane noises as "thuds," "snores," and the sounds of brooms, knives, saws, washboards, towels, and shoes. However, as with many of Mamoulian's so-called innovations, the device came straight from Vakhtangov. As Vera Gottlieb notes, the Vakhtangov Studio's orchestra "had to come from the School or Studio's resources— hence the instrumental use of combs, and pots and pans."[24] Similarly, Worrall notes that in a scene from Vakhtangov's production of *The Wedding*,

Everything was conducted in strict tempo with strong acoustical effects. . . . A lackey arranged wine and hors d'oeuvres to the opening rhythm of the music as Aplombov pounded the back of a chair while conducting an argument with the mother, both in time to the music and in accompaniment to his own words. The dialogue between the romantic Zmeyukhina and the telegraphist, Yat, was accompanied by a rattling waltz on the piano whilst she fanned herself in a rapid, nervous tempo. When her voice broke on a high note while singing a romance, Yat took over the fanning . . . his stylish pince-nez vibrating on his nose in time to his movements. The production opened at a brisk tempo with a rousing quadrille. The group danced to the commands of the MC . . . Vakhtangov suggested that each actor perform some simple, initial action like moving a chair, adjusting something on the table so as to produce the necessary auditory effect.[25]

As Aviv Orani notes, Vakhtangov's company "in effect, became an orchestral ensemble conducted by the director so as to sharpen and increase the audience's sensitivity."[26] A striking similarity to this orchestral analogy can be found in Philip K. Scheuer's 1932 article "Rhythm Rouben," in which he writes that

> like a good many people who got rhythm, Rouben Mamoulian would like to lead an orchestra. Only, practically, the fact that he has never had an orchestra to lead has stood in his way . . . as a matter of fact, he has found a surprising number of unofficial uses for the baton: anyone who saw his productions of "Porgy" . . . or before that, his "Sister Beatrice" at George Eastman's theatre in Rochester . . . will appreciate that, orchestra or no, there is more than one way to get rhythm . . . Mamoulian conducts whole scenes literally, symphonically.[27]

The shared analogies about conducting only confirm the obvious fact that Mamoulian's art, while regularly promoted as his own idiosyncratic inspiration, in fact derived from the methods of his teacher.[28]

Mamoulian's brilliance, however, was in recasting these avant-garde Russian aesthetics as being fundamentally American ones: "The ideal theatre should be a combination of dance, music and the spoken word, inextricably woven together. This country is, of course, the most rhythmic country in the world. And rhythm is the most important thing in the theatre. It's up to us to evolve a new form of typically American theatre."[29] Noticeably, this modulation of Russian values into American ones required reframing the concept of rhythmic integration as something distinctly American, which he did as far back as 1927, when he directed *Porgy* for the Theatre Guild. As a play with spirituals, *Porgy* was essentially a musical that focused on African American characters. Described in one review as a "cyclorama of negro life, directed, you will remember, by a Russo-American,"[30] *Porgy* gave Mamoulian the vehicle through which he would effect this transposition of rhythmic integration into an American domain: black bodies.

Press accounts built on Mamoulian's own claim that black performers were perfectly suited to his conceptual practice. As one such article baldly phrased it, "'Porgy,' a story full of Negro rhythm, gave Mamoulian his first real chance to try out some of his theories . . . ."[31] Critics were particularly impressed by the "Noise Symphony." Noting that "rhythm is really a built-in element with blacks," Mamoulian said that this scene was inspired by "two black masons building a wall around the garden in Charleston and they sat astride the way you ride horseback facing each other and they tried to finish the wall in between the two—and the one would put a brick on and the other would slap cement on—and the first one would tap it down and the second one would put another brick on. The whole thing was done rhythmically while they were singing. Oh, this was part of life. . . . So, of course this fired my imagination. This was perfect for the idea of stylized rhythmic productions."[32] One account of the "Noise Symphony" reported that Mamoulian "believes firmly in what he calls an 'orchestra of actors,'" and "he doubted whether he could have done that opening scene in Porgy with a white cast. The colored actors looked at him in utter amazement, he said, the first time he staggered on the stage at rehearsal with an armful of noise-making devices . . . but they soon got the idea and entered into it whole-heartedly."[33]

Asked about his interest in an "all-colored" cast, Mamoulian replied that "working with a colored cast has been to me one of the most gratifying and exciting experiences in the theatre. . . . They have a wealth of emotions and dynamic energy to give to the stage."[34] Discussing the rehearsals of Porgy, Mamoulian recalled "the utter passionate devotion of all those people to their work, the inborn sense of rhythm which they possess and which is so important in the theatre."[35] Indeed, Mamoulian's concept of rhythm—which actually traced itself to Russian theories—was being reframed as the rhythm of blackness.

Mamoulian troublingly touted his quick study of black life, telling an interviewer that "when the Theatre Guild handed me the script of 'Porgy,' my only contact with the colored people was a shoeblack who shined my shoes in Rochester."[36] He waxed rhapsodically about the five days he spent in Charleston "wandering around the streets, going into little churches, talking to the fisherman and generally trying to absorb that rich and colorful atmosphere."[37] Newspaper accounts luxuriated in the meeting of the two cultures; as one writer put it,

> he took a train to Charleston, to acquaint himself at first hand with the subject. It was midsummer, July; Rouben Mamoulian, tall, lean, and perspiring behind his spectacles, looking like some Jewish divinity student out of his *métier*, peered up and down streets almost deserted under the sun. His nose crinkled to the odors of rotting fruit and frying fish. He was still there when the trade winds blew in, bearing night like a caress, and the Negro men and women stretched their bodies and came out to meet it.[38]

This sentiment was repeated in other accounts: "The young foreign director studied the American negro; found there was music in his soul and in his speech; that there was rhythm in his body and in his movements."[39]

The "young foreign director" will not only "study" the "rhythm in [the] body," but he will attempt to control it—for the "orchestra of actors" invoked by the newspaper columnist is exactly what Mamoulian wished to conduct with his much-discussed baton. As early as 1926, he claimed that "as in a symphony orchestra, the players are united by the conductor into one rhythmic, musical whole, so the actors on the stage should be all brought into a rhythmic unified design of movement and emotions by the director."[40] He frequently wrote that theatre is the art of "collective action," and that "the Stage is a dramatic art of coordinated acting by live actors."[41] While this seems quite unremarkable to our contemporary sensibilities, Mamoulian in his day felt the need to elaborate: "For the sake of clarity, I would like to mention that whenever we talk of collective acting, we mean acting controlled by the director."[42] In a similar vein, he wrote in 1937 that "the stage is the art of collective acting . . . and the play is expressed almost solely through a collective performance of flesh and blood actors as controlled by the director."[43] Mamoulian did nothing less than bring the modern concept of direction to musical theatre, framing it as the orchestration of bodies—and he introduced this radical theory through the orchestration of black bodies in particular.

Mamoulian's baton became the symbol of the way in which directorial control could restrain—but also unleash the creative potential of—the black performing bodies that were both desired and feared. As one account put it, "there was something about this patient young director that inspired their confidence—even when, clutching a devil-stick and waggling it in their scared faces, he commanded them to start beating their carpets, scraping their knives, thwacking their kettles, pounding their hammers, clanging their bells . . . in four-four time."[44] Of course, it is unclear that Mamoulian ever clutched a devil-stick, much less waggled it in anyone's face—it seems quite unlikely that he did—but the rhetoric of this account testifies to how his directorial vision was understood more generally.

To be fair, Mamoulian always spoke in positive terms of his work with black performers. He was hired to direct not only *Porgy*, but also *Porgy and Bess, St. Louis Woman,* and *Lost in the Stars*, all productions with predominantly black casts.[45] He often championed African American performers, and his correspondence with Todd Duncan and Pearl Bailey suggests that he felt strongly about civil rights. Nonetheless, the emergence of his integrated theatre was predicated on the exploitation and negotiation of blackness.

And it was not only the alleged integration of *Porgy*, but the integration of Mamoulian as well. Mamoulian's control over blackness is indeed *his own* deployment of blackness. This phenomenon is articulated most explicitly in one report that "he put [the black actors] into rehearsal, and saw at once that these colored actors of New York were going to have a lot of trouble in relearning the dialect of their own race."[46] By this account, Mamoulian must construct the blackness that he is then said to recover as a natural essence. In so doing, Mamoulian is essentially partaking in a directorial form of blackface, an American cultural form that has an even broader and more substantial relationship to musical theatre.

Blackface was the first major form of popular culture in America, often as presented in minstrel shows, which were a mainstay of entertainment not only during their nineteenth century heyday but well into the middle of the twentieth century. The minstrel show format generally featured a series of songs, dances, and comic skits—often with an olio presentation that was essentially a condensed musical drama—by performers dressed in black make-up, frequently with exaggerated white lips and eyes. The political origins of blackface were complex. The scholarly work of Alexander Saxton, David Roediger, and Eric Lott has revealed that the early minstrels were often Northerners, often the sons of upwardly mobile middle-class officials and bureaucrats.[47] Faced with the accelerating replacement of agrarian life with an industrialized one, the minstrels idealized black bodies as close to "Nature." By projecting certain kinds of fantasies—the "natural," the "primitive," the sexualized—onto black bodies and then embodying these fantasies, the minstrels found a way to escape the strictures of urban life. Indeed, the fantasy of the sexualized black body was the vehicle for a carnivalesque liberation from the demands of an increasingly bureaucratized and impersonal city.

In the context of musical theatre, a crucial aspect of blackface is its function as a vehicle of carnal fascination that unsettles identity. As Eric Lott phrased it, "to wear or even enjoy blackface was literally, for a time, to become black, to inherit the cool, virility, humility, abandon, or gaieté de coeur that were the prime components of white ideologies of black manhood."[48] Black women were presented as hypersexualized as well, as for example in the famous song "Lucy Long" that was a staple of blackface entertainment. Because the act of blackface worked to indulge a heightened surfeit of sexual energy attributed to black bodies, the assumption of blackness permitted a range of hypersexualized energies to emerge. Saxton, for example, noted that blackface manuals sometimes referred to homosexuality and masturbation, pointing to the "tolerance of sexuality in general . . . the flexibility of standards which flourished behind the false façade of blackface presentation."[49]

The minstrels thus traded on fantasies that they projected onto black bodies—fantasies that they then embodied. At the same time, it was the ability to embody these fantasies *and then become white again* that was the defining operation of minstrelsy. As David Roediger writes, "minstrelsy's genius was then to be able to both display and reject the 'natural self,' to be able to take on blackness convincingly and to take off blackness convincingly."[50] Blackface was indeed essential in the construction of "whiteness," as it permitted a diverse group of ethnic immigrants to define themselves as "white" in opposition to the blackness that they performed—and then disavowed. The mutability was central to minstrelsy's pleasures: as Roediger writes, "the simple physical disguise . . . of blacking up served to emphasize that those on stage were really white and that whiteness really mattered. One minstrel pioneer won fame by being able to change from black to white and back in seconds. Playbills continually featured paired pictures of the performers in blackface and without makeup—rough and respectable, black and white."[51]

To return to the context of Mamoulian, this kind of mobility, this potential for ethnic or racial transformation, was phrased rather explicitly in one 1927 review that noted that Mamoulian

> admits that there is enormous fun in directing a negro cast. His attitude towards the negro residential sections is not that of the intelligentsia. Having come from the Caucasus, whose race is so conglomerate that if you leave the house a Czech in the morning, you never know if you will return in the evening a Tatar, he takes these matters neither too importantly nor too unimportantly.[52]

This article perceptively links the "enormous fun" that Mamoulian has when directing black bodies to his own ethnicity, which is marked as being fluid. And indeed Mamoulian—whose ethnicity was frequently foregrounded in descriptions like "Jewish divinity student out of his métier"— intuitively found a way to use black bodies to effect a different kind of fluidity: not from Czech to Tatar, but from Jewish immigrant to American. As Michael Rogin has argued about the entertainment industry in the 1920s and 1930s, the blackface tradition "moved settlers and ethnics into the melting pot by keeping racial groups out," "turning Europeans into Americans."[53]

Mamoulian's fantasy of rhythmic blackness—and his ability to indulge, control, and harness that fantasy—reveals the minstrelization that governed the origin of integration. For Mamoulian, musical theatre direction—and the integration it facilitated—was understood through the control of a fantasized blackness. Mamoulian's ostensible control of that force became central to his own identity as an American, as the creator of a musical form that was said to be "as American as 'Yankee Doodle Dandy.'" Just as conceptual blackface was central to the operation of Mamoulian's integration, conceptual—as well as literal—blackface also appeared in another early landmark of musical integration: *Show Boat*, the 1927 musical by Jerome Kern and Oscar Hammerstein.

In his survey of musical theatre history, John Bush Jones writes of an "irony" in *Show Boat*: "in a musical of otherwise scrupulously authentic mixed-race casting, the original Queenie—the main female African American character—was played not by a black woman but by white Tess Gardella, a popular blackface entertainer who performed so consistently as 'Aunt Jemima' that Ziegfeld's programs credited Aunt Jemima, not Gardella, as playing Queenie."[54] Jones attributes this "irony" to Ziegfeld "obviously going for some measure of star power rather than racial authenticity."

While director Florenz Ziegfeld's intentions are unknowable, the presence of this blackface performer should not be dismissed as an outlier. I would propose that it is instead a trace of the minstrel aesthetic whose latent and repressed energies suffuse the claims of integration that surround *Show Boat*.[55] More significantly, in a show that takes up the issue of "mixing," Gardella's blackface models exactly the kind of control suggested by integration. Just as blackface performers traditionally gained their power precisely from their ability to take off the mask, Gardella's presence seems all the more logical in this show whose lauded "integration" permitted spectators to disavow and purportedly control the identifications that were in fact the source of so much pleasure.

*Show Boat* has long been considered an anchor of modern musical theatre, often cited as the first integrated musical. The pioneering historian and critic Cecil Smith wrote that *Show Boat*'s "integration of music and drama" makes it "the great classic fore-runner of the modern musical theater,"[56] a sentiment echoed years later in Mark Steyn's claim that *Show Boat* was the first musical whose "constituent elements fus[ed] to create a unified, indissoluble identity."[57] Even the earliest of commentaries on *Show Boat* traffic in this kind of assertion: when Ziegfeld revived the show in 1932, for example, Brooks Atkinson remarked that it was "still the most beautifully blended musical show we have had in this country."[58] What, though, is being blended? Just as Mamoulian's rhythmic integration was generated through his negotiation of blackness, I argue that the integration of *Show Boat* worked to disavow the kinds of relationships that the form encourages with black bodies. I examine how the plot depicts black bodies, and how these plot depictions contrast with the experience of watching *Show Boat* in production, in order to better understand the power of spectacular musical bodies—and the anxieties that they provoke.

Based on Edna Ferber's novel, Oscar Hammerstein's book for *Show Boat* focuses on life upon the *Cotton Blossom*, an itinerant showboat that would drop anchor in various river ports and present shows for audiences of the towns.[59] As the play opens, Magnolia, the daughter of Cap'n Andy, the showboat's impresario, falls in love with Gaylord Ravenal. Magnolia and Gaylord become the leading actors on the showboat when the leading lady, Julie, is revealed to be "a miscegenation case," prompting Julie and her husband to leave the boat. Gaylord strikes it rich, but eventually loses it all and abandons Magnolia, forcing her to find work and return to the stage. The show's abrupt conclusion reunites the couple as their daughter achieves stardom herself.

The plot of *Show Boat* is itself fundamentally concerned with the function of music. When Magnolia confides to Julie the details of her first encounter with Ravenal, Julie warns her about the dangers of love by singing "Can't Help Lovin' Dat Man."[60] Upon hearing Julie launch into this song, the boat's cook Queenie "stops in her tracks and looks puzzled." When Queenie asks Julie how she knows this song, Julie "stops abruptly, a swift terror steals across her face, and quickly vanishes." Julie's "swift terror" manifests because her knowledge of the song has ostensibly telegraphed her blackness. Queenie gives the audience its first major clue in this regard when she remarks, "ah didn't ever hear anybody but colored folks sing dat song—Sounds funny for Miss Julie to know it." This moment of bursting into song is thus treated as an eruption of raced desire. (The song is treated as an eruption of raced desire not only because it is framed as Julie's, and Magnolia's, desire to participate in black culture, but also because Julie's knowledge of the song is our first clue to her lineage, which testifies to an instance of presumably mutual desire between the white and black bodies of her parents.) Significantly, this raced desire generates yet more raced desire: as Julie and the black workers jubilantly sing, Magnolia "gradually starts to do coon shuffle," prompting Joe's approving remark, "Look it dat little gal shuffle!" The dangers of this kind of musical transfer are evident to Parthy, who disdains Magnolia's contact with Julie. In fact, Parthy asks

Julie to abandon giving Magnolia piano lessons, as she "[didn't] want [her] daughter mixed up with you—or anybody like you."⁶¹ Parthy senses correctly that "mixing up" is precisely the kind of activity in which Julie and Magnolia are engaged through this musical exchange.

If Julie's offstage performance of this song is fraught, her stage work will provoke an even greater crisis. The fourth scene opens onto a rehearsal of the *Cotton Blossom* show in which she stars. As Cap'n Andy directs the troupe in a slapdash rehearsal, Ellie warns Julie and her husband, Steve, that the sheriff is making his way to the boat after having been summoned by Pete, an erstwhile showboat worker whose romantic interest in Julie was spurned. Following up on Pete's assertion that Julie was born to a white father and a black mother, the sheriff interrupts the rehearsal, announcing that there's a "miscegenation case" on the *Cotton Blossom*, a "case of a negro woman married to a white man. Criminal offense in this state."⁶² However, in the most melodramatic moment of the entire play, everyone on the boat has just seen Steve "seiz[e] Julie's hand in his left one and ru[n] the blade across the tip of her finger . . . ben[d] his head and pressing his lips to the wound suc[k] it greedily."⁶³ Windy, the boat's captain, testifies to Vallon that "that white man there's got n***** blood in him."⁶⁴ Having just noted that "one drop of n***** blood makes you a n***** in these parts," the sheriff cannot arrest Julie and Steve for a mixed marriage.⁶⁵ He exits by warning the troupe not to "try to give your show tonight with mixed blood in it—or you'll be riding out of town on something that don't sit so easy as a boat."⁶⁶ The so-called miscegenation case thus becomes a prohibition not of marriage or of sex—but of performance!

In this moment, *Show Boat* has subtly—yet significantly—conflated miscegenation and "mixed" performance. Sexual contact and performance contact are interchangeable, and through this elision, the sheriff reveals a fundamental principle of the show: in *Show Boat*, every moment of performance is mediated by raced bodies. Within the world of the play, songs are eruptions of raced desire, eruptions that generate excitement, but that also disrupt and threaten the show. The sheriff's warning is clear: the evidence of this desire must never materialize onstage, or the show will quite literally be stopped. Indeed, when Julie is told that the sheriff is en route, she immediately replies, "No—no, I can't play tonight. Don't ask me."

These two moments of terror will find echoes in a third moment that occurs at the climax of the play, which takes place years later at the Trocadero Rehearsal Room, where the now destitute Magnolia auditions for a show. The show, unbeknownst to her, stars Julie, now "a hollow-cheeked woman—looking older than she really is—with all the ear-marks of one who is down and out," who "from time to time . . . opens her hand-bag and takes out a pint flask . . . and furtively takes a drink."[67] After threatening to "be off on a tear," Julie rehearses her number, "Bill," in some ways a negative complement to "Can't Help Lovin' Dat Man." Jim and Jake, the two men who run the Trocadero, are trying out acts when Frank arrives with Magnolia and asks them to audition her. When Jim asks her what kind of singing she does, Magnolia replies, "Why—I—I do negro songs." Magnolia "throws back her head, half closes her eyes," and sings "Can't Help Lovin' Dat Man."[68] As Magnolia sings, Julie "enters quietly . . . recognizes Magnolia and takes a couple of quick steps up to her, but directly behind her. [She] stands there during [the] song till [the] next to last line when she seems to arrive at a decision. She makes a shy hesitant little gesture which is half-throwing a kiss. She disappears quickly and softly."[69] Julie's "decision" is announced by a theatre employee who reports that their "prima donna" has fulfilled her promise to go on a tear; leaving the production, Julie urges them to let the girl who was just performing take her place.

Jim, the theatre impresario, suggests that Magnolia might be a suitable replacement "if we could only teach you some up-to-date numbers," which prompts his colleague to suggest that Magnolia's song is not so bad—if they "trick" it, as he demonstrates by singing it in syncopation.[70] Magnolia, the stage directions indicate, is bewildered, but attempts to sing along with Jake. She can't quite get the time, and Frank tries stamping his foot to give her the tempo. In her next attempt, she still can't quite keep up—and finally quits to watch Frank dance. Despite her weakness, despite the fact that Frank essentially auditions on her behalf, she gets the job. However, Magnolia—despite having auditioned as a singer of "Negro songs"—sings anything *but* that repertoire in her tentative debut. In fact, although this audition suggests that Magnolia will be required to perform before an audience with this syncopated repertoire, her opening night performance is of the stately period number, "After the Ball," a decidedly un-ragged number. When the managers insist on re-marking the song through ragtime, they reinforce the show's emphasis on the raced dimensions of musicality. Ultimately, however, the show evacuates Magnolia's interest in black performance, leaving her to sing the prim and antiseptic "After the Ball" without a hint of the tutelage that Julie gave her during her formative years.

*Show Boat* thus depicts a melodramatic world in which eruptions of raced desire are titillating, yet dangerous: though we see Julie rehearse, her blackness can never take the stage before an audience. Even when her blackness is channeled within the "pure" vessel of Magnolia, as in the Trocadero rehearsal, it still retains much of its volatility and must be exiled. However, the audience watching the 1927 musical *Show Boat* watches a musical that, by contrast, *foregrounds* and *indulges* black performance, and is thereby elevated *above* the discriminatory world depicted in the plot. The production's ongoing investment in black bodies was clear, as evidenced in the response of contemporaneous reviewers: Leonard Hall, for example, reviewing the out-of-town tryout in Washington, wrote that *Show Boat* features "a huge company of colored performers, including a hot double sextet of creamy skinned dancing girls whose 'Dahomey' number early in Act II, dressed in yellows and reds against a dark drop, is a genuine gem."[71] The black female bodies of *Show Boat*, doubly marked as spectacular, were a particular source of fascination, as for example in the *San Francisco Examiner*'s comments about the "dusky coryphées."[72] Writing in *Rob Wagner's Script*, Paul Gerard Smith enthused, "Particularly let me wave a flag for that colored group. How they sing—and how they dance. And how, above all, they seem to enjoy it. Kenneth Spencer, who did the Old Man Rivering, had a tough assignment . . . but Spencer did it well, and he was greatly aided and abetted by that swell singing chorus."[73] Unlike the world depicted in the plot, the production of *Show Boat* places black performance front and center. A crucial affective element of the experience of *Show Boat* is a feeling of superiority over the world depicted therein.

This feeling of superiority extends to the form as well.[74] Critics have long hailed the melodrama scene as a favorite in *Show Boat*, but the pleasure of this scene similarly derives from the manner by which it permits the audience of *Show Boat* to feel superior to the ostensibly primitive performance traditions of melodrama, whether those be artificial acting styles, illogical sound effects, or the folksy interruption of the show to notify an audience member of a sickness in his family. The primitive nature of the theatrical experience extends to the framed spectators, who cannot restrain their visceral reactions to what is unfolding before them: as the troupe performs, the framed audience of the showboat freely hisses at the entrance of the drunken ex-husband, with one rowdy spectator of the melodrama becoming so enraptured by the production that he begins to confuse it with real life, ultimately threatening Frank, who is playing the villain, by drawing his gun.

Crucially, melodrama is by definition a musical drama, and the melodramatic performance on the boat is also a conventional one in which Magnolia, playing piano as taught to her by Julie, "starts to play for no reason." Thus, the slapdash melodramatic performances depicted in the plot—ones that act on their audience so palpably that they are thought to be real—feature haphazard musicality inextricably linked with eruptions of raced desire—a world of fragmentation and segregation that the experience of *Show Boat* in *production* will purport to transcend. When critics and spectators describe *Show Boat* as integrated, they disavow the raced dimensions of bursting into song, suggesting instead that they can exercise a certain kind of psychic control—precisely because integration claims that these erstwhile disjunctive moments are now a seamless part of the narrative under the precise control of the author.

In other words, the world of the *Cotton Blossom* presents songs as volatile eruptions of raced desire. *Show Boat,* by contrast, presents this dynamic as a regressive relic of the melodramatic past and encourages its spectators to feel distance from, and superiority over, this form. The framed spectators on the showboat, presented as clueless rubes who cannot tell make-believe from real life, further elevate the spectators of *Show Boat*, whose sophisticated theatrical detachment allows them to experience the play without the same kind of direct engagement. These feelings of distance and superiority enable spectators to disavow the identifications that *Show Boat*, and by extension the form, demands.

Sometimes this kind of claim is modulated into a musical register that finds composer Jerome Kern harnessing—and exercising control over—African American musical forms: one San Francisco critic, for example, noted that "the operetta has been modernized with hi-de-ho and hey-hey rhythms in its final darky melodies . . . ."[75] Reviewing the original production, Arthur B. Waters lauded Kern for blending "the Negro spirituals of the Southland with the jazz of today."[76] In an article about Kern titled "Ol' Man River Himself," author Sylvia Rosenberg wrote that "in the rehearsals of *Show Boat*, it was difficult to convince the negro chorus that the negro music written for the show, including 'Ol' Man River,' was not authentic folk music," thus suggesting that Kern's work was imbued with a fundamental blackness that he channeled—though Kern was quick to assert that he was inspired by the characters of the story.[77] The goal here is the replacement of raced eruptions of desire with the organizing vision of the composer, thereby precluding the eruptions from affecting the spectator. In this way, in a genre that structurally demands the labor of spectacular (black) bodies, integration suggests that the musical episodes—and with them, the spectacular bodies who not only bring them to life but who (in this telling) generate the raw material—are no longer spectacular, but have instead been contained and subsumed into the narrative order. Of course, nothing could be further from the case—but the discourse of integration enables this misapprehension.

Indeed, integration—as seen in both Mamoulian's ideas and *Show Boat*—suggests that the black bodies embodying the eruptions of desire—the black bodies that stop the show—are in fact now under authorial, directorial, spectatorial control. In suggesting that these musical moments are not raced eruptions of desire but are instead a narrative vehicle, both *Show Boat* and the discourse of integration deny the very possibility that unnerved Parthy: the "mixing" that the musical form prompts its spectators to undertake in its moments of song and dance. This denial, though, merely gives cover to the inevitable indulgence of this "mixing," and to the identifications and pleasures it brings.

However, the plot pointedly denies the pleasures and opportunities of mixing to Julie, while offering them to virtuous Magnolia, who has tremendous mobility, as seen in the range of performances she is permitted to give, from the raced "shuffle" to the staid "After the Ball." In other words, Magnolia, celebrated for her black-coded dance, can perform such numbers as she desires, and then perform again as white. Julie, meanwhile, is punished for "passing," for performing, as white. That Julie is denied this mobility is all the more remarkable since she is the one who makes Magnolia's mobility possible—both through her performances of blackness, which inspire Magnolia, and through her abdication of the stage. In other words, Magnolia's mobility is enabled by her exploitation of blackness, a blackness denied this mutability. Magnolia's deft control over her experiments in performing blackness works to assure spectators that they too can indulge, yet exercise control over, a parallel kind of psychic play with blackness that is taking place in the experience of watching *Show Boat*. In this way, *Show Boat* and *Oklahoma!* feature plots that—like the discourse of integration—work to assure spectators of their control. Thus, the presence of Tess Gardella in blackface works to assure spectators that the kinds of psychic blackface in which the genre invites spectators to participate, can, like Gardella's own makeup, ultimately be dismissed. By insisting that the spectator, like Magnolia and Tess Gardella, can experience these pleasures safely, *Show Boat* invites its spectators to partake of the very same pleasures of identifications that Magnolia enjoys. However, Magnolia enjoys these pleasures precisely because she is white. The show suggests that just as Magnolia can exploit blackness, so too can the white spectator, who is the primary (psychic) beneficiary of this exploitation of spectacular blackness.

The show's reliance on the labor of black bodies for these pleasures and for this identificatory work prompts an extraordinary anxiety about this debt. The very opening lines of *Show Boat* announce that "N****** all work on de Mississippi / N****** all work while de white folk play"; this parallel between black labor and white "play" will receive further elaboration when the lyrics juxtapose the *Cotton Blossom* showboat with the plant of the same name. In bringing these two economic enterprises into the same moment, the show skillfully draws attention to the fact that black bodies sustain the economy of musical performance as fully as they do more traditional lines of (exploited) labor. The opening image of the play is of the *Cotton Blossom* juxtaposed with the steamboat that pulls it, reminding us from the beginning that the showboat does not provide its own energy. This places an interesting spin on the famous "Ol' Man River" lyric in which Joe sings, "Tote dat barge!" Years later, Richard Bissell would complain that the lyric was "idiotic" since "nobody in the long history of the Mississippi . . . has ever picked up and carried a barge."[78] However, I would argue that

Hammerstein, knowingly or not, intuited precisely whose labor generated the power for the *Cotton Blossom* showboat, the barge that floated down the river giving shows.

The show generally works to absolve itself of this debt. It does so by depicting these moments of appropriation as either voluntary or remunerated.[79] Thus, Julie's moments of exile are treated as voluntary. When Magnolia asks Andy why Julie is being banished from the boat, Julie interrupts to answer that "he's not sending me, Nola dear—Steve and I want to go."[80] Her departure from the Trocadero stage years later mirrors this moment: "When Magnolia begins to sing, Julie enters quietly . . . stands there during song till next to last line when she seems to arrive at a decision. . . . She disappears quickly and softly."[81] Julie's decision, of course, is to leave, and to let Magnolia take the spotlight. In both cases, the martyred Julie voluntarily abdicates the stage to make way for virtuous Magnolia. Her decision to do so is framed within a discourse of love: when Julie is exiled from the showboat, "Magnolia runs to kiss her. Julie turns her head away, but holds Magnolia close to her."[82] If Julie turns her head away as she leaves, Julie will complete this gesture years later at the Trocadero, when, right before she leaves, she—unbeknownst to Magnolia—"makes a shy hesitant little gesture which is half-throwing a kiss." The love remains mutual: when Frank reminds Magnolia at the Trocadero that Julie gave her her first break on the showboat, Magnolia replies, "Yes, I remember . . . I often wonder what ever became of her. I loved Julie . . . ."[83] The resolution of the show comes not from the cursory reunion of Ravenal and Magnolia at the curtain, but instead from Magnolia's reunion with Julie in their shared spotlight. Ultimately, *Show Boat* inoculates itself from claims of exploitation by framing Julie's desertion of the stage as a voluntary action, one motivated by love.

The other strategy found in *Show Boat* is its suggestion that blackness is a commodity whose purchase was appropriately compensated. In the World's Fair scene, we visit an exhibition that will introduce us to the ostensible "wild men" of Dahomey. Their number begins with some nonsense chanting of "African" syllables—"Dyunga doe / Dyunga hungy ung gunga"—which prompts the white customers to sing that they are frightened by this display: "For tho they may play here, / They're acting vicious— / They might get malicious; / And though I'm not fearful / I'll not be a spearful / So you'd better show me / The way from Dahomey."[84] As soon as the "[white] Crowd exits in fear," the Dahomeyans celebrate and sing that their home "ain't Dahomey at all," but is instead "Avenue A / Back in old New York."[85] They are thus black performers from New York, paid to imitate "primitive" Africans. In this case, the desire for black performance is treated comically, but in suggesting that proper compensation has been rendered, *Show Boat* absolves itself of any sense of exploitation.

The "In Dahomey" episode of *Show Boat*, set at the World's Fair of 1893, wasn't entirely the invention of Hammerstein. The actual Chicago World's Fair of 1893 did in fact have a Dahomey Village on the Midway, part of a tradition of displaying black bodies that had developed in the nineteenth century. Before the fair had opened, journalist Julian Ralph predicted that the Midway "will be a jumble of foreignness—a bit of Fez and Nuremberg, of Sahara and Dahomey and Holland, Japan and Rome and Coney Island. It will be gorgeous with color, pulsating with excitement, riotous with the strivings of a battalion of bands, and peculiar to the last degree."[86] The Midway offered not the coherent synoptic view of the "informative" Anthropological Building, but instead a cacophonous and disconnected series of spectacles, all predicated on "exotic" bodies. As H. H. Bancroft noted in his 1894 *Book of the Fair*, fairgoers

> would pass between the walls of medieval villages, between mosques and pagodas, Turkish and Chinese. . . . They would be met on their way by German and Hungarian bands, by the discord of Chinese cymbals and Dahomey tom-toms; they would encounter jugglers and magicians, camel-drivers and donkey-boys, dancing-girls from Cairo and Algiers, from Samoa and Brazil, and men and women of all nationalities, some lounging in oriental indifference, some shrieking in union or striving to outshriek each other, in the hope of transferring his superfluous change from the pocket of the unwary pilgrim.[87]

At the time of the fair, the spectacle of blackness—depicted here as exotic, foreign, and beyond reason—was treated as a commodity that was deeply appealing and profitable.

What's more, the trope of the fake Dahomeyans in *Show Boat* could trace its lineage even beyond the 1893 World Fair to a broader series of

African spectacles that had been produced earlier in that century. By 1853, A. T. Caldecott produced a show featuring South African performers who posed as "Zulu Kaffirs." Caldecott advertised that the show would display "in an extensive and unexampled manner this wild and interesting tribe of savages in their domestic habits, their nuptial ceremonies, the charm song, finding the witch, hunting tramp, preparation for war and territorial conflicts."[88] The show, and the genre of "Zulu" display that it inaugurated, generated interest—indeed so much interest that the demand for Zulus exceeded the supply, prompting unscrupulous showmen to pay black performers to pose as Africans. As circus impresario George Middleton, for example, recalled in his memoirs,

> In the side show we had a big negro whom we had fitted up with rings in his nose, a leopard skin, some assegais and a large shield made out of cow's skin. While he was sitting on the stage in the side show, along came two negro women and remarked, "See that n***** over there? He ain't no Zulu, that's Bill Jackson. He worked over here at Camden on the dock. I seen that n***** often.[89]

Claims were even made that some were "Irish immigrants, cunningly painted and made up like savages."[90] Bernth Lindfors reports that some showmen "found it more convenient to continue to employ pseudo-Zulus who could be more easily controlled and disciplined."[91] The prevalence of the "fake" Africans led to the term "Zulu"—the very term that Captain Andy used to describe the Dahomey performers—becoming circus jargon for "a black laborer or musician employed by the circus . . . [who] don[ned] a costume and parad[ed] around the hippodrome track in the grand opening pageant." As Lindfors notes, "Pseudo-Zulus proliferated, emerging as a stock character type that eventually entered the standard vocabulary of ethnic imagery projected by such powerful media as Hollywood films."[92]

This is essentially the path pursued by Hammerstein, a path depicting the Dahomey entertainers as black New Yorkers fraudulently presenting themselves as Africans. However, two actors—who themselves performed as fake Dahomeyans in 1893—would take this trope in an entirely different direction, revealing the radical opportunities afforded by the form precisely to those who were exploited by it. In 1906, performer George

Walker recalled that "in 1893, natives from Dahomey, Africa, were import-ed to San Francisco to be exhibited at the Midwinter Fair. They were late in arriving in time for the opening of the Fair, and Afro-Americans were employed and exhibited for native Dahomians."[93] Speaking of himself and his performing partner, Bert Williams, Walker wrote that "Williams and Walker were among the sham native Dahomians." However, once the actual Africans arrived, Williams and Walker were fascinated by them and decided that they would "delineate and feature native African characters as far as we could."[94]

This desire to perform a different kind of theatrical representation seemed to link back to Walker's desire to transcend the minstrel tra-ditions in which he participated as a young member of an amateur minstrel troupe in his hometown of Lawrence, Kansas. When Walker decided to leave Lawrence to seek his fortune in San Francisco, he did so by performing as medicine show entertainment, drawing crowds for itinerant "quack" doctors who sold medicine. Walker recalled that he would "mount the wagon and commence to sing and dance, make faces, and tell stories, and rattle the bones."[95] Walker's experiences in these earlier forms of entertainment would inspire the minstrel-style medicine show scene that opens his 1902 musical—itself titled *In Da-homey*.

This prologue of *In Dahomey* features Dr. Straight hawking "Straightaline," which he says will cure not only dandruff and various other maladies, but "most wonderful of all, Straightaline straightens knappy or knotty hair— . . . in three days." In addition to this hair tonic, Dr. Straight also sells "Oblicuticus," a "wonderful face bleach" that "removes the outer skin and leaves in its place a peach-like complexion that can't be duplicated—even by peaches. Changing black to white and vice versa."[96] This mocking portrayal of racial transformation—"changing black to white and vice versa"—and racial commodification announces the ways in which the show will deploy minstrel tropes against themselves, a project made possible by the musical form itself, with its structural opportunities for transformation.[97] Nowhere is this more evident than in the third act of *In Dahomey*, which presents a Transformation Scene, echoing in many ways similar scenes in shows like *The Black Crook*. In Walker's and Williams's show, the scene opens onto

Practical moon effect. Small body of water in perspective. Dark stage at rear of curtain. Light gradually works up to medium moonlight. Ballet or chorus, costumed as frogs, color scheme of costumes and scenery to be the same. Chorus or ballet to be posed in entrance to stage with back to audience. Back made up of foliage. Song ["My Lady Frog"] sung in boat that passes, refrain taken up by chorus or ballet. At finish of refrain chorus or ballet turn faces to audience, form picture and dance. At finish of dance exit and lights out. Change to Gardens of Dahomey. Enter Amazons—drill. Exeunt. Customs of Dahomey explained by characters. At cue the Caboceers are approaching. . . . Chorus enters as African chiefs, soldiers, natives, dancing girls. After much chorus come to front of stage, kneel and sing chorale descriptive of glories of Cannibal King and Caboceers . . . .[98]

While Walker confessed that his long-standing goal had been to "delineate and feature native African characters as far as we could, and still remain American," this glorious, fantastical finale presents something far more complex. The show's fantastical depiction of "real" Africa reveals this "nature" to be itself a construction, and the profound transformations permitted by the musical form enable a total denaturalization to take place. Like the minstrel medicine show prologue that opened *In Dahomey*, this Transformation Scene would give voice to the show's "secret—that the Ethiopian could, indeed, change his own skin," to quote Daphne Brooks's brilliant reading of the play.[99] In this way, the musical extends to the performers whom it has exploited the possibility to rewrite the narrative in which the form has enveloped them. The power of the musical form is that it can permit a revaluation of spectacle, transforming its audience just as it transforms itself. Thus, while the musical may depend structurally on raced bodies, the uses to which it may deploy its eruptions of raced desire complicate any simple claims regarding the structures of power implicit in the disintegrated logic of musical theatre—a topic that will be considered further later in this book.

In exploring the operation of "changing black to white and vice versa," *In Dahomey* radically suggests that the tropes of minstrelization can be subverted, that racial transformation is possible—and thereby challenges the idea of race itself. This potentiality of the musical form is precisely the one denied by the claims of integration. Just as the discourse of integration works to contain radical energies, *Show Boat* works to contain the radical potential of *In Dahomey* precisely by reminstrelizing the reference. In integrating the "In Dahomey" trope into *Show Boat*, the integrated *Show Boat* works to deny the power of the musical form—a power borne of provoking new identifications and thereby challenging identities—available to the bodies who generate those pleasures. The issues of exploitation raised implicitly by Mamoulian—and explicitly by *Show Boat*—point toward the complex ethical dilemma regarding the identificatory play central to the experience of musical theatre. The discourse of integration insists that spectators can indulge—and yet maintain control over—psychic fantasies and relationships with performing bodies. Integration is thus an attempt to negotiate a complex relationship that, as *Show Boat* demonstrates, can be predicated on the exploitation of spectacular bodies. Given that integration is a response to anxieties generated by the form, I now turn to a deeper consideration of what I will term the "disintegrated" aesthetic of musical theatre, and to the ethical dilemmas posed by a form that may secure its most profound effects—precisely as Magnolia did—by exploiting spectacular bodies.

The eponymous Gentlemen of the 1971 musical *Two Gentlemen of Verona*. Photograph by Friedman-Abeles, ©Billy Rose Theatre Division, New York Public Library for the Performing Arts.

# 5

# THE EXOTIC AND EROTIC ECONOMY OF MUSICAL IMPERSONATION

The World's Fair scene in *Show Boat* features several exhibits, including the iconic ferris wheel, the Dahomey Village, and The Streets of Cairo, often referred to as the "Hoochie-Coochie Booth." Having just dismissed a member of the "Congress of Beauty" as a "hussy," Parthy moralizes as men exit the hoochie-coochie booth: "Couchie-couchie. . . . A man ought to be ashamed t' be seen near the place. I wouldn't have any respect for— My God. Look, Nola, is that your father?"[1] Andy emerges from the booth, oblivious to the presence of Parthy and Magnolia because he "is so deeply engrossed trying to master the couchie-couchie movement." Andy mutters that "I'll be darned if I see how she does it," as he tries to imitate the dance, much to Parthy's dismay. As a barker announces that another performance will take place, Andy is distracted by one of the women and says that he wants to attend the performance again. Parthy has to "pul[l] him away as he starts once more to follow the magnetic appeal of the dancer." The magnetism of the dancer not only attracts Andy but also compels him to *imitate* and *embody* her movement.

Andy's failed attempt to imitate the (exoticized) burlesque dancer is thus presented alongside the Dahomeyans, who are themselves performing a complex form of "failed" (racial) impersonation. The juxtaposition of these failed imitations is not coincidental and is but one example of what I will call the exotic/erotic dynamic of musical theatre, in which different forms of failed gendered and raced impersonations lead into one another. This exotic/erotic trope is virtually ubiquitous in musical theatre, uncannily bubbling to the surface in show after show. The exotic/erotic dynamic explains how, for example, *Guys and Dolls*—a show rooted squarely in New York—suddenly finds itself in Cuba. This dynamic generates the turning point in the play, when Sarah, eager to save her job, travels with Sky to Havana, where she sees a "very sexy Cuban dancing girl" who, with two "Cuban dancing men," do a "sexy routine as they pass and exit."[2] Inspired to imitate this sexualized burlesque performance, the tipsy Sarah "rises and imitates their routine as she exits doing bumps." Even more incredibly, Sarah's imitation of the Cubans inspires Sky to imitate *her*: "Sky rises and places hand to his head in amazement, quite shocked at her. Then he does the same movement as he exits." Wherever and whenever the exotic/erotic dynamic appears, it points us toward the essential psychic operations of musical theatre—ones that involve performance across different types of bodies.

Significantly, this exotic/erotic dynamic—and the psychic operations indexed by it—bring together the concerns of the previous chapters. The preceding four chapters have explored the shows generally cited as landmarks of integration: the Princess Theatre Shows, *Show Boat,* and *Oklahoma!* Through historical investigation, I have shown that the so-called integration of these shows is an attempt to disavow the profound identifications—across gendered, raced, and sexualized bodies—solicited by the musical form in the moment of bursting into song and dance. Indeed, integration is an attempt to discipline bodies—to discipline the gendered, raced, and sexualized bodies that create, perform, and experience musical theatre. The fundamental work of this discourse, then, is to mitigate, misapprehend, and insulate against the radical relationships—relationships across different types of bodies—imagined and made possible by the musical form.

With the first four chapters having thus considered how "integration" works, I now move to a consideration of "disintegration," which encompasses the radical power of these profound relationships across bodies, a power suggested by the exotic/erotic dynamic. In this way, the structural logic of disintegration articulated in this chapter is precisely what generates the anxieties that prompt the discourse of integration. The exotic/erotic dynamic provides an aperture through which I will investigate the musical's radical operations upon the workings of gender, race, and sexuality, as well as its persistent interest in the laboring bodies of musical theatre. I pursue this through five major case studies. The first three—*Where's Charley?*, *Lady in the Dark*, and *Gypsy*—demonstrate not only the presence of this dynamic across a wide range of styles but also its presence at different points in the creation, performance, and spectatorship of musical theatre. Through a close reading of *Where's Charley?*, I will show how the plots of musical comedy explicitly explore both the operation and the stakes of the exotic/erotic dynamic. Having shown how this dynamic structures the plot of *Where's Charley?*, I then explore how it structures not only the plot of *Lady in the Dark* but also the scene of its construction and performance. The last reading in this series, *Gypsy*, reveals how this dynamic persists in the relationship between the audience and the performer. The other two major case studies, *The Fantasticks* and *A Chorus Line*, show how this logic relates to the *labor* of spectacular bodies. Meanwhile, other shows—*Promenade*, *Bells Are Ringing*, *Two Gentlemen of Verona*, *The Grass Harp*—make appearances along the way as I consider the exotic/erotic economy at the heart of musical theatre.

As the focus moves from integration to disintegration, it is worth remembering that all musicals—whatever the critics may claim—are necessarily disintegrated. The claims of integration made by critics do not describe a particular form of musical, but instead work to frame how the musical works upon its spectators. With this in mind, I am not concerned in this chapter with whether critics have claimed that these pieces are integrated (or not). In fact, a cursory look at the first series of case studies reveals the ultimate incoherence of such claims, as each of the three shows has elements that have been the subject of disputes about integration. Writing about *Where's Charley?*, critic John Chapman understandably referred to the "Pernambuco" number as a "fantasy not connected with the plot,"[3] while producer Cy Feuer argued that the number "was essential to the story."[4] In a similar vein, *Herald-Tribune* critic Howard Barnes referred to the "'Pernambuco' interlude" as a "welcome brea[k] in a dreary exposition," while another critic commented that the show is "constructed in a form that lets every production number become an integral progression of the show."[5] As for *Lady in the Dark*, Moss Hart, noting that he and composer Kurt Weill set out to write "a show in which the music carried forward the essential story," mused in the published edition of the score that "for the first time—at least so far as my memory serves—the music and lyrics of a musical 'show' are part and parcel of the basic structure of the play."[6] Sidney Whipple's opening night review, however, referred to the song "Tschaikowsky" as "an interpolated number that has nothing to do with the play but which provides its most exciting diversion."[7] Further, it is precisely the show's sequestering of the musical numbers into discrete dream sequences that is the show's principal innovation. Meanwhile, Walter Kerr concisely articulates the incoherence surrounding "integration" in his comment that he was "not sure whether 'Gypsy' is new fashioned, or old-fashioned, or integrated or non-integrated."[8] Consequently, I will be focusing in this chapter on the mechanisms of *disintegration* in order to explore the complex politics of bursting into song.

Perhaps the clearest articulation of the logic of disintegrated bodies can be seen in the plot of *Where's Charley?*, a musical whose central premise focuses on precisely this confluence of impersonation and performance. In 1948, George Abbott adapted Brandon Thomas's farce *Charley's Aunt* into *Where's Charley?*, for which Frank Loesser, in his first Broadway outing, wrote the music and lyrics, which included "Once in Love with Amy," a song that long served as star Ray Bolger's signature tune.[9] The premise of the show is simple and introduced straightforwardly as the curtain rises: Jack and Charley are two Oxford students interested in entertaining their girlfriends one afternoon. Since social protocol demands a chaperone, Jack uses the imminent arrival of Charley's aunt, Donna Lucia D'Alvadorez, as an excuse for the two pairs of lovers to spend time together. The girls arrive before Charley's aunt does, and so in an attempt to maintain decorum and etiquette, they leave when they discover that she has yet to arrive. As they wait, Mr. Wilkinson pays a visit to Jack and Charley. Identified as having "charge of the theatricals," Mr. Wilkinson arrives to check in on the preparations for the (otherwise undiscussed) "performance" the following night and asks Charley to try on his costume.[10] Charley goes offstage and promptly returns dressed as a female character. Wilkinson briefly coaches Charley on his one line—"Be gone, my good man, and don't bother me any longer"—before exiting.[11]

Then, just as a telegram arrives from Charley's aunt saying that she will not arrive as expected and will "surprise [him] at later date," the girls return.[12] Jack, desperate to spend time with the girls, demands that Charley—already in drag—present himself as his aunt from Brazil. Meanwhile, Jack's father arrives, as does Amy's uncle, Mr. Spettigue. Shortly thereafter, Charley's real aunt Lucy arrives, recently widowed and traveling under her "new name," Mrs. Beverly Smythe. Immediately perceiving Charley's mischief, she says nothing but takes comic advantage of the situation by making Charley respond to her too-close-for-comfort queries and comments—telling him, for instance, that "You see, I knew your late husband intimately."[13]

Jack's father, newly impoverished by inherited debts, and the always greedy Mr. Spettigue both try to woo Charley's wealthy aunt. Taking advantage of Spettigue's romantic inebriation, Charley-as-his-aunt promises to wed him if he will sign a note permitting the girls to marry the boys. Just after the note is signed, Charley's subterfuge is revealed. As the stage directions indicate, "Skirt falls off—Crowd is amazed," and Spettigue protests that this fraud invalidates his note.[14] However, they are saved when Mrs. Beverly Smythe reveals that she is in fact Charley's aunt, and, having now herself received the note intended for Charley's aunt, declares the note valid. The couples embrace as the curtain falls.

Much of the piece's humor stems predictably from Charley's bumbling attempts to portray his Brazilian aunt.[15] When Jack's father is taken aback to hear that Charley's aunt is from Brazil, Charley-as-his-aunt replies, "Brazil, where the nuts come from,"[16] and, as she goes to leave, parts with "As they say in Brazil, 'Goodbye.'"[17] In another scene, Charley shakes his fist at Jack—but when Jack's father turns at that moment toward Charley, Charley-as-his-aunt rapidly "converts the shake into a Spanish dance . . . turns around, kicks foot up . . . does samba towards him."[18] Once the real aunt shows up, she clearly enjoys turning up the heat on Charley-as-his-aunt, as for example when she asks him which part of Brazil he lived in. Charley's reply: "The residential part."[19] When she exhorts him to "tell [her] about the Brazileros," Charley leans in and says that "only the nicer girls wore them," and laughs.[20]

It is around this time that Charley begins to ease into his part—and the show's other main generator of humor is the growing acceptance that Charley makes of his role. At times, his comments play on his desire for the girls—as when he tells Jack to leave him with Amy and Kitty because "we three girls want to be alone"[21]—or on a general joy in the deception, as when Spettigue exits and Charley remarks, "what devils we women are!"[22] However, Charley clearly begins to delight openly in the performance, and to assimilate it quite fully. For example, he-as-she declares, "I'm not going to marry old Spettigue. I could never be happy with a man like that."[23] He takes two steps and then says, "What a horrible thought."[24] (In the same exchange, Charley tells Jack that he can't tell him the things Spettigue has said because Jack is "too young."[25]) Indeed, Charley's initial attempts at a ladylike walk ultimately develop into an elaborate flirtatious pantomime between Spettigue and Charley-as-his-aunt, which concludes with Charley declaring, "You're cute."[26]

The show delights in the manner by which bad and awkward performances—like that of Charley himself—can in fact be pleasurable, even featuring a whole production number based on this premise. The first grand production number focuses on the endearingly incompetent "New Ashmolean Marching Society and Students' Conservatory Band," whose members "march only slightly out of tempo" and "play just a trifle out of tune." However, while the oboe may sound like "a hound beneath the moon," and "though the trombone's a little independent / And the drummer is not exactly choice," Jack sings, "to me it's bully, it satisfies me fully," and indeed the song concludes with everyone singing, "By George! What a band!"[27] Charley's own awkward yet enjoyable performance could receive no greater validation than this number, which itself is introduced with only the slightest regard for narrative motivation.

The other great production number imagines Pernambuco, the Brazilian town of Charley-as-his-aunt. Conjuring up a fantasy of Brazilian romance, Charley muses:

> Pernambuco. I'd be happy to tell you about it, but you'd hardly believe me. Picture if you will, the life that greeted me. I stepped off the boat with high ideals and a small travelling bag. At first, I was frightened, especially of that wonderful man with the big moustache. Whom I

afterward married. He was brutal, but attractive. He was a good boy, a fine boy, a rich boy, so I married him. Ah, the romance of it all. We used to make love all night long—(Pause. He dances.)—and sit in the hot sun all the next day—(Pause. He dances.)—cooling off! . . . Ah, the romance of it all. And sometimes I can still hear those sounds. . . . And smell those smells—and wish I could live the whole thing over again.[28]

This leads into the production number that describes Pernambuco as an "unbelievable town / Where the crops go to seed / And the bank is in need of financing / Still the people keep dancing." Similarly, "the farmers all play the guitar. . . . But there's nobody farming. . . . Where they hum and they strum / And they drum 'til the feeling is frantic / And they call it romantic."[29]

"Pernambuco"—a song about how its residents ignore needs because of their desire to perform, and their desire to desire—is itself a moment that dismisses the plot in order to indulge the ecstasy of performance. Like its subject, it is motivated only by the desire to perform. But the "desire to perform" is also the desire to desire. Indeed, in the musical, the desire to perform is precisely a desire to experiment with performance by taking on bodies other than one's own. To desire to perform, then, is to desire relationships beyond the discrete self, to engender affect across different bodies, and to desire them. Song and dance become the vehicles of desire, the vehicles through which we imagine and feel potential relationships across bodies. The musical genre is thus structurally built to indulge and facilitate that desire.

Indeed, Charley's performance is not just any type of performance, but in particular it is the performance of bodies that are clearly marked as the projections of his desires as fabulated in his fantasy of Brazilian romance. This desire to perform, and the desire to desire, exist in a kind of feedback loop that begins to affect Charley's very identity. Though the play begins by framing his costume as being necessary for a "theatrical," it swiftly posits that the performance must be realized in Charley's life, and through his growing delight in his role, Charley permits the role to confuse his identity. Regarding his aunt, Charley admits at the beginning of the play that he's "never seen the woman."[30] And though her name would lead one to believe that she *was* Brazilian, she is of course his own aunt, born a British woman. Charley's own fantasies construct the aunt he goes on to perform, thereby permitting him the opportunity to embody these desires. The line that he practices repeatedly—"Be gone, my good man, and don't bother me any longer"—becomes in fact a mantra that he preaches to himself, its incantations relieving him of his rigid identity. Charley's "failed" performance as a Brazilian and as a woman makes possible the failure of his own identity.

It is worth emphasizing that Charley is not only in drag—but in a kind of exoticized drag. Doubly spectacular, his impersonation of a Brazilian woman is a concentrated instance of what I call the logic of exotic/erotic performance, a logic that deploys in *close proximity* the exotic, inspired by minstrelsy, and the erotic, inspired by the relationship between burlesque and drag. Often, these follow one another, as in the case of "The Rain in Spain," where the trio's impersonation of Spaniards precedes Colonel Pickering's assumption of psychic drag, or as in the case of Cap'n Andy, who imitates the burlesque dancer while next to the Dahomey Village. The confluence of these related forms of impersonation proves central to the politics of musical theatre, as will be seen through the course of this chapter. Indeed, this exotic/erotic dynamic that suffuses *Where's Charley?* is not merely a plot device. Instead, its presence in *Where's Charley?*—and in countless other musicals—merely makes explicit the energies that structure the genre at every level. A closer look at the 1941 musical *Lady in the Dark* reveals how this presence of gendered and ethnicized performance in the plot is mirrored by its presence in the act of making and performing musical theatre.

*Lady in the Dark* shares the exotic/erotic logic of *Where's Charley?*, but the circumstances of its creation reveal how this logic of failed gendered and ethnic performance profoundly suffuses the act of *making* musical theatre. One of the most conceptually ambitious musicals ever devised, *Lady in the Dark* was written by Moss Hart, with a score by Kurt Weill and Ira Gershwin. *Lady in the Dark* explores the life—conscious and unconscious—of fashion magazine editor Liza Elliott, who seeks the care of a psychiatrist when she begins to suffer increasingly frequent episodes of extreme panic.[31] Through therapy sessions with Dr. Brooks during which he explores Liza's relationship to her own femininity, she begins to unravel the cause of her anxieties. At the same time, she is forced to confront her indecisiveness, both in making professional decisions as well as in settling her romantic life.

When Liza submits to Dr. Brooks's care, she lies down on the couch and says, "How curious—how very curious! Out of all the millions of little pieces of which my life is made up, one silly little thing keeps going round and round in my mind. It's the first thought I had and it keeps turning."[32] This "silly little thing" is a childhood song whose lyrics Liza cannot quite recall, a song that comes to mind during episodes of depression or panic. When she mentions that the song appeared in a dream that she had had the night before, Dr. Brooks invites her to hum a few bars. As she hums the snippet of melody, we are ushered into the world of her dreams. This is the stunning conceptual ingenuity of *Lady in the Dark*: it begins by presenting its musical numbers as part of huge sequences that are sequestered, entirely set apart from reality and framed as either Liza's fantastic dreams or her memories of years past. The published edition of *Lady in the Dark* only reinforces the segregation of these fantasy sequences, printed as they are in a "Biblical" style, with the "reality" portions in black type and the fantasy sequences in red.

Significantly, we discover that Liza's anxiety is more precisely a kind of "performance anxiety." Over the course of her therapy, her dreams prompt her to recount to Dr. Brooks three episodes from her past, all of which reveal traumatic relationships to her femininity within the context of musical and theatrical performances. The first involves young Liza's father batting away compliments about her appearance when she is brought out at one of her parents' parties to sing the song. After he calls her "Daddy's little ugly duckling," little Liza tries to sing the song—the same song that now appears in her dreams and at the moments of panic—but she suddenly "breaks into sobs and runs from the room."[33] The second scene involves seven-year-old Liza being cast as the princess in a school play. When the boy cast as a prince complains that Liza is not attractive enough to play a convincing princess, she runs from the room in tears. The third scene occurs at a high school dance, when Liza sings the childhood song to a boy, noting to him that she has never before remembered all the words. Shortly thereafter, he abandons her and leaves her waiting for him, rejected.

The structural link between Liza's various forms of "performance anxiety"—whether musical, theatrical, or gendered—is reinforced when she begins another session with her familiar introduction: "How curious! How very curious! Of all the things I could be thinking of at this moment . . . ." This time, however, the object of her obsessive thought is not her song, but instead "a little school play I acted in when I was a child. . . . It was called 'The Princess of Pure Delight.'"[34] The stage directions indicate that a "Persian Prince, a little child, appears, along with other children. They bow, then proceed to enact Liza's narrative."[35] And Liza's narrative it is, the sing-song fairy tale of a princess and her three suitors clearly functioning as an allegory for Liza's own situation in the present. The conclusion of the school play will lead, within the dream, into a terrifying wedding scene that becomes "a bizarre combination of oratorio and mysterious and ominous movement winding up in a cacophonous musical nightmare."[36]

While this climactic and dystopic first act finale—a moment of *sexualized* panic catalyzed by Liza's recollection of the *Persian* prince—references the logic of exotic/erotic performance, an even more demonstrative moment of such performance will effect the resolution to the play. The key to Liza's resolution comes in the figure of Russell Paxton, described in the stage directions as "the staff photographer—the Cecil Beaton of *Allure* [Magazine]. He is still in his early twenties, but very Old World in manner and mildly effeminate in a rather charming fashion."[37] When we first encounter Russell, he is "hysterical, as usual," this time fawning over the film star Randy Curtis: "Girls, he's God-like! I've taken pictures of beautiful men, but this one is the end—the *end*! He's got a face that would melt in your mouth . . . ."[38] Later, when everyone in the office is waiting for Liza, Russell "is sprawled full length on the couch, a ladies' evening cape thrown across him as a coverlet, a rather outrageous lady's hat over his face."[39] In another scene, Russell surveys a suit of armor being used in a photoshoot. Telling an assistant that he's "going to make Elmer pretty," Russell "begins, with great concentration, to drape the chiffon over the suit of armour."[40]

Thus established as, in the words of one reviewer, a "swishy" character,[41] Russell—whose performance of "swishiness" is understood as a kind of cross-gender performance, a performance across bodies—will permit Liza to reconfigure her own femininity precisely by performing "across" him, a dynamic enabled by exotic/erotic performance. In the circus dream, the one that represents the climax of the play, Russell is the ringmaster, the orchestrator of the whole spectacle. He also assumes the penultimate place on the bill, picking up right after Liza sings, "When a maid gives her heart but does not give her word, / How on earth can that maid have betrayed him?"[42] When Russell asks who wrote the music just played, the jury's answer prompts him to exclaim, "Tschaikowsky! I love Russian composers!"[43] This inspires Russell-as-the-Ringmaster to recite, at breakneck speed, the names of over fifty Russian composers.[44] The number was a tour de force, and was met with universal acclaim, as in Sidney Whipple's opening night review, which drew attention to "'Tschaikowsky,' an interpolated number that has nothing to do with the play but which provides its most exciting diversion."[45] This seemingly inexplicable act of gendered and ethnic (Russian) performance immediately precedes Liza's turn,[46] "The Saga of Jenny," in which she recounts the various ways that a woman named Jenny made up her mind—to her peril—concluding with an exhortation: "Don't make up your mind!"[47]

These performances represent the cathartic release of the play, and in their wake, Liza's performance anxiety is ultimately cured. Newly able to perform in real life, she bursts into song: the play concludes when Liza hums the song, and Charley, her new beau, "suddenly singing," supplies the words.[48] The two sing as the curtain slowly descends. Thus, the goal of the piece is to permit Liza to be able to perform—and in so doing, to reposition herself in the economy of desire. This is precisely the kind of "mental acrobatics" that the erotic/exotic logic of performance has permitted Liza to do; indeed, it is the otherwise inexplicable Russian number—sung by an effeminate man—that makes this possible. Given the importance of the exotic, ethnic dimension of this number, it comes as no surprise to discover that the Circus Scene was, in the first drafts of the piece, a minstrel show, but "it was decided that minstrel costume and background weren't novel enough." They settled instead on a circus setting since "there could be more riotous color and regalia."[49] In its place, though, we find a structurally equivalent moment of Russell's cross-ethnic (Russian) and cross-gender ("swishy") performance that unleashes the desire to perform, and the desire to desire—here embodied in the single image of the play's conclusion—thereby transforming the character.

And just as these desires transformed Liza, the very act of embodying them also transformed the actress playing her, Gertrude Lawrence. Reflecting years later on the show's first performance during its out-of-town tryout, lyricist Ira Gershwin recounted that Danny Kaye's performance of "Tschaikowsky" received "thunderous applause . . . for at least a solid minute."[50] A staff member standing with Gershwin at the back of the theatre muttered, "Christ, we've lost our star!," feeling that "nothing could top Danny's rendition, that 'Jenny' couldn't compete with it, and that either [star Gertrude] Lawrence would leave the show or that Danny Kaye would have to be cut down to size."[51] However, Gershwin recalled that as if by some strange theatrical alchemy,

> "Jenny" began. She hadn't been singing more than a few lines when I realized an interpretation we'd never seen at rehearsal was materializing. Not only were there new nuances and approaches, but on top of this she "bumped" it and "ground" it, to the complete devastation of the audience. At the conclusion, there was an ovation which lasted twice as long as that for "Tschaikowsky."[52]

Hart similarly recalled that after Lawrence stared at Kaye, she "saluted and walked to the footlights and then sang 'Jenny' as she had never rehearsed it. She did it with bumps, grinds, [like] a strip tease, and completely topped him."[53] Significantly, Lawrence's body—inspired by the participation of the audience at the conclusion of the Russian number—here makes explicit her own song's foundation in the logic of burlesque. Critic Richard Watts, Jr., noted in his review that "the way in which Danny Kaye stops the show with the song made up of the names of Russian composers and Miss Lawrence proceeds to top him with her story of Jenny, the girl without inhibitions, is one of the remarkable things about 'Lady in the Dark.'"[54] This remarkable thing—the manner by which Lawrence builds on Kaye's performance—is remarkable precisely because it taps into the most primal logic of musical theatre—the exotic/erotic logic of musical performance—and executes it with remarkable efficiency.

Given that this logic of performance across bodies, this logic of performing desire, was present in the plot and the production of *Lady in the*

*Dark*, it is no surprise to discover that it structured the scene of its creation as well. As Hart recounted in 1941, "over the last few years I've literally sabotaged every serious idea I've had for a play. And so my psychoanalyst made me resolve that the next idea I had, whether it was good or lousy, I'd carry through. This was my next idea, and it was about the toughest one I've ever had to realize."[55] Hart frames *Lady in the Dark* as his *own* attempt to overcome a performance anxiety—just like the ones Liza will confront over the course of the play. And just as Liza's psychoanalyst, Dr. Brooks, solicits her musical performances (in the form of her dreams), Hart's own psychoanalyst solicits the play into being.

The structural link between Liza's and Hart's predicaments is made explicit in the published version of the play, which features a preface written by Hart's own psychiatrist, Dr. Lawrence Kubie, under the pseudonym of Dr. Brooks. There, in terms that echo how Hart described his own issues, Kubie writes that "in this gay and tender play, perhaps for the first time on any stage, the struggle of a vigorous and gifted human spirit to overcome deep-seated, unconscious, self-destructive forces is portrayed accurately."[56] While Kubie was of course describing Liza's situation, he noted that "the story of this woman, of her illness and of her recovery is the saga of what can happen to any woman—and, with some transposition of forces, to any man."[57] Such "transposition of forces" was precisely the creative work that Hart was undertaking in bringing the play to life. Hart's onetime lover, Glen Boles, felt that the show "grew directly out of the sessions with Kubie as an extension of the therapy, a reinforcement of it."[58] The resonance of Liza's psychoanalytic dilemma—choosing among three men—becomes all the more tragic when we learn that the sexually conflicted Hart autographed a copy of *Lady in the Dark* for Boles with the inscription: "You always wanted to know what goes on inside me. Here it is."[59] This would likely come as no surprise to the other artists working on the production—certainly not to Irene Sharaff, who was hired to create the costumes for the dream sequences and who had a longstanding professional relationship with Hart. In 1941, Kurt Weill reported her as observing that "Moss can only write about himself—and [*Lady in the Dark*] is certainly about Moss Hart again."[60]

Hart would be afforded the opportunity to test Sharaff's hypothesis when Gertrude Lawrence was stricken with a siege of influenza during tech rehearsals. With no understudy prepared to go on in her place as they ironed out the glitches in the technologically ambitious show, Hart volunteered to take on the part of Liza. As Hart biographer Steven Bach writes,

> A volunteer stepped forward. Moss would play Liza for the tech rehearsals, beginning to end, and did. He reclined on the psychiatrist's couch in the book scenes, went sophisticated and languid for the Glamour Dream, and bumped and ground his way through "The Saga of Jenny" ... Danny Kaye remembered it as "the greatest performance, I think, ever done on the New York stage."[61]

Hart was thus afforded the opportunity to physically embody the character whom he had already psychically inhabited. This physical and psychic substitution of Hart for Lawrence (the actress) and Liza (the character) represents one link in the transitive chain of impersonations—of identifications across bodies—that unleashes the profound potential of musical theatre. When Hart bumps and grinds as Lawrence playing Liza, he accesses a socially unsanctioned desire, becoming through Liza an entirely different character. As Hart becomes Liza, we in the audience inhabit the position of Dr. Brooks, where we perform precisely the work of the psychoanalyst: through an act of transference, the catalyzing force of our applause delivers Liza—through the performances of Moss Hart and Gertrude Lawrence—to the solution. If Hart began *Lady in the Dark* because he had sabotaged all his other ideas, he fully realizes his goal when he writes the part with his own body.

It is worth noting that Hart's play features a heroine who, like Laurey in *Oklahoma!*, is ultimately contained: the resolution of the play finds Liza submitting, personally and professionally, to Charley. As Maya Cantu has observed, *Lady in the Dark* is one of a number of musicals that "focused on the necessity of its heroine to, in the words of Kaye's Ringmaster, 'decide who she wants to be'—masculine or feminine, powerful or glamorous."[62] In this way, Liza's *burlesque* might be seen as the cathartic *release* of her erotic energies that permits them to be contained—and as a similarly structured closet for Hart's desires. In one possible understanding of the situation, Hart's ability to perform as Liza might give him a socially permissible situation in which to exorcise and sublimate his desire, thereby sustaining him in the absence of a means of expressing, or finding an object for, that desire. The conclusion *does* restrain Liza, just as it presumably provides a mechanism for Hart that might preclude the eruption of his own desire into his quotidian life. However, I would argue that the facile coda of *Lady in the Dark*, which presents Liza's domestication—her sudden realization that she likes the office cad—is hardly believable. The conclusion feels arbitrary, as though it were merely a functional conclusion, an inconsequential narrative obligation that pales next to the profound complexity of Liza's spectacle. Tellingly, Burns Mantle, in his opening night review, referred to *Lady in the Dark* as an "unusual spectacle," writing that "spectacle, too, is the word, for there is more show than substance in it."[63] It is the *show*, the *spectacle*, that compels us, that delivers us, that affects us.

The centrality of our ovation in this disintegrated logic, as for instance in its catalyzing of Gertrude Lawrence's burlesque, should not be understated.[64] The musical emerges from melodrama; but whereas melodrama attained its most profound affective charge in its static tableaux, we spectators of the musical align ourselves instead with the dancing, singing bodies whose performances—informed by the performing traditions of vaudeville, burlesque, and ethnic and racial minstrelsy—puncture its narrative surface. Thus, every musical must be understood as a play that, every few minutes or so, features an explosive eruption of performance that is fundamentally inspired by burlesque or minstrelsy.

Yet, even as the melodramatic tableau evolves into song and dance, the static melodramatic tableau ironically remains in the musical, in the most privileged and culturally prominent depiction of the genre—the iconic image of the performers who, at the climactic moment of a song, freeze into an ecstatic tableau with arms extended. Notably, as they freeze, we move, we applaud—indicating our participatory transference, our extension of their kinetic explosion. Their outstretched, frozen hands invite us to extend our own in a jubilant ovation, and in so doing, we signal our eager transformation, our willingness to "join in" and participate in the impersonation, in the performance. Through this embodiment of the energies unleashed when the narrative fragments, we demonstrate the psychic process by which we experience the drama. The applause is the manifestation of the energies unleashed when the narrative fractures. The ovation, then, is a corporeal link in a psychic and material chain that forms the disintegrated logic of musical theatre.

Just as ovation completed the logic of *Lady in the Dark*, it will prove crucial to *Gypsy*, a show that thematizes the role of the audience in the transference central to musical theatre. This dynamic materializes most conspicuously in two creative disagreements that emerged during the show's out-of-town tryout in 1959, both of which involve fascinating juxtapositions of the exotic/erotic dynamic and its concern of performance across bodies. The first disagreement concerned "Little Lamb," the melancholy number that Louise sings on her birthday. Significantly, director Jerome Robbins had tried to cut the tender ballad, replacing it with, as librettist Arthur Laurents put it, "a big dance number in the hotel corridor utilizing all the unnecessary people he had hired."[65] These "unnecessary people" were the "acrobats, jugglers, comics, strippers, showgirls, and dancers" who had been part of a Minsky's Christmas Show burlesque sequence that Robbins had begrudgingly cut. As Laurents remembered in a roundtable discussion years later, "Jule asked Jerry to put 'Little Lamb' back in, Jerry said no. He said, 'It doesn't work. It's out.'" After Styne threatened to withdraw his entire score unless "Little Lamb" was restored, "it was put back, and that was the end of that."[66] According to Sondheim, Robbins's issue with the song was that the number "was not getting a hand."[67] In fact, all of the issues with *Gypsy* will center precisely on this issue of "getting a hand"—theatrical parlance for the act of soliciting bodies.

To discover the deep significance of "Little Lamb," we must consider its juxtaposition with "Mr. Goldstone, I Love You," a joyful production number that Rose sings to Mervyn Goldstone, as part of a musical sequence that interrupts Louise's chaotic birthday celebration. At the height of the birthday frenzy—which includes Rose's ostensibly comic allegations of having been raped by the hotel manager—Herbie arrives with Mr. Goldstone, a "mild little man" to whom Rose immediately apologizes for the paltry birthday spread: "I'm sorry it's such a small cake and—."[68] Herbie interrupts Rose to explain that Mr. Goldstone is from the Orpheum vaudeville circuit. As Rose slowly comprehends Goldstone's significance, her inventory of the feast grinds to a halt: "There's only one egg roll and some fried . . . rice

... and ... sub ... gum ... chow ....”[69] As Herbie announces that Mr. Goldstone has booked the act, the stage directions indicate “a long pause. Rose stares, numb with a growing happiness. Mechanically, she picks up a plate from the trunk and holds it out.”[70] With that, Rose begins the explosive “Mr. Goldstone,” a beautiful moment of nonsense in which Rose fêtes the titular character with everything at her disposal: “Have an egg roll, Mr. Goldstone / Have a napkin, have a chopstick, have a chair!” The madness builds to a climax when the entire company exclaims, “Mervyn Goldstone, we love you! / Goldstone!”[71] Then, the stage directions indicate, “the lights black out in the larger bedroom and fade in slowly on the small room, where a forgotten Louise sits with the lamb.” In this small room, Louise sings, “Little lamb, little lamb, / I wonder how old I am. / I wonder how old I am ....”[72]

The stark contrast between these two numbers leads to the central issue of “getting a hand.” The effect of “Little Lamb” cannot be separated from its juxtaposition with “Mr. Goldstone,” a cross-racial number which is about nothing *but* performing. Significantly, the arrival of Mr. Goldstone—who here embodies the theatrical circuit on which Rose has long dreamed of performing—is quite literally an invitation to performance. From Rose’s very first song, we know that she “had a dream.... All about June and the Orpheum Circuit,” and with Mr. Goldstone’s arrival, that dream has come true.[73] Noting that “Mr. Goldstone” is “one of those songs in which you just take one idea and repeat it as cleverly or as interestingly or as wittily as possible,” Sondheim ultimately calls the song a “stage wait,”[74] a fitting term since everything has stopped for this moment of musical ecstasy.[75] Significantly, this ecstasy takes the form of the verbal dexterity by which Rose, “hysterical with excitement,” incants her litany of Chinese foods, ultimately turning the otherwise unassuming Mr. Goldstone into a Chinese food himself: “Have a goldstone, Mr. Egg Roll.... Have some fried rice, Mr. Soy Sauce ....”[76] This cross-racial performance is of course neither the first nor the last time that Rose will project onto other less inclined bodies her desire to perform. As a cross-racial moment of soliciting performance, “Mr. Goldstone” prepares the audience for a chain of impersonations to unfold, but *Gypsy* will thwart this expectation. As this ecstatic moment of cross-racial (Chinese) performance concludes, Sondheim recounted, the number “got a really nice hand.”[77] However, the applause for “Mr. Goldstone" will imminently be cut off when Louise begins to sing plaintively to her little lamb.

In moving so swiftly from this jubilant scene of performance to the "small room, where a forgotten Louise sits with the lamb,"[78] the show cultivates two attitudes simultaneously: first, it allows a non-performer, Louise, to perform while denying the exhibitionism at the core of all performance, and makes the audience feel intrusive and voyeuristic, as though it were interrupting Louise's crushingly introspective moment. Second, the emotional depth of this song and the effect of interiority created by its staging conspire to cast Rose's joyous "Mr. Goldstone" as the kind of theatrical vacuity whose emotional bankruptcy harms Louise. In indicting the exhibitionist and presentational nature of "Mr. Goldstone," "Little Lamb" also indicts the spectators whose ovation it stifles by force, as if punishing them for their outburst. Performance here is framed negatively, and audiences are invited to feel shame over their complicity with it. In both denigrating performance and denying performance, "Little Lamb" creates Louise's psychic depth as much by its own content as by its placement following "Mr. Goldstone." Far from continuing a chain of impersonations, "Little Lamb" makes spectators feel guilty for desiring this transference and these relationships with other bodies.

However, "Rose's Turn"—the subject of the other great creative dispute—will present the audience with the opportunity for revenge, as the spectators' defiant applause will insist that, like the exotic/erotic logic invoked by the song, the experience of musical theatre is fundamentally about performing through other bodies. Oscar Hammerstein, visiting the show's Philadelphia tryout as a favor to his protégé (and *Gypsy* lyricist) Stephen Sondheim, took great issue with the final moments of "Rose's Turn," Ethel Merman's climactic showstopper that precedes the play's brief closing scene.[79] According to Laurents,

> *Gypsy* is so designed that Rose is on stage alone after a number ends only once in the entire evening. Thus there is only one place for the star to receive her applause and bow in direct response to her audience—at the end of "Rose's Turn." As written, however, just as Rose finishes and starts to bow, Louise comes on applauding, thus killing the audience's hand before it can start and getting the final scene

under way. This was exactly what we all wanted. Oscar, however, felt Ethel Merman wasn't getting the applause the audience had been waiting all night to give her; and because they had been waiting in vain, they were frustrated and didn't listen to the last scene.[80]

Laurents writes that the creators heeded Hammerstein's advice, allowing Ethel Merman to take her bows. As Laurents phrased it, pitting the character of Rose against that of Merman, "Rose left the stage while Ethel Merman took her bow. Bows. Endless. She brought the house down and the show went out the window."[81] Laurents, though, was determined to rescue this moment from the clutching talons of the diva, and he got his chance fourteen years later when he directed a London revival of the show starring Angela Lansbury, whom he hailed as being not "just a musical star but a superb actress and a courageous one."[82] Laurents reasoned that the number should communicate that Rose's strip, unlike Louise's, is "by a desperate, crazed middle-aged woman who doesn't actually strip because it's all taking place in the only place she *could* strip: in her recognition-hungry head."[83] As imagined by Laurents,

> The stage is ablaze with ROSE in huge lights. There's a huge spotlight on Rose as she bows to thunderous applause, even cheers. . . . And bows again. The spot goes with her as she moves to one side and bows again. Then the ROSE lights begin to drop out. She bows again. Now the ROSE lights are gone and the stage light is diminishing. Still, she bows again. Only her spot is left now; the applause is dying out. Her spot is reduced to a dim glow. A work light comes on; the applause peters out, then ends—but not for Rose: she still hears it. She takes a slow, deep, regal bow to deathly silence—and at that moment the audience gets it: there never was any applause for Rose; it was all in her head.[84]

Describing Angela Lansbury's performance of his direction, Laurents writes that "[b]y the time all the ROSE lights were gone and she was taking the last bow in a dim spot, she had made the by-now-unsettled audience aware something was awry; just what, they weren't sure. And then, as she took that last deep bow, she *smiled* to no applause—to a dead silence."[85] He concludes by noting that "she was acknowledging what wasn't there. It was frightening, chilling; it brought an audible gasp from the audience. They got it."[86]

Indeed, this final scene, just like "Little Lamb," was intended to "kil[l] the audience's hand,"[87] thereby obliterating—almost chastising—the audience's recognition of Merman's burlesque performance. It is an attempt to deny the musical's fundamental desire to perform through other bodies. The creators had wanted to send Louise onstage applauding herself, so as to return the applause to the world of the character, presumably forcing Merman to cede the stage to Rose, the character—and thereby forcing the audience to remove itself from the theatrical situation. After Hammerstein intervened and urged the creators to indulge the audience's desire to applaud, Laurents tried to devise a way to reconceptualize that applause, claiming to have rendered it "imaginary"—suggesting that, in a sense, it had never even happened. This profound desire to neutralize the audience's applause represents Laurents's (paradoxical and impossible) goal of removing the audience from the theatrical situation, which for him would ideally unfold voyeuristically.

The desire of the creators in 1959 to refuse the audience becomes, in 1973, an attempt to force them into Rose's world. In either case, the fundamental desire is to diminish the distinctly theatrical elements of the presentation and, by dissolving the audience's presence as such, to diminish spectacle and envelop it within narrative. This gesture is the logical fulfillment of the play's opening salvo—that, by having Rose enter from the back of the theatre and charge through the aisle, we, the audience, are already *in* the *empty* vaudeville theatre at the beginning of the play. Disembodied as we are inside Rose's theatrical world, it is only one small step further to become disembodied figments of her own imagination. With each step, the play presents more complications to our attempts to identify with Rose through our own bodies—through our own applause. Laurents's goal of removing the audience—of preventing its identification with Rose—in "Rose's Turn" mirrors and extends the way in which "Little Lamb" was used to stifle the applause prompted by the (cross-ethnic) "Mr. Goldstone." Indeed, "Rose's Turn" can be understood as a fiery rejection of Rose's broader logic of performance, which, like that of the entire genre, always involves projection across bodies. Even in her first scene, we find her "singing along with her girls,"[88] and in her first song,

"Some People," she confuses herself and June: "Rose! Get *yourself* some new orchestrations. . . . Good riddance to all the socials *I* had to go to, all the lodges *I* had to play . . . ."[89]

"Rose's Turn," however, challenges this logic: while her ecstatic (cross-ethnic) explosion with Mr. Goldstone found her projecting performance onto him, "Rose's Turn" will find her demonstratively excluding him. Rose flaunts that she has no further need to project onto Mr. Goldstone: while she initially addressed the "mild little man" from the Orpheum Circuit as "Mr. Egg Roll," she now has no use for him since she embodies him in her stripper's breasts—"How d'ya like them egg rolls, Mr. Goldstone?"[90] In turning her cross-ethnic performance into the beginning of a burlesque act, Rose prepares the audiences to expect a volatile act of psychic transference. However, her violent incantations of "For me!" aim to deny this, as does Laurents's desperate directorial strategy of denying applause. "Rose's Turn" thus presents the genre's own nightmare: an inert moment of performance that insists on its own isolation by disavowing the spectator. This mission is doomed to fail, however. If *Gypsy* has insisted through Rose that we perform through others—casting this dynamic in the captivating yet carnivorous form of the stage mother—her final declaration is meant to deny this: "FOR ME!" she howls.[91] But the applause for "Rose's Turn" is always explosive and deafening, deafening as though to drown out the ostensible message. The ovation is so enthusiastic precisely because it is the audience's defiant rejection of the song's premise, and our affirmation of the star's *performance*.

Tellingly, just as our booming applause for "Rose's Turn" insists on its transference across bodies, so too "Rose's Turn" has been the subject of stories that attempt to re-mark its genesis as an act of transference. In echoes of Moss Hart embodying Eliza for Julie Andrews, one account suggests that Merman learned the role by working through it with Robbins in her place, with her "mimick[ing] him mimicking her."[92] A parallel account of Merman's inspiration comes from Barbara Seaman's *Lovely Me*, a biography of Jacqueline Susann, in which she writes that "when Ethel admitted she was having trouble with the bumps and grinds she had to do in one scene, Jackie dug out her infamous bikini from *Between the Covers* and put it on under a button-down dress. She wore it to Ethel's apartment at the Park Lane Hotel, and once inside dropped the dress and gave a private performance of everything she had learned from Margie Hart, Christine Ayers, and even Dovita. . . . It was a highly erotic performance, and whether it taught Ethel how to strip or not, it certainly turned Jackie on."[93] Whatever may have actually happened, these stories work to situate the development of "Rose's Turn" as itself a performance across bodies.

In applauding the number, we assert our presence, and our own participation in this act of transference. Our defiant applause insists that Rose, and *Gypsy*, and in fact all musicals demand that we perform through the bodies of others. *Gypsy* is thus a musical at war with itself. It chafes at the degree to which the musical is fundamentally about impersonation and performance, and denies this source of pleasure even as it must indulge it. This structural ambivalence was felt, for example, in Walter Kerr's perceptive comment on opening night that he wasn't "sure whether 'Gypsy' is new fashioned, or old-fashioned, or integrated or non-integrated."[94] Another distinguished critic, Brooks Atkinson, observed that "there are some sticky scenes toward the end when 'Gypsy' abandons the sleazy grandeur of show business and threatens to become belles-lettres. It deserts the body and starts cultivating the soul. Things look ominous in the last ten minutes. But trust Ethel. She concludes the proceedings with a song and dance of defiance."[95] It is through Ethel, through her "song and dance of defiance," that the audience is delivered to the body, precisely through applause, directed at and through these moments of impersonation. Oscar Hammerstein was right.

Significantly, when we in the audience applaud, it is *we* who burst into song. The transitive contagion of the song prompts us, and it does so with such force that we often quite literally burst *into* the song—unable to wait for a clean ending before we explode into ovation. This applause testifies to the manner by which *we* ourselves have burst. The musical's narratological disintegration is a psychic and bodily disintegration, and it is *our* psychic bodies that are disintegrated. In this sense, the song is you: the song's relationship to the narrative catalyzes and mirrors similar ruptures to our own sense of identity.

To understand how this dynamic works, I return to "Rose's Turn," which, for Arthur Laurents, represented a kind of impossibility since Rose would never be asked to strip anywhere except in her mind. However, the number—which features an impossible, unthinkable, failed performance at its core—is nonetheless considered by many to be the greatest moment in all of musical theatre. In other words, a depiction of a failed performance is paradoxically considered to permit the supreme performance. This is no anomaly. The genre of musical theatre returns continually to this theme of bad and failed performance. No one bats an eye, for example, when the musical *Grey Gardens* will sustain an entire act on the absurd premise that Edith Beale's singing embarrasses everyone in earshot—all while we in the audience eagerly await every crystalline vocalization by Christine Ebersole, the incomparable singer and actress portraying this allegedly mortifying performer.

In fact, all three of the plays examined in this chapter focus on a kind of endearingly bad or failed performance: the New Ashmolean Conservatory Band members stand alongside Charley fumbling in his dress, just as the mute, paralyzed Liza takes her place in the pantheon with Louise's laughably wretched Toreadorables, the tacky strippers, and Rose herself. The predicaments of Charley, Liza, and Rose exemplify the genre's interest in misfires and glitches—what might in theatrical terms be called turkeys or flops—in the performance of identity.

The failed performances that populate the genre are quite often performances of gender, race, and sexuality—reified categories of identity that govern social life. The obsession with failed performances emerges precisely from the fissures of the form, which itself is founded on its own kinds of failure of performance and identity. It is a commonplace that characters burst into song when words no longer suffice to carry the emotion; however, I argue that characters burst into song and dance when their expressive needs can no longer be satisfied by a single body and, in this way, thereby experience failure. Thus, characters burst into song as a means of performing across and through other bodies. These complex negotiations of "across and through" in fact produce the defining affect of musical theatre. In every gap between song, story, and dance, the audience is invited to try on a kind of "bad" performance, and inevitably made to enjoy it, to desire it, to thereby become something else. Undertaking this process relentlessly, the ultimate power of musical theatre is to suggest the failure of identity itself. To be sure, the musical's obsession with gender, race, and sexuality is not incidental to the genre, nor is it merely the result of certain subcultural reading practices. The genre's endless play with these categories is as constitutive of musical theatre as is the eruptive structure that makes this play possible—both of which work in concert to destabilize the very category of identity itself.

Thus, the genre thematizes not merely the failure of a single mode of expression—hence the need to "burst into song and dance"—but also the failure, the insufficiency, of a single and discrete subject to articulate certain modes of thought and feeling. The genre, with its constitutive ruptures, performs this kind of failure with every explosion into kinetic and musical energy. These moments of "bursting" are themselves the product of a kind of failed performance—a moment when the narrative, and the stable subject who undergirds it, must be fragmented. It is the radical instability of the form, with its predilection for "bursting into song," and the radical instability of the subject it brings into being, that prompts the desperate detection of the inoculating powers of "integration" at every turn. By denying a stable subject position, the musical forces one to exist in the protean field of bodily cross-identifications and desire that constitutes the disintegrated logic of musical theatre. Integration suppresses and denies that these ruptures occur, and thereby disavows the radical personal and social transformations embedded in the generic structure and embodied in the performers and spectators who experience them.

The radical transformations are made possible in part from the structural residues of burlesque and minstrelsy that populate the musical's melodramatic structure. The moments of burlesque and minstrelsy function precisely as bad performances, failed performances of other kinds of gendered and raced bodies. As I noted in chapter 4, minstrelsy worked to *consolidate* identity precisely through the putting on *and taking off* of blackface. It was through the performance of not-blackness that the ethnic immigrant became white. However, the incorporation of minstrelsy into the broader musical form—with its relentless sequences of transformations across gendered, raced, sexualized bodies—deploys minstrelsy to a different end. Unlike minstrelsy, the musical eschews any binary logic and never works to *stabilize* identity. Indeed, it accomplishes precisely the opposite, undermining any sense of stable subjectivity.

The form thus proliferates a range of spectacular identifications that unsettle any straightforward sense of narrative identification. The structure of musical theatre must be seen as a narrative form punctuated at regular intervals by the eruption of transformative erotic energies, which are themselves inspired by and not unlike the kinds of energies that attend burlesque and minstrel traditions. Each of these eruptions demands that spectators shift the nature of their identifications, inviting identification across different kinds of bodies—both the bodies of the performers onstage, and the bodies imagined by the performance. The genre's greatest pleasures, and its most potent politics, emerge from the complex network of desires and identifications made possible by these erotic energies, all unleashed in the moment of "bursting into song and dance." While the narrative scenes do not preclude identification, they do not present—as songs and dances do—the unconstrained erotic energy of the bodies that stop the show, which carry with them unparalleled identificatory powers and complexities.

The form amplifies this dramatic energy by unleashing *chains* of imitations—ethnic, gendered, racial, among others—that mutually enable each other and unsettle any sense of stable, permanent, or baseline identity, as, for example, in the case of Moss Hart imitating Gertrude Lawrence imitating Liza imitating Persian royalty. Indeed, the form emphasizes the lack of any stable identity and distributes this transitive energy widely. The 1971 musical *The Grass Harp* opens onto a scene featuring Collin Talbo, a daydreaming fifteen-year-old, and Catherine Creek, a "black woman . . . dressed up in flamboyant, somewhat self-invented, Indian regalia—a long 'squaw' dress, an apron, and moccasins; she is festooned with turquoise bracelets and necklaces, and her cheeks are highly rouged."[96] One of the main concerns of this opening scene is Collin's obsession with "floozies," as seen for example in his interest in the book "Confessions of a Harem Princess." As Collin describes his nightly visions of "imaginary harems full of doozies" whom he watches "salaam," his fantasy takes him even further: as the stage directions indicate, "acting out his floozy fantasy, Collin 'becomes' a floozy."[97] Collin's desire to embody—to "become"—the eroticized "floozy" is matched by Catherine's own failed impersonation of Indian-ness, which is an ongoing concern of the play. While Collin has already queried Catherine as to "which side of [her] family were Indians," it is the haughty Verena who finds Catherine's imitation most unsettling. Announcing the impending arrival of an important guest, Verena says, "Catherine, I'd appreciate it if you'd scrape the paint off your face, and take off your costume jewelry"—prompting Catherine to "jangl[e] her bracelets in Verena's face" and note that they are "genuine Indian bracelets, passed down to [her] on account of [her] Indian princess blood."[98] Catherine's impersonation is picked up later in her musical lament, "Indian Blues," in which she sings, "Since I'm a princess, wish I had a pile of wampum / If someone tried to treat me mean, my braves'd whomp him."[99] Shortly thereafter, Verena notes that "she's not Indian, and the whole town knows it"—a sentiment disavowed by Verena's sister, who says, "She's not pretending. She feels Indian."[100] The play not only legitimizes Catherine's clearly imagined impersonation of Indian-ness but it also invites its spectators to identify with Catherine identifying with the Indian princess, as with Collin who "becomes" the exoticized floozy of his imagination.

This distribution of this urge to play with impersonation also occurs in the 1971 musical *Two Gentlemen of Verona*, which was constructed with a diverse cast in mind: as the authors noted, "for the original production, we cast a Puerto Rican for Proteus and Speed, a Cuban for Julia, Valentine and Silvia and the Duke and occasionally Lucetta were played by Blacks, Launce was originally done in Yiddish, then went Country Western in a cast change, Eglamour was Chinese, Thurio was an Irishman, Lucetta a Russian-Danish girl. The chorus was every color under the sun."[101] Noting the production's success in representing the diversity of the city, *Newsweek* writer Jack Kroll remarked that "under a chunk of open sky the scared New York of the '70s achieved a rare moment of glowing amity as John Guare and Mel Shapiro's adaptation used Shakespeare's very first comedy to reintroduce the fragmented city to its own piebald, polyglot dramatis personae."[102] Another reviewer wrote that *Two Gentlemen* was the epitome of the form: "if the musical form did not exist they would have needed to invent it"[103]—an unsurprising sentiment given that the organizing principle of its plot, as articulated concisely in a rhymed compendium to the play written by John Guare, was that

> Everyone falls in love
> Even milkmaids in the field.
> Everyone can be metamorphosed:
> That is the secret of life,
> And that secret is revealed.[104]

This process of metamorphosis is exploited in the show's brilliant title number, as Julia wonders how she can tell Proteus, now in the "big city" of Milan, that she is pregnant. After Julia laments that "I'm not a young man / So I never can travel," Lucetta exhorts her to "throw off all the fears you have / We'll dress like men." Julia's reply: "Ay sie cuanto cuanto la gusta / This hen's become a rooster."[105] Thus empowered by this eruption of ethnic difference, Julia dresses like a man and assumes her place as one of the eponymous gentlemen of Verona. This eruption of chains of difference—of (our identification with) a Cuban American woman portraying an Italian woman who, in a moment of Spanishness, becomes a man—enables the metamorphosis of Julia, mirroring the process whereby the musical asks us to constantly change our positions, to change our relationships to bodies, to desire and identify anew. This economy of metamorphosis might be articulated most concisely in a lyric from María Irene Fornés's extraordinary musical *Promenade*: "Be one and all. / Be each and all. / Transvest, / Impersonate, / 'Cause costumes / Change the course / Of life."[106] Imitation begets imitation, and as the rhythm of impersonation accelerates, and as the ruptures multiply, the form delivers its full potential. As a show demands, with ever greater acceleration, that the audience identify with this body, and then that body, and then yet another, the vertiginous frenzy dizzyingly unsettles any sense of terra firma upon which the spectator can stably rely.

The musical thus works to unsettle identity through its deployment of bodies that it positions as objects of sensuous spectacle and erotic contemplation. The discourse of integration, meanwhile, denies the identifications that take place with those bodies. However, just as musicals require a narrative to fragment, so too do they posit a subject position *precisely in order to dismantle it.* This is the unmarked subject—generally a white heterosexual male position—in opposition to which the musical will determine which bodies are the repositories of sensuous spectacle.

The musical is invested in its own heterosexual narrative only insofar as that narrative fails, and, in the same manner, it pursues this unmarked subject position only so that the subject can fail. Thus, the musical invites its spectators to assume this position, but the pleasure comes precisely in its immolation, in the pleasurable dissolution of a hegemonic subject, a dissolution that can be freeing for all. While musical theatre offers this sundering of the subject as one of its greatest pleasures, this may not ultimately be pleasurable for every spectator, hence the discourse of integration, which represents the attempt to shore up this subject position, to suggest that the deployment of the other bodies in no way threatens—and in fact affirms—the narrative subject.

Integration is merely a reaction to the genre's formal structure, which dismantles the idea of identity as a stable phenomenon, enabling the spectator to rehearse new ways of conceiving their identity and their relationships to other bodies. As the form shatters identities, it pushes the spectators not toward a new, or better, singular identity but toward a still more dizzying shuffle of impersonations. Take, for example, the charmingly absurd premise of the 1956 musical *Bells Are Ringing*, in which Ella Peterson is a switchboard operator who takes a deep personal interest in the lives of the clients at her telephone answering service. From the very beginning of the play, she is trailed by two members of the Vice Squad, who surmise that the answering service is essentially a cover for a prostitution ring—the dangers of working women!—but who later suspect that the operators are actually a ring of counterfeiters. The counterfeiting suspicion is not entirely off the mark, since much of the pleasure of the piece comes from the humor of finding Ella imitating all sorts of characters, whether Santa Claus, a French restauranteur, or a "Brando" wearing "flats and leather jacket and motorcycle cap," spouting Beatnik phrases and snapping her fingers. Ella's predilection for spinning a hodgepodge of identities finds an interesting parallel in a series of geographic and ethnic flights of fancy that take place around her. When Ella's client Jeffrey Moss sits down to write a scene of his new play, he dictates "Act Twelve, Scene Nine. Senor Mendoza's Hacienda in Iceland." This laughable mishmash will be echoed by Sandor, Sue's con man suitor, who sings with "gypsy passion" of the incredible time awaiting them in Salzburg. His ode to Salzburg, however, turns out to celebrate a city of geographic and ethnic implausibility. His Salzburg is the "Salzburg on the shore. . . . Where Geisha girls keep coming back for more," where he says that he and Sue will dine on "goulash for two as we barge down the Nile."[107] The song concludes with a lusty "Liebchen! By the sea! Olé!"[108] The genre is constantly generating, and ostensibly taking pleasure in, the endless proliferation of gendered and ethnic identities—a proliferation that almost inevitably accelerates into a collision of identities.

However, as the play nears its conclusion, Ella laments that "playing all kinds of imaginary characters" ultimately led to complications because "*I* wasn't real."[109] Reiterating that "I don't really know myself who I am," she sings "I'm Going Back," a song in which she playfully announces her return to the Bonjour Tristesse Brassière Company, where she can undertake "a little modeling on the side." While her goal is ostensibly to discard her "imaginary characters" and discover who she "is," the song that will supposedly accomplish this in fact consists of yet more imitations: first, with "exaggerated 'blues' mannerisms," and then "changing to French chanteuse style," with a final transformation in which she sings "in all-out 'Mammy' style." The eruption of minstrelsy announces and prepares the moment of burlesque, with her Jolsonesque cry that she will discover "what Ella Peterson is all about / In that Shangri-la of lacy lingerie."[110] While the endless set of "imaginary characters" prompts Ella's crisis, the solution to this crisis is merely to indulge her desire for imitation even more, as articulated unsurprisingly in a moment of exotic/erotic performance. Ella's self-discovery thus results not in a conclusive moment of self-identification, but in an even more protean state of flux. Indeed, the musical theatre form resists Ella's search for an *identity*.

While Ella's search is a kind of utopian playing with identities, the mechanisms by which Ella realizes her non-resolution are not so utopian. The transformations of the genre—the very source of its pleasures—are produced by bodies that stop the show. While Ella's joyful explosion works to liberate her, it does so through her invocations of lingerie modeling, blues singing, and "Mammy" vocalizing. In other words, her citations of blackness and of her own history of exhibiting her body serve as the currencies that purchase her ability to transform. Because musicals always rely on bodies that stop the show to generate its pleasure and to effect its transformations, the genre is thus structurally founded on bodies marked as spectacular, bodies consumed not principally as narrative vehicles but as erotic vehicles of fantastic projection and identification. While these bodies, as the ones who stop the show, wield the greatest power in musical theatre, the applause through which audiences venerate them is always to some degree self-interested—testifying to their utility—provoking a tremendous anxiety over these bodies whose labor and whose display permit others to experience the profound possibilities of the form.

This dilemma prompts the musical's greatest anxiety: that it can never fully and absolutely dissociate its most progressive utopian politics from the possibility of exploiting the bodies through whom these very politics are effected. This is not to say that these moments are necessarily exploitative, but instead that the possibility of exploitation can never be fully evacuated from the eruptive site of musical performance. The transformations catalyzed by these bodies are so profound that the genre has developed an entire repertoire of strategies for mitigating and denying this potential for exploitation. *Show Boat*, as we have seen, suggests that networks of love and compensation excuse its dependence on spectacular bodies. These two thematic rationalizations, (voluntary) love and (remunerated) compensation, recur again and again as the genre subtly addresses its own dramaturgical logic and assuages the specter of guilt.

Nowhere is the theme of compensation brought up so playfully—or so explicitly—as in the musical *The Fantasticks*, a show distinguished by having run continuously off-Broadway from 1960 until 2002.[iii] In this musical, two fathers, wanting their children to marry each other, purport to be feuding so that their children will fall in "forbidden" love. Once the children fall for each other, the fathers seek a way to end the feud. One father announces that he has found a "very theatrical" answer: an "abduction" by a professional abductor. Essentially, the mysterious abductor will pretend to kidnap the girl, giving the boy an opportunity to heroically save her. The abductor, El Gallo, announces that he will undertake "the Rape," which he insists, citing Alexander Pope, is the "proper word" for the abduction. The show's climax thus depends, predictably, on El Gallo's sexualized eruption of foreignness—aided by two comrades, both notoriously bad (failed) performers, who help to carry out the abduction: Mortimer, an "Indian" who speaks with a "thick Cockney accent," and Henry, an "ancient actor" who can barely remember lines. *The Fantasticks* could not make any clearer that all of its performances—including that of the exoticized/eroticized El Gallo—are precisely ones of "bad acting," as they are in the cases of (the also exoticized) Mortimer and Henry.

After a romantic moment between the boy and girl, the "Rape Ballet" begins, with Henry yelling, "Indians, ready? Indians—Rape!" The "abduction" unfolds as planned, and once Matt disposes of El Gallo, "the young lovers rush upon the little platform and embrace in a pretty tableau. The Fathers rush in too. And embrace too. And get upon the platform to finish off the 'Living Statues' type of tableau."[112] As the lovers and parents hold their positions, El Gallo asks the audience a question that unknowingly takes this moment back to the very birth of the entire genre: "Very pretty, eh? Worthy of Watteau. A group of living statues: What do they call it? A tableau. Hmmm. I wonder if they can hold it." After a second act of tribulations and growth, the lovers are united—though it is worth noting that the animating desire is the one between the two fathers. They too "embrace over the 'wall,'" and they mirror the antics of the lovers: Bellomy, for example, "yips with delight" as Hucklebee approaches the wall.[113]

Significantly, El Gallo introduces the "rape"—the exotic/erotic Spanish threat that will accomplish the profound reorientation of desire the fathers seek—through an obsessive meditation about the compensation of his labor. When one of the fathers asks about the cost, El Gallo explains that the cost will depend on the "quality of the Rape," prompting the song "It Depends on What You Pay," an elaborate litany of the fifteen types of rape that the fathers could purchase. During an interlude in which the fathers, Bellomy and Huck, dance with El Gallo, Bellomy exclaims, "It's so Spanish; that's why I like it!" to which Huck replies, "I like it, too. Ay, yi, yi!"[114] All three build to a climactic "Ra-aa-aa-pe! Olé!" This performed eruption of exoticized sexuality—the Spanish rape—is thus excused by the suggestion that it is being compensated "with regular Union rates."

While *The Fantasticks* assuages its anxieties by suggesting that its labor has been properly remunerated, the other principal practice suggests that the spectacular labor is a manifestation of voluntary love, as Julie, for example, does with Magnolia in *Show Boat*. This is also the route undertaken by director Michael Bennett's 1975 musical *A Chorus Line*, which Ken Mandelbaum refers to as a "continuous theater piece" that "represents perhaps the most seamless blending of all the elements of musical theatre yet achieved by a theatre artist."[115] Noting the show's "theatrical seamlessness," Frank Rich echoed Mandelbaum's claims when he wrote that the tremendous effect of *A Chorus Line* could be traced to the "stitching together of all its elements in that purest of theatrical arenas, a deep and empty stage, by its director-choreographer."[116] If Mamoulian's theatre of integration represented the emergence of the unifying director, Bennett represents its maturity and ascendance. And fittingly, *A Chorus Line* features Zach—a director-choreographer strongly resembling Bennett himself—who gives voice to the desires of integration.

Just as *A Chorus Line* was celebrated for blending its elements, Zach famously seeks an ensemble that will "blend": as he tells the auditioning dancers, "Now—this is important! I want to see *Unison Dancing*. Every head, arm, body angle, *exactly the same*. You must blend."[117] Zach claims that "this is one of those numbers where you back the star," but of course *A Chorus Line* never highlights a star; in fact, the whole show is predicated not merely on the absence of stardom, but on its negation. Zach orders that since the unison dance is in service of the star, "I don't want anybody to pull my eye." However, as Frank Rich rightly notes, "in *A Chorus Line*, the show as an entity was a star."[118] Thus, the uniformity demanded of the dancers is in service of turning the show into an entity; in asking that no one "pulls his eye," Zach is seeking to accomplish precisely what integration aims to do: preclude any point of (errant) identification with spectacular bodies. Nonetheless, while the show essentially functions as a set of vaudeville turns that feature the auditioning performers, its major narrative moments revolve around two characters—Paul and Cassie—who challenge Zach's desire to preclude any points of identification. It is not accidental that Paul and Cassie embody the exotic and erotic spectacularity that challenges Zach's desire for integration, and therefore must be addressed in the course of the play. While the other characters are interrogated as part of a group exchange, Paul and Cassie are "singled out"—before these two unruly spectacular bodies are forced to negotiate with the demands of group discipline under the integrating eye of their director-choreographer.

Much of the dramatic energy of the piece comes from the question of whether Zach will cast Cassie, who has returned to New York after an unsuccessful attempt at a career in Hollywood. Noting that Cassie "stopped two shows cold" in the past, Zach tells her that she is "too good for the chorus." The result of Cassie's star-like talent, this ability to stop shows, becomes clear when Zach tells her, "You don't fit in. You don't dance like anybody else—you don't know how."[119] While the dialogue implies that he was the one who long ago urged her to transcend the chorus and aim for stardom, Zach's interactions with Cassie in the show focus instead on taming the diva. As the group rehearses, Zach nags Cassie: "Too high with the leg, Cassie . . . Too much plié, Cassie . . . You're late on the turn, Cassie . . . Don't pop the hip, Cassie . . . Do it again, Cassie . . . Don't pop the head, Cassie . . . ," culminating in his shouting, "you're distorting the combination, Cassie. Pull in. Cool it. Dance like everybody else."[120] Cassie ultimately reins her "unique" talents in, and she has a climactic moment in which she insists that everyone in the chorus is as "special" as she, the erstwhile star, is. Through this disavowal of her ostensibly unique talents, Cassie is integrated into the line.

Thus, by working to prevent Cassie's body from escaping from the line into the spotlight, the show suggests that she can be successfully disciplined. Paul's exotic/erotic spectacularity, however, will be more forcefully restrained after his discussions with Zach about his gender and ethnicity. For example, Zach questions why Paul, being Puerto Rican, would adopt an Italian name—to which Paul replies that he "just wanted to be somebody new. So I became Paul San Marco."[121] Paul similarly confesses that he was "terribly effeminate" and "didn't know how to be a boy." These anxieties are amplified in his climactic monologue in which he discusses how he became interested in performing, recalling that his father would take him to see musical films on 42nd Street. Aligning these early experiences of musical performance with queer desire, Paul recounts that he would "move down front and these strange men would come and sit beside me and 'play' with me."[122]

The most fascinating moment in the entire show comes when Paul breaks down after revealing how his father reacted to discovering his son performing in a drag revue, where "we were doing this Oriental number and I looked like Anna May Wong."[123] Strangely, this deeply emotional moment occurs not in a song, but in a monologue, a necessarily impoverished vehicle in a genre focused on song and dance. Crucially, then, *A Chorus Line* permits Paul—himself an ethnic "invention" who invokes his gender and sexuality—to *describe* how exotic/erotic performance, in his guise as Anna May Wong, brought him to a transformative personal experience; but it performatively denies him a platform to *enact* this experience, or to *transfer* it to the audience, in song and dance. The show demonstratively hammers home this "inability" to perform, when Paul injures himself as the group is learning a number. This is the fate of the exotic/erotic spectacular body in Zach's theatre of integration.

Fully denied the chance to dance, Paul's unruly body is removed from the stage, prompting the performers to reflect on the precariousness of their labor. Having achieved Zach's idea of integration by eliminating the exotic/erotic Paul, the show then brings to a climax its complete obsession with labor, which began in the opening montage, in which the dancers endlessly incant, "I really need this job. Please, God, I need this job. I've got to get this job."[124] Cassie, once a star, is now forced to beg Zach for work, noting that "I don't need a handout. I need a job."[125] Further, one of the show's most famous tableaux, that of the dancers holding their headshots in place of their faces, as though they were nothing but jobseekers, was a moment that Ken Mandelbaum wrote "represents the perfect blend of theme, staging concept, musical underscoring, lighting, and set design" that characterizes all of the show.[126] However, the significance of this image—paired with the famous line, "Who am I anyway? Am I my resume?"—leads to the existential crisis that accompanies Paul's demise: what is a dancer to do when there is no work? After Richie notes that he "love[s] being in this business," he concedes that "there's no security in dancing . . . no promotion and no advancement . . . there's no work anymore." Mike laments that even if you get a job, "nothin' runs forever," to which Richie adds, "then you have to start all over again—'cause the only chorus line you can depend on in this business is the one at un-em-ploy-ment!"[127] It is Diana, the dancer who celebrates her Puerto Rican heritage in "Nothing," who absolves all of these feelings of exploitation through the saccharine ballad "What I Did For Love," claiming, "I can't regret / What I did for love. . . . The gift was ours to borrow. It's as if we always knew. . . . Won't forget, can't regret / What I did for love."[128] What is this song if not Diana suggesting—and accepting—that the dancers were motivated by love? Indeed, the culmination of *A Chorus Line* is this pronouncement that the process by which dancers are made into an integrated unit—which requires exploiting and then purging the points of exotic/erotic spectacularity—is one in which the dancers willingly participate because they love to perform. As the chorus of dancers echo the word "Love" one last time, Zach begins to eliminate dancers and form his line. With Cassie tamed and Paul excised, Zach has created—as Bennett himself aimed to do—an ensemble that has ostensibly blended all the elements under his control. Here, the bodies of the show embody the form that Bennett sought to develop.

The discourse of integration is precisely a discourse of unity, of wholeness, of making "one." And of course *A Chorus Line* will close with "One," a number whose subject is never identified. The ostensible star described in "One" will certainly not be identified in the curtain call, for *A Chorus Line* prescribes an abrupt termination of the music with "no additional 'Bows' after this."[129] Having worked to excise all the various indices of the disintegrated aesthetic—the diva, the exotic/erotic logic, the applause—*A Chorus Line* is left to celebrate the virtues of "one" in its unison ensemble and in its attempts at montage, continuity, cinematic staging, and long sequences. But just as the subject of "One," though trumpeted by an endless kickline, is embodied by an absent void—so too the aesthetic of unity is precarious, a precarity that will be explored further in chapter 7.

As seen in this chapter, the musical deploys the (potentially exploited) spectacular bodies of the genre to pleasurably fracture the subjectivity of the spectator. Integration, meanwhile, works to shore up the stable subject, precisely by denying the work of these spectacular bodies. However, might those who have been exploited by the musical theatre form paradoxically desire "integration" insofar as it might hold out the promise of wholeness and coherent subjectivity? In other words, might integration paradoxically also offer up a strategy for those artists who have been relegated to the spectacular? I now move to consider two different strategies of "integration" that artists have used as they implicitly deal with the fraught ethics of the musical theatre form. First, I consider David Henry Hwang's *Flower Drum Song* in order to see whether the musical form, as it currently exists, can be used to present a more "authentic" content. Then, the focus moves to *Hamilton*, to contemplate what political possibilities are offered by the through-sung musical's resistance to bursting into song and dance. In this way, the remainder of this book will think through how artists have addressed the central ethical dilemma of musical theatre—that its progressive effects are accomplished by regressive means—and consider ways to move forward.

Miyoshi Umeki and Larry Blyden in *Flower Drum Song*. Photograph by Ralph Morse/LIFE Picture Collection via Getty Images.

# 6

# "GET OUT OF THAT DRESS"

*David Henry Hwang's* Flower Drum Song

In 1958, Rodgers and Hammerstein sought to give voice to San Francisco's Chinatown in their musical *Flower Drum Song*. While the reactions to their effort varied widely, critic Albert Johnson memorably dismissed the show's book as "veritable neo-Chinese torture," writing that "one is finally forced to recognize a major fault of this show, and that is simply the fact that it has absolutely nothing to do with Chinese-Americans."[1] However, the kind of performance that Johnson criticizes—projections of fantasies of exoticized bodies—is, as we have seen, not only endemic to the genre but also responsible for its most profound effects, possibilities, and anxieties. The genre's exploitation of these bodies can alienate spectators; Donatella Galella, for example, has written about her reactions to yellowface performance in a contemporary production of *It's a Bird . . . It's a Plane . . . It's Superman*, reporting that such performances prompt in her feelings of "indignant anger, profound sadness, and racial alienation, typically in that order."[2] This is precisely the kind of reaction that prompted Asian American playwright David Henry Hwang to revise *Flower Drum Song*, such that it might be more authentic. Hwang's project enables us to see how an artist, seeking to resist the spectacularization of bodies, might rewrite the narrative which enveloped this spectacularization.

Significantly, Hwang's project was framed simultaneously as one of bodily authenticity and as one of integration. The playbill for the Los Angeles production of Hwang's revision noted that the original "*Flower Drum Song* was less a tightly integrated, dramatic 'musical play' . . . and more a traditional musical comedy in which the songs, while delightful, didn't always have sufficient dramatic motivation or purpose."[3] By contrast, Hwang's play was "intended to be an integrated and complete musical drama."[4] Here again, claims about integration are inseparable from claims about bodies.

In this context, consider Hwang's own description of his project: "I tried to write the book that Oscar Hammerstein would have written if he were Asian-American."[5] And indeed, in so many ways Hwang seeks to accomplish the same effect that "integration" sought to secure for shows like Hammerstein's *Show Boat* and *Oklahoma!*: to stabilize the subject of musical theatre. In Hwang's pursuit to resist Orientalism and render Asian bodies whole by instating them as the subject of musical theatre, he is pursuing the long-standing goal of stable subjectivity that integration had always been deployed to secure. The question of this chapter is whether the musical's disintegrated structure precludes any such "authenticity," indeed whether "integration" functions as a mirage for Hwang as he seeks to install an Asian American subject. In other words, are the politics baked into the form, such that the musical inevitably cultivates a certain kind of relationship across bodies—or can changes in the content fundamentally change the structural work of the genre? And more broadly, can revising the content of musicals salvage ones that may become unperformable?

In chapter 5, I showed how the exotic/erotic dynamic was the trope that signaled the musical's fundamental work across bodies. Unsurprisingly, then, the deepest implication of Hwang's *Flower Drum Song* can be understood precisely by following how he negotiates this dynamic in his revision. I situate the exotic/erotic dynamic of his *Flower Drum Song* in the context of his earlier *M. Butterfly*, a play he "envisioned . . . as a musical," to see how the musical structurally *resists* the production of a stable subject—and therefore cannot fulfill Hwang's avowed goal. Indeed, discourses of identity and authenticity cannot be comprehensibly mapped onto a form whose very structure works to dissociate artistic forms, bodies, and identities. At the same time that the musical form thwarts his stated goal of authenticity, the genre's structural investments in the performance of failure present an especially potent vehicle for Hwang to critique stereotype, which is nothing if not a type of failed performance.

When Rodgers and Hammerstein's *Flower Drum Song* opened on Broadway in 1958, critics applauded the show as "colorful, tuneful, and lively," judging it to be a "good, routine musical comedy of the conventional school."[6] As the latter comment might suggest, the piece was not received as a groundbreaking masterpiece in the style of the authors' earlier *Oklahoma!* or *Carousel*—but there was a general consensus that the duo had managed, in the phrasing of Brooks Atkinson, to "make something pleasant out of something that does not have the distinction of their great works."[7] Hammerstein himself even confessed in a magazine article that the show "doesn't break any new dramaturgical ground."[8] Still, opening night critic John McClain predicted that the show would become a "big, fat Rodgers and Hammerstein hit" regardless of any lukewarm reception, and he was right: the show ran for six hundred performances before being adapted into the popular 1961 film starring Nancy Kwan.[9]

Despite this healthy run, the show never attained the canonical status of other Rodgers and Hammerstein shows, which receive countless productions year after year. While *Flower Drum Song*'s dramaturgical weaknesses did not help matters, the casting demands of the piece—with its nearly all Asian cast of characters—likely contributed to its neglect as well. These casting demands were certainly tricky in 1958, when *Time* noted that hiring the members of the *Flower Drum Song* chorus "took on a scope that recalled nothing less than the recruitment of Kublai Khan's harem," a comment with sexual overtones that portend some of the broader issues surrounding the exotic/erotic dynamic that underpins the genre.[10] The production's creative staff raided nightclubs, theatres, and high schools for talent, while librettist Joseph Fields even served as a judge at a Chinatown beauty pageant in San Francisco, hoping to find women suitable for the show. In the *New York Times Magazine,* Joanne Stang suggested that the piece was difficult to cast because of the low regard that Asian American families held for careers in performance: "the motives which impel some mothers to drag small children down the byways of Broadway, and teach them spelling by neon sign, move the Chinese not at all."[11] Stang, like others, noted the paucity of responses to advertisements seeking performers, and the "number of doors politely but effectively slammed in [the] faces of [*Flower Drum Song* company management]."[12]

Despite these allegedly herculean efforts to secure Chinese performers for the Chinese roles, the show would ultimately feature a mélange of ethnicities:[13] Japanese actresses performed the two lead roles; African American Juanita Hall, who had portrayed Bloody Mary in *South Pacific*, would take the part of Madame Liang; and Hawaiian Ed Kenney would undertake the part of Ta. While the critics noted the nature of the casting choices, they generally did not seem to care about faithfulness or authenticity, as seen for example in Walter Kerr's comment that the Chinatown of *Flower Drum Song* was "filled with wide-eyed Chinese, semi-Chinese, and not very Chinese faces—all of them pleasant."[14] Critic Richard Watts, Jr. earnestly commented that "the cast playing the minor Chinese roles even included a few Chinese," as though this were a novel accomplishment.[15] The most unexpected casting was of Caucasian actor Larry Blyden as Sammy Fong. Blyden's performance, though, was praised—with most critics seemingly indifferent to his cross-ethnic portrayal. As John McClain phrased it, Blyden "doesn't look much like a tenth-generation Chinese-American, but it doesn't really matter."[16] Actor Ed Kenney, who played the part of the older son Wang Ta, was similarly received, as in one reviewer's comment that Kenney, "said to be Hawaiian, Chinese, Irish and Swedish in his ancestry . . . fits the role of Wang Ta quite nicely if not Orientally."[17] *Herald* critic Elinor Hughes was more direct, arguing that Kenney "looks solidly unoriental, and something should be done with make-up to suggest that he is the son of Keye Luke."[18] A 1961 production at the St. Louis Municipal Opera garnered similar appraisals: critic Myles Standish wrote that the production featured the "biggest outpouring of black wigs and slanty-painted eyes since 'Chu Chin Chow,'" judging "some of the racial effects . . . a little forced" since "only three members appear to be of Chinese extraction."[19] However, while he complained that the actor playing Ta, James Stephenson, "looks about as Chinese as Paddy O'Murphy," Standish still praised Stephenson's performance. The acceptance of "bad" casting was present even at the creation of the piece: Rodgers wrote "Fan

Tan Fanny" for Canadian Anita Ellis, who was hired as, in the words of one newspaper writer, "an Occidental stand-by," or understudy, for lead actresses Miyoshi Umeki and Pat Suzuki.[20]

For some, the implausible casting of *Flower Drum Song* was consistent with the show's broader problems in representation. Stanley Eichelbaum, reviewing a 1963 production at San Francisco's Garden Court Dinner Theatre, referred to the show as a "counterfeit version of East meets West in San Francisco's Chinatown."[21] As noted at the beginning of this chapter, critic Albert Johnson memorably dismissed the show's book as "veritable neo-Chinese torture," writing that "one is finally forced to recognize a major fault of this show and that is simply the fact that it has absolutely nothing to do with Chinese-Americans."[22] The strongest criticism came from Kenneth Tynan, who rejected the 1958 show as a "stale Broadway confection wrapped up in spurious Chinese trimmings."[23] He took the authors to task, writing that "it seems to have worried neither Mr. Rodgers nor Mr. Hammerstein very much that the behavior of war-torn Pacific Islanders [in *South Pacific*] and nineteenth-century Siamese [in *The King and I*] might be slightly different from that of Chinese residents of present-day California." (This same indifference, Tynan wrote, led them to see no problem in casting Japanese actresses in the lead roles—though he was quick to note that audiences likely would not notice the difference).[24]

Even these critics who objected to the show's casting or to its representations of Asian Americans did not generally dismiss the show altogether. This ambivalence, though, was unsustainable, and by the 1980s these issues would be impossible to ignore. When the San Francisco Musical Stage Company announced its intention to revive *Flower Drum Song* in 1983, debates erupted about the representations of Asian Americans perpetuated by the musical. As Patrick Anderson noted in an article in *Asian Week*, "the company emphasized that it intended to cast Asians in the leading and supporting roles"; ultimately, Asian actors—ranging from Chinese to Japanese to Filipino performers—comprised all but a slight fraction of the company.[25] However, even as the production made significant strides in casting, sharp debates remained about the particular representations of the play itself. Fred Van Patten, the director of the production, told journalist Sheri Tan that he "didn't want to do [*Flower Drum Song*] the way it was, with its elements of racism and sexism. . . . The play needed to be reworked, songs like 'Chop Suey' left out and lots of lines which could in any way be construed as racist or sexist cut out."[26] Van Patten worked with members of the cast and the company's cultural advisor, Chen Ling-Ehr, to construct a culturally sensitive version of *Flower Drum Song*. However, these changes did not satisfy the musical's critics. In a letter to the editor of *Asian Week*, Forrest Gok and Dennis Kinoshita-Myers wrote that *Flower Drum Song* "utilizes racist and sexist images of Asian Americans and no amount of revision can change that basic premise."[27] The tensions surrounding this production made it clear that the piece might be destined for exile from the regular rotation in amateur, regional, and professional productions.

Yet the musical attracted the attention of renowned Chinese American playwright David Henry Hwang, for whom the musical held a special place. "As a child," he noted, "I wouldn't watch anything in film or on television that had Asian characters, and I couldn't articulate to myself at the time why they made me feel bad. But *Flower Drum Song* was the singular exception, because it had Asian characters—at least the younger generation—who were clearly American. It had a love story between an Asian man and an Asian woman, which you still don't much see today."[28] By the time he was in college, though, he and others "started to emphasize and discover the ways the work felt sometimes patronizing and sometimes stereotypical."[29] For Hwang, his early fascination with the piece's "revolutionary" depiction of Asian Americans would, by his college years, give way to his view of the piece as "inauthentic." However, after having seen the 1996 Broadway production of *The King and I*, which sought to sensitively depict that play's Siamese setting, Hwang was inspired to reimagine *Flower Drum Song*. Setting out with the "intention of creating a more 'authentic' *Flower Drum Song*," he ultimately wrote an entirely new book that used not a single line of the original Hammerstein-Fields libretto.[30] If the 1958 musical was faulted for its fetishized version of Chinatown, its dramaturgical weakness, and its awkward casting, Hwang's revisal would seek to address all these concerns.

Rodgers and Hammerstein's 1958 musical was itself an adaptation—if a loose one—of a novel by Chinese American writer C. Y. Lee. The original novel focuses on Wang Ta and his father, juxtaposing the son's journey as a sensitive young man finding his way in America alongside his conservative father's own negotiation of Western values. While the 1958 musical invokes some of the novel's characterization of the father—such as his disdain for banks and his affinity for traditional Chinese clothing—it ignores the novel's complex character arc, which finds him ambivalently adjusting to Western ways.[31] Indeed, the novel concludes not with Ta's romantic union, but instead with his father's acceptance of Western medicine as the solution for his chronic cough. When Ta, a student of Western medicine, initially tries to get his sick father to see germs using a microscope, the elder Wang recoils: "I am not interested in any of your foreign black arts. Take it away!"[32] However, the concluding image of the book will find him giving up his herbalist and entering the Tung Wah Hospital, where American medicine is on offer.

When musical book writers Oscar Hammerstein and Joseph Fields adapted Lee's book in 1958, they refocused the show's East-meets-West conflict through the romantic travails of Wang Ta, whose amorous interests lead him into conflict with his father's traditional ways. The show opens as Ta sings a poem he plans to recite to Linda Low, the "thoroughly Americanized Chinese girl" with whom he has fallen in love.[33] After Ta leaves, smarmy nightclub emcee Sammy Fong arrives. Knowing that Ta's father hopes his son will marry an Asian woman, Fong offers up his own "picture bride," Mei Li, who has just arrived from Hong Kong—and whom Fong doesn't want to marry. Ta's father accepts Sammy Fong's offer and plans to wed Ta and Mei Li. Meanwhile, however, Ta proposes to Linda Low, who accepts—much to the chagrin of Sammy Fong, whom she's been dating for five years. Sammy, furious at Linda's betrayal, sets a trap by inviting the Wang family to his club that night. At the Celestial Bar, everyone arrives, only to discover Linda working essentially as a burlesque dancer. Horrified, Ta's father storms out in disgust, leaving Ta humiliated. The second act is devoted to Ta's discovery that Mei Li is right for him after all.

The two librettists looted the novel for themes and images—such as the aunt's immigration classes or the playful rebelliousness of the younger son, Wang San—but reshuffled them into their own narrative structure. Perhaps the most amusing bit of reinvention occurs with Mei Li's flower drum song, which, in Hammerstein's version, famously celebrates a "hundred million miracles," including "children . . . growing," "rivers . . . flowing," and various haiku-like descriptions of sun and rain.[34] However, in the novel, the song is a dialogue between two characters played by May

Li [sic] and her father. When May Li complains that she "married a man with a flow'r drum [who's] stupid and dumb," her father replies that "Of all the women you ever did meet, My wife has the largest pair of feet."[35] The treacly modulation of insults and podiatric barbs into "A Hundred Million Miracles" bespeaks the musical's broader saccharine transformation by Hammerstein's pen.

Hwang's 2002 revision, meanwhile, retains all the songs—and the character names—but radically revises the libretto. In Hwang's version, the conflict of assimilation plays out at the Golden Pearl Theatre, a run-down Chinese opera theatre owned by Ta's father, Wang. Faced with declining revenue, Ta's father permits his son to transform the theatre into a night-club once a week. When Ta presents a number in which Linda Low begins singing in a Chinese opera costume before stripping down to a bikini and singing, the nightclub achieves greater prominence and success. This in turn attracts Madame Rita Liang, an entertainment agent who turns the Golden Pearl Theater into Club Chop Suey. Despite Wang's initial horror at the desecration of his theatre, he is impressed at the success of the nightclub and makes a swift about-face, performing at the club and chris-tening himself "Uncle Sammy Fong." The second act finds Ta struggling with, and ultimately reconciling, the uneasy balance between tradition and assimilation. While the end of the play finds his father running Club Chop Suey, Ta and Mei-li are given one night a week there to host "opera night," where they "us[e] the traditions of [Wang's] old opera days to tell new stories—of life in America."[36]

As Hwang assigns the Rodgers and Hammerstein songs to different characters and different circumstances, they undergo varying degrees of transformation. Several songs retain the same tone and intent as they did in 1958: "You Are Beautiful," "Sunday," and "Love, Look Away," for exam-ple, are all delivered earnestly, just as they were in 1958. Others receive more substantial recontextualization through new introductions: "I Enjoy Being A Girl" is now prefaced by Linda's vaguely feminist declaration that "we're not in China anymore. No more stuffing daughters down a well, or selling us into slavery. And foot binding—what was *that* all about? No, this is the land of opportunity."[37] Hwang transforms "A Hundred Million Miracles" fairly profoundly, staging it quietly before ironizing it against scenes of Mei-li's father's protest of Mao and her own travel as a refugee on a boat. "Grant Avenue," meanwhile, sets up a montage in which the Golden Pearl opera house is converted into Club Chop Suey.

Hwang's transformation of "Gliding Through My Memoree," a song performed at Club Chop Suey, reveals much about his own anxieties surrounding the disintegrated logic of musical theatre, and the means by which he will attempt to transform it. In Rodgers and Hammerstein's treatment of the sequence, "Gliding Through My Memoree" functions as a textbook case of the exotic/erotic dynamic that models the transitive chains of impersonation that fuel musical theatre. In that 1958 version, Sammy Fong, scheming to make Linda Low disreputable in the eyes of the Wang family, invites the entire family to the Celestial Bar, a "typical San Francisco Chinese night club designed to attract tourists."[38] The Wangs arrive at the nightclub just as "a chorus of girls in idealized coolie costumes" finish singing "Fan Tan Fanny." As the Wangs are being seated, Frankie, the emcee, begins performing "Gliding Through My Memoree," a song in which he plays the role of a sailor singing of all the girls he has met while on a tour of duty. As he recalls the various girls from Ireland, Sweden, and Spain, they enter, but "in spite of his descriptions of them, they are all undeniably Asian." Their performances are purposefully bad—the "Irish" girl, for example, when prompted to say something Irish, says, "Ellin go blah." The Spanish girl will offer up a similarly ironic "Olé." This ethnic and racial impersonation is a prelude to Linda's performance of "Grant Avenue," which develops into a striptease.[39] The 1958 version thus juxtaposes failed ethnic performance and burlesque, which, as seen with Brecht, raises the specter of male identification with the female body.

This number—with its exotic/erotic dynamic that foregrounds the genre's work across bodies—is precisely the kind of number that might be thought to offend Hwang. However, he does not excise the number, nor does he fundamentally alter its function. Instead, his revision merely makes explicit the fear about burlesque—that it prompts men to identify with women's bodies—before proceeding to regulate this kind of performance. In other words, he deploys the number—itself about bad ethnic and racial performance—as a moment of ("bad") *gendered* performance.

In Hwang's revision, "Gliding Through My Memoree" is presented as a montage of several performances of the song. When we first encounter the number, it is being sung by a character of Hwang's invention: Harvard, a fey costume designer who agreed to make the costumes for free if he were given a featured place on the bill. Harvard, in the words of *New York Times* reviewer Ben Brantley, is "a swishy gay costume designer and a font of the pastel humor found on sitcoms like 'Will and Grace.'"[40] When the elder Wang learns that the mayor will see the act, he is clearly uneasy with Harvard, the effeminate costume designer, portraying a "vagabond sailor" who sings of his various heterosexual fantasies and conquests. Wang confronts Rita Liang about finding "anyone more convincing to play a sailor," arguing that "that number is never going to work until you put the right actor into the part."[41] "Where is your integrity?" he demands. In Hwang's revision, integrity—which is itself about getting the right person to play the part so as to stabilize racial representation—comes in the form of excising any unauthorized male performances. This "integrity" is precisely the "integration" of the show. Indeed, the real work of Hwang's *Flower Drum Song* is in its reconception of the Asian (male) body—a reconception undertaken in relation to anxieties around men who perform in the context of musical theatre.

Hwang thus generates a plot that articulates and embodies the otherwise latent fears that we have explored in the course of this book, fears that the musical theatre form would enable male spectators to identify with women's bodies. Hwang makes this fear a quite literal element of his plot, repeatedly invoking the danger of men being effeminized in and through the act of performance. Though Harvard in particular functions as an extreme externalization of the play's—and the genre's—broader anxiety about male performance, Wang and Ta are endangered by this logic as well. While the original 1958 musical focused on female performance—as in the contrast between the innocence of Mei Li's flower drum songs and the capitalist vulgarity of Linda's nightclub act—Hwang's revision will locate anxiety in male performance: not only through Wang's uneasiness with Harvard's queer-coded performance on- and offstage but also through Wang himself in his guise as Uncle Sammy Fong. When Linda leaves the show, she complains to Harvard that "Uncle Sammy's made himself the star of this show. Before you know it, he'll be doing the stripping, too.

You should've seen this coming the night he first stole your costume," a sentiment with which Harvard concurs.[42] This threat—that Wang will imitate women stripping—is indeed the danger when men are in close proximity to burlesque performance, a danger first articulated by Brecht.

These same concerns about male performance appear in Ta's anxieties about the traditional form of Chinese opera. When we first encounter the Chinese opera, Ta is playing the female ingénue part opposite his father. For Ta, the Chinese theatre's financial troubles are related precisely to this unorthodox presentation of gender: as he tells his father, "Look, you wanna *maybe* put some butts in those seats? Why don't you find a girl to play the girl?"[43] When Mei-li emerges as a suitable replacement for Ta, he tells her, "I've been waiting all my life to get out of that dress."[44] Later in the play, Ta tells Mei-li, "Here's the kind of love I'd wish for you: when I was a kid, I used to daydream about what it'd be like to have a normal family—with a mom, and a dad who didn't walk around the house all day with his makeup on."[45]

These various fears represent classic ones about male bodies in musical theatre, but they take on an especial charge in the context of *Asian* bodies in a *Western* theatrical form. Writing about "Gliding Through My Memoree," Josephine Lee argues that Hwang "maintains the racialized comedy of this song," which she describes as Chinese American chorus girls being presented as "inadequate representations of European females."[46] Ultimately, she argues, Hwang's revision "preserves the way such novelty acts stage Asian bodies as comically incompatible with American song and dance." However, I would argue that this view of the number misapprehends its function in the show. The show in fact labors—for better or worse—to suggest the very opposite, to suggest that Asian bodies are entirely assimilable to the conventional American musical theatre form. Indeed, in reviews of the 1958 production, particular attention was drawn to the number "Don't Marry Me," in which Larry Blyden enticed Miyoshi Umeki into joining him in a soft-shoe routine. As critic Walter Kerr wrote in his opening night review:

> As the fetching rhythm of "Don't Marry Me" begins to make itself felt, [Umeki as Mei Li] is willing to follow her renegade suitor [Blyden as Sammy Fong] into a lazy investigation of light and easygoing Ameri-

can footwork. Unaccustomed as she is to soft-shoe shenanigans, and feeling a bit sheepish about her inexperience, she takes Mr. Blyden's hat into her upraised hand and waves it loyally as she joins him in a delectable double-truck. The moment . . . is a joyful experiment in innocence flirting with sophistication. It outlines, in a few graceful and grinning vaudeville gestures, nearly everything that librettists Oscar Hammerstein and Joseph Fields have to say. . . . By the time Mr. Blyden and Miss Umeki have drifted into the wings, a gentle and genial meeting of cultures has been impishly accomplished.[47]

To be sure, it is precisely this capacity to be *assimilated* into the musical form that prompts the broader anxieties about how the form deploys and acts upon Asian bodies, fears that are especially potent in the case of men, as seen in the narratives of Ta, Wang, and Harvard.

To think about these dangers of formal assimilation—particularly as they relate to Asian men—I now turn to the Hammerstein version of "Chop Suey," the song that, inspired by the "Chinese dish that the Americans invented," celebrates the diversity of America, especially in its popular culture. In the 1958 version, Madam Liang is a student of the Marina American Citizenship School. Upon winning the school's Senior Medal of Excellence, she declares, "I am proud to be both Chinese and American."[48] Wang replies that she is like chop suey, "that Chinese dish that the Americans invented," which he characterizes as "everything is in it, all mixed up." Madam Liang says that this quality is exactly what she likes about America and launches into "Chop Suey," a "virtual anthem of assimilation," to quote Steven Oxman, that celebrates the motley diversity of America and American life: "Hula Hoops and nuclear war / Doctor Salk and Zsa Zsa Gabor" stand alongside late late movies, potato chips, and weather that can range from chilly to clammy, depending on the city.[49]

Of course, as a drama about Chinatown written by Rodgers, Hammerstein, and Fields, *Flower Drum Song* is *itself* a "Chinese dish that the Americans invented," and thus the epitome of the "chop suey" aesthetic. As the song celebrates the motley assortment of things juxtaposed in American culture, it prompts perhaps the most unexpected moment of the entire 1958 show, when—amidst a joyous celebration of these collisions of American life—Ta's younger brother, Wang San, sings, "Dreaming in my Maiden-Form Bra, Dreamed I danced The Cha Cha Cha."[50] What prompts this young Chinese man—described by Ta in the play as "completely American" and depicted as thoroughly and happily assimilated—to fantasize about performing a Latin dance in a woman's undergarment?[51] It is precisely San's assimilation that produces this exotic/erotic fantasy. This remarkable moment of gendered and racial play, or mixing-up, is made possible by the related form of mixing-up offered by American popular culture—the unmooring from and reshuffling of traditions, circumstances, customs. The "assimilation" of "Chop Suey" is, among many things, the ability of Asian bodies to participate in, to be subsumed into, the disintegrated aesthetic of musical theatre, which unsettles (Asian and heterosexual male) identity.

This is precisely Hwang's anxiety, an anxiety about the role of Asian bodies in musical theatre—and about Asian male bodies in particular. In the forty years since Rodgers and Hammerstein wrote *Flower Drum Song*, the musical genre had become associated in the popular imagination with queer audiences. Further, prominent cultural depictions of musical fandom—often in the form of diva worship and drag impersonation—only amplify the gendered anxiety that governs how musical theatre is received. However, this concern would take on additional significance in the case of *Flower Drum Song*: what does it mean for Asian bodies, especially male ones, to be subjected to a Western form associated with queerness? As Hwang himself once noted, in the context of colonialism, "because they are submissive and obedient, good natives of both sexes necessarily take on 'feminine' characteristics in a colonialist world."[52] This gendered anxiety is distilled in a comment Harvard makes when he brings Wang the Uncle Sam costume that will become his performing persona: "You're on, Lady Liberty."[53] In giving Wang this campy sobriquet, Harvard implicitly recognizes and gives voice to the idea that anyone participating in the American burlesque show will be feminized by it. Despite Wang's initial disdain for Harvard's effeminized performance, Wang's enthusiastic embrace of the "Americanized" form will ultimately lead him to the same place: to assuming the effeminized place of the Asian body in a Western form. Therefore, the deployment of Asian (male) bodies in western musical theatre can be seen not only as an act of cultural appropriation by a capitalist entertainment, but also as one more operation in the pernicious castration, in the effeminization, of Asian cultures by the West. This confluence of anxieties about capitalist exploitation, Asian bodies, and the musical help to explain the dual concerns of Hwang's *Flower Drum Song*: gender and cultural appropriation.

Meanwhile, Hwang's use of the Chinese opera as a plot device does much more than merely provide a metatheatrical trope for a culture clash. The crucial element of the Chinese opera trope is in fact the *dan*, the male actor who performs as a woman. The presence of the *dan* in *Flower Drum Song* makes possible two important maneuvers: first, it links race and gender, such that traditional Asian culture is linked with the (otherwise subversive "contemporary") act of cross-dressing. By linking two forms of Asian cross-dressing—Ta's theatrical Chinese opera cross-dressing and Harvard's fey performance in everyday life—*Flower Drum Song* modernizes Asian America through the play's heterosexual conclusion, itself facilitated by the elimination of cross-dressing. Second, Ta-as-the-*dan* stands in for Hwang, who has a similarly conflicted relationship to the gendered and sexualized dimensions of musical theatre, thereby giving him a vehicle to disavow the queerness of the form, in both its deployments of, and its effects upon, the Asian male body.

Ironically, while Hwang's revision contains a thematic critique of Communist China—as seen, for example, in the play's opening image of Mei-li's father being beaten by soldiers after tearing up Mao's Little Red Book—the play's attitude toward the performance of cross-dressing actually mirrors that of the Communist party.[54] Though the figure of the *dan*, the male performer who performs as a woman, has a long and distinguished history, the People's Republic set out a general policy against cross-gender performance. In his 1964 "Speech Given at the Seminar on the Festival of Beijing Opera on Modern Themes," Premier Zhou Enlai asserted that a "man playing [a] woman will have to be gradually terminated . . . it is certain that this is *not* the direction we *encourage*."[55] Colin Mackerras reported in 1981 that Deputy Minister of Culture Hi Jinzhi suggested three rationales for discontinuing the training of *dan*: "First, people act better if portraying those of their own sex; second, it is unnatural for men to play the roles of women; and third, the custom of the male *dan* arose in a feudal society and reflects conditions no longer applicable to China."[56]

The deputy minister's invocation of the "unnatural" elements of the performance points to the incompatibility of the *dan* within a heteronormative, binary view of gender and sexuality. As Siu Leung Li writes, the *dan* "virtually embodies boundless ambiguity and anxiety concerning the transgression of gender and sexual boundary," a position echoed in attitudes in mainland China at the time that Hwang was writing.[57] One study of sexual culture in China links theatrical transvestism with the "psychological anomaly" of transvestism in daily life, observing that the cross-dressing in ancient theatre "reinforced" similar behaviors in daily life.[58] Hwang's characters give voice to the same anxieties about cross-dressing—a similarity Hwang would have known, since he invoked the Party's attitude toward cross-gender performance in his landmark 1988 play *M. Butterfly*.

In fact, Hwang's use of the Chinese opera form, one of the trademarks of his aesthetic, can be traced even beyond *M. Butterfly*, to his very first work, *F.O.B.* First staged in 1980 by lauded Japanese American actor and director Mako, the play featured actor John Lone, who had trained extensively in Peking opera while living in Hong Kong. Lone incorporated elements of the Peking opera form into the production of Hwang's play, elements which Hwang made part of his permanent script. While Hwang had never before been acquainted with Chinese opera, his encounter with Lone would prove integral to the development of his aesthetic.[59]

To better understand the significance of the Chinese opera form to Hwang's *Flower Drum Song*, I return to his most celebrated use of the device, in *M. Butterfly*, which concerns the story of Gallimard, a diplomat who pursues a relationship with—and shares government secrets with—a Chinese man whom Gallimard thought to be a woman. In her study of *Flower Drum Song*, scholar Josephine Lee writes that Hwang's musical and *M. Butterfly* both "fram[e] racial stereotypes as deliberate enactments rather than true revelations of character and . . . repurpos[e] song and themes in ways that highlight contemporary Asian American sensibilities."[60] While Lee's observation is undoubtedly true, I will argue that there are even more profound parallels between the two pieces. Crucially, Hwang conceived of both as musical theatre. Indeed, he wrote of *M. Butterfly* that he "envisioned the story as a musical."[61] Having already completed a draft, though, and fearing the amount of time it would take to pursue a musical collaboration, Hwang decided to abandon his plans to make the piece a musical. However, he wrote, "I would like to think . . . that the play has retained many of its musical roots."[62]

And the relationship between the two productions goes even further: seen in a certain light, they are in fact the same narrative—the narrative of the cross-dressing male actor—and they both use this gendered narrative to negotiate *racial* representation. However, there are crucial differences: *M. Butterfly* affirms a heteronormative conclusion precisely to draw attention to the failures of heteronormativity, while *Flower Drum Song* embraces the heteronormative conclusion; *M. Butterfly* eagerly disavows identity categories, while *Flower Drum Song* attempts to shore them up. These differences play out in a way that elucidates the politics of gendered and racial representation, the geopolitical implications of Asian performance, and the capacity of musical theatre to represent the discourses of authenticity and identity.

Hwang's *M. Butterfly* and his *Flower Drum Song* both follow the course of an actor, tracking his rehabilitation as he moves from *playing* a woman to *being* a man while a paired character moves from *being* a man to *playing* a woman—all under the specter of homosexuality. In *M. Butterfly*, the actor is Song, who, as his name would suggest, is a musical actor whom we first encounter as he sings Puccini in his guise as a woman. Song's presentation as a woman is framed as central to his identity as an actor. When Song, wearing a dress, declares to Comrade Chin, "I'm an actor," Chin asks, "Is that how come you dress like that?"[63] After Song protests that his dress is a disguise, Comrade Chin declares, "Actors, I think they're all weirdos," before admonishing him that there is no homosexuality in China.

Both plays are deeply concerned with rehabilitating the cross-dressing actor, with their plots tracing the transformation from playing a woman into "being" a man. As the plot of *M. Butterfly* advances to 1966, during the Mao regime, we find Song kneeling onstage as Comrade Chin "walks across the stage with a banner reading: 'The Actor Renounces His Decadent Profession!'"[64] In a public humiliation in which Song is beaten and soldiers "lampoon the acrobatics of the Chinese opera," Song is addressed as an "actor-oppressor" who indulged in luxuries and "engaged in the lowest perversions with China's enemies." When prompted to confess what these perversions were, Song exclaims, "I let him put it up my ass!" However, Song repents and announces that he "want[s] to serve the people," whereupon the dancers unfurl a banner: "The actor is rehabilitated!"[65] Complaining that Song's prior work serving the people was merely the action of "Homos! Homos!," Chin forces Song to track down Gallimard in France. In the next scene, Song appears dressed as a man.

Song's renunciation of acting—of performing as a woman—will be paired with Gallimard's newfound interest in performance. The final scene of *M. Butterfly* might be said to take place in three locations: in Gallimard's prison cell, where it is ostensibly set; in his mind, which generates the "world of fantasy where I first met her"; and in the theatre, which will enable, through his enactment, his return to this fantasy world. There, he notes, "I've played out the events of my life night after night, always searching for a new ending to my story. . . . Tonight I realize my search is over. That I've looked all along in the wrong place."[66] Gallimard, finding renewed faith in his own fantasy, narrates it to the audience: "I have a vision. Of the Orient. That, deep within its almond eyes, there are still women. Women willing to sacrifice themselves for the love of a man. Even a man whose love is completely without worth."[67] As he articulates his fantasy, he embodies it, donning a kimono and wig and making up his face. Here we watch not merely a role reversal—Song as a man, Gallimard as Butterfly—but indeed the *taking on* of a role. While Song may have ostensibly renounced his profession, Gallimard now becomes an actor.

I would argue that this final scene is the logical conclusion to the play's initial scene of performance, early in *M. Butterfly* when Gallimard first encounters Song. The encounter takes place at the German ambassador's house in Beijing, where Song, dressed as a woman, is performing the final scene of *Madama Butterfly*. Why, we might ask, is a Chinese opera performer, a man dressed as a woman, undertaking an aria from an Italian opera? And, in a further elaboration, why would a Chinese opera performer sing an aria from an Italian opera—itself about a Japanese woman—in the Beijing residence of the German ambassador to China? Put differently, why must Hwang invent such a scene—a scene that is essentially one of exotic/erotic performance? Nowhere does Hwang's play fulfill his goal of having "roots" in musical theatre more so than in his invention of this scene—and in the outcome to which it leads.

This exotic/erotic scene of *M. Butterfly* prepares the work of the play's final scene, when the identities dissolve, when the layers of masquerade and complex reversals of performance undermine any sense of the Real. The realms of projection in performance—as externalized in the jumbled ethnic context of Song's initial performance—are ultimately no different from those in the performance at the end of the play, when we see the complex and intertwined nature of gender, race, sexuality, and geopolitics. Gallimard's willingness to believe Song's racialized enactment of gender as "real" is made possible by—and in spite of—the realm of performance that undergirds it. Performance makes possible the layers of projection and imagination needed to realize a fantasy, while it also points out the constructed, performative nature of such fantasies. Song even poses the question explicitly: "Why, in the Peking Opera, are women's roles played by men?"[68] He ultimately answers his own question: "Because only a man knows how a woman is supposed to act." Song here gives voice to the show's broader insistence that "woman" is a collective fantasy constructed by men.[69] Both men—through the act of performance—will embody this collective fantasy.

As Hwang deploys exotic/erotic performance in *M. Butterfly* in order to dissolve the concept of identity, it might be juxtaposed with a remarkably similar moment of exotic/erotic performance in *Flower Drum Song*: "Gliding Through My Memoree," which he deploys to critique queer performance. The similarity between the two numbers makes their differences all the more significant. *M. Butterfly*, as in the classic musical theatre tradition to which its formal structure is indebted, deploys its moment of musical performance to unsettle any sense of terra firma—to reveal the usefulness of (musical) performance to unsettle the question of identity through its manifold layers of identifications and projections. Hwang's *Flower Drum Song*, however, will take its number, "Gliding," in a very different direction, using it to set up anxieties about male performance more broadly, anxieties that the play will seek to quell.

His *Flower Drum Song* attempts to resolves its anxieties predictably through its insistence that male performance can be successfully regulated. Having raised issues concerning the gendered performances of Harvard and Ta, the musical resolves itself when Ta finally assumes the "male" role in Chinese opera. As Ta rehearses a Chinese opera, Wang goes to join him; the stage directions indicate that "Ta starts to step into his familiar Maiden's role, but Wang takes that position instead," prompting Ta to exclaim, "Dad! You're really gonna play the girl?"[70] "Someone's got to," Wang replies, "if you're ever going to learn to play the man. But I refuse to wear the costume."[71] The stage directions then indicate that "Father and Son dance together." The fundamental work of this dance is to stabilize Ta—to resolve the Oedipal drama by having Ta assume his father's position—which, in this case, requires the father to assume the role of the girl, which he can disavow by refusing to dress as a woman. This stabilization of Ta—who can now play a man—and his subsequent wedding bring the play to a close. Unlike *M. Butterfly*, which celebrates the radical play of identity, *Flower Drum Song* attempts to create a positive depiction of "Asian American" identity precisely through its heteronormative narrative.

*M. Butterfly* depicts the work of musical theatre while *Flower Drum Song* depicts the work of integration; both do this through their radically different approaches to the performativity of gender and race. While *M. Butterfly* suggests that gender and race are collective fantasies embedded within networks of power, the plot of *Flower Drum Song* works to legitimize these categories as stable identities—precisely the work of the discourse of integration. These different attitudes, I argue, are functions of the radically different aims of the two works: one focusing on properly deconstructing the concept of identity, the other on shoring up a very particular, authentic (Asian American) identity.

*M. Butterfly* works to interrogate the concept of "the East" and "the Orient," with the show's engagement with gender facilitating the show's engagement with the raced body. The case of Bernard Boursicot—the diplomat whose affair inspired the show—announces nothing if not the ultimate "unknowability" of gender, and, through a transitive operation, an epistemological critique of race. *M. Butterfly* works to negate the concept of identity—as reified in the concepts of "woman" and the "Orient." At the same time that *M. Butterfly* reveals the general performativity of identity, it also indicts the very specific logic of identity performance that is enacted. As the characters of *M. Butterfly* remain trapped within these representational systems of "Orient" and "West," of "woman" and "man," the inability of these characters to escape these systems is used to illuminate the tragic dimensions of these categories, in both their arbitrariness and in their profound power. The conclusion depicts Gallimard's profound desperation to maintain the heteronormative dynamics of man and woman. Indeed, as Gallimard plunges the knife into his body, he testifies to the lethal dimensions of his inability to escape the binary representational logic. Song, too, falls prey to this pernicious and persistent logic, his domination in Armani slacks a token of what is nothing but a reversal of the previous heterosexist hierarchy. The mere reversal of their "male"-"female" relationship is one tragedy of the play.

If *M. Butterfly* thereby indicts this system of representation, *Flower Drum Song* embraces it. Ta's assumption of the male role in the theatre presages his wedding—the obvious setting to affirm not only heterosexuality but also the Asian American identity shored up thereby. *Flower Drum Song* works toward a positive conception of identity in the form of "Asian American," precisely by anchoring gender as a fixed identity in a logic of heterosexuality.

While the plot's insistence on its conclusion feels desperate, the play's heterosexual closure is similarly fraught: even though the play draws to a close with Ta's wedding, it is the peculiar romantic dance between Ta and Wang, between son and father, that haunts the play's heterosexual closure. Indeed, Wang—the character who voiced the concerns about Harvard— more generally complicates any real resolution of the play, not only through his relation to his gender but also in his relation to Asian America. The complexity of this relationship can be traced through Hwang's revision of *Flower Drum Song*'s most iconic number, "Chop Suey," a song described in *Asian Week* magazine in 1983 as having "raised the ire of many Chinese Americans as the most tasteless and racist part of the musical."[72]

While the 1958 musical treats the song as a joyous celebration of American culture—and implicitly of assimilation—Hwang deploys the song as a montage showing the club's accelerating "Americanization." The "Chop Suey" number features Wang in his Sammy Fong stage persona, fitted "in a giant take-out container . . . dressed as a chef, and backed-up by Chorus Boys who dance with giant chopsticks." The giant chopsticks are in fact bamboo poles that had been used as swords in Chinese opera at the Golden Pearl, thereby symbolizing the complete transformation of the opera house into a nightclub.[73] The "showgirls," meanwhile, are "wearing giant take-out containers which light-up from within." "And don't forget MSG," Wang adds, clarifying that it means "more—stunning—girls." Shortly after "Chop Suey," Wang proposes a "Swinging Confucius" number, peppering his speech with offensive Confucius jokes. These scenarios prompt Ta to confess, "Sometimes I think we're turning into some kind of weird Oriental minstrel show."[74]

In critiquing Club Chop Suey as a minstrel show, Ta gives voice to Hwang's broader concerns about the metaphorical—and literal—yellowface of the original. However, the conclusion of Hwang's *Flower Drum Song* does not end with the elimination of this Club Chop Suey minstrel show. If anything, the play sympathizes with Wang, as in one spoken interlude during "Chop Suey," when he looks "upward" and addresses his wife: "My dear wife in heaven: it didn't turn out quite like we'd planned, did it? You know how hard I tried. But I couldn't get them to love our opera here—I couldn't even convince our own son. And you know how much I love the sound of an audience. So can you please forgive me, that I have finally begun to find happiness?"[75] It is applause and not authenticity that governs Wang—a sentiment only confirmed by his otherwise absurd and slapdash marriage to Rita Liang, the agent who orchestrates the entire spectacle. While the play initially sets the nightclub up as a tension, it ultimately indulges its pleasures. Wang's eager submission to the demands of American entertainment parallels the way in which Hwang's interest in authenticity seems to yield before a range of formal pressures.

Meanwhile, Wang's "Chop Suey" reveals an even greater complexity surrounding the deployment of stereotype in the piece. In response to the plausible critique that parody may be ineffective in a genre predicated on moments of heightened spectacularity, Karen Wada writes that the "kaleidoscope of scantily clad chorines who don oversized Chinese takeout-food boxes . . . is not an attempt, as some critics say, to have one's cheesecake and eat it too."[76] In other words, these critics question whether Hwang's particular mode of critique—humorous caricature—can be effective. After all, isn't this precisely the same mechanism that caused the anxiety in the first place? Wada's reply to these critiques is fascinating in the context of the logic of transformation that we have seen in musical theatre:

It's done just for fun, as satire (ah, Asian women as tasty dishes), and as an homage to the classic musicals of the past. More subtly, Asians and non-Asians can appreciate moments that transcend race and yet carry a special kick because of it, like watching a great performance of a great role—as happens when Jodi Long milks the most out of her character. By playing the agent as a Chinese Ethel Merman, she honors a theatre tradition, while busting an ethnic stereotype (an Asian with chutzpah!).[77]

Crucially, Wada argues that Jodi Long's "great performance of a great role" carries an enjoyable "special kick" because it "transcends race." This transcendence seems to be accomplished precisely through the kinds of impersonations—"a Chinese Ethel Merman," "an Asian with chutzpah"—that have always done this work of transcendence in musical theatre. In other words, Wada reveals that part of the pleasure of Hwang's piece is precisely in its deployment of stereotype—itself a kind of failed performance—in song and the consequent feeling of "transcend[ing] race."

In this way, I would argue that Hwang has not challenged the fundamental disintegrating logic of musical theatre, but instead exploited it. Asian American bodies are being deployed as spectacle, but the spectacle is being orchestrated by an Asian American.[78] Hwang, like those before him, generates theatrical excitement—and "busts stereotypes" and "transcends race"—precisely through his use of other theatrical tropes, which themselves are indebted, like the "Chinese Ethel Merman," to the legacies of other moments of bursting into song.

There is thus a fundamental ambivalence at the core of Hwang's project: the narrative of Wang—which represents a mitigated acceptance of the capitalist exploitation of Asian bodies, with the trace of cross-gender performance not fully evacuated—precludes any firm resolution of Ta's narrative. And at the level of form, Hwang himself critiques cross-ethnic performance while also indulging it. Hwang's goal of an authentic Asian American musical seems, then, to be a fraught project, precisely because it works against the musical's formal tendency to unsettle identity categories. *Flower Drum Song* thus undertakes a mission that its form resists.

This is a conundrum that Hwang seems to have implicitly acknowledged. After working on the piece, he wrote, "I discovered the search for authenticity and identity to be more mysterious, complicated, and rich than I had anticipated."[79] And indeed, he seems to root this in the material and in the form itself, conceding that he "realized the authors had a very strong point of view and that it was impossible to change some things. That's because Rodgers and Hammerstein were geniuses of their craft."[80] *Flower Drum Song* ultimately revealed to him that "perhaps the riddle of identity is not one that we are ever meant to answer definitively."[81] This is precisely the lesson of musical theatre, one that challenges the very premises of his revision. Despite these failures, though, Hwang succeeds elsewhere—ironically in his embrace of the same kind of failed stereotype featured in "Gliding Through My Memoree." His Chinese take-out number, for example, deftly brings attention to the kind of spectacularization of Asian bodies that was most problematic.

As the form limits the mechanisms by which Hwang can affirm Asian America, he attempts one final strategy to secure it. In the final moments of the play, Mei-li and Ta give thanks at their wedding ceremony. After they express gratitude for their families, Mei-li gives thanks to her ancestor "whose legacy was passed down to me the day I was born *(Turns to face the audience)* in Soochow, China." Then, each member of the cast "step[s] forward to address the audience," stating "the actual place of his or her birth."[82] His other attempts to reconfigure Asian American performance having been thwarted by the form, Hwang moves to secure authenticity by recognizing the laboring bodies onstage.

In revising the 1958 musical to tell a contemporary story, Hwang clearly undertakes the same task as Ta, who himself infuses an antiquated music theatre tradition—Chinese opera—with contemporary values. The arc of Hwang's revision traces Ta's evolution from his initial embarrassment over the Chinese opera form to his ultimate embrace of it, just as Hwang himself moves from ambivalence to acceptance. As the play begins, Ta complains that "this theatre is dying." Upon hearing reports of his parents' success as Chinese opera performers, he replies, "Must've been tough to breathe life into those corny old stories," dismissing one mythic narrative as not being "credible." Mei-li, however, helps Ta to see that "to create something new, we must first love what is old."[83] Over the course of the play, he begins to see the value of the form, and ultimately remains a performer himself, "us[ing] the traditions of [his father's] old opera days to tell new stories—of life in America."[84] The "something new" that Hwang has created is precisely a new understanding of identity, something the musical creates every time it bursts into song.

Hwang's project exposes the limits of the musical form to facilitate the production of a stable identity. His *Flower Drum Song* reveals that one cannot simply populate the musical theatre form with an "authentic" content. Given that the *form* resists such work, the question becomes whether it will take a reinvention of the form itself in order to contest how the musical works across bodies. Put differently, if this transformation happens every time the musical bursts into song, what happens when the musical no longer wishes to burst into song? This is the circumstance to be confronted in chapter 7—the paradox of the through-sung musical.

"The Eccentricities of Davey Crockett" from *Ballet Ballads*. Photograph by Gjon Mili/LIFE Picture Collection via Getty Images.

# 7

## THE THROUGH-SUNG MUSICAL

*From* Ballet Ballads *to* Hamilton

In a 1929 article, music critic Robert Simon complained that most musical comedies "are not composed; they are assembled."[1] Dismissing composers who wrote with the popular song trade in mind, and producers who interpolated numbers by other tunesmiths into shows, Simon argued that composer Jerome Kern was "virtually the only one who looks on his score as an entity."[2] Believing Kern already to have transcended many of the limitations of musical comedy, Simon envisioned the ultimate horizon for Kern's talent, arguing that "if theatrical circumstances permitted, [Kern] would dispense entirely with dialogue." For Simon, the elevation of musical theatre would involve eliminating dialogue, concentrating authorial control in Kern alone, the composer who himself saw his score as an "entity," as an integral whole. As dialogue is eliminated, which began to occur not long after Kern's death in 1945, the musical moves toward a through-sung aesthetic, the emergence of which challenges the disintegrated aesthetic—an aesthetic that Simon dismisses as "'book and music' entertainment"—that has been explored through the course of this book. As seen in the preceding chapters, the disintegrated logic is fundamentally about transference across different kinds of bodies. This chapter will show

how the through-sung musical, with its emphasis on authorial control, eschews the genre's aesthetic of failure, thematizing not transference across different bodies but the distillation of disparate energies into a single body. By examining the writings of Andrew Lloyd Webber and the works of Jerome Moross and John Latouche, I articulate the relationship of the through-sung musical to the aesthetic of disintegration that we have been charting through the course of this book. I conclude by thinking about *Hamilton* in the context of whether the bodily politics of the through-sung genre might provide a way of resolving the ethical dilemma regarding the genre's potential exploitation of bodies.

The through-sung aesthetic might be said to have come into prominence with the premiere of Andrew Lloyd Webber's *Joseph and the Amazing Technicolor Dreamcoat*, the first of several through-sung musicals that would dominate Broadway in the 1970s and 1980s. Commissioned by choir director Alan Doggett to compose a cantata for a student concert at St. Paul's Preparatory School in London, Lloyd Webber collaborated with Tim Rice on a musical piece that told the Biblical story of Joseph. Lloyd Webber recounted that his "trademark" through-sung aesthetic emerged "unwittingly" out of the necessity of writing for schoolchildren, as he required them to sing continuously in an "attempt to write music that would never allow its kid performers to get bored."[3] After following *Joseph* with the similarly through-sung *Jesus Christ Superstar*, Lloyd Webber briefly experimented with writing a book musical, securing Alan Ayckbourn to write the book for a musical based on the Jeeves stories of P. G. Wodehouse. However, Ayckbourn had little facility with musical theatre, telling reporters, "I've tried with *Jeeves* at least to make it dramatically viable . . . I said to Andrew, 'The only thing I can do is to write a book I could put on the stage if your music didn't happen to arrive in time. I've just got to write something that will work regardless and hope the music comes as a bonus.'"[4] Many attribute the failure of *Jeeves* to Ayckbourne's book, and as Michael Walsh notes, this lack of control surrounding the narrative drove the composer even further from the idea of a conventional book show. As Lloyd Webber told Mark Steyn, "I did learn that, frankly, the book musical, in the sense of dialogue interrupting the musical line, is not for me."[5] However, it was not merely Ayckbourne's inexperience that soured the composer on the classic structure of musical theatre.

Lloyd Webber's disinclination to write conventional book musicals stemmed precisely from his dissatisfaction with the interruptive aesthetic of musical theatre: he once noted that he prefers musicals "where the music and words can get uninterrupted attention without jolts from one style to another."[6] In the same piece, he complained of a "snag with the musical," referring to "that awkward moment when you see the conductor raising his baton and the orchestra lurching into life during the dialogue which indicates the impending approach of music."[7] His through-composed musicals eliminated this allegedly awkward moment of "bursting into song," a moment his description tellingly embodies in the conductor—the stand-in for the composer—who, while powerful, must often cede control of the stage to the actors who alone give voice to the playwright. Lloyd Webber would remedy what he called "that ghastly moment when the violins are lifted and the dialogue stops" precisely by never letting those violins down.[8]

Lloyd Webber's anxiety is clearly one regarding authorial control. He noted that once he and Rice agreed on a general plot and song placement, "it was down to [Lloyd Webber, the composer] to control the rhythm of the piece."[9] Elsewhere, he wrote that the "most important thing for the composer is to be able to control the piece from A to B. If you have any dialogue, no matter how brilliant, that interrupts the flow, it means the composer is not in the driver's seat."[10] This rhetoric recurs in his thought, as in his comment years later that "the fact that there was no spoken dialogue [in *Joseph*] meant that I was in the driving seat."[11] Lloyd Webber felt that this control was a control not only over the construction of the piece but also over the audience: discussing the balcony scene in *Evita*, he wrote, "I knew that its construction used music as manipulatively as you can get, but that's what a through-composed score can do and I felt good about it."[12]

In Lloyd Webber's vision, authorial control meant that the composer was responsible for the flow "from A to B"—in other words, responsible for *narrative* motion. While composers traditionally orchestrated the realm of *spectacle*, Lloyd Webber sought to use music throughout a piece, thereby dissolving the binary of narrative and musical spectacle. In his view, he had unlimited purview to tell the *story*, without the jarring interruptions that marked the coming and going of spectacular musical numbers. The genre of "megamusicals" written or inspired by Lloyd Webber thus have an extremely complicated relationship to spectacle. While they sought to reconfigure spectacle—and indeed eliminated its traditional marker of "bursting into song and dance"—they were often criticized precisely for their emphasis on spectacle. However, they trafficked in spectacle no more nor less than their predecessors. The crucial difference is that these shows relied less on bodies—and more on scenery—to mark the spectacular order.[13] The surfeit of lavish scenery, though, did nothing to affect the through-sung musical's emphasis on musical narrative, which precludes the profound ruptures of the traditional musical form that prompt new bodily relationships. By avoiding the moment of "bursting into song and dance" that ushers in the spectacular order, Lloyd Webber dismisses the genre's trademark disintegrated aesthetic, its emphasis on failure, and with it the genre's profound capacities for transformation.

When Lloyd Webber told Mark Steyn that "the book musical . . . is not for me," he added, "Whether you like it or not, this *is* opera." Here, Lloyd Webber perceptively distinguishes his genre of work from the genre of musical theatre. Of course, there are many subspecies of opera, and not all completely eliminate dialogue, so his use of the term might provoke taxonomic quibbles. He is certainly right, though, in calling attention to the distinctions between conventional musical theatre and his genre of through-sung musical theatre. However, Lloyd Webber was not the first composer to experiment with the through-sung aesthetic in musical theatre, nor the first to loosely term it opera.

Twenty years before Lloyd Webber would write *Joseph*, composer Jerome Moross and lyricist John Latouche premiered two extraordinarily experimental pieces, *Ballet Ballads* (1948) and *The Golden Apple* (1954). In an interview with John Caps, Moross called *The Golden Apple* "pure opera for Broadway. It's completely sung through and no dialogue. And it worked, it ran on- and off-Broadway for five months, which is, you know, kind of unusual for an opera."[14] A deeper examination of these two groundbreaking shows can help us to think through the relationship of the through-sung aesthetic to the musical's traditional cultivation of relationships across bodies.

An attempt to rework the Homeric epics into a decidedly American vernacular, *The Golden Apple* was produced by Norris Houghton's and T. Edward Hambleton's Phoenix Theatre, a non-profit theatre company that mounted creative theatrical pieces that were unlikely candidates for commercial production. In Moross and Latouche's retelling, Helen becomes a town squeeze kidnapped by traveling salesman Paris, who absconds with her in his hot air balloon. Ulysses and his men, freshly back from the Spanish-American War, go out in search of Helen, their travels helping them appreciate anew the joys of home.

When the piece was initially produced in 1954, both Moross and Latouche identified the structure of their "integrated" work as a modulation of musical comedy, as opposed to opera. Latouche wrote that while Moross through-composed the piece so as to keep the "episodic" script from seeming "choppy," "the result is completely different from such forms as opera and ballet. It develops out of musical comedy, consisting of what can be called a series of interlocking production numbers."[15] Similarly describing *The Golden Apple* as "a series of continuous musical-comedy production numbers," Moross wrote in 1954 that he and Latouche shared "an old quest, the marriage of words, music and movement to tell a story on the stage."[16] While he wrote that their approach was to "use the best in musical comedy, opera and ballet forms with gay abandon," Moross noted that "our starting point had always been from the 'musical comedy' rather than the 'operatic' theatre."[17]

However, despite their early desire to associate their piece with musical comedy—a desire that might have been motivated by a sociological desire not to repel audiences through an association with the highbrow term "opera"—Moross went on years later to distance himself, and *The Golden Apple*, from the world of musical theatre. During an interview with Moross in 1970, Paul Snook invoked the highbrow provenance of *The Golden Apple*, referring to it as "the only American musical comedy that's been written on a Guggenheim fellowship," to which Moross responded that he "would hardly call it a musical comedy." Snook agreed, pronouncing it "a new genre, really," prompting Moross to discuss this "new genre":

Yeah . . . I wanted to fool around with the opera form. I love to fool around with the opera form. I think it's a great form and I've done a great deal of experimenting with it. And the idea was to do a Broadway piece using idioms that would not push the audience out, you know . . . make them feel part of it . . . and still utilize the opera form to present our ideas on war and peace, on love, on hate, good and evil and all the rest of it . . . and actually write an opera for Broadway, and we did.[18]

Despite their ambivalence about the terms "musical comedy" and "opera," Moross and Latouche were clear that the aesthetic of *The Golden Apple* had clearly emerged from their earlier landmark piece, *Ballet Ballads*. Calling *Ballet Ballads* "an attempt at a new approach to musical theatre," Moross referred to *The Golden Apple* as a "full-length piece expanding the 'Ballet Ballads' pattern. Every word in it, you know, is sung, and the score runs the gamut of American musical styles."[19] Meanwhile, Latouche, in the introduction to the published libretto, calls *The Golden Apple* "a musical in the manner of our *Ballet Ballads*, developing the style of those pieces into a framework that could tell a unified story."[20] To understand the significance of *The Golden Apple* and Moross's through-composed aesthetic, I move now to look more closely at *Ballet Ballads* and its unique challenge to the disintegrated aesthetic.

*Ballet Ballads* would eventually consist of a series of three pieces based on folk tales or legends: "Susanna and the Elders," "Willie the Weeper," and "The Eccentricities of Davey Crockett." While the first episode, "Susanna and the Elders," was composed by 1940,[21] Latouche was then drafted into the Navy, and, as he put it, "the war came and bore me away to the murky wilds of the Belgian Congo. . . . Every now and then, during an elephant hunt, or lounging on a termite heap in the Ituri, I would think of some way to alternate action by dance or song, scribble a note and forget it."[22] The show had taken shape by 1944, and it was first produced in 1948 by New York's Experimental Theatre company, an early off-Broadway company helmed by Cheryl Crawford. Crawford's production was such a rousing success that, according to newspaper reports, five producers were interested in transferring the production to a Broadway theatre. Ultimately, Alfred Stern and T. Edward Hambleton offered the money to mount the production, and during the very week that *Oklahoma!* finally closed, *Ballet Ballads* opened at the Music Box.[23]

As is often the case when considering adventurous pieces, the critics had a difficult time categorizing the show. As one reviewer put it, "Watching 'Ballet Ballads' is a lot easier than defining it. . . . But however you define their finished product, librettist John Latouche and composer Jerome Moross have successfully compressed song, dancing, and legend into a sly and racy bit of theatre."[24] For Richard Watts, Jr., the show was "a happy amalgamation of the gayest features of ballet, music, and folk drama."[25] Reviewers characterized the show as "acted-danced-sung interludes,"[26] "a combination of song and dance which is ingratiating and refreshing,"[27] and "three lengthy pieces of popular Americana that blend song, dance, and pantomime."[28] Others, meanwhile, emphasized the terpsichorean component of the piece by referring to *Ballet Ballads* as "dancing operas,"[29] "dance-dramas,"[30] or "dance narratives."[31]

However awkward these characterizations might have been, though, nearly every review hailed the unprecedented interrelationship—the alleged integration—of the various components of *Ballet Ballads*. *New York Post* critic Richard Watts, Jr., wrote that "all the talents involved in the enterprise have combined their achievements so cooperatively that the result is a winning amalgamation of three acts of the theatre into a finely integrated whole."[32] Dance critic Frances Herridge echoed Watts, arguing that *Ballet Ballads* is "an attempt to revive the ancient lyric theatre in modern idiom, to blend singing, dancing, acting, and decor into an integral art form, so that each is necessary to the other."[33] For Walter Terry, *Ballet Ballads* was "the first, or at least the most successful, experiment in fusing not two but three theatrical arts and maintaining that fusion, or at the minimum a concept of fusion, throughout an entire production."[34] Terry concluded his appraisal by noting that *Ballet Ballads* "has given fresh focus to the concept of theater-art synthesis." Meanwhile, music critic Miles Kastendieck wrote that "as a synthesis of story, song, and dance, 'Ballet Ballads' . . . is a crystallization of something in the making for almost a quarter of a century—a new art form American in creation."[35]

This was certainly what Moross and Latouche had hoped to do. Just after the piece had opened, librettist Latouche wrote in the *New York Times*: "our intention was to blend several elements of the American theatrical, dance and musical heritage into a pattern adapted to the contemporary stage."[36] Moross would later call the show an attempt at a "new kind of amalgam of singing and dancing," referring in the same note to a "fusion."[37] When Paul Snook interviewed Moross in 1970, Snook mentioned *Ballet Ballads* and said that "[people] talk a lot about the integrated musical comedy today but you were integrating long before it became fashionable."[38] Moross replied that "as a matter of fact, the *Ballet Ballads* started the whole talk about integration. They were a seven day wonder, and while their whole life in New York lasted eight weeks, it was, for the intellectuals in the city, very influential. And every time I go to a show now, I see something which developed out of *Ballet Ballads*."

Of course, *Ballet Ballads* did not start "the whole talk about integration"—far from it. While *Ballet Ballads* was merely the latest in a long line of shows to claim this revolutionary mantle, I wish to claim that *Ballet Ballads* is nevertheless a revolutionary show. The powerful effect of integration that audiences and critics felt in the show relates precisely to its unique *manipulation* of the disintegrated logic of musical theatre explored in the previous chapters. The disintegrated musical structure exists in two related registers: the structural disintegration of the narrative by song and dance, and the disintegrating psychic relationships across the various bodies that perform and enjoy musical theatre. *Ballet Ballads* creates a radical revision of this structure by ultimately eliminating the break between song and dance, presenting a through-composed work that thematizes not relationships across different bodies, but instead the unification and concentration of different bodies into one. *Ballet Ballads* thus sought to foreclose all of the musical's points of rupture—narratological and bodily—to present a piece that lived up to its creators' ambition to create a "fusion."

The narrative elements of *Ballet Ballads* were fused through the creators' idiosyncratic approaches to the eruption of song and dance. By eliminating the musical's trademark sources of failure—its divisions between speech and song—Moross saw himself as writing a kind of hybrid genre that he imagined would "make the theater operatic."[39] While there were no independent "numbers" of which to speak, *Ballet Ballads* was ultimately a mosaic of songs. This through-sung structure was very much a conscious choice for Moross, who, in reference to another project, wrote to Latouche in 1947 that he "would prefer it, of course, if the whole thing were sung. The alternation of singing and speaking always seems doubly artificial."[40]

The eruptive element of dance, too, was eliminated. Rather than featuring danced interludes, *Ballet Ballads* was through-choreographed, with continuous movement and dance throughout the piece. The movement was universally acclaimed, with reviewer Walter Terry ecstatically announcing that "'Ballet Ballads' has been a long time coming. Ever since Agnes de Mille created the now-historical dances for 'Oklahoma!' our theatre has been reaching toward a form which might be described as choreographed folk opera."[41] While noting that a few shows had made achievements in this regard, he wrote that "the Experimental Theater's new production has come closest to arriving at the desired integration of drama, song and dance." Miles Kastendieck similarly hailed *Ballet Ballads* with the claim that "ever since ballet first broke into the Broadway show, it has been groping for the right outlet. This is it. As a synthesis of story, song, and dance, *Ballet Ballads* provides both entertainment and art in the same package."[42] Walter Terry went on to remark that Hanya Holm "has done a magnificent job of choreography, highlighting dance when action was required and subduing movement when it was right for song or acting to take the lead."[43] Richard Watts, too, lauded the ways in which *Ballet Ballads* had finally created a kind of integration through its unique deployment of dance: "I suppose," Watts wrote,

> that Jerome Robbins' Keystone Comedy number in "High Button Shoes" has done more than anything else, including the pioneering work of Agnes de Mille in "Oklahoma!" to make ballet fit comfortably into musical comedy. But it required "Ballet Ballads" to provide a form of stage entertainment in which the ballet would be neither an intrusion nor an interlude but an authentically component part of a complete amalgamation of drama, dance and music in a new form of American art.[44]

This sense that dance—and music—functioned as "neither an intrusion nor an interlude" stood in direct opposition, of course, to the genre's constitutive sense that, at any moment, performers could burst into song and dance. This effect of "neither an intrusion nor an interlude"—"integration" by another name—is an effect that *Ballet Ballads* cultivates through its unique formal structure.

As the disintegrated structure of conventional musical theatre matched narrative failure with bodily failure, the ostensibly "integrated" form of *Ballet Ballads* paired its narrative fusion with the semblance of a bodily one. If disintegration is the affect produced "across bodies," *Ballet Ballads* pursues instead an affect produced by the converse: the concretizing and focusing of disparate bodily energies into a coherent, discrete unit. *Ballet Ballads*, in fact, thematized this very process in the way that it deployed its performers across the arc of the show. Indeed, while the show ostensibly consisted of three independent one-acts, there was actually a powerful formal arc uniting the three episodes and providing a logic of its own. Thus, we might return to critic Richard Watts's comment that "all the talents involved in the enterprise have combined their achievements so cooperatively that the result is a winning amalgamation of three acts of the theatre into a finely integrated whole."[45] The three acts have no shared subject matter; their integration into a whole comes precisely through the combinations of the "talents" and "achievements"—the singing, dancing, and acting—of the various artists who brought it to life. As the authors explained in a production note,

> The BALLET BALLADS were produced in New York as dance-operas; they were intended to fuse the arts of text, music, and dance into a new dramatic unity. When performed in sequence, the fusion takes place gradually, proceeding from SUSANNA AND THE ELDERS, which suggests the typical choral-ballet until the chorus is drawn into the action, to the ECCENTRICITIES OF DAVEY CROCKETT, where the action and characters move independently of logical space and time.[46]

The piece begins with "Susanna and the Elders," in which the title character is split, portrayed by two performers—a singer and a dancer. Meanwhile, the chorus tentatively begins to function as actors in the drama. As Latouche observed, "at first, the congregation are spectators, with certain members acting out the text with the improvised solemnity of a Sunday school pageant. Gradually, however, their collective imagination transforms them into the children of Israel, and they come downstage to participate in the action."[47] The title character of the second piece, "Willie the Weeper," is also portrayed by two performers, although Latouche writes that at certain points, the singing Willie and the dancing Willie sync up and become fused. As for the chorus in this piece, "the singers and dancers are freely intermingled," and are therefore increasingly portrayed as individual characters.[48] According to Latouche, "'The Eccentricities of Davey Crockett' integrates the use of song and dance still further. Here the chorus arbitrarily portrays frontiersmen, the singing walls of a house, trees, Congressmen, and whatever else is necessary; the dancers communicate the plot; Davey and his wife both sing and dance their roles. In this final piece there is a completely free use of all the theatrical elements. . . . ."[49]

Thus, *Ballet Ballads*, while consisting of three otherwise independent acts, creates a formal arc that begins with a segregation of the arts—as embodied in the separate singing and dancing choruses—and climaxes with their integration, as each chorus member both sings and dances. The show similarly thematizes this "integration" in its portrayal of the main characters. Susanna is portrayed by a singer as well as a dancer, as is Willie—but in Willie's case, the two different Willies, each representing a different artistic faculty, begin to merge at points. This tentative merging will reach its full potential in the third act, when Davey essentially functions as a "triple threat," a performer who can sing, dance, and act with equal facility.

Given that this arc of integration culminates in Davey's unification, it is unsurprising that critics felt this last act of the show to be particularly successful. Indeed, several seemed to discern the uniquely "integrated" quality of the "Davey Crockett" piece, with Walter Terry noting that "in 'The Eccentricities of Davey Crockett,' the most successful of the three works, one was rarely aware of switches from one medium of theater expression to another. Transitions were smooth, for a phrase of acting, a gesture expanded logically into dance or the lift of a dance movement extended itself into song."[50] He concluded by arguing that "'The Eccentricities of Davey Crockett' had integrity of form, a new form in which three major arts united to create compelling theatre." Thus, the integration of the piece was embodied in Davey's "integrity," in his being an integral whole in whom the component arts have been united. Elsewhere, Robert Garland tried to pin down the source of Davey's charm, suggesting that "in 'The Eccentricities of Davey Crockett' . . . there's freshness, excitement, and Americanism that none of the others so overwhelmingly achieves. Much of these attributes are to be credited to the acting-dancing-singing abilities of Mr. Lawrie, who's as right as right in the exacting title role."[51] *Sun* critic Irving Kolodin pronounced that "the best of the works . . . unquestioningly [is] 'Davey Crockett,'" later noting that it "plainly has the happiest balance" of the three acts.[52] Looking back at the Experimental Theatre's 1948 season, *Brooklyn Eagle* critic George Currie noted that the production of *Ballet Ballads* "added a tasty touch of interest and really introduced something pretty close to the sensational in 'The Eccentricities of Davey Crockett.'"[53] The astute perception that Davey was the most "integrated" of the three pieces no doubt stems from the fact that this piece thematized the integration of the arts in the single body of its titular character.

The effect of integration in *Ballet Ballads* is to be found in the manner by which the show reconceived how the genre deployed the bodies of its performers. Musical theatre had long indulged a series of conventions that separated singers and dancers into a singing chorus and a dancing chorus—and as one chorus gave way to the other, the audience had to imaginatively conjure any continuity between these two types of performance. Similar conventions held for de Mille's celebrated dream ballet in *Oklahoma!*, which relied on dancers—a "Dream Laurey," "Dream Curly," and "Dream Jud"—to dance where their narrative counterparts had left off.[54] However, *Ballet Ballads* structurally presented the fusing, the melding, the unifying of these discrete faculties into the body of a single performer—into what we would now call "triple threats." As Gwen Verdon would recall years later, "It used to be that a show needed eight dancers and eight singers. Today a performer in a musical has to be multifaceted, able to dance, sing, and act as well."[55]

The uniqueness of *Ballet Ballads* in the history of integration—and of the triple threat—can be found in a 1948 column by Mildred Norton about the show, in which she writes that

> the unusual inter-relation of the staging elements . . . helped to weld the show into a solid unit. Moross had long objected to the immobility of the usual chorus, so the "ballad" singers were taught to move as part of the dancing, although their chores were naturally less demanding. The first time a line of singers was asked to take a "fall," two of the members dislocated their knee-caps but they persevered until now

the entire ensemble appears to be both singing and dancing as an indivisible unit. This increased mobility, Moross feels, is likely to be one of the major features of the future's footlight entertainment.[56]

Norton's comment that the company, now singing *and* dancing, is an *indivisible* unit perceptively identifies the true locus of integration: the bodies in which all the arts have become unified. Meanwhile, her last line testifies to the perceived uniqueness of this presentation, a uniqueness also noted in William Hawkins's comment that *Ballet Ballads* is "demanding work for the ensemble as well as the principals, because they are expected to act, sing and dance, often all at the same time."[57]

The critics were clearly apprehending what the writers had intended. In Paul Snook's 1970 interview with Moross, the composer emphasized this "integrated" quality of the performers, telling Snook that "the *Ballet Ballads* were an attempt by John Latouche and myself to really create a multimedia, or mixture, so that you wouldn't know who were the dancers, who were the singers. The singers had to move and mix with the dancers." "The idea," he continued, "was to do a stage work in which the whole story was told through dance and song but so mixed up that it was not the usual pattern of singers at the side."[58] Moross's remark subtly but correctly elides the artistic "media" and the bodies, suggesting that the integrated "multimedia" that he wishes to make is precisely a fusion of *bodies.*[59]

Just as the disintegrated aesthetic is cultivated simultaneously in the narrative structure of a piece and in the arrangements of bodies that it engenders, Moross and Latouche created in *Ballet Ballads* a unique form that aims to do precisely the opposite: it eliminates the divisions among singing, speaking, and dancing, both in the piece and *perforce in the bodies* of its performers. While Moross and Latouche were extraordinary stylists who, by dint of their unusual geniuses, remain idiosyncrasies on Broadway, their explorations in the through-sung aesthetic powerfully illuminate the bodily politics of the through-sung aesthetic. Their exploration of these bodily politics can prove useful in regards to the ethical dilemma presented in this book, a dilemma regarding the potential exploitation of the spectacular bodies that facilitate psychic projection across bodies every time the musical bursts into song. Given that the through-sung musical never bursts into song and does not pursue the same kind of work across bodies, might it provide a strategy for escaping this dilemma? This is precisely one of the issues at stake in Lin-Manuel Miranda's *Hamilton*.

Perhaps it is fitting that *Hamilton*, a musical about colonial America, should make something British its own—with a bit of help by way of the French. And so it is that the show, according to its creator Lin-Manuel Miranda, was deeply influenced by the 1985 musical *Les Misérables*, perhaps the most popular and venerable of the through-sung works to appear in Lloyd Webber's wake. Miranda told an interviewer that "the things that you can see in *Hamilton* that are affecting people are also present in *Les Mis*," citing its epic scope and its dark colors. Just as Lloyd Webber admired the capacity of the through-sung musical to "manipulate" the audience's emotion, Miranda called *Les Miserables* "a masterclass in how to use themes in order to take a short circuit to someone's tear duct or heart or gut."[60] It is on this ground that Lloyd Webber, *Les Miserables*, and *Hamilton* meet: they share a through-sung structure that effectively functions as a medium of authorial control.

To think about this issue of control, we might look at *Hamilton: The Revolution*, the authorized "Hamiltome" that includes the script of the show as well as a series of behind-the-scenes vignettes, in which author Jeremy McCarter writes that

> . . . Lin proposed that I write this book. It tells the stories of two revolutions. There's the American Revolution of the 18th century, which flares to life in Lin's libretto . . . .There's also the revolution of the show itself: a musical that changes the way that Broadway sounds, that alters who gets to tell the story of our founding, that lets us glimpse the new, more diverse America rushing our way.[61]

The book follows through on its promise to link the two "revolutions." Sometimes, it does so movingly—as, for example, when McCarter observes that creator Lin-Manuel Miranda "realized that if Eliza's struggle was the element of Hamilton's story that had inspired him the most, then the show itself was a part of her legacy. To borrow an image from his script, she had planted seeds in a garden that she didn't get to see, and one of them turned out to be *Hamilton*."[62] At other moments, the comparison between the two revolutions feels forced or even absurd, as, for example, when the meeting among Hamilton, James Madison, and Thomas Jefferson to decide the location of the capital of the United States is compared to the meeting in which the *Hamilton* producers decided to transfer the production uptown from the Public Theater to Broadway: "In a series of meetings in the days leading up to the press conference, a handful of people—Lin, Tommy, Jeffrey, and Oskar—had made big decisions in a little room."[63]

Perhaps the most significant analogy comes when McCarter notes that both Hamilton the man, and *Hamilton* the show, sought to achieve a kind of integration. McCarter suggests that Alexander Hamilton would have approved of the show, since, to quote Henry Cabot Lodge, "the dominant purpose of Hamilton's life was the creation of a national sentiment, and thereby the making of a great and powerful nation from the discordant elements furnished by thirteen jarring States."[64] The book similarly revels in the degree to which *Hamilton* has ostensibly unified the potentially discordant and jarring elements of theatrical production. Musing about a change made during the creative process, McCarter observes that "the rewrite . . . illustrates what all those creative impulses, all those pragmatic experiments, were trying to achieve: to ensure that every single element in the show, at every moment, was serving The Story," the capitalization suggesting the deference required to the all-important narrative.[65] This sentiment was echoed by journalist Jeff MacGregor, who wrote that *Hamilton* "is so good largely because of Lin-Manuel Miranda. His secret is that he writes in service of character, to advance story."[66] Later, McCarter notes that "Lin and his collaborators needed the creativity to generate thousands of ideas and the pragmatism to test them all—both of which are key Hamiltonian virtues. But the show only works because they possessed a quality that their subject lacked: self-restraint. Again and again they sacrificed little pleasures (a beautiful melody, a big laugh) in pursuit of an overarching goal."[67] MacGregor surmises that "maybe Miranda's genius lies in his willingness not to *behave* like a genius—an outlier, a singularity—but rather to dissolve himself into the group, the collective in which ideas and improvements are argued on their merits."[68]

In detailing the cooperation required to pull off a particular moment, McCarter explains, "it took extraordinary integration, many veteran artists working in harmony."⁶⁹ However, it is worth noting that despite the many obviously remarkable collaborations that did exist in the production, one collaboration failed during the development of the piece. When *Hamilton* was in its infancy, Miranda recalled, they experimented with a first act that contained dialogue between songs, but "found that if you start with our opening number, you can't go back to speech. The ball is just thrown too high in the air."⁷⁰ As McCarter writes, Miranda and director Tommy Kail had "assumed that they would need spoken dialogue to connect the songs . . . Tommy asked a playwright they both respected enormously to write a libretto. But a single reading with a few scenes of spoken dialogue . . . convinced them that . . . everyday speech couldn't sustain the energy of the rapped lyrics. That meant that all of the writing duties would fall to Lin."⁷¹ This decision, McCarter writes, was "an important break with precedent . . . the most important, maybe, in the entire development of the show."⁷² In deciding to dismiss the librettist, Miranda and Kail thus decided that their show would never burst into song. As Rebecca Mead noted in the *New Yorker*, the show "is sung-through, as in most operas, so there is never a sense of a character shifting register into rap."⁷³

In other words, *Hamilton* does not participate in the musical's logic of stopping the show, a logic that structurally facilitates a dizzying series of identifications with bodies as the musical relentlessly oscillates between narrative and spectacular modes. Instead, just as *Ballet Ballads* cultivated its effect of integration by uniting all of the arts within the body of a single performer, I would argue that the powerful effect of integration in *Hamilton* comes not from "many artists working in harmony," as McCarter suggests, but instead through its very opposite: a single body, that of its deified creator, Lin-Manuel Miranda. As McCarter notes, "*Hamilton* is Lin's show to an extent that almost no Broadway musical in living memory is one person's show: idea, story, music, lyrics, lead performance."⁷⁴ Discussing collaboration, Miranda noted that musical theatre "is not a singular art form—it's 12 art forms smashed together . . . [collaboration is] enormously gratifying because you can build things so much bigger than yourself."⁷⁵ However, in abandoning the collaboration with the playwright, *Hamilton* actually became all the more about Miranda himself.

In replacing the book writer with himself—indeed, with his own body—Miranda exercises an extreme form of authorial control, taking Andrew

Lloyd Webber's anxieties to their logical conclusion. By regulating not merely the narrative but indeed the bodies that bring it to life onstage, Miranda mirrors the show itself, which is about nothing if not narrative control. This explains the power of *Hamilton*'s closing scene, which concludes a show that is dramaturgically quite episodic, following Hamilton's life from one situation to the next, with no particular thematic unity or singular arc. The final scene—which concerns "who lives, who dies, who tells your story"—derives its power not from any climactic resolution of the (virtually non-existent) plot, but instead from its striking confluence with *Hamilton*'s structural work of reconfiguring the narrative bodies of the genre through the show's most visible and most discussed feature: its casting conceit.[76] As the producers noted, "it is essential to the storytelling of *Hamilton* that the principal roles, which were written for nonwhite characters (excepting King George), be performed by nonwhite actors."[77] The effect of this has been widely noted: *Rolling Stone* journalist Mark Binelli referred to the "almost indescribable power in seeing the Founders . . . portrayed by a young, multiracial cast,"[78] and Helen Lewis, writing in *The New Statesman*, referred to the casting choices as the show's "sublime" "political act."[79]

Thus, when Eliza says, "I put myself back in the narrative," she might as well be referring to the performers' own relationship to the act of narration. Ben Brantley perceptively noted in his opening night review that "*Hamilton* is, among other things, about who owns history, who gets to be in charge of the narrative," noting that the young performers demonstrate that they have "every right to be in charge of the story here."[80] I would argue that this being "in charge of the story" refers not merely to the Revolutionary War narrative at hand, but to a much more general *narrative* capacity in the genre. Fascinatingly, the performers have even echoed Eliza's comment as they reflected on their own relationship to the material as storytellers: cast member Leslie Odom Jr., for example, who portrayed Aaron Burr, commented, "We are saying we have a right to tell [the story of America's creation] too."[81] And Miranda makes the connection all too explicit when he was asked by an interviewer about when the original cast would leave the show: "It was a year contract. So I don't know who's staying and who's going. Who tells our story [*laughs*]."[82]

Miranda's comment, discussing the storytelling in relation to contractual issues of labor, mirrors broader concerns about racialized labor voiced by *Hamilton*. The show's casting conceit of having the Founding Fathers be portrayed by actors of color certainly derives its effects from the relationship of these actors' bodies to the historical ones that they are portraying. Indeed, much of the show's power comes from the dissonance between the commanding (performing) labor of these performers, and the kinds of enslaved and disenfranchised labor to which they would have been conscripted during the period of the play. The play itself is deeply concerned with this labor, giving voice to critiques through these bodies, as seen especially in two lines singled out by Miranda. The most famous line of the entire play—Lafayette's and Hamilton's "Immigrants: we get the job done"—prompted such a response from the audience that the creators "added two bars just to absorb the reaction."[83] The other line that generates a remarkable reaction is Hamilton's rejoinder to Jefferson that "we know who's really doing the planting," a riposte that Miranda describes as pleasurable to performers and spectators alike: "I cannot tell you how cathartic it is to get to express this to Jefferson every night. The audience's reaction is similarly cathartic."[84] The cathartic dimensions of these lines—which echo in substance the song of *Show Boat*'s stevedores— attest to *Hamilton*'s shared investment in the questions of racialized labor that permeate the genre.

Further, as we have seen, the musical's cross-racial and cross-ethnic performances have historically functioned to suggest the broader kinds of cross-bodily identifications solicited by the eruptive structure, indeed to provide points of identification that, as part of a series, enable the spectator to undertake an exhilarating dissolution of identity. *Hamilton* references the cross-body performance tradition of the genre but detaches it from the eruption of song—as if to thwart any expectation of the characteristic transformations. Miranda's formal control over the narrative—as in his through-sung structure—is mirrored by the control he exercises over the bodily performances that will enact it. In deploying the bodies onstage as narrative vehicles for his continuous theatrical tapestry, Miranda precludes the kind of transference that the musical had previously indulged every time it burst into song and dance, foiling the expectations of the genre and its spectators. The show's conservative attitude toward gender similarly works to diminish the kind of work across bodies that is central to the musical's disintegrated aesthetic. While it is worth noting that the chorus is called upon to enact a number of roles, some of which occasionally entail cross-gender performance, Miranda remains reticent about cross-gender performance in the principal roles. When queried by a fan if he could imagine women assuming the roles of men, Miranda replied that "it's a complicated answer," before placing the blame on the difficulty of changing keys! (He conceded that "no one's voice is set in high school. So I'm totally open to women playing founding fathers once this goes into the world. I can't wait to see kick-ass women Jeffersons and kickass women Hamiltons once this gets to schools.")[85]

Meanwhile, Ben Brantley notes elsewhere in the review that "you never feel that any single performer is pushing for a breakout moment . . . with one exception. That's King George III . . . but ultimately, it's not his story."[86] Indeed, the closest *Hamilton* comes to spectacular isolation is its treatment of the white King George—thereby inching its way toward inverting the customary hierarchy, with black bodies as narrative bodies and King George's white body as the isolated spectacular body. However, the show's singular musical and theatrical tapestry never permits him the kind of "breaking out" that a traditional musical does in the moment of stopping the show and bursting into song, effectively denying him a privileged position outside the narrative. *Hamilton*'s through-sung structure insists that artists of color enact narrative at the same time that it precludes spectatorial identification with white bodies.

While *Hamilton*'s casting is billed as revolutionary, I would argue that it is but a complex modulation of the (always-revolutionary and ever-present) paradigm of cross-bodily impersonation that defines the genre. The source of *Hamilton*'s potency is that it attempts to rewrite this convention. *Hamilton*'s singular musical fabric—and its control over bodies and bodily relationships—prevent the kind of exploitative spectacularization that has troubled the genre. By dissociating cross-racial or cross-ethnic performance from the moment of bursting into song, *Hamilton* thereby works to deny the spectator's expectation of transitive exchanges among bodies that are unleashed by the traditional musical theatre aesthetic. Indeed, in denying the disintegrated subjectivity of musical theatre that bursts into song, *Hamilton* promulgates instead a conservative model of stable subjectivity. It reconfigures the possibilities of the bodies of its actors of color, but it actively precludes the kind of imaginative play made possible by the eruptive structure with its deployment of spectacular bodies and the related relentless changes of subject position. The through-sung aesthetic has thus enabled Miranda to escape the musical's exploitative practices, precisely by embracing a *conservative* model of stable subjectivity—a subjectivity that formally mirrors the conservative subjectivity advanced by the plot, which reduces major structural issues to matters of individual agency, matters that are under the control of a single body. By detaching these impersonations from the eruptive moment, *Hamilton* achieves its goal of precluding the exploitation of spectacular bodies—but its cautious approach thereby forecloses the opportunities offered by the form: the opportunity to break down identity through the musical's endless psychic play with impersonation. This cautious approach represents the safety, but also the limitation, of through-sung musical theatre.

As they undertake different projects under the sign of "integration," David Henry Hwang's *Flower Drum Song* and Lin-Manuel Miranda's *Hamilton* do not resolve the dilemma that haunts the genre, as they are thwarted in their attempts to fashion a different, more unequivocally progressive content or form of musical theatre. However, this does not mean that the ethics of the genre are intractable, that the genre cannot be transformed. Instead, I now consider a third approach to thinking about how to address the genre's potentially problematic deployment of spectacular bodies— one that paradoxically contains a more radical embrace of the structure of musical theatre.

Gregory Hines and Savion Glover as Jelly and Young Jelly in *Jelly's Last Jam*. Photograph by Martha Swope, ©Billy Rose Theatre Division, New York Public Library for the Performing Arts.

# CONCLUSION

*Rethinking the "Delivery System"*

This book began by examining the great landmarks of integration—the Princess Theatre shows, *Show Boat, Oklahoma!*—to understand how "integration" operated. Through these case studies, I articulated a logic of identification, control, and labor that forms the essence of the discourse. Integration was motivated by the pleasurable identifications that the form solicits with the gendered, raced, and sexualized bodies that the genre marks as spectacular. A defensive response to these identifications, integration insists that authors and spectators retain control over these bodies and can therefore safely indulge such otherwise forbidden psychic relationships. At the same time, integration works to deny any exploitation of these bodies through its insistence that spectacular performance has been properly remunerated or is a gift freely given.

In this way, integration inoculates one from understanding what is actually transpiring every time the musical bursts into song. If every musical outburst prompts a radical play with identity, integration works to counteract this, to shore up the stable subject. Integration is thus a systematic disavowal of the radical nature of the genre, and, in the same stroke, a disavowal of the ethical dilemma that lurks at the center of the genre: that the genre's most progressive effects are powered by the (potential) exploitation of spectacular bodies. In the paranoid logic of integration, there is no identification anyhow, much less an exploitative identification, and yet even if there were, the labor underpinning these non-existent identifications has been properly addressed. Though such claims could never bear much scrutiny, they served their function and were a widely accepted part of common parlance. Today, however, integration no longer exercises the conceptual hegemony it once did. As it becomes increasingly difficult to sustain a belief in integration, however, there is no bulwark against recognizing the ethical dilemma that haunts musical theatre. Thus exposed, the dilemma becomes the central concern in what we might term the post-integration era.

We explored two attempts at redressing the genre's problematic ethics, as seen in Hwang's *Flower Drum Song* and Miranda's *Hamilton*. Both exist on the cusp of the post-integration era, attempting to resolve the dilemma—but through strategies that still cling to "integration." Hwang's integration seeks to situate an Asian American subjectivity as the integrated subject of musical theatre, while *Hamilton* seeks to create an integrated form that resists the eruptive, disintegrative aesthetic of musical theatre. Neither, I would argue, is particularly successful. Hwang's revision seeks to populate the existing musical theatre form with a more authentic content, but even as he writes a more sensitive book, the form still works to generate cross-bodily performances and cannot accommodate the earnest portrayal of "identity." *Hamilton*, meanwhile, looks to abandon the form of bursting into song, but in so doing forecloses the progressive possibilities of the form. In much the way that Miranda's plot promulgates a story that I would argue is fundamentally conservative, so too his form is ultimately a conservative retreat from the radical possibilities of musical theatre.

However, three relatively recent productions—*Passing Strange* (2008), *Jelly's Last Jam* (1992), and *Soft Power* (2019)—pursue an entirely different approach to addressing the dilemma. The artists of these brilliant pieces do so by working through the form itself to expose the mechanisms by which it accomplishes its effects. In other words, they exploit the musical's own aesthetic of failure in order to address the failures of the form. This, I believe, is the kind of innovation that will keep the form alive as we move past the illusions of integration.

The extraordinary 2008 musical *Passing Strange*, written by Stew and Heidi Rodewald in collaboration with Annie Dorsen, makes explicit this engagement with failure. In this remarkable and unusual piece of musical theatre, Stew—the writer who also performs as the narrator—reflects on a young black artist's journey from his early years in suburban Los Angeles to his travels in Europe, and then to his return back home upon the death of his mother. This journey prompts him to reconsider his relation to his family, his identity, and himself. Stew's presence as both the writer and the narrator is introduced at the outset of the evening: "Now you don't know me, / And I don't know you, / So let's cut to the chase, / The name is Stew. / And I'll be narrating this gig," he sings.[1] Stew's position as a narrator already creates a fascinating tension in which narrative itself is made into a spectacle.

A powerful musical—by turns hysterically funny, movingly sentimental, and profoundly insightful—*Passing Strange* is all the more remarkable for having been written by Stew, an artist who "not only had . . . never actually written a play before, but the number of shows he claimed to have seen could be counted on one hand."[2] Stew's collaborator, Heidi Rodewald, similarly wrote that "the reason I think we ended up on Broadway was that Stew, Annie Dorsen and I never wanted to do anything that resembled something you'd normally see there. Because that's never what we wanted. To be on Broadway. But we ended up doing what we'd want to see on Broadway."[3] Their disavowal—which telegraphs not only the failure of the genre, but also their ostensible failure as "traditional" musical theatre artists—camouflages how their piece will deploy their purported insufficiencies to tremendous effect. Paradoxically, it is precisely through their failure at the form that they are most inside its structure, which, as we have seen, is one of failure. Their vehement disavowals hide their profound if intuitive engagement with, and reinvention of, musical theatre.

The artists of *Passing Strange* reinvent the form of musical theatre at the same time that they reinvent the (African American) identity of the central character, the "Youth." The play concerns the young artist grappling with—and playfully critiquing—the idea of an authentic blackness. The Youth's first revelation comes when he joins the choir of Mr. Franklin, the preacher's queer son who, we are told, undertook an (exotic/erotic) performance of "'Onward Christian Soldiers' as a rhumba."[4] When Mr. Franklin gets the Youth high on pot, Mr. Franklin likens their situations: "So, in this corner, the sensitive, artistic soul . . . and in this corner, moi, La Franklin . . . the wicked Baptist rebel. Yet in the end we're just two brothers . . . passing. Like your high yellow grandma back in the day, only we're passing for black folks."[5] This revelation of "black folks passing for black folks" will prompt the Youth first to create a band, "The Scaryotypes," and then to travel to Europe.

The play's remarkable performance of failure is distilled in the Youth's exchange with his mother when he announces that he is travelling to Europe. When the Youth dramatically announces, "I'm moving there for good!", the Narrator says, "At this point in the play we were planning a show tune! An upbeat 'gotta leave this town' kinda show tune! But we don't know how to write those kind of tunes . . . ."[6] It is precisely in his inability to conform to the conventions of musical theatre that Stew metaphorizes his own escape from the confines of his suburban middle-class upbringing. Then, they perform a parody of existentialist film dialogue before singing "Merci Beaucoup, M. Godard." Here, Stew's rejection of musical theatre tropes—just like his own disavowal of the genre—camouflages his own brilliant reinvention of it, a reinvention that is at the same time the Youth's reinvention of himself and of his black identity. Through the form, he conceives of blackness itself as a kind of performance.

Like *Passing Strange*, George C. Wolfe's extraordinary 1992 musical *Jelly's Last Jam* also calls into question the tropes of musical theatre and takes pleasure in denying audiences the pleasures they expect. At the same time, Wolfe suggests another way of challenging the narrative/spectacle binary, as he investigates what might be called the narrative of spectacle. The musical explores the life of Jelly Roll Morton, a jazz pianist and composer who was born into an aristocratic Creole family in New Orleans. Wolfe's book traces Morton's musical career from his early assimilation of African American cultural forms to his subsequent disavowal of them in his claim that he alone "invented jazz." The second act follows Jelly as he eventually acknowledges the debt that he owes to African American forms. As the show explores the various forms of hierarchy among skin tones within the African American community, it suggests that these kinds of dynamics were related to an identification with whiteness and a denial of blackness—and questions the relationship of black bodies to the minstrel stereotypes put forward in blackface performance and, by extension, musical theatre.

Fascinatingly, the idea for the show originated with Margo Lion and Pamela Koslow-Hines, two producers who sought to develop a musical based on Alan Lomax's interviews with Jelly Roll Morton. When the piece originally premiered at the Mark Taper Forum in 1991, actor Obba Baba-tundé portrayed Jelly. However, the Broadway incarnation would be wholly reworked, as Jelly was to be played by Koslow-Hines's husband, the legendary tap dancer Gregory Hines. Hines's casting led to a brilliant conceit: Morton's music would now be modulated into embodied form, precisely through the vehicle of tap dance. Indeed, Morton "plays" his music in the show through the kinetic energy of Hines's dancing. The show thus thematizes the kind of link across different modes of expression that characterizes the genre; only here, it might be said, he "breaks into dance when music will no longer suffice." Indeed, the manic energy splits across modes—music to dance—and across bodies, as Jelly divides in two, into Jelly and Young Jelly. However, Wolfe deploys this tap conceit even further, as a way to give bodily expression to the racial dynamics explored in the plot. Just as Jelly is forced to confront "the black soil from which that rhythm was born," *Jelly's Last Jam* insists not only upon the generative energy of blackness to the form, but also upon the genre's defining relationship to tap dance, with its complex negotiation of blackness and minstrelsy.[7]

The first act finale directly addresses the toxic nature of these represen-tations. Though Jelly has finally attained success and opened a rollicking nightclub, he retains deep trauma around his blackness, trauma that has haunted him since he was a child. When he arrives at his club, he presents his friend Jack with a box containing "a bright red doorman's coat." The gift confuses Jack, prompting Jelly to explain that a white man he once knew said, "Jelly, I can't explain it, but havin' a li'l n**** in a red coat opening that door, makes me feel like I belong."[8] Jelly thus elevates himself precisely by sub-jecting his friends to the dehumanizing effects of minstrel representation. This exchange is followed by "Dr. Jazz," a number in which Jelly celebrates his own genius as the sui generis inventor of jazz. The stage directions in-dicate that "on Jelly's signal, lights reveal the Crowd as a Chorus of Coons, in white lips and red doormen's jackets and caps." In their minstrel garb, the chorus announces, "Front n' center the inventor of jazz! . . . Only name that you need to know—."[9] Jelly thus uses the denigrating form of blackface to distance himself from the blackness that is the source of his art. As the Chorus of Coons appeases Morton's desire to see himself as the inventor of jazz, the stage directions indicate, "[Morton's] rage releases itself as a manic 'showstopper'—driving himself and the Chorus of Coons in a dance break that is as exuberant as it is emotionally raw."[10] The showstopper invites its audiences to explode in applause even as it problematizes that response, provoking the audience to question why it should respond so powerfully to a number that involves such troubling representations.

As the plot forces Jelly to confront the sources of his glorious aesthetic, Wolfe's musical ultimately forces the genre to confront one of the principal sources of its own theatrical energy: black bodies. As John Lahr suggests in the introduction to the published edition, the show "indicts Jelly Roll Morton for a moral amnesia that mirrors the commercial musical's practice of removing pain for gain."[11] However, I would argue that this amnesia is not merely the musical's alleged disinclination to address serious issues. It runs much deeper, indeed to the heart of the genre, as Wolfe forces spectators to confront the spectacularity of black bodies in musical theatre. As Hines noted in an interview in *Ebony*, "For too long on the musical stage we have perpetuated the myth that African Americans are always singing and dancing and happy."[12] This myth is precisely what Wolfe undermines, a myth that undergirds the spectacular mode to which black bodies were assigned by the genre. Wolfe works to unsettle the narrative-spectacle binary precisely by exploring what we might call the narrative of spectacle, or what Wolfe often refers to as "context." As Wolfe told the *New York Times*,

> There are tons of people who would prefer to come see a show where you have black people just singing and dancing. Often, when black entertainment is presented, what happens is what I call cultural strip mining, where you don't go through the dirt to get the jewel, you just scoop down and put it on top. The performance is stripped of its context. But the context is what's so exciting—it's not just somebody riffing, but where is that riff coming from?[13]

For Wolfe, exploring the "context" can promote healing: "America is this giant dysfunctional family that is perpetually denying there's something wrong with itself. So therefore you go and see a bunch of happy people singing and dancing, and it reassures you. But in fact you can never heal. *Jelly's Last Jam* is about healing."[14] In a television interview, Wolfe similarly referred to the "transformational and healing power of darkness."[15]

Much of Wolfe's work focused precisely on challenging the expectations of audiences. At the same time, the popular press made much of the fact that the show still aimed to entertain, a sentiment with which Wolfe concurred. Wolfe told an interviewer that "musicals are a peculiar thing. By their very nature you have to maintain a certain buoyant energy. Here, we've set into motion a certain rhythm and a certain dynamic, and that's what you obey: not the audience but the dynamic."[16] This idea of "obey[ing] not the audience, but the dynamic" points to his radical project to entertain using the structure of musical theatre—and yet simultaneously to interrogate and thereby evacuate the way in which the form works to satisfy certain desires in the audience. Thwarting the audience's desires—from within the musical theatre form—becomes central to Wolfe's project. Lahr notes, for example, that "a number of black shows from *Ain't Misbehavin'* to *Bubbling Brown Sugar* to *Five Guys Named Moe* have brought black music and black talent to Broadway but refused to put the ravishing energy in a proper historical context. The shows are another form of shucking . . . that robs black expression both of context and of ideas."[17] It is not coincidental that many shows celebrating black composers were revues, a series of songs and dances with little if any narrative conceit. These shows yet again relegated black bodies to the realm of the spectacular and suggested that they were not points of *narrative* identification. The prevalence of such revues that were focused on black composers led to confusion over whether *Jelly's Last Jam* was one as well. In one *Newsday* article, Wolfe notes that "this is Gregory Hines in *Jelly's Last Jam*, not Gregory Hines doing a revue. He has a good voice, he's an extraordinary actor. He's playing a very complicated character and doing it quite wonderfully. We are not trying to fulfill everybody's secret wish to have all their fantasies served in one evening."[18] Wolfe's comments subtly hint at the fact that Hines's presence as a title character in the traditional musical theatre form—where he is involved in narrative scenes—would *frustrate* the fantasies of some in the audience.

Wolfe seems to insist on keeping black bodies from being identified as principally narrative or spectacle, and instead uses the form to move them between modes. He seems to do this especially with the black women of the show, performers whose bodies are doubly marked as spectacular. Central to Wolfe's vision are "The Hunnies," three black women who function as the show's "chorus girls—ethereal and low."[19] During the show, they re-emerge as "Storyville Whores" or "Low Girls," among other incarnations. The *Orange County Register* review of the show's tryout referred to them as a "trio of long-stemmed dancing beauties [who] suppl[y] steaming, strut-and-grind spice,"[20] while *New York Times* writer Anna Kisselgoff referred to them as "three self-mocking and hip-gyrating furies."[21] They too reference the traditional spectacular nature of female bodies, a nature that Wolfe will seek to deny: one feature article recorded Wolfe in a moment of direction, as he told them that "The Hunnies aren't chorus girls. They're agenda girls. Any time you appear, you have an agenda."[22]

In all of these strategies, Wolfe does not discard the form, but rather doubles down in order to think *through* it. For Wolfe, "simply because a silhouette is deemed offensive, you don't throw away the silhouette or the content, you reclaim it."[23] This project of "reclaiming" the musical theatre form is precisely what Wolfe undertakes in *Jelly's Last Jam*. For Lahr, the show "astutely renegotiates the audience's idea of black culture and the nature of the musical itself," and he notes elsewhere that it "thrills an audience by bending the musical's structure to assert its gorgeous authenticity."[24] As Frank Rich writes, the show aims to "remake the Broadway musical in a mythic, African-American image."[25]

Like *Jelly's Last Jam*, David Henry Hwang's "play with a musical," *Soft Power*, also reclaims the musical theatre form precisely by challenging spectators to address the sources of their pleasure. If Hwang's *Flower Drum Song* was inspired by the 1996 revival of Rodgers and Hammerstein's *The King and I*, the 2015 Lincoln Center revival of that piece would cue his most recent production, *Soft Power*. Hwang reported that when he attended the recent revival, "I became more aware than I have in previous iterations of the show the degree to which some aspects of the premise are sort of questionable—particularly the central premise portraying Anna as the central force who helps the king bring his country into the modern age."[26] At the same time, however, Hwang notes that these fraught issues, ones of exoticism and yellowface, "did not preclude [him] from feeling very moved and still crying at the end." Arguing that such a dynamic—"the experience of feeling simultaneously uncomfortable with content, yet seduced to some extent by the skill at which this content was delivered"—was particularly familiar for people of color, Hwang notes that he wanted to "create a piece that would create that same effect for a mainstream Western audience."[27] The result is *Soft Power*, a musical written with composer Jeanine Tesori that opened at the Public Theater in the fall of 2019 after workshops in Los Angeles and San Francisco.

As produced at the Public, *Soft Power* begins with "DHH," a stand-in for the author, being invited by Chinese producer Xūe Xíng to write a Broadway-style musical to inaugurate the Dragon Palace, a new theatre in Shanghai. Initially commissioned to adapt a Chinese romantic comedy (titled "Stick With Your Mistake"), DHH invites the producer to accompany him to a campaign fundraiser for Hillary Clinton that features a performance of *The King and I*. Walking home after the campaign event, DHH is stabbed, prompting a fever dream in which he writes the musical "Soft Power." In this dream musical, which reconceives elements of *The King and I* from the Chinese point of view, Xūe Xíng visits Hillary Clinton as she campaigns and loses. As the two fall in love, Xūe essentially asks Hillary whether democracy can truly be superior to authoritarianism, given that the democratic process evidently sows chaos and disruption. The piece concludes with a desperate affirmation of the values of democracy.

The show is billed as a "play with a musical," which is generally interpreted as referring to a straight play framing the musical fantasia. However, I would suggest that this invocation of the word "play" is better understood as a verb—indeed, an imperative one—as *Soft Power* is precisely about playing with the structure of the musical and demanding that we do so as well. To think more about the way in which *Soft Power* "plays" with a musical, we might look more closely at the moment when the play becomes a musical—indeed, when it finally bursts into song.

After DHH, Xūe Xíng, and his girlfriend Zoe Samuels attend *The King and I*—described in the play as a "classic American musical"—Xūe Xíng tells DHH to "write a musical play just like this one." The characters then give voice to the *Soft Power* creators' own real-life thoughts—as reported in the press—on the musical form, including Hwang's feelings about representation and Tesori's thoughts on the "delivery system."[28] In the play, DHH critiques the condescendingly colonialist East-West narratives, the bad accents of the performers, and the factual inaccuracies. "Even today sometimes, Asian characters still get played by white actors," Zoe adds. DHH adds that he is nonetheless still emotionally moved by these plays, a conundrum that Zoe explains by discussing the "delivery system" of musical theatre. However problematic the narrative might be, she explains, the delivery system works to endear these stories to us: "There's the story there and then there's the delivery system—and musicals have gotta be the best system ever. I mean, once those violins start playing, those shows go straight to our heart."[29] When DHH and Zoe initially critique *The King and I*, Xūe Xíng defends it: "Someone has to be the King, and someone has to be the I!", prompting DHH to question why "the white character always [has] to be the 'I.'" After Zoe discusses the "delivery system," Xūe Xíng says that DHH should use the delivery system and make China the "I."

The morning after the 2016 election, DHH asks in a monologue whether he'll "be able to live in this country anymore" since half the country voted for a candidate who thinks "that we should be nothing more than sup- porting characters in someone else's story." Lamenting an earlier period when Asian actors only ever played supporting characters—"bad guys, sexy women, or jokes"—DHH recalls, "Whenever I saw a face like mine, I braced myself because I knew something terrible was going to—." Before he can finish this sentence, something terrible *does* happen: he is stabbed. As he fades into unconsciousness, DHH visualizes the musical Xūe Xíng wanted him to write: a reverse *King and I*, with China as the "I."

The curtains part to reveal a twenty-two–piece orchestra—which includes, of course, the violins that Zoe used to characterize the "delivery system," the same musical instruments that Lloyd Webber used as shorthand for the fracturing of the musical form. If these issues of bursting into song are always bodily ones, *Soft Power* is insistently about the laboring bodies that bring the show to life. The play's own narrative disintegration—the play bursting into a musical—is prompted by an act of bodily disintegration: the stabbing of DHH. This stabbing is a literalization of the symbolic violence of represen- tation that, as Hwang puts it in his monologue, reduces him to a supporting character. The reparative dimension of *Soft Power* is to question this process precisely by inverting the normal tropes of musical theatre representation.

*Soft Power* brilliantly foregrounds the cross-bodily performance tradition of musical theatre, precisely by alienating this process: its stock American characters are portrayed by Asian actors in whiteface, indeed in painfully bad performances of whiteness. Imagining an awkward Chinese vision of America, the show includes not only such laughably flawed references as the "New York airport" whose vista includes the Golden Gate Bridge, but more significantly a series of stereotypical Americans—including Bobby Bob and Randy Rae—embodied by Asian American actors in blonde wigs, Adidas track suits, leather jackets, and backward baseball caps. The politics of these alienated performances are far more subversive and radical than those featured in *Hamilton*, which link the performers of color, and the white historical characters, in a mutually affirming subjectivity.

Just as *Soft Power* reframes the laboring bodies of musical theatre, it also references a wide range of Broadway traditions, never more compellingly than in a number prompted by Hillary's inability to pronounce Xūe Xíng's name. As he gives her a language lesson on tones, the orchestration references both "Do Re Mi" (*The Sound of Music*) and "Just in Time" (*Bells Are Ringing*)—but the song's premise is taken right from "The Rain in Spain."[30] After Hillary's failures to imitate Xūe Xíng, she stumbles onto the right intonation accidentally—when she screams "Son of a whore!" Prompted by him to repeat her success, she incants "Whore! Whore! Whore! Whore!" This joyous incantation—related to sexualized labor in the context of ethnicized imitation—returns us to the primal scene of musical theatre, and foregrounds how *Soft Power* deploys the tropes of musical theatre to make its audiences consider anew the sources of the genre's pleasures.

*San Francisco Chronicle* critic Lily Janiak writes that *Soft Power* aims to "dissect the 2016 election, detoxify us, and offer a path forward."[31] The very same can be said of its formal structure, which aims to dissect the spectacularization of bodies in musical theatre, to detoxify the genre, and offer a path forward. Hwang himself seemed to suggest that the epistemological accomplishment of *Soft Power*—its exposure of the mechanics and politics of musical theatre form—is especially significant in a time when people are increasingly uncomfortable with the representations in classic musical theatre. The playwright noted that there are "wonderful things, craft-wise" in many musicals, so it's important "to see them through kind of a dual lens—to both understand the value of the craft and be able to understand how the delivery system was flawed."[32] The delivery system, of course, consists precisely of the bodies of its performers. When critic Frances Baum Nicholson makes the somewhat typical response that "a highly versatile cast makes this extremely episodic and somewhat fractured story work," she nonetheless points to the fact that it is precisely the versatility of the cast—their ability to transform—that makes the "fractured" story function.[33] The show invites its spectators to think about this fractured form and the precise nature of the performing labor.

Celebrating the craft of these works, Hwang remarked that he does not "advocate the retirement of plays."[34] However, he also noted that "it's quite possible some of these works will be retired as they outlive their usefulness. But in the meantime, it's fine to be aware of what we're seeing and to be rigorous about understanding the context in which they were made." Notably, Hwang did this precisely by working through the form, by challenging the pleasures that exist in the structure of musical theatre. *New York Times* critic Jesse Green wrote that "it's a strange complication that 'Soft Power' critiques the seductive persuasiveness of musicals . . . while also trading in it."[35] However, this is exactly the point: to critique the musical effectively, one must work through its pleasures. And in so doing, Hwang accomplishes what he aimed—but failed—to do nearly two decades earlier with *Flower Drum Song*: : "I tried to write the book that Oscar Hammerstein would have written if he were Asian American."[36]

*Variety* critic Frank Rizzo, writing that *Soft Power* upsets our expectations in a "thrilling, moving, and revolutionary way," suggested that those who view *Soft Power* "may never look at an American musical the same way again."[37] The same could be said of *Passing Strange* and *Jelly's Last Jam*. The brilliant work of Hwang, Stew, and George C. Wolfe reveal that the musical's structural investments in failure and escape make it possible to show the musical's *own* failures, and to thereby *escape* from this dynamic. As these artists reimagine musical theatre, they abandon the quest for authenticity and work instead to interrogate how the musical works upon identity. They reconceive not only the relationship of narrative and spectacle but also the manner by which the musical creates relationships across bodies—emphasizing how the musical can still work across bodies, without reifying those bodies, without working across *types* of bodies. They indulge the pleasures of the musical form, inviting applause at the same time that they problematize it. The genre thus offers the materials for this self-critique precisely in the moment of bursting into song. This is the extraordinary and radical potential of the musical, and why the goal of every performer, of every musical number, is to "stop the show"—for when the show stops, the work of musical theatre begins.

# NOTES

## INTRODUCTION

1. Robert Coleman, "'My Fair Lady' Is a Glittering Musical," *New York Daily Mirror*, March 16, 1956.

2. Richard Watts, Jr., "When Everything Goes Just Right," *New York Post*, March 16, 1956.

3. John Chapman, "'My Fair Lady' A Superb, Stylish Musical Play with a Perfect Cast," *New York Daily News*, March 16, 1956.

4. For examples of this discourse, see, among others, Cecil Smith, *Musical Comedy in America* (New York: Theatre Arts Books, 1950); Richard Rodgers, *Musical Stages* (New York: Random House, 1975), 227, 229; Oscar Hammerstein II, *Lyrics* (New York: Simon & Schuster, 1949), 15; Gerald Mast, *Can't Help Singin': The American Musical on Stage and Screen* (Woodstock: Overlook Press, 1987), 146–47; Lehman Engel, *The American Musical Theater: A Consideration* (New York: CBS Legacy, 1967), 76; or Andrew Lamb, *150 Years of Popular Musical Theatre* (New Haven: Yale University Press, 2000), 258. Geoffrey Block offers a very useful essay on the topic in *Histories of the Musical: An Oxford Handbook of the American Musical*, vol. 1, ed. Raymond Knapp, Mitchell Morris, and Stacy Wolf (New York: Oxford University Press, 2018), 153–76.

5. Alan Jay Lerner, *The Street Where I Live* (New York: Norton, 1978), 119.

6. Lerner, *The Street Where I Live*, 87.

7. Qtd. in Dwight Blocker Bowers, *American Musical Theater: Shows, Songs, and Stars* (Washington, DC: Smithsonian Collection of Recordings, 1989), 76.

8. Alan Jay Lerner, *My Fair Lady: A Musical Play in Two Acts* (New York: Coward-McCann, 1956), 25, italics mine.

9. Lerner, *My Fair Lady*, 30.

10. Lerner, 86.

11. Lerner, 88.

12. Lerner, 88.

13. Lerner, 90.

14. Lerner, 81.

15. See John Storm Roberts, *The Latin Tinge: The Impact of Latin American Music on the United States* (New York: Oxford University Press, 1999).

16. Brian Herrera, *Latin Numbers*, 49.

17. The same might be said of Middle Eastern numbers, which often fixated on the eroticism of the "sheik," who was "a virile, sensual male, a priapic violent lover who masters females by prowess and physical force." Billie Melman, *Women and the Popular Imagination in the Twenties: Flappers and Nymphs* (Basingstoke: Macmillan, 1988), 89. Such numbers come and go over the years, and while we might note that the popularity of T. E. Lawrence gave rise to characterizations like that of the Red Shadow in *The Desert Song*, a whole range of similar representations—such as that of Rajah Bimmy in *On the Town* and Ali Hakim in *Oklahoma!*—are ones that I examine as structurally equivalent to the eruptions of Latin-ness. The question that I ask is what it means that such bodies are positioned (through the erotic energy of their portrayal) as spectacular points of identification.

18. Walter F. Kerr, "My Fair Lady," *New York Herald-Tribune*, March 16, 1956.

19. Qtd. in Myrna Katz Frommer and Harvey Frommer, *It Happened on Broadway: An Oral History of the Great White Way* (Lanham: Taylor, 2015), 170.

20. Lerner, *My Fair Lady*, 118.

21. Nancy Olson Livingston, "How to Stop a Show," *Lincoln Center Review* 71 (Spring 2018): 11.

22. Steven Bach, *Dazzler: The Life and Times of Moss Hart* (New York: Knopf, 2001), 355.

23. Bach, *Dazzler*, 356.

24. Lerner, *My Fair Lady*, 130.

25. Meanwhile, despite the initial motivation that Eliza receive phonetic training so that she might secure employment, the text works to foreclose the need and possibility of her labor. Eliza herself complains that she is now fit only to "sell herself," and Higgins has indeed set in motion a world that subtly removes Eliza from the economy of employment. Then Eliza warns that she'll marry Freddy "as soon as I'm able to support him." Higgins dismisses Freddy as "that poor devil who couldn't get a job" and fantasizes that Eliza will end up selling flowers "while her husband has his breakfast in bed!"

26. Lerner, 161.

27. In addition to the critics discussed in the pages that follow, other important critiques of integration include Tim Carter, Oklahoma!*: The Making of an American Musical* (New Haven: Yale University Press, 2007); and Dan Rebellato, "'No Theatre Guild Attraction Are We': *Kiss Me, Kate* and the Politics of the Integrated Musical," *Contemporary Theatre Review* 19, no. 1 (2009): 73.

28. See, for example, Bertolt Brecht, "The Modern Theatre is the Epic The-

atre," in *Brecht on Theatre: The Development of an Aesthetic*, trans. John Willett (New York: Hill and Wang, 1964), 33–43.

29. D. A. Miller, *Place for Us: Essay on the Broadway Musical* (Cambridge, MA: Harvard University Press, 1998), 1–2.

30. Miller, *Place for Us*, 3.

31. Scott McMillin, *The Musical as Drama* (Princeton: Princeton University Press, 2006), 2. In general, as in these quotations, McMillin's argument is admirably clear in its critique of integration. However, he softens his critique by admitting exceptions: the pantomime of the opening waltz of *Carousel*, "A Weekend in the Country" from *A Little Night Music*, and the opening scene of *West Side Story*, which he writes is "a true example of the integrated musical" (130, 141). In suggesting that integration *is* in fact an attainable aesthetic, he complicates many of his other claims about the implausibility of integration as an aesthetic category. He ultimately argues that "coherence" is a more appropriate standard for the genre, since "coherence means things stick together, different things, without losing their difference" (209).

32. McMillin, *Musical as Drama*, 8.

33. Millie Taylor, *Musical Theatre, Realism and Entertainment* (Farnham: Ashgate, 2012), 71.

34. McMillin, *Musical as Drama*, 179.

35. McMillin, 191.

36. Stacy Wolf, *A Problem Like Maria: Gender and Sexuality in the American Musical* (Ann Arbor: University of Michigan Press, 2002), 32. See also Wolf's *Changed for Good: A Feminist History of the Broadway Musical* (Oxford: Oxford University Press, 2011).

37. David Savran, *A Queer Sort of Materialism: Recontextualizing American Theater* (Ann Arbor: University of Michigan Press, 2003), 29.

38. Savran, *A Queer Sort*, 32.

39. Savran, 34.

40. Note also that I am not discussing "integration" as an aesthetic style of musical theatre. According to some early critics of integration, musicals *could* be integrated, but these critics pushed back against the sense that such stylistic choices were in any way superior to other kinds of choices, such as those that characterized musical comedy. This track is pursued in Margaret Knapp's 1978 critique that the "widespread acceptance" of the integrated musical "led some chroniclers of the musical stage to view the entire history of the American musical as a single evolutionary process, with the integrated musical as its final, perfect product." (See Margaret Knapp, "Integration of Elements as a Viable

Standard for Judging Musical Theatre," in *Focus on Popular Theatre in America*, ed. Henry F. Salerno [Bowling Green, OH: Bowling Green State University Popular Press, 1978], 114.) Like Knapp, Bruce Kirle also validates the idea that some musicals really *are* genuinely integrated, while also insisting upon the value of non-integrated forms. (See Bruce Kirle, *Unfinished Show Business: Broadway Musicals as Works-in-Process* [Carbondale: Southern Illinois University Press, 2005], xxi.) Andrea Most's brilliant work on the Jewishness of musical theatre takes advantage of a similar attitude toward integration as a style, arguing that champions of the "integrated" style advocate an aesthetic mode as well as an implicitly "problematic mode of understanding American identity." (See Andrea Most, *Making Americans: Jews and the Broadway Musical* [Cambridge, MA: Harvard University Press, 2004], 31.)

41. See Block, "Integration," 153–76.

42. See Marvin Carlson, *Theories of the Theatre: A Historical and Critical Survey from the Greeks to the Present* (Ithaca: Cornell University Press, 1993), 310.

43. Nancy Olson Livingston, "How to Stop a Show," 11.

44. John Guare and Ira Weitzman, "An Ordinary Man: An Interview with Jerry Adler," *Lincoln Center Review* 71 (Spring 2018): 14.

## CHAPTER 1

1. Lewis Nichols, "'Oklahoma!' a Musical Hailed as Delightful, Based on 'Green Grow the Lilacs,' Opens Here at the St. James Theatre," *New York Times*, April 1, 1943.

2. Howard Barnes, "Lilacs to 'Oklahoma!,'" *New York Herald-Tribune*, April 1, 1943.

3. Gerald Bordman, *American Musical Theatre: A Chronicle*, 3rd ed. (Oxford: Oxford University Press, 2001), 589.

4. Joseph Swain, *The Broadway Musical: A Critical and Musical Survey* (Oxford: Oxford University Press, 1990), 74.

5. John Bush Jones, *Our Musicals, Ourselves: A Social History of the American Musical Theatre* (Hanover: Brandeis University Press, 2003), 142.

6. Stanley Green, *The World of Musical Comedy: The Story of the American Musical Stage as Told Through the Careers of Its Foremost Composers and Lyricists* (South Brunswick: A. S. Barnes and Company, 1968), 269.

7. Burns Mantle, "'Oklahoma!' Links the Ballet with the Prairie Beautifully," *New York Daily News*, April 1, 1943.

8. Burton Rascoe, "The Guild's 'Oklahoma!' Opens at the St. James," *New*

York *World-Telegram*, April 1, 1943.

9. Peter H. Riddle, *The American Musical: History and Development* (Oakville: Mosaic, 2010), 73. Riddle notes in the same paragraph that *Oklahoma!* "would tell the story in a straightforward narrative manner."

10. "Disastrous Conflagration," *The New York Times*, May 22, 1866.

11. For an excellent discussion of *The Black Crook* and its relationship to the ballet production, see Raymond Knapp, *The American Musical and the Formation of National Identity* (Princeton: Princeton University Press, 2006), 20–29.

12. See M. B. Leavitt, *Fifty Years in Theatrical Management* (New York: Broadway Publishing, 1912), 158.

13. Joseph Whitton, *"The Naked Truth!": An Inside History of the Black Crook* (Philadelphia: H. W. Shaw, 1897), 10. Whitton's short book has long been one of the principal sources of information about the show, with its authority coming from Whitton's position as the manager of Niblo's. However, the July 21, 1866, edition of the *New York Clipper* reports that "Joseph Whitton, treasurer for a long time for Manager Wheatley, in Philadelphia at the old Arch, and at Niblo's, in this city, has resigned the position, and taken up his abode in the country. He is succeeded at Niblo's by Jacob Zimmerman, a young man connected with Mr. Wheatley in his management for some time." This would still place Mr. Whitton in Mr. Wheatley's company at the time of the acquisition of *The Black Crook*, though he would seem to be out of the picture well before the ballet troupe arrived in America.

14. Charles Barras, *The Black Crook*, in *Nineteenth Century American Plays*, ed. Myron Matlaw (New York: Applause, 1967), 326.

15. George C. D. Odell, *Annals of the New York Stage*, vol. 8 (New York: Columbia University Press, 1936), 152.

16. Smith, *Musical Comedy*, viii. *The Black Crook* also inaugurates Stanley Green's chronicle of musical theatre, with Green observing that "although there were earlier attempts to present dramas on the same program with music and dancing, *The Black Crook*, in 1866, was the first successful venture in America to combine the two forms of entertainment." Green, *The World of Musical Comedy*, 1.

17. Smith, *Musical Comedy*, 20.

18. Julian Mates, "The Black Crook Myth," *Theatre Survey* 7, no. 1 (May 1966): 31–32.

19. Mates, "The Black Crook Myth," 38.

20. Christopher Morley, "Hoboken Nights," *Saturday Evening Post*, July 13, 1929.

21. David J. Denby, *Sentimental Narrative and the Social Order in France, 1760–1820* (New York: Cambridge University Press, 1994), 74–75, emphasis Denby's.

22. Anne Patricia Williams, "Description and Tableau in the Eighteenth-Century British Sentimental Novel," *Eighteenth-Century Fiction* 8, no. 4 (1996): 471.

23. Peter Brooks, *The Melodramatic Imagination: Balzac, Henry James, Melodrama, and the Mode of Excess* (New Haven: Yale University Press, 1976), 48.

24. Barras, *The Black Crook*, 367.

25. See, for example, Nicole Anae, "Poses Plastiques: The Art and Style of 'Statuary' in Victorian Visual Theatre," *Australasian Drama Studies* 52 (April 2008): 112–30; Sara Stevenson and Helen Bennett, *Van Dyck in Check Trousers: Fancy Dress in Art and Life, 1700–1900* (Edinburgh: Scottish National Portrait Gallery, 1978), 45–63; and Alison Smith, *The Victorian Nude: Sexuality, Morality and Art* (Manchester: Manchester University Press, 1996), especially 47–67.

26. Philippe Hamon, "Rhetorical Status of the Descriptive," *Yale French Studies* 61 (1981): 3.

27. Denby, *Sentimental Narrative*, 76.

28. See Kenneth Gross, *The Dream of the Moving Statue* (Ithaca: Cornell University Press, 1992).

29. Johann Wolfgang von Goethe, *Goethe on Art*, ed. John Gage (Berkeley: University of California Press, 1980), 81.

30. William Hazlitt, "Flaxman's Lectures on Sculpture," *Edinburgh Review* 50 (1829): 245.

31. When the author Mark Twain saw *The Black Crook*, he was especially struck by the Transformation Scene, recalling "beautiful bare-legged girls hanging in flower baskets; others stretched in groups on great sea shells; others clustered around fluted columns; others in all possible *attitudes*; girls—nothing but a wilderness of girls—stacked up, pile on pile, away aloft to the dome of the theatre . . . ." Twain's description of the "tableau" and "attitudes" of women's bodies, echoed in other descriptions of the show, reveals how relevant this context is for understanding *The Black Crook*. Mark Twain, *Mark Twain's Travels with Mr. Brown*, eds. Franklin Walker and G. Esra Dane (New York: Knopf, 1940), 85–86, italics mine.

32. See Volker Schachenmayr, "Emma Lyon, the Attitude, and Goethean Performance Theory," *New Theatre Quarterly* 49 (February 1997): 3–17; and Ismene Lada-Richards, "'Mobile Statuary': Refractions of Pantomime Dancing from Callistratus to Emma Hamilton and Andrew Ducrow," *International Journal of the Classical Tradition* 10, no. 1 (Summer 2003): 3–37.

33. Jack W. McCullough, *Living Pictures on the New York Stage* (Ann Arbor: UMI Research Press, 1983), 11; and A. H. Saxon, *The Life and Art of Andrew Ducrow* (Hamden: Archon Books, 1978).

34. See McCullough, *Living Pictures*, 16.

35. Mary Chapman, "'Living Pictures': Women and *Tableaux Vivants* in Nineteenth-Century American Fiction and Culture," *Wide Angle* 18, no. 3 (1996): 31, ellipsis hers.

36. Chapman, "'Living Pictures': Women," 32.

37. "Amusements," *New York Times*, September 17, 1866.

38. *New York Clipper*, September 29, 1866; December 29, 1866.

39. *New York Times*, September 13, 1866.

40. "Naughty Things That a Preacher Saw," *New York Clipper*, December 1, 1866.

41. "Naughty Things That a Preacher Saw."

42. Qtd. in John Russell David, "The Genesis of the Variety Theatre: *The Black Crook* Comes to Saint Louis," *Missouri Historical Review* LXIV, no. 2 (January 1970): 135.

43. *New York Daily Tribune*, September 24, 1866.

44. Olive Logan, *Apropos of Women and Theatres, With A Paper or Two on Parisian Topics* (New York: Carleton, 1869), 134–35, emphasis in original.

45. *New York Clipper*, October 13, 1866.

46. "Naughty Things That a Preacher Saw."

47. Twain, *Mark Twain's Travels*, 84–85.

48. Twain, 86.

49. Barbara Barker, *Ballet or Ballyhoo: The American Careers of Maria Bonfanti, Rita Sangalli, and Giuseppina Morlacchi* (New York: Dance Horizons, 1984), 14.

50. Barker, *Ballet or Ballyhoo*, 126.

51. Barker, 167.

52. James Weldon Johnson, *Black Manhattan* (New York: Arno and the New York Times, 1968), 95.

53. Jayna Brown, *Babylon Girls: Black Women Performers and the Shaping of the Modern* (Durham, NC: Duke University Press, 2008), 93, 191.

54. Richard Kislan, *Hoofing on Broadway: A History of Show Dancing* (New York: Prentice Hall, 1987), 75. In this regard, see also Anthea Kraut's argument regarding de Mille's pursuit of copyright in Anthea Kraut's *Choreographing Copyright: Race, Gender, and Intellectual Property Rights in American Dance* (Oxford: Oxford University Press, 2015).

55. Ethan Mordden, *Beautiful Mornin': The Broadway Musical in the 1940s* (New York: Oxford University Press, 1999), 75.

56. Roger Copeland, "Broadway Dance," *Dance Magazine* (November 1974): 34.

57. Oscar Hammerstein II and Richard Rodgers, *Oklahoma!* (New York: Random House, 1942), 18.

58. Hammerstein and Rodgers, *Oklahoma!*, 61.

59. Hammerstein and Rodgers, 74.

60. Hammerstein and Rodgers, 62.

61. Hammerstein and Rodgers, 27.

62. Hammerstein and Rodgers, 34.

63. Hammerstein and Rodgers, 21, 66.

64. Andrea Most, *Making Americans*, 108.

65. Qtd. in Kara Ann Gardner, *Agnes de Mille: Telling Stories in Broadway Dance* (Oxford: Oxford University Press, 2016), 24.

66. Qtd. in Gardner, *Agnes de Mille*, 32.

67. Qtd. in Gardner, 31.

68. Agnes de Mille, *And Promenade Home* (Boston: Little Brown, 1958), 221–22.

69. De Mille, *And Promenade Home*, 226.

70. Qtd. in Max Wilk, *Ok!: The Story of* Oklahoma! (New York: Applause, 2002), 114.

71. Hammerstein and Rodgers, *Oklahoma!*, 88.

72. Hammerstein and Rodgers, *Oklahoma!*, 89–90.

73. Anthea Kraut has argued that while de Mille's work in *Oklahoma!* employed both ballet and tap traditions, her claim to authorship was predicated on disavowing the importance of what were dismissed as mere tap "routines." Thus, de Mille attained legal rights precisely through her denigration of the African American forms that inspired some of her work. In this way, we might see how Laurey's subjectivity comes into being through a disavowal of racialized influence/desire just as de Mille's legal subjectivity did. See Kraut, *Choreographing Copyright*, especially 165–218.

74. Hammerstein and Rodgers, *Oklahoma!*, 146.

75. David Savran, "Towards a Historiography of the Popular," *Theatre Survey* 45, no. 2 (November 2004): 211–17.

76. Christopher Morley, "Hoboken Nights," 110–12.

77. Morley, 112.

78. Edward B. Marks, *They All Had Glamour: From the Swedish Nightingale to the Naked Lady* (New York: Julian Messner, 1944), 13.

79. Gilbert Millstein, "How The First Musical Was Born," unattributed. New York Public Library Collection.

80. *The Girl in Pink Tights*, souvenir program.

81. Robert Coleman, "'The Girl in Pink Tights' Is a Tuneful Frolic," *New York Daily Mirror*, March 8, 1954, 28.

82. Millstein, "How the First."

83. Coleman, "'The Girl in Pink Tights.'"

84. George Jean Nathan, "The Show in Split Tights," *New York Journal-American*, March 28, 1954.

85. Frances Herridge, "Dance Differences in Two Musicals," *New York Post*, April 26, 1954.

86. Walter Terry, "Dance: Golden Apple, Pink Tights," *New York Herald-Tribune*, March 21, 1954.

87. John Chapman, "'One Touch of Venus' Brings a Touch of Life to Broadway," *New York Daily News*, October 8, 1943.

## CHAPTER 2

1. Qtd. in Barker, *Ballet or Ballyhoo*, 18.

2. George Abbott and Richard Bissell, *The Pajama Game* (New York: Random House, 1954), 3.

3. Abbott and Bissell, *Pajama Game*, 4.

4. Abbott and Bissell, 42.

5. Abbott and Bissell, 150.

6. Jerome Weidman and George Abbott, *Fiorello!* (New York: Random House, 1960), 12.

7. See David Foil, liner notes to *Can-Can*, Angel Records, 1992, 7.

8. Michael Stewart and Jerry Herman, *Hello, Dolly!* (New York: DBS, 1964), 9.

9. Stewart and Herman, *Hello, Dolly!*, 24.

10. Barras, *The Black Crook*, 374.

11. Jerry Herman and Ken Bloom, *Jerry Herman: The Lyrics, A Celebration* (New York: Routledge, 2003), 55.

12. Michael Stewart, Manuscript of "Dolly," Box 43, Michael Stewart Collection, New York Public Library, Act 2, Scene 2, p. 19.

13. Stewart and Herman, *Hello, Dolly!*, 26.

14. David Payne-Carter, *Gower Champion: Dance and American Musical Theatre* (Westport: Greenwood Press, 1999), 93–94.

15. Stewart and Herman, *Hello, Dolly!*, 89–90.

16. Stewart, Manuscript, unpaginated addition to script.

17. Stewart and Herman, *Hello, Dolly!*, 35.

18. In "So Long, Dearie," Dolly seems to note that her marriage with Horace will preclude her return to burlesque: if, on the other hand, she goes "as far away from Yonkers as a girl can get," she will "learn to dance and drink and smoke a cigarette." Stewart and Herman, 106.

19. Qtd. in Reuel Keith Olin, "A History and Interpretation of the Princess Theatre Musical Plays: 1915–1919" (Ph.D. diss., New York University, 1979), 21.

20. Olin, "A History and Interpretation," 22.

21. Souvenir program of *Oh, Boy!* in the Museum of the City of New York Collection.

22. Jones, *Our Musicals, Ourselves*, 46.

23. Elisabeth Marbury, *My Crystal Ball* (New York: Boni & Liveright, 1923), 253.

24. Elisabeth Marbury, introduction to *Modern Dancing*, by Mr. and Mrs. Vernon Castle (New York: Harper & Brothers, 1914), 26–27.

25. Marbury, introduction to *Modern Dancing*, 25.

26. Marbury, 25.

27. Marbury, 29, italics hers.

28. Marbury, 24.

29. Marbury, 19.

30. Marbury, 19.

31. Marbury, *My Crystal Ball*, 243.

32. Marbury, *Modern Dancing*, 20.

33. Marbury, 22.

34. Marbury, 23–24.

35. Marbury, 22.

36. Souvenir program of *Oh, Boy!* in Museum of the City of New York Collection.

37. Guy Bolton and Paul Rubens, *Nobody Home* manuscript, New York Public Library Collection, Act 1, p. 13.

38. Bolton and Rubens, *Nobody Home*, Act 1, p. 3.

39. Bolton and Rubens, *Nobody Home*, Act 1, p. 24.

40. Bolton and Rubens, *Nobody Home*, Act 1, p. 4.

41. Bolton and Rubens, *Nobody Home*, Act 1, p. 25.

42. Marbury, *My Crystal Ball*, 253.

43. Glenmore Davis, "The Ladies of the Chorus," *Green Book Magazine* (May 1911): 1020.

44. Marbury, *My Crystal Ball*, 254.

45. Marbury, 254.

46. Elisabeth Marbury, "My Girls – As I Know Them," *Harper's Bazaar* (August 1917): 42.

47. Marbury, "My Girls," 43.

48. Marbury, 43.

49. Archie Bell, "Woman Making Theater Her Own Institution, Says Bell," *Mary B. Miller Women's Interest*, undated, New York Public Library Collection.

50. Elisabeth Marbury, "My Girls," 42.

51. Marbury, *My Crystal Ball*, 254–55.

52. See Newman Levy, *The Nan Patterson Case* (New York: Simon & Schuster, 1959).

53. Ned Wayburn, "The Chorus Girl—Old and New," *Theatre* (May 1920).

54. Marbury, *My Crystal Ball*, 256.

55. Marbury, 255.

56. Souvenir program of *Oh, Boy!* Collection of the Museum of the City of New York.

57. "Miss Marbury, Who Produced 'Very Good Eddie,' Speaks," Clipping in the files of the Museum of the City of New York.

58. Clipping held in the Robinson Locke collection of the New York Public Library.

59. See Thomas Postlewait, "George Edwardes and Musical Comedy: The Transformation of London Theatre and Society, 1878–1914," in *The Performing Century: Nineteenth-Century Theatre's History*, ed. Tracy C. Davis and Peter Holland (Basingstoke: Palgrave Macmillan, 2007), 80–102.

60. Alan Hyman, *The Gaiety Years* (London: Cassell, 1975), 6.

61. Hyman, *The Gaiety Years*, 67.

62. Qtd. in Hyman, 63.

63. Qtd. in Michael Goron, *Gilbert and Sullivan's 'Respectable Capers': Class, Respectability and the Savoy Operas, 1877–1909* (Basingstoke: Palgrave Macmillan, 2016), 59.

64. Goron, *Gilbert and Sullivan's*, 60.

65. Marbury, *My Crystal Ball*, 156.

66. "Elisabeth Marbury Discovers A New Type of Entertainment," typescript of press release, Shubert Archive.

67. "Garrick," undated clipping in the Alice Dovey scrapbook, New York Public Library Collection.

68. "'Nobody Home,' Musical Comedy Entertainment Amusement," clipping held in the Robinson Locke Collection, New York Public Library.

69. Bell, "Woman Making Theater."

70. Marbury, *My Crystal Ball*, 253.

71. More generally, it is worth noting that musical theatre, a genre tradition-ally associated with gay men, was suffused in one of its foundational moments with a different kind of queer desire.

72. See Kim Marra, "A Lesbian Marriage of Cultural Consequence: Elisabeth Marbury and Elsie de Wolfe, 1896–1933," in *Passing Performances: Queer Readings of Leading Players in American Theater History*, ed. Robert A. Schanke and Kim Marra (Ann Arbor: University of Michigan Press, 1998), 112.

73. Elsie de Wolfe, *After All* (New York: Arno Press, 1974), 48–49.

74. De Wolfe, *After All*, 49.

75. De Wolfe, 51.

76. De Wolfe, 52.

77. De Wolfe, 67.

78. For an argument about de Wolfe's investment in femininity as expressed through design, see Penny Sparke, "The Domestic Interior and the Construc-tion of Self: The New York Homes of Elsie de Wolfe," in *Interior Design and Identity*, ed. Susie McKellar and Penny Sparke (Manchester: Manchester Uni-versity Press, 2004), 72–91; and Penny Sparke, "Elsie de Wolfe and Her Female Clients, 1905–1915: Gender, Class, and the Professional Interior Decorator," in *Women's Places: Architecture and Design 1860–1960*, ed. Brenda Martin and Penny Sparke (London: Routledge, 2003), 47–68.

79. "'Nobody Home,' A Musical Comedy at the Princess," Clipping in the files of the Shubert Collection.

80. Channing Pollock, "Revive Us Again," *The Green Book Magazine* (1915): 59.

81. "Urbanity of the Follies," *Arts and Decoration* 11, no. 6 (1919): 302.

82. Cecil Smith quotes Bolton's rationale without question, though he also quotes one review that mentions the "'individualized' chorus." Smith, *Musical Comedy*, 122. Meanwhile, Gerald Bordman notes that "Bolton has suggested that he and Kern set out to change the mindlessness of musical comedy from the very start. The show's early history belies his recollections. . . . That these pronouncements were still a bit utopian in 1917 or 1918 scarcely detracted from their essential truth." Bordman, *American Musical*, 104.

83. "The Improvement in Musical Comedy Standards," *The Dramatic Mirror*, February 23, 1918, 7.

84. "The Improvement in Musical Comedy Standards."

85. "The Improvement in Musical Comedy Standards."

86. P. G. Wodehouse and Guy Bolton, *Bring on the Girls: The Improbable Story of Our Life in Musical Comedy, with Pictures to Prove It* (London: Herbert Jenkins, 1954), 88.

87. "The Improvement in Musical Comedy Standards."

88. Wodehouse and Bolton, *Bring on the Girls*, 11.

89. Wodehouse and Bolton, 11–12.

90. Stewart, Manuscript of "Dolly," Act II, Scene 2, p. 21. The spirit of this remains in the 2017 production. The choreography for "Motherhood" has Barnaby fitted by Irene and Minnie Fay in a lady's hat so that he can briefly sing with them in a trio and evade detection by Vandergelder.

91. Stewart, Manuscript of "Dolly," Act II, Scene 2, p. 23; Act II, Scene 3, p. 27–28.

## CHAPTER 3

1. Rodgers, *Musical Stages*, 227.

2. Barnes, "Lilacs to 'Oklahoma!'"

3. Howard Barnes, "The Theatre: Old Season Sets Pace for New," *New York Herald Tribune*, August 8, 1944.

4. Robert Pollak, "'Oklahoma!' flows on like river of delight," *Chicago Sunday Times*, December 5, 1943.

5. "Oklahoma!" *Boston Globe*, October 12, 1945.

6. William Hawkins, "'Oklahoma!' Revisited Is Still a Great Show," *New York World-Telegram*, December 24, 1947. To be sure, the depreciation of hierarchy among musical comedy performers is a hallmark of integration: both *Oklahoma!* and *On The Town*, another oft-cited bulwark of integration, thrived without stars. Ward Morehouse, for example, commented in the *New York Sun* that "there are no overpowering names in the cast of this new production, but it's a company that works well together." Ward Morehouse, "'On The Town' Is a Festive Musical Show—Has Freshness and Vitality," *New York Sun*, December 29, 1944.

7. Samuel Marx and Jan Clayton, *Rodgers & Hart: Bewitched, Bothered, and Bedeviled* (London: W. H. Allen, 1977), 265.

8. Burton Rascoe, "The Guild's 'Oklahoma!'"

9. Jones, *Our Musicals, Ourselves*, 46.

10. Wolf, *Changed for Good*, 11.

11. Richard Wagner, *Opera and Drama*, vol. 1, trans. Edwin Evans, Sr. (London: W. M. Reeves, 1913), 136.

12. Qtd. in Piero Weiss and Richard Taruskin, eds., *Music in the Western World* (Belmont: Schirmer, 1984), 301.

13. Richard Wagner, *Correspondence of Wagner and Liszt*, vol. 1, trans. and ed. Francis Hueffer (London: H. Grevel, 1888), 92, emphasis Wagner's.

14. Richard Wagner, *Opera and Drama*, 181.

15. In this context, it is worth noting conductor Jay Blackton's comment that "it was fascinating to watch [Agnes de Mille] at work. What amazed me was how she took Dick and Oscar's lyrical songs and used them as the framework, the roots, the sperm of her choreographic devices." Qtd. in Gardner, *Agnes de Mille*, 33.

16. Wagner, *Opera and Drama*, 185.

17. Wagner, 186.

18. Brecht, "The Modern Theatre is the Epic Theatre," in *Brecht on Theatre*, 35.

19. Brecht, 35–36.

20. Brecht, "On the Use of Music in an Epic Theatre," in *Brecht on Theatre*, 89.

21. Brecht, 89.

22. Brecht, 89.

23. Brecht, 87.

24. Brecht, 87.

25. Brecht, "On Gestic Music," in *Brecht on Theatre*, 104.

26. Brecht, "The Modern Theatre is the Epic Theatre," 37.

27. Brecht, 37.

28. Brecht, 35.

29. Brecht, 38.

30. Brecht, "On the Use of Music in an Epic Theatre," 87.

31. Brecht, "A Short Organum for the Theatre," in *Brecht on Theatre*, 203.

32. Burt Shevelove, Larry Gelbart, and Stephen Sondheim, *A Funny Thing Happened on the Way to the Forum* (New York: Dodd, Mead & Company, 1963), 19.

33. Shevelove, Gelbart, and Sondheim, *A Funny Thing*, 43.

34. Shevelove, Gelbart, and Sondheim, 73.

35. Shevelove, Gelbart, and Sondheim, 36.

36. Shevelove, Gelbart, and Sondheim, 59.

37. Shevelove, Gelbart, and Sondheim, 85.

38. Shevelove, Gelbart, and Sondheim, 71.

39. Shevelove, Gelbart, and Sondheim, 87.

40. Shevelove, Gelbart, and Sondheim, 90–91.

41. Shevelove, Gelbart, and Sondheim, 91.

42. Shevelove, Gelbart, and Sondheim, 101.

43. Stephen Sondheim, *Finishing the Hat: Collected Lyrics (1954–1981) with Attendant Comments, Principles, Heresies, Grudges, Whines and Anecdotes* (New York: Alfred A. Knopf, 2010), 79.

44. Sondheim, *Finishing the Hat*, 79.

45. Sondheim, 80.

46. Stephen Sondheim, "The Musical Theatre," in *Broadway Song and Story: Playwrights/Lyricists/Composers Discuss Their Hits*, ed. Otis L. Guernsey, Jr. (New York: Dodd Mead, 1986), 233.

47. Sondheim, *Finishing the Hat*, 80.

48. Sondheim, 80, 55.

49. Judith Roof, *Come as You Are: Sexuality and Narrative* (New York: Columbia University Press, 1996), xxvii.

50. Roof, *Come as You Are*, xxii.

51. Roof, 8.

52. Roof, 69.

53. Roof, 85.

54. Arthur Laurents, Stephen Sondheim, and Jule Styne, *Gypsy* (New York: TCG, 1994), 106–7.

55. See also Stacy Wolf's discussion of homosocial duets in "The 1950s: 'Marry the Man Today,'" in *Changed for Good*, 34.

56. Laurents, Sondheim, and Styne, *Gypsy*, 78.

57. Oscar Hammerstein II, Joshua Logan, and Richard Rodgers, *South Pacific: A Musical Play* (New York: Random House, 1949), 45–46.

58. Hammerstein, Logan, and Rodgers, *South Pacific*, 120.

59. Hammerstein, Logan, and Rodgers, 42–43.

60. Hammerstein, Logan, and Rodgers, 128.

61. Hammerstein, Logan, and Rodgers, 18, 129.

62. Hammerstein, Logan, and Rodgers, 129.

## CHAPTER 4

1. George Brooks, "Revolution in the Rhythm Department," *Stardom* (October 1943), 16.

2. "America's Little House," transcript of CBS interview, October 28, 1935. Mamoulian Collection of the Library of Congress.

3. Edwin Schallert, "Grand Opera Gives Mamoulian His Cue," *Los Angeles Times*, August 8, 1943.

4. "Eastman Theater Singers to Put On Excerpts from One of Wagner's Music Dramas," *Rochester Democrat and Chronicle*, March 2, 1924. See also a 1923 profile of Mamoulian that posits that "in its true sense Opera is musical drama and Operatic Art is human emotion expressed through singing, music, and movement, these being united in a common rhythm." Rouben Mamoulian, *The Note Book* 3, no. 5 (December 17, 1923): 1.

5. "In or Of the Broadway Scene: Introducing the Young Russo-American Who Staged an American Negro Play, and a Dancer from Philadelphia," *New York Times*, October 30, 1927.

6. Schallert, "Grand Opera."

7. Schallert, "Grand Opera."

8. Paul Horgan, *A Certain Climate: Essays in History, Arts, and Letters* (Middletown: Wesleyan University Press, 1988), 214.

9. "Eastman School Gives Health Dance Course for Teachers," *Rochester Journal*, July 15, 1925.

10. "A New Form of Theatrical Art," *Rochester Democrat and Chronicle*, December 15, 1925.

11. George Fisher, "Radio Interview," December 18, 1947, Mamoulian Collection of the Library of Congress.

12. "R. M. Director," ca. 1944, Mamoulian Collection of the Library of Congress.

13. "Adventure in Musical Americana: Rouben Mamoulian," *Coronet*, undated, Mamoulian Collection of the Library of Congress.

14. Ruth Moore, "Mr. Mamoulian from Tiflis," October 27, 1945, Mamoulian Collection of the Library of Congress. Mamoulian noted that "El Greco, the most expressively Spanish painter, was a Greek. Lafayette, a Frenchman, felt more closely and keenly the American ideal of liberty and mode of living than thousands of Americans who worked against it."

15. Eddie Egan, "Columbus of Americana," undated, Mamoulian Collection of the Library of Congress.

16. George Fisher, "Radio Interview."

17. Edward Braun, *The Theatre of Meyerhold: Revolution on the Modern Stage* (New York: Drama Book Specialists, 1979), 54–55.

18. Nick Worrall, *Modernism to Realism on the Soviet Stage* (Cambridge, UK: Cambridge University Press, 2008), 110.

19. Yosef I. Yzraely, "Vakhtangov Directing *The Dybbuk*," (Ph.D. diss., Carnegie-

Mellon University, 1971), 39.

20. Myles Fellows, "Rhythm, Music, and the Theatre: An Interview with Rouben Mamoulian," *Etude* (April 1945): 187.

21. Rouben Mamoulian, "Importance of Rhythm on the Screen," *The Film Daily*, March 15, 1934.

22. Philip K. Scheuer, "Rhythm Rouben," 1932, Mamoulian Collection of the Library of Congress. In other tellings, the clock serves as a rhythm "to which in his day dreams knights in shining armor marched to its infallible tempo." Bill Adamson, "Rouben Mamoulian on 'Summer Holiday,'" clipping dated 1946, Mamoulian Collection of the Library of Congress.

23. "Gershwin Trans. Copy," transcript of interview with Rouben Mamoulian, Mamoulian Collection of the Library of Congress.

24. Vera Gottlieb, "Vakhtangov's Musicality: Reassessing Yevgeny Vakhtangov (1883–1922)," *Contemporary Theatre Review* 15, no. 2 (2005): 265.

25. Worrall, *Modernism to Realism*, 105.

26. Aviv Orani, "Realism in Vakhtangov's Theatre of Fantasy." *Theatre Journal* 36, no. 4 (December 1984): 473.

27. Scheuer, "Rhythm Rouben."

28. Mamoulian performed the same appropriative work with the metronome. Time and time again, we hear Mamoulian citing his work with Greta Garbo: "My ambition as a director is to convey the rhyme and cadence of poetry in pictorial images. The scene in the tavern room of 'Queen Christina' is like a poem. I had a metronome on the set to maintain a precise rhythmic relation between the music, the moods in the scene, and the mechanical interchange of camera movement . . . I believe profoundly in the esthetic and emotional satisfaction to be derived from rhythm." "Rhythm on the Screen," *New York Times*, February 11, 1934. Notably, these devices not only echo Vakhtangov's theatrical strategies but also mirror ones used by filmmaker Lev Kuleshov, a contemporary of Mamoulian's who was widely recognized as Russia's first cinematographer and film theorist.

29. Mary Braggiotti, "Roubenchik Has Fun," *New York Post*, May 10, 1943, 31.

30. Brooks Atkinson, "The Play: Back Comes 'Porgy,'" *The New York Times*, September 14, 1929.

31. Margaret Case Harriman, "Mr. Mamoulian of Tiflis and Oklahoma!," *The New York Times Magazine*, July 25, 1943.

32. "Gershwin Trans. Copy," Mamoulian Collection.

33. "From Armenia to Catfish Row: Rouben Mamoulian Travels Far . . . . ", *The Baltimore Sun*, March 17, 1929.

34. "Rouben Mamoulian on KFI with Helen Colley," transcript dated January 31, 1938, Mamoulian Collection of the Library of Congress.

35. "Rouben Mamoulian on KFI."

36. "Rouben Mamoulian on KFI."

37. "Rouben Mamoulian on KFI."

38. Philip K. Scheuer, "Rhythm Rouben."

39. Bob Wachsman, "Salute . . . This Week: To a Citizen of Beverly Hills Who Will Soon Deliver a Golden Boy," 1939, p. 2, Mamoulian Collection of the Library of Congress.

40. "Theater Guild Calls Eastman Act Producer," unattributed 1926 clipping, Mamoulian Collection of the Library of Congress.

41. Rouben Mamoulian, "Stage and Screen," *The Screen Writer* 2, no. 10 (March 1947): 4.

42. Mamoulian, "Stage and Screen," 4.

43. Rouben Mamoulian, "The World's Latest Fine Art," *Cinema Arts* 1, no. 1 (June 1937).

44. Philip K. Scheuer, "Rhythm Rouben."

45. *Porgy and Bess* was seen as the fulfillment of the promise of *Porgy*. As Ruth W. Sedgwick wrote, "Just as it was inevitable . . . that *Porgy* should one day be placed within the frame of a musical score, it was inevitable that when that happened Mamoulian should be called back from Hollywood . . . . With *Porgy and Bess* he is at last able to carry rhythm to its logical conclusion on the wings of George Gershwin's songs." Ruth W. Sedgwick, "Two Adventures in Direction," *Stage* (October 1935): 61.

46. "From Armenia to Catfish Row."

47. See Alexander Saxton, "Blackface Minstrelsy and Jacksonian Ideology," *American Quarterly* 27, no. 1 (March 1975): 3–28; David R. Roediger, *The Wages of Whiteness: Race and the Making of the American Working Class* (New York: Verso, 1991); and Eric Lott, *Love and Theft: Blackface Minstrelsy and the American Working Class* (Oxford: Oxford University Press, 1993).

48. Lott, *Love and Theft*, 52.

49. Saxton, "Blackface Minstrelsy," 12.

50. Roediger, *The Wages of Whiteness*, 116.

51. Roediger, 117.

52. "The Man Who Staged Porgy," transcript of October 4, 1928 article in Newark *Ledger*, Mamoulian Collection of the Library of Congress.

53. See Michael Rogin, *Blackface, White Noise: Jewish Immigrants in the Hollywood Melting Pot* (Berkeley: University of California Press, 1998).

54. Jones, *Our Musicals, Ourselves*, 77.

55. For a different reading of the compensatory functions of the stereotypes in *Show Boat*, see Lauren Berlant's argument that "*Show Boat* would argue that the shell of the stereotype secures the capacity to survive in America and counters the same powerfully dislocating forces of modernity the dramatic texts virtually celebrate. In this sense . . . *Show Boat* demonstrated enormous faith in the vitality of conventionality to provide a world for the disenfranchised, to encode and protect their optimism for living, and to produce aesthetically a sense of comfort akin to that which cannot be provided by the material world of inequality and the political world that destroys life." Lauren Berlant, *The Female Complaint: The Unfinished Business of Sentimentality in American Culture* (Durham, NC: Duke University Press, 2008), 97–98.

56. Cecil Smith, "'Show Boat' Drops Anchor at 1st and Grand," *Los Angeles Times*, September 21, 1967. See also Howard Barnes's comment: ". . . put comedy and music together in an integrated entertainment and toss in dances and odd turns for good measure and 'Show Boat' is the show—a miraculous musical comedy," in Howard Barnes, "The Theater: Greatest of All Musical Comedies," *New York Herald-Tribune*, January 13, 1946. Peter Riddle baldly refers to Hammerstein being able to "attain the fullest possible integration of the songs and the story." Riddle, *The American Musical*, 48. Gerald Bordman hedges admirably in writing that "once again the matter of integration arises. Given the exigencies of the commercial theatre, the aim of a subtle, seemingly inevitable blend of dialogue, song, and dance is a probably unattainable goal, at least in its purest form. But if inevitability is replaced by reasonableness, a number of our best shows certainly attain it. And *Show Boat* is high among the best." Bordman, *American Musical Theatre*, 485.

57. Mark Steyn, *Broadway Babies Say Goodnight: Musicals Then and Now* (New York: Routledge, 2000), 21.

58. Brooks Atkinson, "'Show Boat' As Good As New," *New York Times*, May 20, 1932.

59. For a comprehensive account of *Show Boat*, see Todd Decker's Show Boat: *Performing Race in an American Musical* (Oxford: Oxford University Press, 2012).

60. Oscar Hammerstein II and Jerome Kern, *Show Boat*, in *American Musicals 1927–1949: The Complete Book and Lyrics of Eight Broadway Classics*, ed. Laurence Maslon (New York: Library of America, 2014), 23.

61. Hammerstein and Kern, *Show Boat*, 13.

62. Hammerstein and Kern, 36.

63. Hammerstein and Kern, 36.

64. Hammerstein and Kern, 37.

65. Hammerstein and Kern, 37.

66. Hammerstein and Kern, 37–38.

67. Hammerstein and Kern, 76.

68. Hammerstein and Kern, 79.

69. Hammerstein and Kern, 79.

70. Hammerstein and Kern, 80.

71. Leonard Hall, "Mister Ziegfeld Shows Us One: The Leviathan," *Washington Daily News*, November 16, 1927.

72. "'Show Boat' Makes Bow at Curran With Huge Cast," *San Francisco Examiner*, October 31, 1933.

73. Paul Gerard Smith, "Drama and Music: Show Boat," *Rob Wagner's Script* 10, no. 248 (December 9, 1933).

74. Wilella Waldorf, for example, wrote that "if one scene stood out amid the general opulence, it was that showboat interior with a pretty good burlesque of good old melodrammer [sic] going on. Miss Terris and Mr. Marsh did splendidly by the burlesque, even carrying the spirit of it, perhaps unconsciously, into their subsequent scenes." Wilella Waldorf, undated, *New York World-Telegram* clipping in the files of the New York Public Library. A similar sense of old-fashioned melodrama permeating the proceedings can be found in a review of a 1960 production in Los Angeles, featuring Joe E. Brown, Jacquelyn McKeever, Virginia Capers, and Eddie Foy, Jr. Reviewer Albert Goldberg noted that "the [actors, excepting Lawrence Winters] are mostly decorative, and if they sing rather better than they act, that is all to the good. Sometimes, in fact, it was hard to distinguish between the parody of the play within the play and the characterizations of the straight drama." Albert Goldberg, "'Show Boat' Revival Opens to Full House," *Los Angeles Times*, August 16, 1960.

75. Fred Johnson, "'Show Boat' Given Opulent Production at Curran," *San Francisco Call Bulletin*, November 1, 1933.

76. Qtd. in Miles Kreuger, *Show Boat: The Story of a Classic American Musical* (New York: Oxford University Press, 1977), 55. Canadian critic M. NourbeSe Philip writes that "Kern's music supports the practice of appropriating the products of Black and African culture so as to enrich white life culturally and financially. The same music and rhythms that Magnolia affected—'coon' music—which brought her fame, Kern would incorporate in his music; this in turn would bring him fame. . . . This is the classic case of life imitating art imitating life." I would argue that what Philip senses in the music was the same kind of

control that constitutes the discourse of integration. In M. NourbeSe Philip, *Showing Grit: Showboating North of the 44th Parallel* (Toronto: Poui Publications, 1993), 36.

77. Sylvia Rosenberg, "Ol' Man River Himself," Clipping in files of the Museum of the City of New York.

78. Qtd. in Otis L. Guernsey, Jr., ed., *Playwrights Lyricists Composers On Theater* (New York: Dodd Mead, 1974), 105–6.

79. Tamsen Wolff explores a similar theme in a passage in *Mendel's Theatre: Heredity, Eugenics, and Early Twentieth-Century American Drama* (Basingstoke: Palgrave Macmillan, 2009).

80. Hammerstein and Kern, *Show Boat*, 41.

81. Hammerstein and Kern, 79.

82. Hammerstein and Kern, 42.

83. Hammerstein and Kern, 80.

84. Hammerstein and Kern, 69–70.

85. Hammerstein and Kern, 67–68.

86. Julian Ralph, *Harper's Chicago and The World's Fair* (New York: Harper & Brothers, 1893), 207.

87. Qtd. in Curtis M. Hinsley, "The World as Marketplace: Commodification of the Exotic at the World's Columbian Exposition, Chicago, 1893," in *Exhibiting Cultures: The Poetics and Politics of Museum Display*, ed. Ivan Karp and Steven D. Lavine (Washington, DC: Smithsonian Institution Press, 1991), 353.

88. Qtd. in Bernth Lindfors, "Ethnological Show Business: Footlighting the Dark Continent," in *Freakery: Cultural Spectacles of the Extraordinary Body*, ed. Rosemarie Garland Thomson (New York: New York University Press, 1996), 214.

89. Ruth Middleton, *Circus Memoirs: Reminiscences of George Middleton* (Los Angeles: George Rice and Sons, 1913), 69.

90. J. G. Wood, "Dime Museums from a Naturalist's Point of View," *The Atlantic* 55, no. 332 (June 1885): 760.

91. Lindfors, "Ethnological Show Business," 216.

92. Lindfors, 217.

93. George W. Walker, "The Real 'Coon' on the American Stage," *Theatre* (August 1906): 224.

94. Walker, "The Real 'Coon,'" 224.

95. Walker, 224.

96. Thomas L. Riis, ed., *The Music and Scripts of* In Dahomey (Madison: A-R Editions, 1996), xlix.

97. See Daphne Brooks, *Bodies in Dissent: Spectacular Performances of Race and Freedom, 1850–1910* (Durham, NC: Duke University Press, 2006).

98. Riis, *The Music and Scripts of* In Dahomey, lxvii.

99. Brooks, *Bodies in Dissent*, 238.

## CHAPTER 5

1. Hammerstein and Kern, *Show Boat*, 66.

2. Jo Swerling, Abe Burrows, and Frank Loesser, *Guys and Dolls: A Musical Fable of Broadway*, in *American Musicals: 1950–1969*, ed. Laurence Maslon (New York: Library of America, 2014), 44.

3. John Chapman, "Main Query in 'Where's Charley' Is Where's Bolger?— He's There!" *New York Daily News*, October 12, 1948.

4. Cy Feuer and Ken Gross, *I Got the Show Right Here* (New York: Applause, 2005), 102–3.

5. Howard Barnes, "Here's Bolger," *New York Herald-Tribune*, October 12, 1948; William Hawkins, "'Where's Charley' Out of This World," *New York World-Telegram*, October 12, 1948.

6. Moss Hart, preface to *Lady in the Dark*, ed. Alfred Sirmay (New York: Chappell, 1941).

7. Sidney B. Whipple, "'Lady in the Dark' Triumph for Miss Lawrence," *New York World-Telegram*, January 24, 1941.

8. Walter F. Kerr, "First Night Report: 'Gypsy,'" *New York Herald-Tribune*, May 22, 1959.

9. Producer Cy Feuer seems also to take some credit for the adaptation; see Feuer and Gross, *I Got the Show*, 81.

10. George Abbott and Frank Loesser, *Where's Charley: A Musical Comedy in Two Acts* (New York: Frank Music, 1948), 12.

11. Abbott and Loesser, *Where's Charley*, 14.

12. Abbott and Loesser, 15.

13. Abbott and Loesser, 56.

14. Abbott and Loesser, 88.

15. While the show's investment in Brazilian imitation takes place in the wake of a number of Latin American performances popularized during the Good Neighbor Era, it is part of a broader tradition of Latin American imitation in musical theatre and indeed takes place after the geopolitical imperatives of the Good Neighbor Policy had waned, leaving in its place a broader "camp incoherence." See Herrera, *Latin Numbers*.

16. Abbott and Loesser, *Where's Charley*, 21.

17. Abbott and Loesser, 27.

18. Abbott and Loesser, 41.

19. Abbott and Loesser, 59.

20. Abbott and Loesser, 59.

21. Abbott and Loesser, 50.

22. Abbott and Loesser, 83.

23. Abbott and Loesser, 48.

24. Abbott and Loesser, 48.

25. Abbott and Loesser, 48.

26. Abbott and Loesser, 81.

27. Abbott and Loesser, 25–26.

28. Abbott and Loesser, 60.

29. Abbott and Loesser, 61.

30. Abbott and Loesser, 5.

31. See Maya Cantu's "'Make Up Your Mind': Boss Ladies and Enchantresses in the 1940s Broadway Musical," in her *American Cinderellas on the Broadway Musical Stage: Imagining the Working Girl from* Irene *to* Gypsy (Basingstoke: Palgrave Macmillan, 2015), for a broader contextualization of the panicked working woman figure.

32. Moss Hart, Ira Gershwin, and Kurt Weill, *Lady in the Dark* (Cleveland: World Publishing, 1944), 15.

33. Hart, Gershwin, and Weill, *Lady in the Dark*, 140.

34. Hart, Gershwin, and Weill, 68.

35. Hart, Gershwin, and Weill, 68.

36. Hart, Gershwin, and Weill, 73.

37. Hart, Gershwin, and Weill, 46–47.

38. Hart, Gershwin, and Weill, 47.

39. Hart, Gershwin, and Weill, 86.

40. Hart, Gershwin, and Weill, 98.

41. Richard Watts, Jr., "Dreaming Lady," *New York Herald-Tribune*, January 24, 1941.

42. Hart, Gershwin, and Weill, *Lady in the Dark*, 126.

43. Hart, Gershwin, and Weill, 127.

44. It is worth noting that the presence of "exotic" elements suffused the other dream sequences as well. As bruce d. mcclung has shown, "each dream sequence was conceived with a specific dance"—the "Glamour Dream" featured an Afro-Cuban rumba, while the "Wedding Dream" was organized around a

Spanish bolero. Thus, with the "Russian" number in the "Circus Dream," we can see how each of the dreams features an eruption of "exotic" desire in the form. See bruce d. mcclung, *Lady in the Dark: Biography of a Musical* (Oxford: Oxford University Press, 2007), 62–63.

45. Sidney B. Whipple, "'Lady in the Dark.'"

46. For more on the performance of Russian-ness, see Choi Chatterjee, "The Russian Romance in American Popular Culture, 1890–1939" and Beth Holmgren, "Russia on their Mind: How Hollywood Pictured the Soviet Front," in *Americans Experience Russia: Encountering the Enigma, 1917 to the Present*, ed. Choi Chatterjee and Beth Holmgren (New York: Routledge, 2013).

47. Hart, Gershwin, and Weill, *Lady in the Dark*, 134.

48. Hart, Gershwin, and Weill, 181.

49. Ira Gershwin, *Lyrics on Several Occasions* (New York: Limelight, 1997), 207.

50. Gershwin, *Lyrics on Several Occasions*, 209.

51. Gershwin, 209.

52. Gershwin, 209.

53. Bach, *Dazzler*, 226.

54. Watts, Jr., "Dreaming Lady."

55. Robert Rice, "Rice and Old Shoes," *New York PM*, February 3, 1941.

56. Lawrence Kubie, preface to *Lady in the Dark*, by Hart, Gershwin, and Weill (Cleveland: World Publishing, 1944), viii.

57. Kubie, preface to *Lady in the Dark*, viii.

58. Bach, *Dazzler*, 216.

59. Qtd. in Bach, 216.

60. Lys Symonette and Kim H. Kowalke, eds. and trans. *Speak Low (When You Speak Love): The Letters of Kurt Weill and Lotte Lenya* (Berkeley: University of California Press, 1996), 276.

61. Bach, *Dazzler*, 227–28.

62. Cantu, *American Cinderellas*, 102.

63. Burns Mantle, "'Lady in the Dark' Evening of Dreams for Gertrude Lawrence," *New York Daily News*, January 24, 1941.

64. It is worth noting that the audience was central to *Where's Charley?* as well: the trademark gimmick of "Once In Love With Amy" was that it became a sing-a-long.

65. Arthur Laurents, *Mainly On Directing: Gypsy, West Side Story, and Other Musicals* (New York: Knopf, 2009), 20.

66. Terrence McNally, Arthur Laurents, Stephen Sondheim, and Jule Styne, "Gypsy," in *Broadway Song and Story: Playwrights/Lyricists/Composers Discuss*

*Their Hits*, ed. Otis L. Guernsey, Jr. (New York: Dodd Mead, 1986), 74.

67. McNally, Laurents, Sondheim, and Styne, "Gypsy," 73.

68. Laurents, Sondheim, and Styne, *Gypsy*, 29.

69. Laurents, Sondheim, and Styne, 29.

70. Laurents, Sondheim, and Styne, 29.

71. Laurents, Sondheim, and Styne, 29–30.

72. Laurents, Sondheim, and Styne, 31.

73. Laurents, Sondheim, and Styne, 11.

74. McNally, Laurents, Sondheim, and Styne, "Gypsy," 64.

75. For an account that suggests how these "stage waits" (as in the case of *Lady in the Dark*'s "Tschaikowsky" and *Gypsy*'s "Mr. Goldstone") might themselves be queer, see David Savran, "You've Got That Thing: Cole Porter, Stephen Sondheim, and the Erotics of the List Song," *Theatre Journal* 64, no. 4 (December 2012): 533–48.

76. Laurents, Sondheim, and Styne, *Gypsy*, 30.

77. Guernsey, *Broadway Song and Story*, 64.

78. Laurents, Sondheim, and Styne, *Gypsy*, 30.

79. Laurents, *Mainly On Directing*, 32.

80. Laurents, 32. For Jule Styne's slightly different recollection, see Al Kasha and Joel Hirschhorn, *Notes on Broadway: Intimate Conversations with Broadway's Greatest Songwriters* (New York: Simon & Schuster, 1985), 294. Hammerstein does not figure at all in Styne's memory of the incident; Styne claims instead that he told his collaborators, "She's been screaming for five minutes; you'd better give her some applause." Challenged by Laurents, Styne (allegedly) argued that "this woman deserves a hand. Not one place in the whole show does she get one. . . . You never let her stop the show." In Styne's account, director Jerome Robbins approved Styne's instincts, and Laurents conceded and allowed Merman to take her bows. According to Styne, "The show didn't go on for seven minutes after the number—applause, applause, applause. And I said, 'What's better, Arthur, to have a show like that, or to have her quiet? You've got enough drama in your show.'"

81. Laurents, *Mainly On Directing*, 33.

82. Laurents, 33.

83. Laurents, 34.

84. Laurents, 34.

85. Laurents, 35.

86. Laurents, 35.

87. Laurents, 32.

88. Laurents, Sondheim, and Styne, *Gypsy*, 7.

89. Laurents, Sondheim, and Styne, 11–12, italics mine.

90. Laurents, Sondheim, and Styne, 105.

91. Laurents, Sondheim, and Styne, 107.

92. Laurents, *Mainly on Directing*, 22.

93. Barbara Seaman, *Lovely Me: The Life of Jacqueline Susann* (New York: William Morrow, 1987), 246.

94. Walter F. Kerr, "First Night Report: 'Gypsy.'"

95. Brooks Atkinson, "Theatre: Good Show!," *New York Times*, May 22, 1959.

96. Kenward Elmslie, *The Grass Harp: A Musical Play* (New York: Samuel French, 1971), 9.

97. Elmslie, *The Grass Harp*, 15.

98. Elmslie, 14.

99. Elmslie, 63.

100. Elmslie, 64.

101. Type-script libretto, *Two Gentlemen of Verona*, 1.

102. Jack Kroll, "Avon Rock," *Newsweek*, December 13, 1971, 114.

103. Irving Wardle, "Two Gentlemen of Verona," *London Times*, April 27, 1973.

104. John Guare and Mel Shapiro, *Two Gentlemen of Verona*, in *Great Rock Musicals*, ed. Stanley Richards (New York: Stein & Day, 1979), 76.

105. Guare and Shapiro, *Two Gentlemen of Verona*, 101.

106. María Irene Fornés, *Promenade and Other Plays* (New York: PAJ Publications, 1987), 24.

107. Betty Comden, Adolph Green, and Jule Styne, *Bells Are Ringing* (New York: Random House, 1957), 144–45.

108. The by-now familiar logic of exotic/erotic imitation plays out when Carl, a delivery boy, sees Ella dressed in a fancy dress ready for a night on the town and insists on teaching her how to cha-cha. Removing his jacket, Carl "seems suddenly transformed into a slinky, Latin-type male." Thus begins "Mu-Cha-Cha," a number that absurdly "turn[s] Susanswerphone into a Cuban dance hall." Predictably, this scene of jubilant ethnic imitation is followed by an unexpected eruption of sexual desire, as a man crosses by Jeffrey Moss, who is seated on a park bench. The stage directions indicate that "Jeff, with sudden, happy inspiration, sings 'Hello, hello there!' as the man passes. The latter turns and looks at him with disbelief and extreme suspicion, then dashes off." The scene leads to "Just in Time," a romantic number, the performance of which attracts a crowd who watches and applauds. As the stage directions indicate, "they continue dancing. As the dance reaches a 'torrid' climax, Ella almost

delivers a 'bump.'" Jeff interrupts her, saying, "Hey, wait a minute! Don't give them everything," prompting ad libs from the crowd, who want more. Comden, Green, and Styne, *Bells Are Ringing*, 116–125.

109. Comden, Green, and Styne, *Bells Are Ringing*, 162.

110. Comden, Green, and Styne, *Bells Are Ringing*, 164.

111. It is worth noting that *Fantasticks* author Tom Jones, writing in 1990, recalled that a pivotal moment in the development of the show came when he discarded an earlier draft that used the "Rodgers and Hammerstein model" and structured the show based on their idea of a "presentational theatre which would exalt in theatrical devices rather than trying to hide them." See Tom Jones and Harvey Schmidt, *The Fantasticks* (New York: Applause, 1990), 8.

112. Tom Jones and Harvey Schmidt, *Fantasticks/Celebration* (New York: Quite Specific Media, 1973), 31.

113. Jones and Schmidt, *Fantasticks/Celebration*, 15.

114. Jones and Schmidt, *Fantasticks/Celebration*, 21.

115. Ken Mandelbaum, *A Chorus Line and the Musicals of Michael Bennett* (New York: St. Martin's Press, 1989), 168.

116. Frank Rich, introduction to *A Chorus Line*, by James Kirkwood, Nicholas Dante, and Edward Kleban (New York: Applause, 1995), xv, xiii.

117. Kirkwood, Dante, and Kleban, *A Chorus Line*, 105.

118. Rich, introduction to *A Chorus Line*, xiv.

119. Kirkwood, Dante, and Kleban, *A Chorus Line*, 97.

120. Kirkwood, Dante, and Kleban, 114–15.

121. Kirkwood, Dante, and Kleban, 98.

122. Kirkwood, Dante, and Kleban, 99.

123. Kirkwood, Dante, and Kleban, 103.

124. Kirkwood, Dante, and Kleban, 19.

125. Kirkwood, Dante, and Kleban, 94.

126. Ken Mandelbaum, *A Chorus Line and the Musicals of Michael Bennett* (New York: St. Martin's Press, 1989), 169.

127. Kirkwood, Dante, and Kleban, 131.

128. Kirkwood, Dante, and Kleban, 138.

129. Kirkwood, Dante, and Kleban, 145.

## CHAPTER 6

1. Albert Johnson, "Exposure to 'Flower Drum Song.'" Clipping in files of the New York Public Library.

2. Donatella Galella, "Feeling Yellow: Responding to Contemporary Yellow-face in Musical Performance," *Journal of Dramatic Theory and Criticism* 32, no. 2 (Spring 2018): 70. For some of the musical's spectators, this very spectaculariza-tion may seem to shore up this unmarked white, male, heterosexual subject in a mechanism similar to that described by José Muñoz, who writes of an "'official' national affect," which he describes as "a mode of being in the world primarily associated with white middle-class subjectivity," in contrast to which "Latina/o affect appears over the top and excessive." In such a representational economy that "often attempts to contain Latina/o images as spectacles of spiciness and exoticism," these "mainstream depictions of Latino affect serve to reduce, sim-plify, and contain ethnic difference." See Muñoz, "Feeling Brown: Ethnicity and Affect in Ricardo Bracho's 'The Sweetest Hangover (and Other STDs),'" *Theatre Journal* 52, no. 1 (March 2000): 69.

3. Christopher Breyer, "Vision & Revision: Collaborating with the Past," *Performing Arts Magazine* (November 2001): 9.

4. Breyer, "Vision & Revision," 7.

5. Quoted in Sheryl Flatow, "Culture Clash," *Playbill* 118, no. 10 (10 October 2002): 15.

6. Richard Watts, Jr., "Two on the Aisle," *New York Post*, December 2, 1958.

7. Brooks Atkinson, "Theatre: Oriental Musical," *New York Times*, December 2, 1958.

8. "Special Broadway Report: Back in Lights," *Newsweek*, December 1, 1958, 56.

9. John McClain, "Musical by R & H Garners a Posy," *New York Journal-American*, December 2, 1958.

10. "Broadway: The Girls on Grant Avenue," *Time* 72, no. 25 (December 22, 1958): 42.

11. Joanne Stang, "R & H Brand on a Musical," *New York Times Magazine*, November 23, 1958.

12. Stang, "R & H Brand on a Musical," 18. In an article in *Dance* magazine, Hollis Alpert suggested that Carol Haney's choreographic demands also made it difficult to assemble a cast. "It was easier to find those who could do ethnic work," he wrote, "but many of those, along with more classically trained danc-ers, couldn't 'cut it' to quite the satisfaction of Miss Haney." Hollis Alpert, "Old Friends in New Jobs," *Dance Magazine* (December 1958): 53.

13. In a *Newsweek* article, Richard Rodgers seemed to hint at the ways that the "mélange of nationalities" was itself pleasurable: ". . . the funny thing is, the more mixed up they are, the more attractive they are. We have 13-year-old twin

girls who are as outrageous a combination as oysters and chocolate sauce—Polish and Filipino. Oscar and I think they're wonderful." See "Special Broadway Report: Back in Lights," 53–54.

14. Walter F. Kerr, "First Night Report: 'Flower Drum Song,'" *New York Herald-Tribune*, December 2, 1958.

15. Watts, Jr., "Two on the Aisle."

16. McClain, "Musical by R & H."

17. Cyrus Durgin, "R & H with Chinese Flavor: 'Flower Drum Song' Premiere," *Boston Daily Globe*, October 28, 1958.

18. Elinor Hughes, "The Theatre: Flower Drum Song," *Boston Herald*, October 28, 1958.

19. Myles Standish, "'Flower Drum Song' a Delightful Show," *St. Louis Post-Dispatch*, August 22, 1961.

20. Louis Calta, clipping in the files of the New York Public Library Theatre Collection.

21. Stanley Eichelbaum, "Talented Crew in 'Flower Drum Song,'" *San Francisco Examiner*, February 7, 1963.

22. Albert Johnson, "Exposure to 'Flower Drum Song.'"

23. Kenneth Tynan, "Tiny Chinese Minds," *The New Yorker*, December 13, 1958.

24. Cyrus Durgin similarly referred to the show as being "cannily contrived for the Broadway trade . . . mingl[ing] Oriental fancies with hotcha, strippers, and very simple Americanisms of speech, hoofing, and attitudes." Durgin, "R & H with Chinese Flavor."

25. Patrick Anderson, "'Flower Drum Song' in the 1980s," *Asian Week*, April 7, 1983, 14.

26. Sheri Tan, "'Flower Drum' Critics Haven't Read Script," *Asian Week*, March 31, 1983, 4.

27. Forrest Gok and Dennis Kinoshita-Myers, "Another Opinion," *Asian Week*, April 7, 1983.

28. Qtd. in Flatow, "Culture Clash," 14.

29. Flatow, 14.

30. Hwang, *Flower Drum Song*, xii.

31. For an extremely insightful reading of the sartorial politics of *Flower Drum Song*, see Sean Metzger's *Chinese Looks: Fashion, Performance, Race* (Bloomington: Indiana University Press, 2014), especially 174–82 and 194–202.

32. C. Y. Lee, *The Flower Drum Song* (New York: Farrar, Straus and Cudahy, 1957), 221.

33. Joseph Fields and Oscar Hammerstein II, *Flower Drum Song* (New York: Farrar Straus & Cudahy, 1960), 31.

34. Fields and Hammerstein, *Flower Drum Song*, 27.

35. Lee, *The Flower Drum Song*, 144–45.

36. Hwang, *Flower Drum Song*, 96.

37. Hwang, 27.

38. Fields and Hammerstein, *Flower Drum Song*, 85.

39. The 1958 version opens up at least the possibility of self-critique: through its association of Broadway-style music with Linda Low, the show indicts the genre of musical theatre as capitalist vulgarity—and its own ostensibly humorous portrayal of "bad" casting (as in the case of the Irish and Spanish women) would clearly have echoed the bad casting of the production itself, which was noted in the popular press.

40. Ben Brantley, "Theater Review: New Coat of Paint for Old Pagoda," *New York Times*, October 18, 2002.

41. Hwang, *Flower Drum Song*, 54.

42. Hwang, 84.

43. Hwang, 17.

44. Hwang, 18.

45. Hwang, 44.

46. Josephine Lee, "'Something Beyond and Above': David Henry Hwang's Revision of Flower Drum Song," in *The Theatre of David Henry Hwang*, by Esther Kim Lee (London: Bloomsburg, 2015), 137.

47. Kerr, "First Night Report: 'Flower Drum Song.'"

48. Fields and Hammerstein, *Flower Drum Song*, 61.

49. Steven Oxman, "Revival Tests 'Flower' Power," *Variety*, October 8, 2001, 27.

50. Fields and Hammerstein, *Flower Drum Song*, 63.

51. Fields and Hammerstein, 37.

52. David Henry Hwang, *M. Butterfly* (New York: Penguin, 1989), 99.

53. Hwang, *Flower Drum Song*, 70.

54. In revising the themes and images of the original production, Hwang said early in the process that he intended to "hew more closely to the novel than to the original Broadway production," referring to the C. Y. Lee novel of the same name that provided the source material for Hammerstein and Fields. Lee himself agreed, saying that Hwang "could have a closer feel to my original novel because he's ABC—American-born Chinese." See Claude Brodesser, "Hwang Bangs 'Flower Drum,'" *Variety*, April 27, 1998; and Heidi Benson, "Fortunate Son," *San Francisco Chronicle*, September 18, 2002.

55. Qtd. in Siu Leung Li, *Cross-Dressing in Chinese Opera* (Hong Kong: Hong Kong University Press, 2003), 192.

56. Colin Mackerras, *The Performing Arts in Contemporary China* (London: Routledge, 1981), 184.

57. Li, *Cross-Dressing in Chinese Opera*, 215–16.

58. Li, 23.

59. See Esther Kim Lee, *A History of Asian American Theatre* (Cambridge, UK: Cambridge University Press, 2011), 129–37.

60. Lee, "'Something Beyond and Above,'" 130.

61. Hwang, *M. Butterfly*, 95.

62. Hwang, 96.

63. Hwang, 48.

64. Hwang, 69.

65. Hwang, 71.

66. Hwang, 91.

67. Hwang, 92.

68. Hwang, 63.

69. Significantly, the show suggests—through Gallimard's interactions with this friend, Marc—that this collective fantasy is inspired by homosocial or homosexual fantasies. And it is Marc who affirms the alignment of the gendered fantasy with a racialized one: "Their women fear us." It is precisely this paternalistic attitude that Gallimard invokes when he first sees Song perform: "I believed her suffering. I wanted to take her in my arms—so delicate, even I could protect her, take her home, pamper her until she smiled." See Hwang, *M. Butterfly*, 15–16.

70. Hwang, *Flower Drum Song*, 92.

71. Hwang, 92.

72. Anderson, "'Flower Drum Song' in the 1980s," 15.

73. See Steven Oxman, "Flower Drum Song," *Variety*, October 22, 2001, 45.

74. Hwang, *Flower Drum Song*, 72.

75. Hwang, *Flower Drum Song*, 71.

76. Karen Wada, afterword to David Henry Hwang, *Flower Drum Song* (New York: TCG, 2003), 113.

77. Wada, afterword to *Flower Drum Song*, 113–14.

78. In a similar vein, Hwang resorts to the same kind of racialized humor that Fields and Hammerstein did. For example, when Ta is celebrating how amazing Linda is, Mei-Li asks, "And can she also strangle a chicken?" Later, Chao suggests to Mei-Li that they "celebrate with a big dinner: fish heads and

chicken feet," to which she replies, "Who could resist?" Also, Harvard is so named because his parents want him to attend school there, before becoming a doctor. Hwang, *Flower Drum Song*, 25, 78.

79. Hwang, *Flower Drum Song*, xii.

80. Hwang, 109.

81. Hwang, xiv.

82. Hwang, 97.

83. Hwang, 33.

84. Hwang, 96.


## CHAPTER 7

1. Robert Simon, "Jerome Kern," *Modern Music* (Feb 1929): 21.

2. Simon, "Jerome Kern," 20.

3. Andrew Lloyd Webber, *Unmasked: A Memoir* (New York: Harper Collins, 2018), 134.

4. Qtd. in Michael Walsh, *Andrew Lloyd Webber: His Life and Works* (New York: Harry N. Abrams, 1997), 84.

5. Steyn, *Broadway Babies Say Goodnight*, 277.

6. Andrew Lloyd Webber, "The Music of Evita," in Andrew Lloyd Webber and Tim Rice, *Evita: The Legend of Eva Peron (1919–1952)*, (New York: Avon, 1978), unpaginated.

7. Lloyd Webber and Rice, *Evita*.

8. Judith Weinraub, "Before 'Superstar,' There Was 'Joseph,'" *New York Times*, December 19, 1976. See also Robert Gordon, Olaf Jubin, and Millie Taylor, *British Musical Theatre Since 1950* (London: Bloomsbury, 2016), especially 157–60.

9. Lloyd Webber, *Unmasked*, 134.

10. Qtd. in Glenn Loney, "Don't Cry For Andrew Lloyd Webber," *Opera News* 45, no. 17 (April 4, 1981): 13.

11. Lloyd Webber, *Unmasked*, 134.

12. Lloyd Webber, *Unmasked*, 322.

13. See Stacy Wolf's excellent discussion in "The 1980s: 'The Phantom of the Opera' Is There Inside My Mind," in *Changed for Good*, 127–60.

14. Jerome Moross, interview by John Caps, August 31, 1979, transcript in Moross Collection, Columbia University Rare Book and Manuscript Library, 4.

15. John Latouche and Jerome Moross, *The Golden Apple* (New York: Random House, 1954), xv.

16. Latouche and Moross, *The Golden Apple*, xx, xix.

17. Latouche and Moross, *The Golden Apple*, xix.

18. Jerome Moross, interview by Paul Snook, WRVR-New York, 1970, transcript in Moross Collection, Columbia University Rare Book and Manuscript Library, 17–18.

19. Qtd. in Jack Gaver, "Jerome Moross Is Selective About His Theatre Projects," *New York Morning Telegraph*, April 5, 1962.

20. Latouche and Moross, *The Golden Apple*, xiv.

21. See John Latouche to Jerry and Hazel Moross, July 19, 1940, Moross Collection, Columbia University Rare Book and Manuscript Library.

22. John Latouche, "Items Called 'Ballet Ballads': Some Notes on Their Prolonged Journey to the Music Box," *New York Times*, June 6, 1948.

23. "Visitor Influx Hypoes Dented B'way," *Variety*, undated clipping in scrapbook in Moross Collection, Columbia University Rare Book and Manuscript Library.

24. Mildred Norton, "Stage Review: 'Ballet Ballads,'" *L.A. News*, October 11, 1950.

25. Richard Watts, Jr., "The Creative Freshness of 'Ballet Ballads,'" *New York Post and the Home News*, May 11, 1948.

26. Robert Garland, "'Ballet Ballads': Fresh and Exciting with Bright Music," *New York Journal-American*, May 10, 1948.

27. John Chapman, "Other Hits Might Have Won: 'Sally' Disappoints; 'Ballads' Excites," *New York Sunday News*, May 16, 1948.

28. Robert Coleman, "'Ballet Ballads' Is Modern Dance Hit," *New York Daily Mirror*, May 28, 1948.

29. William Hawkins, "3 'Ballet Ballads' Are Dancing Operas," clipping in files of Moross Collection, Columbia University Rare Book and Manuscript Library.

30. George Freedley, "'Ballet Ballads' Is Most Interesting ET Production," *New York Morning Telegraph*, May 11, 1948.

31. Chapman, "Other Hits Might Have Won."

32. Richard Watts, Jr., "The Creative Freshness of 'Ballet Ballads.'"

33. Frances Herridge, "'Ballet Ballads' Is at Home on B'way," *PM*, May 23, 1948.

34. Walter Terry, "'Ballet Ballads' Is a Synthesis of Music, Dance, Dramatic Text," *New York Herald-Tribune*, May 16, 1948.

35. Miles Kastendieck, "'Ballet Ballads': Three Artistic Worlds in One," *New York Journal-American*, May 19, 1948. *Ballet Ballads* is virtually forgotten in the

secondary scholarship, though it is mentioned in a footnote in Larry Stempel's "The Musical Play Expands," in which he writes that "a non-Robbins work, *Ballet Ballads* (1948), did use dance throughout each of the three 'dance plays' that comprised the show, but the dance for each was by a different choreographer (Katherine Litz, Paul Godkin, Hanya Holm), and the show itself enjoyed only a brief run." Larry Stempel, "The Musical Play Expands," *American Music* 10, no. 2 (Summer 1992): 168 n59. Original production performer Sharry Underwood recalled the details of the production in "Ballet Ballads," *Dance Chronicle* 9, no. 3 (1985): 279–327. See also Howard Pollack, *The Ballad of John Latouche* (Oxford: Oxford University Press, 2017).

36. Latouche, "Items Called 'Ballet Ballads.'"

37. Jerome Moross, "Ballet Ballads Revisited," production notes for a revival of *Ballet Ballads*, Moross Collection, Columbia University Rare Book and Manuscript Library. It is worth noting that the word "singing" takes the place of the word "music," which is scratched out.

38. Jerome Moross, interview by Paul Snook, WRVR-New York, 15.

39. Jerome Moross, interview by John Caps.

40. Jerome Moross to John Latouche, February 16, 1947, Moross Collection, Columbia University Rare Book and Manuscript Library.

41. Walter Terry, "The Ballet," *New York Herald-Tribune*, undated clipping, Moross Collection, Columbia University Rare Book and Manuscript Library. The clipping actually refers to Agnes de Mille's ballets for "Oakland!" but Terry surely meant *Oklahoma!*

42. Miles Kastendieck, "'Ballet Ballads.'"

43. Walter Terry, "'Ballet Ballads' Is a Synthesis of Music, Dance, Dramatic Text."

44. Richard Watts, Jr., "Some Additional Praise for 'Ballet Ballads,'" *New York Post*, June 8, 1948.

45. Watts, Jr., "The Creative Freshness."

46. Jerome Moross and John Latouche, *Ballet Ballads* (New York: Chappell & Co., 1949).

47. Latouche, "Items Called 'Ballet Ballads.'"

48. Latouche.

49. Latouche.

50. Terry, "The Ballet."

51. Garland, "'Ballet Ballads': Fresh and Exciting."

52. Irving Kolodin, "'Ballet Ballads' at the Music Box," *New York Sun*, May 19, 1948.

53. George Currie, "Off Stage: Theater's Experiments This Year Have Amply Rewarded Enthusiasts," *Brooklyn Eagle*, May 16, 1948.

54. Note Tim Carter's discovery that Hammerstein's sketch for the dance indicates "after the manner of 'Coq D'or,'" referencing the Metropolitan Opera's 1918 production of *The Golden Cockerel*, which Carter notes "had singers seated at the side of the stage and dancers and mimes enacting the plot." See Carter, *Oklahoma!: The Making of an American Musical*, 131. Irving Kolodin's review of "Ballet Ballads" (*New York Sun*, May 19, 1948) notes the show's indebtedness to that production: "How 'American,' actually, is the notion of combining vocalists who sing with dancers who mime the action may be recalled from the Metropolitan's production of 'Coq d'Or' twenty-five years ago, which used precisely the same technic."

55. Qtd. in Frommer and Frommer, *It Happened on Broadway*, 136.

56. Mildred Norton, "Mildred Norton," *Los Angeles Daily News*, June 15, 1948.

57. Hawkins, "3 'Ballet Ballads' Are Dancing Operas."

58. Jerome Moross, interview by Paul Snook, WRVR-New York, 14.

59. Moross expressed a similar sentiment in a 1944 letter to Latouche about *Ballet Ballads* in which he enthused that "the chorus is so integrated." Jerome Moross to John Latouche, August 10, 1944, Moross Collection, Columbia University Rare Book and Manuscript Library.

60. Rembert Browne, "Genius: A Conversation with 'Hamilton' Maestro Lin-Manuel Miranda," http://grantland.com/hollywood-prospectus/genius-a-conversation-with-hamilton-maestro-lin-manuel-miranda/.

61. Lin-Manuel Miranda and Jeremy McCarter, *Hamilton: The Revolution* (New York: Hachette, 2016), 10.

62. Miranda and McCarter, *Hamilton*, 277.

63. Miranda and McCarter, 184.

64. Miranda and McCarter, 11.

65. Miranda and McCarter, 206.

66. Jeff MacGregor, "Meet Lin-Manuel Miranda, the Genius Behind 'Hamilton,' Broadway's Newest Hit," *Smithsonian Magazine*, November 12, 2015.

67. Miranda and McCarter, *Hamilton*, 223.

68. MacGregor, "Meet Lin-Manuel Miranda."

69. Miranda and McCarter, 226.

70. Browne, "Genius: A Conversation."

71. Miranda and McCarter, *Hamilton*, 88–89.

72. Miranda and McCarter, 88.

73. Rebecca Mead, "All About the Hamiltons," *The New Yorker*, February 9, 2015.

74. Miranda and McCarter, *Hamilton*, 136.

75. MacGregor, "Meet Lin-Manuel Miranda."

76. Miranda and McCarter, *Hamilton*, 280.

77. Qtd. in Michael Paulson, "'Hamilton' Casting Call Is Criticized by Union," *New York Times*, March 31, 2016.

78. Mark Binelli, "'Hamilton' Creator Lin-Manuel Miranda: The Rolling Stone Interview," *Rolling Stone*, June 1, 2016.

79. Helen Lewis, "Hamilton: How Lin-Manuel Miranda's Musical Rewrote the Story of America," *The New Statesman*, December 4, 2017. See also Brian Eugenio Herrera, "Miranda's Manifesto," *Theatre* 47, no. 2 (2017): 23–33.

80. Ben Brantley, "A More Perfect Union," *New York Times*, August 7, 2015.

81. Binelli, "'Hamilton' Creator."

82. Binelli, "'Hamilton' Creator."

83. Miranda and McCarter, *Hamilton*, 121. Unconsciously echoing the fear of applause that permeates discussions of integration, Miranda noted that they tried adding more bars since the two bars did not accommodate the applause, but then reverted to two bars since "it felt like we were *asking* for applause."

84. Miranda and McCarter, 161.

85. Kelly Lawler, "'Hamilton' Creator Would Love Women to Play the Founding Fathers," *USA Today*, November 13, 2015.

86. Brantley, "A More Perfect Union."

## CONCLUSION

1. Stew, *Passing Strange: The Complete Book and Lyrics of the Broadway Musical* (New York: Applause, 2009), 1.

2. Bill Bragin, foreword to *Passing Strange: The Complete Book and Lyrics of the Broadway Musical*, by Stew (New York: Applause, 2009), x.

3. Heidi Rodewald, preface to *Passing Strange: The Complete Book and Lyrics of the Broadway Musical*, by Stew (New York: Applause, 2009), xv.

4. Stew, *Passing Strange*, 16.

5. Stew, 25.

6. Stew, 36.

7. Jon Pareles, "Theater: Riffing in Context with a Jazzman," *New York Times*, April 19, 1992.

8. George C. Wolfe and Susan Birkenhead, *Jelly's Last Jam* (New York: TCG, 1993), 66.

9. Wolfe and Birkenhead, *Jelly's Last Jam*, 68.

10. Wolfe and Birkenhead, *Jelly's Last Jam*, 69.

11. John Lahr, introduction to *Jelly's Last Jam*, by George C. Wolfe and Susan Birkenhead (New York: TCG, 1993), viii–ix.

12. Laura B. Randolph, "'Jelly's Last Jam' and the Pain and Passion of Gregory Hines," *Ebony* 47, no. 11 (September 1992): 118.

13. Pareles, "Riffing in Context."

14. Pareles, Riffing in Context."

15. "Broadway Show 'Jelly's Last Jam' and Writer-Director George C. Wolfe," *CBS News Transcripts Sunday Morning*, April 26, 1992.

16. Pareles, "Riffing in Context."

17. John Lahr, introduction to *Jelly's Last Jam*, xi.

18. Qtd. in Anemona Hartocollis, "Gregory's New Jam," *Newsday*, April 23, 1992.

19. Wolfe and Birkenhead, *Jelly's Last Jam*, 4.

20. Thomas O'Connor, "Much Music, Little Life Seen in 'Jelly's Last Jam,'" *Orange County Register*, March 8, 1991.

21. Anna Kisselgoff, "Dance View: Dance and Song are Cheek to Cheek on Broadway," *New York Times*, July 5, 1992.

22. Pareles, "Riffing in Context."

23. Qtd. in Lahr, introduction to *Jelly's Last Jam*, xii.

24. Lahr, xiii, ix.

25. Frank Rich, "The Energy and Pain Inside a Man Who Helped Give Birth to Jazz," *New York Times*, April 27, 1992.

26. Lisa Fung, "A Big Bet on 'Soft Power': How David Henry Hwang's Latest Play Takes on China, Trump and More," *Los Angeles Times*, May 3, 2018.

27. Fung, "A Big Bet on 'Soft Power.'"

28. Eric A. Gordon, "'Soft Power' Imagines a Broadway Musical Under Future Chinese Hegemony," *People's World*, May 29, 2018. https://www.peoplesworld.org/article/soft-power-imagines-a-broadway-musical-under-future-chinese-hegemony/.

29. As performed at the Public Theater, New York City, October 20, 2019.

30. *New York Times* critic Jesse Green, for example, notes that the song is "reminiscent of 'The Rain in Spain' from 'My Fair Lady.'" See Jesse Green, "East Meets West in a Feverish Dream," *New York Times*, October 16, 2019.

31. Lily Janiak, "Curran's 'Soft Power' by David Henry Hwang First Defining Musical of Trump Era," *San Francisco Chronicle*, June 22, 2018.

32. Andrew R. Chow, "Playwright David Henry Hwang on Flipping a Flawed Musical on Its Head in *Soft Power*," *Time Magazine*, October 25, 2019. https://time.com/5708556/david-henry-hwang-soft-power/.

33. Frances Baum Nicholson, "'Soft Power' at LA's Ahmanson Is an Original Musical that Works on Several Levels," *Los Angeles Daily News*, May 25, 2018.

34. Chow, "Playwright David Henry Hwang."

35. Green, "East Meets West in a Feverish Dream."

36. Quoted in Flatow, "Culture Clash," 15.

37. Frank Rizzo, "Off Broadway Review: 'Soft Power,'" *Variety*, October 15, 2019.

# BIBLIOGRAPHY

Abbott, George, and Richard Bissell. *The Pajama Game*. New York: Random House, 1954.

Abbott, George, and Frank Loesser. *Where's Charley: A Musical Comedy in Two Acts*. New York: Frank Music, 1948.

Adamson, Bill. "Rouben Mamoulian on 'Summer Holiday.'" Clipping dated 1946. Mamoulian Collection of the Library of Congress.

"Adventure in Musical Americana: Rouben Mamoulian." *Coronet*, undated. Mamoulian Collection of the Library of Congress.

Alpert, Hollis. "Old Friends in New Jobs." *Dance Magazine* (December 1958): 53–55.

"America's Little House." Transcript of CBS Interview, October 28, 1935, Mamoulian Collection of the Library of Congress.

"Amusements." *New York Times*, September 17, 1866.

Anae, Nicole. "Poses Plastiques: The Art and Style of 'Statuary' in Victorian Visual Theatre." *Australasian Drama Studies* 52 (April 2008): 112–30.

Anderson, Patrick. "'Flower Drum Song' in the 1980s." *Asian Week*, April 7, 1983.

Atkinson, Brooks. "The Play: Back Comes 'Porgy.'" *The New York Times*, September 14, 1929.

———. "'Show Boat' As Good As New." *New York Times*, May 20, 1932.

———. "Theatre: Good Show!" *New York Times*, May 22, 1959.

———. "Theatre: Oriental Musical." *New York Times*, December 2, 1958.

Bach, Steven. *Dazzler: The Life and Times of Moss Hart*. New York: Knopf, 2001.

Barker, Barbara. *Ballet or Ballyhoo: The American Careers of Maria Bonfanti, Rita Sangalli, and Giuseppina Morlacchi*. New York: Dance Horizons, 1984.

Barnes, Howard. "Here's Bolger." *New York Herald-Tribune*, October 12, 1948.

———. "Lilacs to 'Oklahoma!'" *New York Herald-Tribune*, April 1, 1943.

———. "The Theater: Greatest of All Musical Comedies." *New York Herald-Tribune*, January 13, 1946.

———. "The Theatre: Old Season Sets Pace for New." *New York Herald Tribune*, August 8, 1944.

Barras, Charles. *The Black Crook*. In *Nineteenth Century American Plays*, edited by Myron Matlaw. New York: Applause, 1967.

Bell, Archie. "Woman Making Theater Her Own Institution, Says Bell." *Mary B. Miller Women's Interest*, undated. New York Public Library Collection.

Benson, Heidi. "Fortunate Son." *San Francisco Chronicle*, September 18, 2002.

Berlant, Lauren. *The Female Complaint: The Unfinished Business of Sentimentality in American Culture*. Durham, NC: Duke University Press, 2008.

Binelli, Mark. "'Hamilton' Creator Lin-Manuel Miranda: The Rolling Stone Interview." *Rolling Stone*, June 1, 2016.

Block, Geoffrey. "Integration." In *Histories of the Musical: An Oxford Handbook of the American Musical*, vol. 1, edited by Raymond Knapp, Mitchell Morris, and Stacy Wolf, 153–75. New York: Oxford University Press, 2018.

Bolton, Guy, and Paul Rubens. *Nobody Home*, manuscript, 1915. New York Public Library Collection.

Bordman, Gerald. *American Musical Theatre: A Chronicle*. 3rd ed. Oxford: Oxford University Press, 2001.

Bowers, Dwight Blocker. *American Musical Theater: Shows, Songs, and Stars*. Washington, DC: Smithsonian Collection of Recordings, 1989.

Braggiotti, Mary. "Roubenchik Has Fun." *New York Post*, May 10, 1943.

Bragin, Bill. Foreword to *Passing Strange: The Complete Book and Lyrics of the Broadway Musical*, by Stew, ix–xiv. New York: Applause, 2009.

Brantley, Ben. "A More Perfect Union." *New York Times*, August 7, 2015.

———. "Theater Review: New Coat of Paint for Old Pagoda." *New York Times*, October 18, 2002.

Braun, Edward. *The Theatre of Meyerhold: Revolution on the Modern Stage*. New York: Drama Book Specialists, 1979.

Brecht, Bertolt. "On Gestic Music." In *Brecht on Theatre: The Development of an Aesthetic*. Translated by John Willett, 104–6. New York: Hill and Wang, 1964.

———. "The Modern Theatre is the Epic Theatre." In *Brecht on Theatre: The Development of an Aesthetic*. Translated by John Willett, 33–42. New York: Hill and Wang, 1964.

———. "On the Use of Music in an Epic Theatre." In *Brecht on Theatre: The Development of an Aesthetic*. Translated by John Willett, 84–90. New York: Hill and Wang, 1964.

———. "A Short Organum for the Theatre." In *Brecht on Theatre: The Development of an Aesthetic*. Translated by John Willett, 179–208. New York: Hill and Wang, 1964.

Breyer, Christopher. "Vision & Revision: Collaborating with the Past." *Performing Arts Magazine* (November 2001): 7–10.

"Broadway: The Girls on Grant Avenue." *Time* 72, no. 25 (December 22, 1958): 42–47.

"Broadway Show 'Jelly's Last Jam' and Writer-Director George C. Wolfe." *CBS News Transcripts Sunday Morning*, April 26, 1992.

Brodesser, Claude. "Hwang Bangs 'Flower Drum.'" *Variety*, April 27, 1998.

Brooks, Daphne. *Bodies in Dissent: Spectacular Performances of Race and Freedom, 1850–1910*. Durham, NC: Duke University Press, 2006.

Brooks, George. "Revolution in the Rhythm Department." *Stardom* (October 1943): 16.

Brooks, Peter. *The Melodramatic Imagination: Balzac, Henry James, Melodrama, and the Mode of Excess*. New Haven: Yale University Press, 1976.

Brown, Jayna. *Babylon Girls: Black Women Performers and the Shaping of the Modern*. Durham, NC: Duke University Press, 2008.

Browne, Rembert. "Genius: A Conversation with 'Hamilton' Maestro Lin-Manuel Miranda." Accessed January 24, 2017. http://grantland.com /hollywood-prospectus/genius-a-conversation-with-hamilton-maestro-lin -manuel-miranda/.

Cantu, Maya. *American Cinderellas on the Broadway Musical Stage: Imagining the Working Girl from* Irene *to* Gypsy. Basingstoke: Palgrave Macmillan, 2015.

Carlson, Marvin. *Theories of the Theatre: A Historical and Critical Survey from the Greeks to the Present*. Ithaca: Cornell University Press, 1993.

Carter, Tim. Oklahoma!: *The Making of an American Musical*. New Haven: Yale University Press, 2007.

Chapman, John. "Main Query in 'Where's Charley' Is Where's Bolger?—He's There!" *New York Daily News*, October 12, 1948.

———. "'My Fair Lady' A Superb, Stylish Musical Play with a Perfect Cast." *New York Daily News*, March 16, 1956.

———. "'One Touch of Venus' Brings a Touch of Life to Broadway." *New York Daily News*, October 8, 1943.

———. "Other Hits Might Have Won: 'Sally' Disappoints; 'Ballads' Excites." *New York Sunday News*, May 16, 1948.

Chapman, Mary. "'Living Pictures': Women and *Tableaux Vivants* in Nineteenth-Century American Fiction and Culture." *Wide Angle* 18, no. 3 (1996): 22–52.

Chatterjee, Choi, and Beth Holmgren, eds. *Americans Experience Russia: Encountering the Enigma, 1917 to the Present*. New York: Routledge, 2013.

Chow, Andrew R. "Playwright David Henry Hwang on Flipping a Flawed Musical on Its Head in *Soft Power*." *Time Magazine*, October 25, 2019. https://time.com/5708556/david-henry-hwang-soft-power/.

Coleman, Robert. "'Ballet Ballads' Is Modern Dance Hit." *New York Daily Mirror*, May 28, 1948.

———. "'The Girl in Pink Tights' Is a Tuneful Frolic." *New York Daily Mirror*, March 8, 1954.

———. "'My Fair Lady' Is a Glittering Musical." *New York Daily Mirror*, March 16, 1956.

Comden, Betty, Adolph Green, and Jule Styne. *Bells Are Ringing*. New York: Random House, 1957.

Copeland, Roger. "Broadway Dance." *Dance Magazine* (November 1974): 33–37.

Currie, George. "Off Stage: Theater's Experiments This Year Have Amply Rewarded Enthusiasts." *Brooklyn Eagle*, May 16, 1948.

David, John Russell. "The Genesis of the Variety Theatre: *The Black Crook* Comes to Saint Louis." *Missouri Historical Review* LXIV, no. 2 (January 1970): 133–49.

Davis, Glenmore. "The Ladies of the Chorus." *Green Book Magazine* (May 1911): 1019–24.

Decker, Todd. Show Boat: *Performing Race in an American Musical*. Oxford: Oxford University Press, 2012.

de Mille, Agnes. *And Promenade Home*. Boston: Little Brown, 1958.

Denby, David J. *Sentimental Narrative and the Social Order in France, 1760–1820*. New York: Cambridge University Press, 1994.

de Wolfe, Elsie. *After All*. New York: Arno Press, 1974.

"Disastrous Conflagration." *The New York Times*, May 22, 1866.

Durgin, Cyrus. "R & H with Chinese Flavor: 'Flower Drum Song' Premiere." *Boston Daily Globe*, October 28, 1958.

"Eastman School Gives Health Dance Course for Teachers." *Rochester Journal*, July 15, 1925.

"Eastman Theater Singers to Put On Excerpts from One of Wagner's Music Dramas." *Rochester Democrat and Chronicle*, March 2, 1924.

Egan, Eddie. "Columbus of Americana," undated. Mamoulian Collection of the Library of Congress.

Eichelbaum, Stanley. "Talented Crew in 'Flower Drum Song.'" *San Francisco Examiner*, February 7, 1963.

"Elisabeth Marbury Discovers A New Type of Entertainment." Typescript of press release, Shubert Archive.

Elmslie, Kenward. *The Grass Harp: A Musical Play*. New York: Samuel French, 1971.

Engel, Lehman. *The American Musical Theater: A Consideration*. New York: CBS Legacy, 1967.

Fellows, Myles. "Rhythm, Music, and the Theatre: An Interview with Rouben Mamoulian." *Etude* (April 1945): 187.

Feuer, Cy, and Ken Gross. *I Got the Show Right Here*. New York: Applause, 2005.

Fields, Joseph, and Oscar Hammerstein II. *Flower Drum Song*. New York: Farrar Straus & Cudahy, 1960.

Fisher, George. "Radio Interview," December 18, 1947. Mamoulian Collection of the Library of Congress.

Flatow, Sheryl. "Culture Clash," *Playbill* 118, no. 10 (10 October 2002): 14–15.

Foil, David. Liner notes to *Can-Can*. Angel Records, 1992.

Fornés, María Irene. *Promenade and Other Plays*. New York: PAJ Publications, 1987.

Freedley, George. "'Ballet Ballads' Is Most Interesting ET Production." *New York Morning Telegraph*, May 11, 1948.

"From Armenia to Catfish Row: Rouben Mamoulian Travels Far . . . ." *The Baltimore Sun*, March 17, 1929.

Frommer, Myrna Katz, and Harvey Frommer. *It Happened on Broadway: An Oral History of the Great White Way*. Lanham: Taylor, 2015.

Fung, Lisa. "A Big Bet on 'Soft Power': How David Henry Hwang's Latest Play Takes on China, Trump and More." *Los Angeles Times*, May 3, 2018.

Galella, Donatella. "Feeling Yellow: Responding to Contemporary Yellowface in Musical Performance." *Journal of Dramatic Theory and Criticism* 32, no. 2 (Spring 2018): 67–77.

Gardner, Kara Ann. *Agnes de Mille: Telling Stories in Broadway Dance*. Oxford: Oxford University Press, 2016.

Garland, Robert. "'Ballet Ballads': Fresh and Exciting with Bright Music." *New York Journal-American*, May 10, 1948.

———. "'On The Town' Opens at Adelphi Theatre." *New York Journal-American*, December 29, 1944.

"Garrick." Undated clipping in the Alice Dovey scrapbook, New York Public Library Collection.

Gaver, Jack. "Jerome Moross Is Selective About His Theatre Projects." *New York Morning Telegraph*, April 5, 1962.

Gershwin, Ira. *Lyrics on Several Occasions*. New York: Limelight, 1997.

"Gershwin Trans. Copy." Transcript of interview with Rouben Mamoulian, Mamoulian Collection of the Library of Congress.

*The Girl in Pink Tights*. Souvenir program in the New York Public Library Collection.

Gok, Forrest, and Dennis Kinoshita-Myers. "Another Opinion." *Asian Week*, April 7, 1983.

Goldberg, Albert. "'Show Boat' Revival Opens to Full House." *Los Angeles Times*, August 16, 1960.

Gordon, Eric A. "'Soft Power' Imagines a Broadway Musical Under Future
    Chinese Hegemony." *People's World*, May 29, 2018. https://www
    .peoplesworld.org/article/soft-power-imagines-a-broadway-musical-under
    -future-chinese-hegemony/.
Gordon, Robert, Olaf Jubin, and Millie Taylor. *British Musical Theatre Since 1950*.
    London: Bloomsbury, 2016.
Goron, Michael. *Gilbert and Sullivan's "Respectable Capers": Class, Respectability
    and the Savoy Operas, 1877–1909*. Basingstoke: Palgrave Macmillan, 2016.
Gottlieb, Vera. "Vakhtangov's Musicality: Reassessing Yevgeny Vakhtangov
    (1883–1922)." *Contemporary Theatre Review* 15, no. 2 (2005): 259–68.
"The Great Fire." *New York Times*, May 23, 1866.
Green, Jesse. "East Meets West in a Feverish Dream." *New York Times*, October
    16, 2019.
Green, Stanley. *The World of Musical Comedy: The Story of the American Musical
    Stage as Told Through the Careers of Its Foremost Composers and Lyricists*. South
    Brunswick: A. S. Barnes, 1968.
Gross, Kenneth. *The Dream of the Moving Statue*. Ithaca: Cornell University
    Press, 1992.
Guare, John, and Mel Shapiro. *Two Gentlemen of Verona*. In *Great Rock Musicals*,
    edited by Stanley Richards. New York: Stein & Day, 1979.
Guare, John, and Ira Weitzman. "An Ordinary Man: An Interview with Jerry
    Adler." *Lincoln Center Review* 71 (Spring 2018): 12–15.
Guernsey, Otis L. Jr., ed. *Broadway Song and Story: Playwrights/Lyricists/
    Composers Discuss Their Hits*. New York: Dodd Mead, 1986.
———, ed. *Playwrights Lyricists Composers On Theater*. New York: Dodd Mead,
    1974.
Hall, Leonard. "Mister Ziegfeld Shows Us One: The Leviathan." *Washington
    Daily News*, November 16, 1927.
Hammerstein, Oscar II. *Lyrics*. New York: Simon & Schuster, 1949.
Hammerstein, Oscar II, and Jerome Kern. *Show Boat*. In *American Musicals
    1927–1949: The Complete Book and Lyrics of Eight Broadway Classics*, edited by
    Laurence Maslon. New York: Library of America, 2014.
Hammerstein, Oscar II; Joshua Logan, and Richard Rodgers. *South Pacific: A
    Musical Play*. New York: Random House, 1949.
Hammerstein, Oscar II, and Richard Rodgers. *Oklahoma!* New York: Random
    House, 1942.
Hamon, Philippe. "Rhetorical Status of the Descriptive." *Yale French Studies* 61
    (1981): 1–26.

Harriman, Margaret Case. "Mr. Mamoulian of Tiflis and Oklahoma!" *The New York Times Magazine*, July 25, 1943.

Hart, Moss. Preface to *Lady in the Dark*, edited by Alfred Sirmay. New York: Chappell, 1941.

Hart, Moss, Ira Gershwin, and Kurt Weill. *Lady in the Dark*. Cleveland: World Publishing, 1944.

Hartocollis, Anemona. "Gregory's New Jam." *Newsday*, April 23, 1992.

Hawkins, William. "3 'Ballet Ballads' Are Dancing Operas," undated. Moross Collection, Columbia University Rare Book and Manuscript Library.

———. "'Oklahoma!' Revisited Is Still a Great Show." *New York World-Telegram*, December 24, 1947.

———. "'Where's Charley' Out of This World," *New York World-Telegram*, October 12, 1948.

Hazlitt, William. "Flaxman's Lectures on Sculpture." *Edinburgh Review* 50 (1829).

Herman, Jerry, and Ken Bloom. *Jerry Herman: The Lyrics, A Celebration*. New York: Routledge, 2003.

Herrera, Brian Eugenio. *Latin Numbers: Playing Latino in Twentieth-Century U.S. Popular Performance*. Ann Arbor: University of Michigan Press, 2015.

———. "Dance Differences in Two Musicals." *New York Post*, April 26, 1954.

Herridge, Frances. "'Ballet Ballads' Is at Home on B'way." *PM*, May 23, 1948.

———. "Miranda's Manifesto." *Theatre* 47, no. 2 (2017): 23–33.

Hinsley, Curtis M. "The World as Marketplace: Commodification of the Exotic at the World's Columbian Exposition, Chicago, 1893." In *Exhibiting Cultures: The Poetics and Politics of Museum Display*, edited by Ivan Karp and Steven D. Lavine, 344–65. Washington, DC: Smithsonian Institution Press, 1991.

Horgan, Paul. *A Certain Climate: Essays in History, Arts, and Letters*. Middletown: Wesleyan University Press, 1988.

Hughes, Elinor. "The Theatre: Flower Drum Song." *Boston Herald*, October 28, 1958.

Hwang, David Henry. *Flower Drum Song*. New York: TCG, 2003.

———. *M. Butterfly*. New York: Penguin, 1989.

Hyman, Alan. *The Gaiety Years*. London: Cassell, 1975.

"The Improvement in Musical Comedy Standards." *The Dramatic Mirror*, February 23, 1918.

"In or Of the Broadway Scene: Introducing the Young Russo-American Who Staged an American Negro Play, and a Dancer from Philadelphia." *New York Times*, October 30, 1927.

Janiak, Lily. "Curran's 'Soft Power' by David Henry Hwang First Defining Musical of Trump Era." *San Francisco Chronicle*, June 22, 2018.

Johnson, Albert. "Exposure to 'Flower Drum Song.'" Clipping in the files of the New York Public Library Collection.

Johnson, Fred. "'Show Boat' Given Opulent Production at Curran." *San Francisco Call Bulletin*, November 1, 1933.

Johnson, James Weldon. *Black Manhattan*. New York: Arno and the New York Times, 1968.

Jones, John Bush. *Our Musicals, Ourselves: A Social History of the American Musical Theatre*. Hanover: Brandeis University Press, 2003.

Jones, Tom, and Harvey Schmidt. *The Fantasticks*. New York: Applause, 1990.

———. *Fantasticks/Celebration*. New York: Quite Specific Media, 1973.

Kasha, Al, and Joel Hirschhorn. *Notes on Broadway: Intimate Conversations with Broadway's Greatest Songwriters*. New York: Simon & Schuster, 1985.

Kastendieck, Miles. "'Ballet Ballads': Three Artistic Worlds in One." *New York Journal-American*, May 19, 1948.

Kerr, Walter F. "First Night Report: 'Flower Drum Song.'" *New York Herald-Tribune*, December 2, 1958.

———. "First Night Report: 'Gypsy.'" *New York Herald-Tribune*, May 22, 1959.

———. "My Fair Lady." *New York Herald-Tribune*, March 16, 1956.

Kirkwood, James, Nicholas Dante, and Edward Kleban. *A Chorus Line*. New York: Applause, 1995.

Kirle, Bruce. *Unfinished Show Business: Broadway Musicals as Works-in-Process*. Carbondale: Southern Illinois University Press, 2005.

Kislan, Richard. *Hoofing on Broadway: A History of Show Dancing*. New York: Prentice Hall, 1987.

Kisselgoff, Anna. "Dance View: Dance and Song are Cheek to Cheek on Broadway." *New York Times*, July 5, 1992.

Knapp, Margaret. "Integration of Elements as a Viable Standard for Judging Musical Theatre." In *Focus on Popular Theatre in America*, edited by Henry F. Salerno, 112–19. Bowling Green, OH: Bowling Green State University Popular Press, 1978.

Knapp, Raymond. *The American Musical and the Formation of National Identity*. Princeton: Princeton University Press, 2006.

Kolodin, Irving. "'Ballet Ballads' at the Music Box." *New York Sun*, May 19, 1948.

Kraut, Anthea. *Choreographing Copyright: Race, Gender, and Intellectual Property Rights in American Dance*. Oxford: Oxford University Press, 2015.

Kreuger, Miles. *Show Boat: The Story of a Classic American Musical*. New York: Oxford University Press, 1977.

Kroll, Jack. "Avon Rock." *Newsweek*, December 13, 1971.

Kubie, Lawrence. Preface to *Lady in the Dark* by Moss Hart, Ira Gershwin, and Kurt Weill, vii–xiv. Cleveland: World Publishing, 1944.

Lada-Richards, Ismene. "'Mobile Statuary': Refractions of Pantomime Dancing from Callistratus to Emma Hamilton and Andrew Ducrow." *International Journal of the Classical Tradition* 10, no. 1 (Summer 2003): 3–37.

Lahr, John. Introduction to *Jelly's Last Jam*, by George C. Wolfe and Susan Birkenhead, vii–xiii. New York: TCG, 1993.

Lamb, Andrew. *150 Years of Popular Musical Theatre*. New Haven: Yale University Press, 2000.

Latouche, John. "Items Called 'Ballet Ballads': Some Notes on Their Prolonged Journey to the Music Box." *New York Times*, June 6, 1948.

Latouche, John, to Jerry and Hazel Moross, July 19, 1940. Moross Collection, Columbia University Rare Book and Manuscript Library.

Latouche, John, and Jerome Moross. *The Golden Apple*. New York: Random House, 1954.

Laurents, Arthur. *Mainly On Directing: Gypsy, West Side Story, and Other Musicals*. New York: Knopf, 2009.

Laurents, Arthur, Stephen Sondheim, and Jule Styne. *Gypsy*. New York: TCG, 1994.

Lawler, Kelly. "'Hamilton' Creator Would Love Women to Play the Founding Fathers." *USA Today*, November 13, 2015.

Leavitt, M. B. *Fifty Years in Theatrical Management*. New York: Broadway Publishing, 1912.

Lee, C. Y. *The Flower Drum Song*. New York: Farrar, Straus and Cudahy, 1957.

Lee, Esther Kim. *A History of Asian American Theatre*. Cambridge, UK: Cambridge University Press, 2011.

Lee, Josephine. "'Something Beyond and Above': David Henry Hwang's Revision of Flower Drum Song." In *The Theatre of David Henry Hwang*, by Esther Kim Lee. London: Bloomsbury, 2015.

Lerner, Alan Jay. *My Fair Lady: A Musical Play in Two Acts*. New York: Coward-McCann, 1956.

———. *The Street Where I Live*. New York: Norton, 1978.

Levy, Newman. *The Nan Patterson Case*. New York: Simon & Schuster, 1959.

Lewis, Helen. "Hamilton: How Lin-Manuel Miranda's Musical Rewrote the Story of America." *The New Statesman*, December 4, 2017.

Li, Siu Leung. *Cross-Dressing in Chinese Opera*. Hong Kong: Hong Kong University Press, 2003.

Lindfors, Bernth. "Ethnological Show Business: Footlighting the Dark Continent." In *Freakery: Cultural Spectacles of the Extraordinary Body*, edited by Rosemarie Garland Thomson, 207–18. New York: New York University Press, 1996.

Livingston, Nancy Olson. "How to Stop a Show." *Lincoln Center Review* 71 (Spring 2018): 10–11.

Lloyd Webber, Andrew. *Unmasked: A Memoir*. New York: Harper Collins, 2018.

Lloyd Webber, Andrew, and Tim Rice. *Evita: The Legend of Eva Peron (1919–1952)*. New York: Avon, 1978.

Logan, Olive. *Apropos of Women and Theatres, With A Paper or Two on Parisian Topics*. New York: Carleton, 1869.

Loney, Glenn. "Don't Cry For Andrew Lloyd Webber." *Opera News* 45, no. 17 (April 4, 1981): 12–14.

Lott, Eric. *Love and Theft: Blackface Minstrelsy and the American Working Class*. Oxford: Oxford University Press, 1993.

MacGregor, Jeff. "Meet Lin-Manuel Miranda, the Genius Behind 'Hamilton,' Broadway's Newest Hit." *Smithsonian Magazine*, November 12, 2015.

Mackerras, Colin. *The Performing Arts in Contemporary China*. London: Routledge, 1981.

Mamoulian, Rouben. "Importance of Rhythm on the Screen." *The Film Daily*, March 15, 1934.

———. *The Note Book* 3, no. 5 (December 17, 1923): 1–4.

———. "Stage and Screen." *The Screen Writer* 2, no. 10 (March 1947).

———. "The World's Latest Fine Art." *Cinema Arts* 1, no. 1 (June 1937).

"The Man Who Staged Porgy." October 4, 1928, Mamoulian Collection of the Library of Congress.

Mandelbaum, Ken. *A Chorus Line and the Musicals of Michael Bennett*. New York: St. Martin's Press, 1989.

Mantle, Burns. "'Lady in the Dark' Evening of Dreams for Gertrude Lawrence." *New York Daily News*, January 24, 1941.

———. "'Oklahoma!' Links the Ballet with the Prairie Beautifully." *New York Daily News*, April 1, 1943.

Marbury, Elisabeth. Introduction to *Modern Dancing*, by Mr. and Mrs. Vernon Castle, 19–29. New York: Harper & Brothers, 1914.

———. *My Crystal Ball*. New York: Boni & Liveright, 1923.

———. "My Girls – As I Know Them." *Harper's Bazaar* (August 1917): 42–43.

Marks, Edward B. *They All Had Glamour: From the Swedish Nightingale to the Naked Lady*. New York: Julian Messner, 1944.

Marra, Kim. "A Lesbian Marriage of Cultural Consequence: Elisabeth Marbury and Elsie de Wolfe, 1896–1933." In *Passing Performances: Queer Readings of Leading Players in American Theater History*, edited by Robert A. Schanke and Kim Marra, 104–28. Ann Arbor: University of Michigan Press, 1998.

Marx, Samuel, and Jan Clayton. *Rodgers & Hart: Bewitched, Bothered, and Bedeviled*. London: W. H. Allen, 1977.

Maslon, Laurence, ed. *American Musicals: 1927–1949*. New York: Library of America, 2014.

Mast, Gerald. *Can't Help Singin': The American Musical on Stage and Screen*. Woodstock: Overlook Press, 1987.

Mates, Julian. "The Black Crook Myth." *Theatre Survey* 7, no. 1 (May 1966): 31–43.

McClain, John. "Musical by R & H Garners a Posy." *New York Journal-American*, December 2, 1958.

mcclung, bruce d. *Lady in the Dark: Biography of a Musical*. Oxford: Oxford University Press, 2007.

McCullough, Jack W. *Living Pictures on the New York Stage*. Ann Arbor: UMI Research Press, 1983.

McMillin, Scott. *The Musical as Drama*. Princeton: Princeton University Press, 2006.

McNally, Terrence, Arthur Laurents, Stephen Sondheim, and Jule Styne. "Gypsy," in *Broadway Song and Story: Playwrights/Lyricists/Composers Discuss Their Hits*, edited by Otis L. Guernsey, Jr. New York: Dodd Mead, 1986.

Mead, Rebecca. "All About the Hamiltons." *The New Yorker*, February 9, 2015.

Melman, Billie. *Women and the Popular Imagination in the Twenties: Flappers and Nymphs*. Basingstoke: Macmillan, 1988.

Metzger, Sean. *Chinese Looks: Fashion, Performance, Race*. Bloomington: Indiana University Press, 2014.

Middleton, Ruth. *Circus Memoirs: Reminiscences of George Middleton*. Los Angeles: George Rice and Sons, 1913.

Miller, D. A. *Place for Us: Essay on the Broadway Musical*. Cambridge, MA: Harvard University Press, 1998.

Millstein, Gilbert. "How The First Musical Was Born," unattributed. New York Public Library Collection.

Miranda, Lin-Manuel, and Jeremy McCarter. *Hamilton: The Revolution*. New York: Hachette, 2016.

"Miss Marbury, Who Produced 'Very Good Eddie,' Speaks." Clipping in the files of the Museum of the City of New York.

Moore, Ruth. "Mr. Mamoulian from Tiflis." October 27, 1945. Mamoulian Collection of the Library of Congress.

Mordden, Ethan. *Beautiful Mornin': The Broadway Musical in the 1940s.* New York: Oxford University Press, 1999.

Morehouse, Ward. "'On The Town' Is a Festive Musical Show—Has Freshness and Vitality." *New York Sun*, December 29, 1944.

Morley, Christopher. "Hoboken Nights." *Saturday Evening Post*, July 13, 1929.

Moross, Jerome. "Ballet Ballads Revisited," production notes for a revival of *Ballet Ballads*. Moross Collection, Columbia University Rare Book and Manuscript Library.

———. Interview by John Caps, August 31, 1979. Moross Collection, Columbia University  Rare Book and Manuscript Library.

———. Interview by Paul Snook, WRVR-New York, 1970. Moross Collection, Columbia University Rare Book and Manuscript Library.

Moross, Jerome, to John Latouche, August 10, 1944. Moross Collection, Columbia University Rare Book and Manuscript Library.

Moross, Jerome, to John Latouche, February 16, 1947. Moross Collection, Columbia University Rare Book and Manuscript Library.

Moross, Jerome, and John Latouche. *Ballet Ballads.* New York: Chappell & Co., 1949.

Most, Andrea. *Making Americans: Jews and the Broadway Musical.* Cambridge, MA: Harvard University Press, 2004.

Muñoz, José. "Feeling Brown: Ethnicity and Affect in Ricardo Bracho's The Sweetest Hangover (and Other STDs)." *Theatre Journal* 52, no. 1 (March 2000): 67–79.

Nathan, George Jean. "The Show in Split Tights." *New York Journal-American*, March 28, 1954.

"Naughty Things That a Preacher Saw." *New York Clipper*, December 1, 1866.

"A New Form of Theatrical Art." *Rochester Democrat and Chronicle*, December 15, 1925.

*New York Clipper*, September 17, 1866.

———, September 29, 1866.

———, October 13, 1866.

———, December 29, 1866.

*New York Daily Tribune*, September 24, 1866.

*New York Times*, September 13, 1866.

Nichols, Lewis. "'Oklahoma!' a Musical Hailed as Delightful, Based on 'Green Grow the Lilacs,' Opens Here at the St. James Theatre." *New York Times*, April 1, 1943.

Nicholson, Frances Baum. "'Soft Power' at LA's Ahmanson Is an Original Musical that Works on Several Levels." *Los Angeles Daily News*, May 25, 2018.

"'Nobody Home,' A Musical Comedy at the Princess." Clipping in the files of the Shubert Collection.

"'Nobody Home,' Musical Comedy Entertainment Amusement." Clipping held in the Robinson Locke Collection, New York Public Library.

Norton, Mildred. "Mildred Norton." *Los Angeles Daily News*, June 15, 1948.

———. "Stage Review: 'Ballet Ballads.'" *L.A. News*, October 11, 1950.

O'Connor, Thomas. "Much Music, Little Life Seen in 'Jelly's Last Jam.'" *Orange County Register*, March 8, 1991.

Odell, George C. D. *Annals of the New York Stage*. Vol 8. New York: Columbia University Press, 1936.

*Oh, Boy!* Souvenir program in the Museum of the City of New York Collection.

"Oklahoma!" *Boston Globe*, October 12, 1945.

Olin, Reuel Keith. "A History and Interpretation of the Princess Theatre Musical Plays: 1915–1919." Ph.D. diss., New York University, 1979.

Orani, Aviv. "Realism in Vakhtangov's Theatre of Fantasy." *Theatre Journal* 36, no. 4 (December 1984): 462–80.

Oxman, Steven. "Flower Drum Song." *Variety*, October 22, 2001.

———. "Revival Tests 'Flower' Power." *Variety*, October 8, 2001.

Pareles, Jon. "Theater: Riffing in Context with a Jazzman." *New York Times*, April 19, 1992.

Paulson, Michael. "'Hamilton' Casting Call Is Criticized by Union." *New York Times*, March 31, 2016.

Payne-Carter, David. *Gower Champion: Dance and American Musical Theatre*. Westport: Greenwood Press, 1999.

Philip, M. NourbeSe. *Showing Grit: Showboating North of the 44th Parallel*. Toronto: Poui Publications, 1993.

Pollack, Howard. *The Ballad of John Latouche*. Oxford: Oxford University Press, 2017.

Pollak, Robert. "'Oklahoma!' flows on like river of delight." *Chicago Sunday Times*, December 5, 1943.

Pollock, Channing. "Revive Us Again." *The Green Book Magazine* (1915): 56–64.

Postlewait, Thomas. "George Edwardes and Musical Comedy: The Transformation of London Theatre and Society, 1878–1914." In *The*

*Performing Century: Nineteenth-Century Theatre's History*, edited by Tracy C. Davis and Peter Holland, 80–102. Basingstoke: Palgrave Macmillan, 2007.

Ralph, Julian. *Harper's Chicago and The World's Fair*. New York: Harper & Brothers, 1893.

Randolph, Laura B. "'Jelly's Last Jam' and the Pain and Passion of Gregory Hines." *Ebony* 47, no. 11 (September 1992): 116–20.

Rascoe, Burton. "The Guild's 'Oklahoma!' Opens at the St. James." *New York World-Telegram*, April 1, 1943.

Rebellato, Dan. "'No Theatre Guild Attraction Are We': *Kiss Me, Kate* and the Politics of the Integrated Musical." *Contemporary Theatre Review* 19, no. 1 (2009): 61–73.

"Rhythm on the Screen." *New York Times*, February 11, 1934.

Rice, Robert. "Rice and Old Shoes." *New York PM*, February 3, 1941.

Rich, Frank. "The Energy and Pain Inside a Man Who Helped Give Birth to Jazz." *New York Times*, April 27, 1992.

———. Introduction to *A Chorus Line*, by James Kirkwood, Nicholas Dante, and Edward Kleban, xi–xvii. New York: Applause, 1995.

Riddle, Peter H. *The American Musical: History and Development*. Oakville: Mosaic, 2010.

Riis, Thomas L. ed. *The Music and Scripts of* In Dahomey. Madison: A-R Editions, 1996.

Rizzo, Frank. "Off Broadway Review: 'Soft Power.'" *Variety*, October 15, 2019.

"R.M. Director." Ca. 1944, Mamoulian Collection of the Library of Congress.

Roberts, John Storm. *The Latin Tinge: The Impact of Latin American Music on the United States*. New York: Oxford University Press, 1999.

Rodewald, Heidi. Preface to *Passing Strange: The Complete Book and Lyrics of the Broadway Musical*, by Stew, xv. New York: Applause, 2009.

Rodgers, Richard. *Musical Stages*. New York: Random House, 1975.

Roediger, David R. *The Wages of Whiteness: Race and the Making of the American Working Class*. New York: Verso, 1991.

Rogin, Michael. *Blackface, White Noise: Jewish Immigrants in the Hollywood Melting Pot*. Berkeley: University of California Press, 1998.

Roof, Judith. *Come as You Are: Sexuality and Narrative*. New York: Columbia University Press, 1996.

Rosenberg, Sylvia. "Ol' Man River Himself." Clipping in files of the Museum of the City of New York.

"Rouben Mamoulian on KFI with Helen Colley." January 31, 1938, Box 191.1, Mamoulian Collection of the Library of Congress.

Savran, David. *A Queer Sort of Materialism: Recontextualizing American Theater.* Ann Arbor: University of Michigan Press, 2003.

———. "Towards a Historiography of the Popular." *Theatre Survey* 45, no. 2 (November 2004): 211–17.

———. "You've Got That Thing: Cole Porter, Stephen Sondheim, and the Erotics of the List Song." *Theatre Journal* 64, no. 4 (December 2012): 533–48.

Saxon, A. H. *The Life and Art of Andrew Ducrow.* Hamden: Archon Books, 1978.

Saxton, Alexander. "Blackface Minstrelsy and Jacksonian Ideology." *American Quarterly* 27, no. 1 (March 1975): 3–28.

Schachenmayr, Volker. "Emma Lyon, the Attitude, and Goethean Performance Theory." *New Theatre Quarterly* 49 (February 1997): 3–17.

Schallert, Edwin. "Grand Opera Gives Mamoulian His Cue." *Los Angeles Times,* August 8, 1943.

Scheuer, Philip K. "Rhythm Rouben." 1932, Mamoulian Collection of the Library of Congress.

Seaman, Barbara. *Lovely Me: The Life of Jacqueline Susann.* New York: William Morrow, 1987.

Sedgwick, Ruth W. "Two Adventures in Direction." *Stage* (October 1935): 60–61.

Shevelove, Burt, Larry Gelbart, and Stephen Sondheim. *A Funny Thing Happened on the Way to the Forum.* New York: Dodd, Mead & Company, 1963.

"'Show Boat' Makes Bow at Curran With Huge Cast." *San Francisco Examiner,* October 31, 1933.

Simon, Robert. "Jerome Kern." *Modern Music* (Feb 1929): 20–21.

Sirmay, Alfred, ed. *Lady in the Dark.* New York: Chappell, 1941.

Smith, Alison. *The Victorian Nude: Sexuality, Morality and Art.* Manchester: Manchester University Press, 1996.

Smith, Cecil. *Musical Comedy in America.* New York: Theatre Arts Books, 1950.

———. "'Show Boat' Drops Anchor at 1st and Grand." *Los Angeles Times,* September 21, 1967.

Smith, Paul Gerard. "Drama and Music: Show Boat." *Rob Wagner's Script* 10, no. 248 (December 9, 1933).

Sondheim, Stephen. *Finishing the Hat: Collected Lyrics (1954–1981) with Attendant Comments, Principles, Heresies, Grudges, Whines and Anecdotes.* New York: Alfred A. Knopf, 2010.

———. "The Musical Theatre." In *Broadway Song and Story: Playwrights/Lyricists/Composers Discuss Their Hits,* edited by Otis L. Guernsey, Jr., 228–50. New York: Dodd Mead, 1986.

Sparke, Penny. "The Domestic Interior and the Construction of Self: The New York Homes of Elsie de Wolfe." In *Interior Design and Identity,* edited by Susie McKellar and Penny Sparke, 72–91. Manchester: Manchester University Press, 2004.

———. "Elsie de Wolfe and Her Female Clients, 1905–1915: Gender, Class, and the Professional Interior Decorator." In *Women's Places: Architecture and Design 1860–1960*, edited by Brenda Martin and Penny Sparke, 47–68. London: Routledge, 2003.

"Special Broadway Report: Back in Lights." *Newsweek* (December 1, 1958): 53–56.

Standish, Myles. "'Flower Drum Song' a Delightful Show." *St. Louis Post-Dispatch*, August 22, 1961.

Stang, Joanne. "R & H Brand on a Musical." *New York Times Magazine*, November 23, 1958.

Stempel, Larry. "The Musical Play Expands." *American Music* 10, no. 2 (Summer 1992): 136–169.

Stevenson, Sara, and Helen Bennett. *Van Dyck in Check Trousers: Fancy Dress in Art and Life, 1700–1900*. Edinburgh: Scottish National Portrait Gallery, 1978.

Stew. *Passing Strange: The Complete Book and Lyrics of the Broadway Musical*. New York: Applause, 2009.

Stewart, Michael. Manuscript of "Dolly." Box 43, Michael Stewart Collection, New York Public Library.

Stewart, Michael, and Jerry Herman. *Hello, Dolly!* New York: DBS, 1964.

Steyn, Mark. *Broadway Babies Say Goodnight: Musicals Then and Now*. New York: Routledge, 2000.

Swain, Joseph. *The Broadway Musical: A Critical and Musical Survey*. Oxford: Oxford University Press, 1990.

Swerling, Jo, Abe Burrows, and Frank Loesser. *Guys and Dolls: A Musical Fable of Broadway*. In *American Musicals: 1950–1969*, edited by Laurence Maslon. New York: Library of America, 2014.

Symonette, Lys, and Kim H. Kowalke, eds. and trans. *Speak Low (When You Speak Love): The Letters of Kurt Weill and Lotte Lenya*. Berkeley: University of California Press, 1996.

Tan, Sheri. "'Flower Drum' Critics Haven't Read Script." *Asian Week*, March 31, 1983.

Taylor, Millie. *Musical Theatre, Realism and Entertainment*. Farnham: Ashgate, 2012.

Terry, Walter. "The Ballet." *New York Herald-Tribune*, undated, Moross Collection, Columbia University Rare Book and Manuscript Library.

———. "'Ballet Ballads' Is a Synthesis of Music, Dance, Dramatic Text." *New York Herald-Tribune*, May 16, 1948.

————. "Dance: Golden Apple, Pink Tights." *New York Herald-Tribune*, March 21, 1954.

"Theater Guild Calls Eastman Act Producer." Unattributed 1926 clipping, Mamoulian Collection of the Library of Congress.

Twain, Mark. *Mark Twain's Travels with Mr. Brown*, edited by Franklin Walker and G. Esra Dane. New York: Knopf, 1940.

Tynan, Kenneth. "Tiny Chinese Minds." *The New Yorker*, December 13, 1958.

Underwood, Sharry. "Ballet Ballads." *Dance Chronicle* 9, no. 3 (1985): 279–327.

"Urbanity of the Follies." *Arts and Decoration* 11, no. 6 (1919).

"Visitor Influx Hypoes Dented B'way." *Variety*, undated. Moross Collection, Columbia University Rare Book and Manuscript Library.

von Goethe, Johann Wolfgang. *Goethe on Art*, edited by John Gage. Berkeley: University of California Press, 1980.

Wachsman, Bob. "Salute . . . This Week: To a Citizen of Beverly Hills Who Will Soon Deliver a Golden Boy." Transcribed copy of August 11, 1939, article in *Beverly Hills Citizen*. Mamoulian Collection of the Library of Congress.

Wada, Karen. Afterword to *Flower Drum Song*, by David Henry Hwang, 99–115. New York: TCG, 2003.

Wagner, Richard. *Correspondence of Wagner and Liszt*, vol. 1., translated and edited by Francis Hueffer. London: H. Grevel, 1888.

————. *Opera and Drama*, vol. 1., translated by Edwin Evans, Sr. London: W. M. Reeves, 1913.

Waldorf, Wilella. *New York World-Telegram*. Undated clipping, New York Public Library Collection.

————. "'Oklahoma!' the Theatre Guild's New Musical Play at the St. James Theatre." *New York Post*, April 1, 1943.

Walker, George W. "The Real 'Coon' on the American Stage." *Theatre* (August 1906): 224.

Walsh, Michael. *Andrew Lloyd Webber: His Life and Works*. New York: Harry N. Abrams, 1997.

Wardle, Irving. "Two Gentlemen of Verona." *London Times*, April 27, 1973.

Watts, Richard Jr. "The Creative Freshness of 'Ballet Ballads.'" *New York Post and the Home News*, May 11, 1948.

————. "Dreaming Lady." *New York Herald-Tribune*, January 24, 1941.

————. "Some Additional Praise for 'Ballet Ballads.'" *New York Post*, June 8, 1948.

————. "Two on the Aisle." *New York Post*, December 2, 1958.

————. "When Everything Goes Just Right." *New York Post*, March 16, 1956.

Wayburn, Ned. "The Chorus Girl—Old and New." *Theatre* (May 1920).

Weidman, Jerome, and George Abbott. *Fiorello!* New York: Random House, 1960.

Weinraub, Judith. "Before 'Superstar,' There Was 'Joseph.'" *New York Times*, December 19, 1976.

Weiss, Piero, and Richard Taruskin, eds. *Music in the Western World*. Belmont: Schirmer, 1984.

Whipple, Sidney B. "'Lady in the Dark' Triumph for Miss Lawrence." *New York World-Telegram*, January 24, 1941.

Whitton, Joseph. *"The Naked Truth!": An Inside History of the Black Crook*. Philadelphia: H. W. Shaw, 1897.

Wilk, Max. *Ok!: The Story of* Oklahoma! New York: Applause, 2002.

Williams, Anne Patricia. "Description and Tableau in the Eighteenth-Century British Sentimental Novel." *Eighteenth-Century Fiction* 8, no. 4 (1996): 471.

Wodehouse, P. G., and Guy Bolton. *Bring on the Girls: The Improbable Story of Our Life in Musical Comedy, with Pictures to Prove It*. London: Herbert Jenkins, 1954.

Wolf, Stacy. *Changed for Good: A Feminist History of the Broadway Musical*. Oxford: Oxford University Press, 2011.

———. *A Problem Like Maria: Gender and Sexuality in the American Musical*. Ann Arbor: University of Michigan Press, 2002.

Wolfe, George C., and Susan Birkenhead. *Jelly's Last Jam*. New York: TCG, 1993.

Wolff, Tamsen. *Mendel's Theatre: Heredity, Eugenics, and Early Twentieth-Century American Drama*. Basingstoke: Palgrave Macmillan, 2009.

Wood, J. G. "Dime Museums from a Naturalist's Point of View." *The Atlantic* 55, no. 332 (June 1885): 759–65.

Worrall, Nick. *Modernism to Realism on the Soviet Stage*. Cambridge, UK: Cambridge University Press, 2008.

Yzraely, Yosef I. "Vakhtangov Directing *The Dybbuk*." Ph.D. diss., Carnegie-Mellon University, 1971.

# INDEX

# STUDIES IN THEATRE HISTORY AND CULTURE